KNOT YOUR DAMN OMEGA

DEVYN SINCLAIR

To The Little Cupcake Bakeshop in New York City, who to this day, has still made the best cupcake I've ever eaten.

Blue velvet and mascarpone will forever haunt my dreams.

AUTHOR'S NOTE

Dear Readers,

Knot Your Damn Omega is not a book that's meant to be dark. However, there are still things which some readers might find objectionable or difficult to read, including primal play, and strong portrayals of grief. If you feel like this could be a problem for you, please protect yourself. No work of fiction is worth your mental health.

The full list of content warnings is available on my website.

CHAPTER ONE

ESME

*T*he man in the suit across from me smelled like burnt popcorn. And not the good kind, when movie theater butter caramelized and gave you that weird but delicious bitter smell. No, this guy smelled like when you left the popcorn bag in the microwave too long, and when you opened it, half the bag was blackened and charred, and you were lucky the whole thing wasn't on fire.

It was an effort not to wrinkle my nose.

The other three Alphas were similar. Honestly, if I didn't look too closely at them they could be carbon copies of each other. Dark suits, neat hair, and smiles that looked as expensive as their watches.

All of their scents were *off*. Not all of them were outright bad, and I knew well enough some lucky Omega out there was going to get a whiff of burnt popcorn and scream *fuck yeah take me now*.

That Omega just wasn't me.

Even if their scents were sending me into a state of orgasmic bliss, I wouldn't choose this pack. Because they weren't actually interested in me. If they were, maybe I'd get closer to examine their scents in detail and see if I could make it work. But they weren't.

I tuned back in to what Katarina was saying. She was

1

wearing a perfectly tailored pink suit, hair tied up in a shiny updo, and was holding her clipboard with manicured hands I would never be able to function with. Even my mother was dressed up where she sat on the other end of the couch. I was the one out of place in jeans and a t-shirt, but I wasn't about to pretend I was something I wasn't.

And there wasn't a chance in hell any pack who wanted me would expect to see me in a suit.

"And Thomas," Katarina gestured to the man on the end whose scent reminded me vaguely of hot copier paper, "is one of the Vice Presidents of Slate City Bank." She looked at me. "Do you have any questions?"

I stared down popcorn guy. "Katarina sent you my file, correct?"

My mother paid Katarina an absurd amount of money in an attempt to match me with a pack. Because apparently being a single Omega in our family was unacceptable. It wasn't that I didn't want a pack—I did want one, more than I would ever admit to anyone who wasn't Eva—it was that everyone who came to meet me actually wanted my sister and didn't have the balls to admit it.

"She did, yes."

I thought his name was Gary. Or maybe Grayden? Probably should have listened closer. Smiling, I made sure I didn't break eye contact. "What's my middle name?"

"May."

Thomas and one of the other guys—there were four in total—closed their eyes and I heard a distinctive *fuck* under someone's breath. My mother let out a long sigh, and Katarina's smile was so frozen on her face I thought it might crack.

"Nope," I said. "That's my sister's middle name. Try again."

He went pale, realizing what he'd done. And deep down, I knew I shouldn't do what I was about to do, but the anger coiling in my gut was the only thing holding me back from sadness I didn't want to face. So fuck it. "You could probably get my birthday right, given it's the same as hers. And you'll probably be able to name all of her movies in alphabetical order. But you do realize you're here for me and not her, right?"

"Of course," the man sputtered, flicking his eyes toward Katarina and my mother as if they could save him from a drowning of his own making. "I'm sorry, I got mixed up. Of course, I know your middle name. I know everything in the file. We all do."

"If you know it, then what's my middle name?"

"Elyse," Thomas blurted out from his spot, looking sick to his stomach. "It's Elyse."

"Very good. Now, what do I do for a living?"

All four of them stared back at me blankly. All four of them, like I'd just zapped them and turned them into clothing store mannequins with the magical, sultry tones of my voice.

"No one? That's too bad. I thought you knew everything about me."

"I think we're done here," Katarina said, her voice a

full octave higher than normal. "Gentlemen, thank you so much for coming. The agency will be in touch."

"Toodaloo," I waved as the four men stood and made their way out of the room. Katarina closed the door behind them as my mother's butler Arnold saw them to the front door. "That didn't even take half as long as normal."

My mother sighed again, rubbing her forehead. "Esme." I'd probably given her another headache she'd have to sleep off.

I stood, pushing off the couch, unable to sit still anymore.

"Don't walk away. Let's talk about this."

"What is there to talk about?" I threw my hands out, gesturing to the big, stuffy living room where I'd had probably thirty meetings with packs from all over the country in the last three years. "They don't *want me*, Mom."

I quickly swallowed back the emotion in those words. There was no way in hell I was going to cry in front of Katrina, and I *certainly* wasn't going to cry in front of my mother.

"You could have given them a chance."

"For what? To illustrate how thoroughly they expect me to be a clone of Eva?"

She floundered, looking for something which could combat the obvious. "Your sister's details are very well known, and he was nervous. He probably just needed some more time without you treating him like a hostile enemy."

"Yeah," I said with a sigh. "I'm sure that's it."

That wasn't it. It wasn't even fucking close. Because being the twin sister to the biggest Omega movie star on the planet came with certain drawbacks, like everyone expecting you to be exactly alike.

I loved my sister, and she wanted me to be happy, too. But now that she'd found her pack and was happily bonded, every Alpha who missed his 'chance' with Eva now thought I would be a good replacement. And for once in my life, I wanted someone to want me for me and not because of who I looked like.

Walking over to my mother, I leaned down and kissed her cheek. Even when she frustrated me, I loved her. "Since I'm here I'll go for a run on the grounds, but I'll see you for lunch next week, okay?"

She managed to pull me into an awkward hug. "Of course, sweetie. Call me."

"I will." I turned away before she could see the tears starting to mist my eyes. That was the thing about my mom. She genuinely did want me to be happily bonded, but she had no clue how to make it happen. I wasn't Eva, and I couldn't ever be. Which probably meant I was going to be alone forever.

My twin sister was pushing in the front door when I'd changed into my running clothes. "Wait, where are you going? I know I'm late, but I wanted to watch some of the action."

I smiled, but it wasn't a good one. "No action. They're already gone. I'm going for a run, but Mom's probably still in there."

5

Eva blinked, and I was out the door, but I didn't quite leave. It was a shitty thing to do, and I knew it, but I went back inside after she made it all the way into the living room, and stepped close enough to the door to hear.

"I just passed Esme and could barely get her to stop for three words in a row. What happened?"

"What do you think?" Katarina snapped. "What always happens. Your sister is so resistant to finding a pack she looks for reasons to turn them down."

"That was uncalled for," my mother said. "And not your place. If you can't discuss this civilly, you're free to leave."

I didn't hear footsteps, so she must have decided the commission she was getting was worth the frustration I was putting her through.

"The men seemed..." Mom paused, and I could almost picture her face trying to find a way to make it more palatable. Finally, she just sighed. "There's no point in sugarcoating it. It was the same as always. Esme quickly and brutally exposed that they weren't really here for her. They were here for you. Or a version of you."

Eva let out a string of curses so long and so loud I wondered if Katarina had passed out from shock, but I smiled. One of the many reasons I loved my sister as much as I hated living in her shadow.

"I'm glad then. These assholes need to realize I am off the market. It's not fair to her."

"She doesn't exactly make it easy, Eva. It could be these men are nervous, and you're more well known so they fall back on what they know. Esme at least could be a little nicer to them. No man, let alone an Alpha, wants an Omega who's going to pick him apart like that."

"I doubt that's true."

"Oh, it is true," Katarina said. "And I'm running out of options for her to meet. If Esme actually wants a pack, she's going to have to settle for one who might not know her middle name after reading a file once. She's getting a reputation. My staff and I are keeping on top of the rumors, but they're still slipping out. That, on top of the footage of her from your bonding ceremony? Esme is practically unmatchable."

Her statement shouldn't have hit me in the chest the way it did. It wasn't like I didn't already know, and it wasn't like I hadn't had the exact same thoughts not even twenty minutes ago. But to hear it laid out like that by the person who—theoretically—was supposed to be helping me find a pack, still stung.

"Esme is smart, beautiful, and talented," Eva said, frustration coloring her tone. "And Jack knew almost everything about me the night after we met. Not because he had a fucking file, but because he cared enough to ask. They all did. They didn't need an incentive to get to know me because when we met, they felt like they already did. It was that natural and that fast. Esme deserves that, too."

"Of course she does, sweetheart. But you know it's not that simple." I peeked through the door just in time to see mom pat Eva's knee. "You got lucky. Not only did you click with them right away, but there weren't any... problems to be avoided."

Meaning the band my sister bonded with, Mindless Delirium, was famous too, and therefore had already been vetted for things which would make our family look bad. I didn't give two shits about that kind of appearance, but when you came from my world, everyone else did.

"All I can say is if Esme ever wants to find a suitable pack, she needs to really think about what life will be like as an Omega *alone* instead of a pack who might not be perfect, but will treat her well." I couldn't stay longer to hear more of Katarina's opinion of me.

I was sassy and prickly and definitely not my sunshine twin, who was the sweetheart of the world. Outside the gates to this estate there was no doubt a crowd of paparazzi trying to catch a glimpse of her through the walls and the security. They were far enough away they wouldn't see me, and I was glad that pack left before the paps got here. Even if I didn't care about appearance, the last thing I needed was another story about me and how I chased away another batch of eligible men.

Pushing off the stairs, I followed the brick path around the house which led to the main grounds. On the outskirts of the city, this estate was massive, and it was easy to get lost in the woods and fields when I needed to run away from... everything for a while.

When I was running, or painting, or mixing a new color, for a little while I could pretend I wasn't me, and this wasn't my life, and every fucking second wasn't lonely.

Katarina was right. It wasn't my choice to be Esme Williams, Eva Williams's less shiny twin. But this is who I was, and it wasn't going to change. I just needed to accept it and find a way to be okay being lonely, even if it felt like my heart was ripping to shreds.

Blinking the beginnings of tears out of my eyes, I turned my music on shuffle, and ran.

CHAPTER TWO

ESME

"Do you really need me to go to this thing with you?" I asked, flopping down on the ludicrously large beanbag in my sister's living room. Having a rock band for a pack definitely had its benefits.

"Yes, I do. And you're going to wear whatever I put you in."

"Eva."

"Esme."

I groaned. "I think I would rather have bamboo shoved under my nails."

"Listen." She sat on the coffee table, identical face looking at me seriously. "Going to this thing and looking fucking fabulous is only going to help you. I know you hate the press attention, but if they think you're happy and thriving they'll back off. People always want to read more about drama than happiness."

I threw an arm over my face, intentionally dramatic. "Why do you have to be right when all I want to do is sulk? I know this will help the 'rumors,' or whatever the hell Katarina was talking about yesterday."

Eva smacked my knee. "I *knew* you were listening."

"You did not."

"I did. And yeah, that bitch was way out of line. The

next time I see Mom alone I'm telling her to dump her ass."

I smirked. Eva had stood up and had her hands on her hips like a superhero. To the rest of the world, she was Eva May Williams, the darling sweetheart. Behind the scenes, she was as snarky as I was. If the paparazzi knew how much Eva swore, her whole career would be different.

"Shut up."

"I said nothing."

The door closed. "Hello? I brought home pizza. Oh, hey, Esme."

I waved to Liam, one of Eva's Alphas. Both their scents immediately got stronger. Eva's roses and coffee, and Liam's bourbon. The good kind. He'd barely put down the stack of pizza boxes before she was in his arms. The way she melted before he leaned down to kiss her— smiling the whole time—made my stomach flip with longing.

Pulling out my phone was the only way to distract myself without leaving the room. A year ago at the Designation Choice Awards, Eva ran into Mindless Delirium backstage and instantly started perfuming.

Scent-sympathetic they called it. A very clinical name for when scents were so compatible you just *knew*. It didn't always work, but this time it had.

They went home together and basically never separated. A few months later, their bonding ceremony was televised—*the event of the decade*—and I was there. Looking like I would do anything to be in her place.

It was the footage Kat had mentioned. Whenever the press deigned to give me attention, it was usually those pictures or videos, with either a true, twisted, or entirely fabricated story about how I'd chased off yet another pack.

Eva and Liam were practically making out now, her twisting up and around him like he was a tree and she was a vine. I heard his purr from here. "Get a room, please."

My sister just flipped me off and kissed him a little more before breaking away with a laugh. "We have to get ready, anyway."

"Get ready for what?" Jack, another one of Eva's Alphas, stood in the doorway to their kitchen, shirtless.

"Studio party, remember? I'm dragging Esme with me."

"Though I'm perfectly willing to just go home."

"No, you're not." She came over and hauled me to my feet, dragging me upstairs into her sprawling bedroom.

Eva lived in a two-story penthouse in one of the most secure buildings in Slate City. I could probably afford to live here if I cared to, but the high-rise life wasn't for me. My place was plenty secure, but it wasn't downtown. I lived on the edge of the city where I could get out easily and run in the park and outside the city boundaries if I needed to.

I frequently needed to.

"Okay, what vibe are we feeling tonight?"

"There are no vibes. I have no vibes. I am not a vibe."

"Sexy as hell it is." She disappeared into the massive closet.

I groaned. Once my sister got a hold of an idea, especially when it came to me and fashion, there was almost no stopping her.

"Here. I've been dying to wear this, but my publicist absolutely forbid it, so I'm going to have to live vicariously through you."

I looked at the dress she was holding and stared at her. "There's no way in hell I can pull that off."

The dress was gold and slinky, ruched at the sides just enough to make sure it would show off every curve I had, and I would be *lucky* if it fell mid-thigh. Spaghetti straps and a cowl neckline, and the outfit would cover just as much of my skin as it revealed. Fifty-fifty.

I wasn't ashamed of my body or showing skin, but I wasn't sure about giving the paparazzi that kind of ammunition if I had a wardrobe malfunction. Which, you know, wasn't unheard of.

"You can one-hundred-percent pull this off. How do I know? Because it looks fucking fabulous on me, and we're identical twins. Put it on."

Sticking out my tongue, I reached for the dress. It wouldn't hurt to try it on. When Eva saw how uncomfortable I was in the dress she would change her mind. "Are your Alphas going to come waltzing in here? Or should I change in the bathroom?"

She laughed, but bit her lip. "I mean, it's not their room," it was, in the sense I knew all of them slept in here most nights, "but yeah, maybe use the bathroom."

That was fine with me. The last thing I wanted tonight was for one of my sister's pack to see me naked.

The dress itself was cool to the touch, made out of a metal mesh on the outside and silk on the inside. There was absolutely no way I could wear a bra with this thing. I slipped it on and looked in the mirror, already cursing.

It looked amazing—there was no way to deny it. The golden tone highlighted my skin and brought out the warmer colors in my hair. Even my eyes looked brighter.

"Just so you know," I called. "I hate you."

"I know. Get your ass out here."

Padding back into the room, her jaw dropped. "Holy *shit*, Esme."

"Have I mentioned I really hate it when you're right? I'm going to need to borrow make-up, though."

She gestured to her cluttered vanity. "Have at it."

Most of the time Eva's team did her make-up and hair, but for smaller events like this she gave them time off. I was glad tonight, since it meant the reveal of the dress was limited to only her. You know, before all of Slate City's paparazzi saw me.

Fine. If I was going to do this? Then I was going to do this. I leaned into the look of the dress, making my eyes dark and smoky with a hint of metallic gold at the inner corners. Just enough gloss on my lips to make people wonder what I'd been doing, and I ran some hairspray through with my fingers, attempting to corral the flyaways in my waves.

"What do you think of this?"

Her dress was white, falling to her knees. It had a

similar neckline to mine, so we wouldn't look completely out of sync, but it was a much more toned-down, wholesome version of what I was wearing. "It's pretty."

She sighed. "I would kill to wear what you're wearing right now. I've been begging Jasmine and Brian to let me go a little edgier, but the whole team thinks it's a bad idea."

"Why?"

"Because I still have three more Summer Saga movies coming up, and they don't want to piss off the studio. Which is one of the reasons we're going to this party."

Grabbing an overflowing jewelry box, I picked through the jewelry until I found some dangly gold earrings which matched.

"Hold on, I have something else perfect for that." She disappeared into the closet again and reappeared with her shoes, gold heels for me, and a gold wire armband that twisted into swirls and rested on my bicep. "God, you're such a badass."

"Remind me why I'm going to this party again?"

This was at the core of my problems with the packs who had come to court me. I wasn't Eva. I didn't love parties, preferring silence or my own music to rooms filled with pounding bass and people. I wasn't afraid of people, but most of the time they exhausted me. On the whole, I was built for a different life than this one.

It wasn't anyone's fault. No one could have seen our lives turning out this way. But sometimes I wished I could simply disappear, if that wouldn't draw even more media attention and make life hell for Eva.

"Don't the guys want to go?"

"They would go if I asked, but I told them not to. I'm trying to help you, remember? Pictures of you in this dress are going to have packs *begging* to meet you. And none of them will think you're me when I'm wearing a white sack."

I rolled my eyes. "It's not a sack."

"You get the point."

Tugging on the shoes, I looked at her. "What if I don't want packs knocking down my door? What if I just want what you have? To meet the right pack at the right time and for everything to be simple. I don't think that's going to happen with Katarina lining up every pack made up of suit-wearing Alphas."

"It'll happen, May-may. Promise."

I wished I could believe her. The ache which lodged itself in my chest yesterday hadn't really left, and I didn't think a party like this was going to help. But Eva was trying to do something for me, and I could help her by making her look wholesome by comparison.

A win-win.

Sort of.

"Okay, I think I'm ready," I said.

"Hold on," she said, holding out a little perfume roller. "Put this on. Scent canceller. Not for you, but these things are just a mess of everyone, so if you need to clear your head it's good. I mean, they'll be spraying scent cancellers, but you can't be too careful."

I raised my eyebrows. I'd never had this stuff before. Only the kind of soap and spray that cleaned other scents off you. And she meant I couldn't be too careful because I was going to this party to help my rumors and my Omega instincts rising in the middle of a party because there were too many nearby Alphas wasn't going to help those.

"I'll keep it with me, if that's okay."

"Sure."

The only other thing I had was my phone, and I shoved it in the little black clutch Eva tossed to me on our way out of the room.

Her four Alphas were all in a line at the bottom of the stairs, waiting to see her off, and the whole room was suddenly a mess of their scents. "I'll wait for you in the hall."

"Looking good, Esme," Tyler called after me, and I waved without turning back. They meant it, but right now they wanted to be with my sister, and she wanted to be with them. If I looked back, I would crack open seeing the kind of love which sang between them.

I stepped out the front door into the hallway which led only to the elevator, and Neil, Eva's head of security, laughed. "I can smell the happiness from here."

"Why do you think I'm not waiting in there?"

Scrolling on my phone, I was suddenly seeing the rumors Katarina had mentioned now that I was looking for them. *Williams sister terrorizes more Alphas?* A blurry looking photo of my family's estate and the guys from yesterday leaving. They wouldn't talk—Kat made everyone sign non-disclosure agreements tighter than a noose—but it was still frustrating. They had no proof it had gone badly, just a guess.

Eva came out of her apartment beaming. "Ready."

I closed the flashy news story before she could spot it on my phone. "How's it looking tonight, Neil?"

"About average. I'm expecting it to be much tighter at the venue. When we get there, straight from the car to the door, no questions."

The elevator dropped, my stomach whooshing in response.

"Yeah, Jasmine said as much. No questions from reporters outside. You too, Esme. We're controlling the story as much as we can for the release next month."

I resisted the urge to laugh, as if I would voluntarily stop and talk to one of the people trying to make me look like a monstrous shrew to everyone in the world.

Sighing, I leaned against the wall of the elevator. Even to me, I was starting to sound like what they accused me of. Maybe I was hangry. I should have grabbed a slice of that pizza Liam brought home.

The cameras started flashing as soon as the elevator doors opened into the glassed-in lobby. Not nearly as many as there would be later.

"Smile on?" Eva asked, looping her elbow through mine like all the times we'd done this before.

I didn't have much of a choice, but I looked amazing, and if I was going to be dragged to this party anyway, I needed to get my head on straight and try to have some fun.

"Smile on."

CHAPTER THREE

ESME

*T*his was insane.

The horde of paparazzi outside nearly blinded us getting out of the car. They were behind barricades and there was plenty of security, but it still felt like being hit with a metric fuck ton of sound.

After making sure I didn't flash my vagina at every camera in the known world, I managed to smile and wave next to Eva while she posed, looking over her shoulder at them and winking.

They were all rapid-fire and toppling over one another, but I could still pick out all the questions.

Esme, who's the latest victim? Which pack now has broken hearts? Are you in the closet? Do you need a female pack? Did the death of your father break you? Are you in therapy? Who helps with your heats? Do you share with Eva?

My sister looped her arm through mine again, her smile now forced. "Fucking assholes." She said it without moving her lips.

"Apparently everyone's thinking the same thing, so I'm not sure they're out of line."

She rolled her eyes as soon as we were out of view. The lobby of the building was echoey and quiet in comparison, even with people milling about, waiting to

21

go upstairs. "They're so fucking far out of line I'm going to have my lawyers rip them a new asshole. I get they have to ask about the relationship stuff, and it sucks. But they don't get to ask about dad or if you're in fucking therapy."

I swallowed and pulled her into a hug. Every day I missed Dad. And yes, I'd gone to therapy, though it was no one's business. But it hit Eva hard, too. He hadn't been gone long, and he hadn't been there to present her at her bonding ceremony.

If—when—my time came, I was sure I would feel the same.

I shoved down the emotions about Dad. Though it had been two years, I hadn't really grieved. I had, and I hadn't. It was too hard, and every time I thought about him I couldn't breathe.

So I did my best not to think about him.

Denial was the best medicine, right?

"Sorry," Eva muttered. "It just pisses me off."

"I know, and I appreciate it. But let's go do this party thing so we can get the hell out of here."

Eva laughed, quickly swiping under her eyes. "Deal."

"Why is this party happening again?"

She snorted inelegantly as we walked to the elevator, Neil close behind. "Honestly? What we just walked through was most of it."

"This was all for pictures?"

"Kind of. Just press in general. You know how it is. A lot of pretty, famous people in one spot draws attention. Wellbridge Studio doesn't have any huge films out until the end of the summer, but they want to keep us in everybody's mind."

Neil pushed the button for the elevator, and we followed him inside.

"I hate that that makes sense."

"Plus," Eva added. "They get to spoil us at these parties, and they're fun. You'll see. Now that I've finally dragged you to one you'll always want to come."

"I highly doubt it."

But I had to admit, the doors of the elevator opening onto what looked like a mix between a circus and a nightclub might be able to change my mind.

Deep red fabric draped from the ceiling, creating a tent. Black chandeliers dotted the space with actual candles flickering in them. The rest of the light came from roving spotlights and patterned beams in warm colors shifting over the tent itself.

An aerial silk performer hung from the ceiling, twisting sensually in time with the music. In the corner I spotted an illusionist, and there was a person painting an elaborate golden mask on someone's face. Eva was right, the studio wasn't holding anything back for this party.

There was an exit to the balcony overlooking downtown, and there were people *everywhere*. Music pulsed under my feet, at once melodic and rhythmic. It was loud enough so that it wasn't awkward, but I also didn't feel the need to beg for earplugs.

Eva was right. It smelled remarkably mild in here for the amount of people. The scent controller they used spread everything out to a sweet, vaguely citrus scent.

Just to test, I lifted my wrist to my nose and inhaled. Nothing but clean air.

Damn.

I needed to ask Eva where she got this.

"There you are!" Jasmine waved, pulling us deeper into the crowd. "I was about to come hunt you down."

"A lot of paps," Eva said. "And do me a favor? Tell the gossip magazines if they ever shout questions at me or Esme about our father, if we've gone to therapy, or anything *remotely* close to that line, I'll make sure they never have a legal photo of us ever again."

She raised her eyebrows. "Got it."

Jasmine was Eva's manager. A Beta with gorgeous dark skin and even darker eyes, she was easily the most badass, competent person I'd ever met. Not once had she done anything to endanger Eva or expose her to the press, and because of that, I trusted her.

"Anything I should know?"

Jasmine waved her hand in a so-so motion before she took both of our clutches for safekeeping. "Mostly just mingle. The studio heads will probably want a few words at some point, but I'll come pull you out when you're needed. There's also an official photographer, and we'd love to get some pictures of the two of you dancing."

"We can do that," I said. The dance floor was a go-to of mine. "When I dance I don't have to talk to people."

Jasmine laughed. "If more of the people in this room had your attitude, I imagine there would be a lot fewer publicity messes."

Eva pulled me away and was immediately flagged down by Dante Norwood. A sweet Beta who somehow managed to *drip* Alpha energy on screen. Pretty sure all the Alphas in the room hated him a bit for it, too. "Darling, you look beautiful." He kissed Eva on both cheeks before he turned to me. "And Esme, you look fucking *fantastic* if I say so myself."

"Thank you."

"I had to force her into that dress since Jasmine wouldn't let me wear it." Eva pouted.

Dante shook his head in mock pity. "Whatever will Eva May Williams do without wearing a ten thousand dollar dress?"

My head swung so fast I thought my neck would dislocate. "This dress cost that much?"

She shrugged. "I didn't pay for it. It was a gift from the designer."

It was moments like these I realized how truly different my sister's life was from mine. I had more money than I knew what to do with thanks to my inheritance, but I wasn't walking around in clothes that cost ten grand. My stomach growled, reminding me I hadn't stolen any of Liam's pizza earlier.

"Have you seen the food?" I asked Dante. "Because I'm about to eat so much this thing will look like a maternity dress."

Dante tilted his head back, throwing laughter toward the ceiling. "If you manage to make that happen, please come straight to me. It's over there." He gestured to the other side of the room. Or the tent.

"Thank you!" I grabbed Eva's wrist and pulled her with me. "I should have stolen your pizza earlier."

"We both should have. Food is a great idea."

A table nearly as long as the room itself was stuffed with food. Mountains of crab puffs, charcuterie, a line of hot, covered dishes full of comfort foods, and down at the end I saw a grocery store's worth of fruit nearby three different chocolate fountains.

All at once, the scent of cake washed over me, like a bakery come to life, and I groaned. "Fuck, do you smell that? I need a cupcake."

Eva looked at me, then she looked all along the table. "What? There aren't any cupcakes here."

"Then Dante must have been wrong because I smell cupcakes and now it's all I can think about." Sweet vanilla frosting and yellow cake. The craving was so strong, I would have eaten the cupcakes you found in plastic containers at a gas station just to make sure my stomach stopped its rebellion.

"Esme," Eva called after me, laughing. "You're having food hallucinations right now."

"It's because I'm so hungry," I said over my shoulder, pushing towards the front of the room where the scent was coming from. I swore they must have come straight out of the oven. "It'll be fine. Just one and my brain will be back to normal."

That wasn't true. With a craving this strong? I'd probably be six cupcakes deep before I felt like stopping.

"Esme—" Eva called out as I crashed into something. Someone. I turned, looking at a man sitting in a chair, while another man sat in front of him with his wrist out. The guy I'd just run into was holding a tattoo machine and in the middle of tattooing some kind of symbol on the guy's wrist.

He was now looking at me, big green eyes and a backwards baseball cap, and he seemed as confused as I was about the fact that I'd just slammed into him like my human brake lines had been cut.

It didn't look like I'd just ruined a tattoo, but I couldn't stop staring in confusion. This was right where the scent was, but there were no baked goods, and my cranky ass couldn't handle that.

"You," I said, "are not a cupcake."

The man smirked. "No, I'm not."

He stood, and Eva finally stepped in next to me. "He may not be a cupcake, but he does have some *serious* cake, if you know what I mean."

I turned my head slowly, staring at my sister, who I was now going to murder. "He can hear you, Eva."

She wasn't paying attention to me at all. "Holy shit. You're Bennett Gray."

"Guilty as charged." The giant in front of me spoke in a voice which was somehow both deep and musical. He was tall and built like a wall, the dark t-shirt he wore doing absolutely nothing to disguise the kind of biceps he had just like his jeans did nothing to hide the ass my sister called out. Biceps covered in tattoos which flowed all the way down to his wrists. I saw some peeking out from the collar of his shirt, too.

Holy. Fuck.

It wasn't just his body which was gorgeous. The man fit perfectly into this room of movie stars and models. But I didn't recognize him, and I was at least halfway familiar with most of the people in Eva's circle. Who was he?

My mind still seemed fuzzy, and I still couldn't seem to wrap my mind around why he was here and not the plate of carbs and sugar my nose had promised me. "You're still not a cupcake."

"He knows, Esme."

Quickly, I lifted my wrist to my nose to clear my head, and when I pulled it away the scent was still there. If anything it was stronger. My stomach flipped, suddenly realizing my mistake.

It was him.

The fucking cupcake scent *was him*.

He was all Alpha, and I felt pulled toward him like a magnet. Oh shit.

Terror so deep I couldn't breathe clawed at my chest, and I took a step back.

"Um," I cleared my throat. "I hope I didn't fuck up your tattoo."

He laughed, the rich sound reaching down inside me and making everything stand at attention. "You got lucky. I was about to grab more ink. So no, you didn't fuck it up."

His eyes slid over me, taking in the hair, the dress, the bracelet Eva had put on my arm, everything. I felt that look like a physical touch, hot honey sliding across my skin. I could have imagined it, but under the music, I thought I heard the low rumble of a purr, and I had to clear my throat to keep myself from letting out a whine which would draw more attention.

"I'm glad about that, for my sake. But I also like hearing Bennett be called a cupcake." The man who was getting the tattoo spoke. He looked familiar, but I couldn't quite place him.

"Okay." I pressed my lips together. "I'm gonna go now."

Before the tattooing cupcake or my sister could stop me, I ducked through the crowd back the way I came, toward the door to the balcony. Scent blockers or not, I needed some fresh fucking air after that mess.

And to maybe bury myself under all the food I *hadn't* eaten in humiliation.

CHAPTER FOUR

BENNETT

*O*mega.

The sweet scent of lilacs and the sharpness of hot tea filled my nose. Over all the scents in this crowd, her scent stood out like a firework in a dark sky. I couldn't stop watching her disappear through the crowd, that gold dress doing things to her body my imagination should *not* be running with.

"Sorry about that," the other Omega said with a grimace. "She doesn't like parties."

I recognized her when I looked more closely. Her hair was much shorter, but she had the same face as the woman who'd just run from me like I was the devil himself. If the devil were made of cupcakes, apparently.

This was the movie star, Eva May Williams, and that... "That's your sister?"

"That's Esme. In the flesh. Sorry about the interruption, Carson."

"That's all right," Carson said, still smirking. "Even a fucked up Bennett Gray tattoo is still a Bennett Gray tattoo."

"For real." Eva looked at me with sparkles in her eyes. "I'm a huge fan of your work, and I'd *love* to have a piece done by you sometime. Something bigger than you can do at a party."

I blinked, trying to focus on the words she was saying. The scent of delicate, purple flowers was still in the air and I was suddenly wondering if we had a kettle back home because I was in the mood for tea.

"Absolutely." I reached over to my table where the supplies were and grabbed one of the cards. "Make an appointment and come in any time. We'll do a consultation."

"Thank you!" She was practically dancing. My eyes were still drawn to the disappearing gold dress I saw slip out the door to the balcony. Eva caught my gaze and followed it. "Do you want me to talk to her?"

No. I wanted to talk to her. I wanted to *inhale* her. "I don't think she's ready to talk to anything that isn't made in a bakery."

Eva laughed. "Don't let her food craving scare you off." Someone called her name across the room, and she waved before holding up the business card. "I'll give the studio a call. Hopefully I'll see you soon."

I stood there for a second after she left, feeling like I'd been flipped upside down and hung by my ankles, and was still hanging there.

"You okay, Ben?" Carson asked, voice carrying under the music.

"Yeah." I turned back, taking my seat once again. I needed to finish his tattoo—an infinity symbol which looked simple but was actually difficult to execute because of the three-dimensional elements I was adding. If she'd bumped into me a second earlier or later, there would have been a thick black line running up the inside of Carson's wrist, and that wouldn't have been good for my reputation.

"So, Esme?"

I glanced up at him and then back down. Carson Lord was one of many actors in the room. An Alpha, but he played the lighter roles. Comic relief, which was why him getting a tattoo on his wrist in the middle of an industry party wasn't career suicide. There were more than enough actors in this room—Alphas and Betas alike —who'd eyed me, clearly wanting to come over before they were inevitably pulled away by whatever publicist had to make sure they kept their image clean.

That was fine. I was getting paid either way.

"What about her?" I asked, trying to disguise the sharpness of my interest. New waves of her scent still lingered in the air. The bitterness of tea steeped too long and the lightness of it when you breathed in the steam. But mostly, the feather-light sweetness of the air in spring when you walked by lilacs in full bloom.

Fuck, I loved that scent.

And I'd purred for her. Hopefully the music had hidden that instinctual bit of Alphaholic instinct, but it felt like the most natural thing in the world. She'd been distressed, and I needed to comfort her.

"You like her?"

I raised an eyebrow. "I've never met her before. How would I know?"

He stared at me, challenging me with his gaze until I relented with a growl. "Fine. She smells amazing, and I'm finding it very difficult to focus on inking you."

"Clearly she likes the way you smell too, cupcake."

"That's a new one," I admitted. "Most people have said some shade of vanilla, but cupcake is very specific."

Carson chuckled. We'd known each other long enough now that his teasing couldn't get under my skin. He already had one of my pieces on his back—the wrist was just a bonus since I was tattooing for 'free' as a part of my fee to be here.

A ridiculously large fee.

"Have you read what the press says about her?"

I snorted. "You know I haven't." Through Carson and some other famous clients I had, I'd seen enough to know what the gossip mags reported was rarely true, and mostly hurtful.

"They say she's an ice queen. Has turned down a hundred packs who've offered to bond, and not been kind while doing it. A complete bitch."

A growl ripped out of me, causing the heads nearest us to turn, and I sat back, stunned. I must still be caught up in her scent. Pure, gorgeous Omega.

Carson held up the hand I wasn't inking. "I didn't say I thought those things. I've never met her in person, cupcake incident aside, but I know Eva. And Eva is amazing. I can't imagine her sister being completely different. Not when they spend so much time together."

Intentionally, I dipped the irons in ink and went back to doing the final touches on his tattoo. I'd been around plenty of Omegas before, and none of them had ever made me react this way. There was always the protective instinct, of course, that natural *leaning in* which made Alphas and Omegas pull toward each other.

But none of their scents had slammed into me like a battering ram. Was this what it was like for Addison when she met Claire? I needed to ask her. Because if it was...

I wasn't sure I could follow that line of thought. It was too complicated. There was so much more than one scent to consider. There was the whole rest of my pack, if Esme was even looking for one. If what Carson said was even a tenth true about her turning down packs?

Shaking my head, I dismissed the thought. Not once had I put stock in what the gossip machine had to say. I wasn't going to start now when it might actually matter.

Finishing the final shading, I wiped away the last bit of ink from Carson's wrist. "There you go."

He grinned. "Stellar. As usual."

"I think you're the only one who's actually going to get one." I bandaged it for him. We'd done enough sessions I knew I didn't have to lecture him about proper care.

"Oh, one-hundred percent. I'd say you're fully clear to go after Miss Cupcake if you want."

I looked at him. "Who says I want to?"

Carson snorted. "Every inch of your body language says you want to. And even with the scent dampeners, I could scent a bit of her. I don't blame you a bit."

Suddenly I was on my feet and I didn't know how I got there, the feral urge to protect against the threat of what was *mine*.

Laughing, Carson just stood and clapped me on the back. "Thank you for proving my point so thoroughly. Now, I have to go show off the tattoo."

I started to put away my equipment. No one else had even spoken to me about ink tonight, and now I had another motivation. As much as it annoyed me to admit Carson was right, he was. I didn't want to be stuck doing a tattoo when I could be closer to a bunch of lilacs.

The smart thing would be to walk away. Pack up the equipment, go home, tell the guys about it and maybe try to meet her the way someone like her should be met. With flowers and courting gifts. Showing her everything we had to offer and laying everything on the table.

Then again, I was one hell of a tattoo artist, but I never claimed to be smart.

Stowing my equipment in the secure space left for the vendors and performers, I took one long, deep breath. The air was filled with a hundred mild scents, all knocked down because of the scent dampeners in the air. All but one. A sweet thread which called to me, pulling me like it had me on a leash.

There was no point in trying to resist. I was already moving, searching for the scent of lilacs and tea.

CHAPTER FIVE

ESME

The night air was cool, fresh, and a hell of a lot easier to breathe. Even with the occasional cloud of cigarette smoke floating around, this was still better. Clearer. I wasn't being driven out of my mind by non-existent cupcakes.

What the hell *was* that?

And why did I want to go back inside, haul him close by his shirt and bury my nose in it?

I shook my head, leaning my back against the railing. Just more proof coming to this party had been a bad idea. Not even ten minutes inside and I'd already made a fool of myself. They'd all probably burst into fits of laughter after I left.

"Stupid," I muttered, ignoring the heat of embarrassment I now felt. In the cool, scentless air it was easy to see how I'd been reacting to the scent of an Alpha. Who the fuck hallucinated about the scent of cupcakes? And never mind that, the universe could have at least given me the saving grace of having him be a troll. Or a monster. Not a tattooed god who looked like he could bench press me with one hand.

"There you are." Eva crossed to me from the door. "You disappeared so quickly I thought you might have ditched me and gone home."

"You know I wouldn't do that," I said quietly. Now that the high of pheromones and hunger was fading, all I felt was embarrassment. "I'm sorry about back there. I didn't realize it was a scent. I should have."

"Why are you sorry?"

"Because that didn't make you look good. Who knows how many people saw me charging across the room in search of *non-existent cupcakes*?"

Eva stepped to the side, leaning against the railing with me. "Esme, do you think I'm angry with you for it?"

Angry? No, I didn't think that. Disappointed maybe. Probably frustrated I'd once again be the center of a news story if the official photographer caught any of it. Just Esme Williams, the fuck-up half of the twins.

"Because I'm not. At all. His scent may not have hit me as strongly, but do you have any idea what it means that it hit you?"

I glanced over at her.

"When I was backstage at the award show? The first one I scented was Tyler. Fucking cinnamon and apples. I didn't think it was pie, but it was like the best candle I'd ever smelled. All I wanted to do was roll around in the scent until I was covered in it, and then I wanted to do it all over again.

"And then I met the rest of them. I don't have to tell you a story you already know. But when a scent hits you like that, it *means* something. Don't be embarrassed because you reacted the way you were supposed to."

I tilted my head back, spotting the couple of stars

which were still visible with the city's light pollution. "I called the man a cupcake, Eva."

"And I said he had a nice ass. So?"

He won't want me.

I cringed at the automatic thought, but it was true. It's where the fear had come from. The realization that my body reacted to him on a visceral level, and there I was standing next to Eva. Cupcake scent aside, I'd done this song and dance too many times for it to be unfamiliar.

"Bennett Gray is a phenomenal tattoo artist," she said. "And I've wanted to get a piece done by him for a long time. He gave me the card to their studio, and I'm going to go for a consultation. You can come with me, and we'll see what happens."

I turned away long enough to roll my eyes. I already knew what would happen, but I just nodded.

"Come on," she pulled one arm out from where I had it crossed and tugged me back towards the party. "Dance with me, eat some *real* food, and then we can go home. Okay?"

"Okay."

I supposed I was still hungry, though I was disappointed my brain didn't get what it wanted. I tried to briefly satisfy the hankering for sugar with some fruit and chocolate from the fountain.

While I did it, I glanced around the room, looking for a tall Alpha in black with gorgeous tattoos. The table where he'd been tattooing was empty, all his equipment gone. My stomach did a disappointed tumble, but it was probably for the best. Nothing had changed on the walk from the balcony to the food table.

The fruit took the edge off, and Eva reached for my hand again. "Let's dance."

Halfway there, Dante ran into us, and we kept going to the dance floor together. Here it was a lot louder, which was just fine. If I wanted to say something I would have to yell, so I just closed my eyes and danced.

The photographer Jasmine mentioned took pictures of the two of us for a few minutes before Dante finally chased the guy away and I could dance the way I wanted without having to half-pose for the camera. This was way more fun, and some of my self-conscious anxiety fell away.

Eva spun me under her arm, and then I saw her face, eyes wide, looking behind me. A second later I was enveloped by the smell of warmth and sugar. The Alpha. I turned, finding him standing so close we were almost touching.

Oh.

I started to move aside so he could move past toward Eva, and he caught me lightly by the upper arm, releasing me immediately. The brief touch was simply to stop me from moving—nothing more—and still his fingerprints felt like pure heat now branded on my skin.

He leaned in, and I was immediately proven wrong about needing to yell to be heard. The deep baritone of his voice cut under the music and made me shiver. "I came for you."

Goosebumps rippled across my skin, and with him so

close, I was absolutely *drowning* in the scent of vanilla. I could close my eyes and see those fucking cupcakes coming out of the oven, and my mouth was practically watering.

He spoke again, mouth even closer this time. "Dance with me?"

How could I say no to that? Well, I couldn't, because my tongue had decided this was the perfect moment to resign her job indefinitely, but I nodded. I glanced back once at Eva—who was smiling so widely it almost looked fake—and she gave me a thumbs up. Dante winked too, looking Bennett up and down with approval.

The music changed to a slower, more rhythmic beat, and suddenly we were dancing together. It didn't feel awkward or like we were trying too hard. It was entirely the opposite. Everything else in the world fell away. My instincts surged to the surface, and this time I didn't fight them.

One of my hands in his, he spun me the way Eva had, and I was aware of every fucking movement. Bennett leaned down to whisper in my ear. "Even with the scent dampeners in here, if I touch you, you're going to have my scent on you. Are you okay with that?"

I should assure him I had scent canceling body wash at home and I would take care of it later. Instead, all I managed was a strangled "Yes," because the last thing I wanted to think about was washing his scent *off* my body.

His hands brushed down my bare arms, raising more goosebumps on my skin. He briefly skimmed over the bracelet on my bicep before turning me again, pulling my back against his chest and locking us together. One arm slipped around my waist, and the other laced with my fingers, crossing our arms around my chest as we swayed. That's what it was now. Swaying. We were no longer dancing, and I didn't give a single Beta's ass.

I sank deeper into the layers of his scent—the sharpness of fresh vanilla and the sweetness of icing. It was factually impossible for someone to smell *this* good—I was sure of it.

He moved, and I moved with him, our swaying deepening to a little more, moving with the music. Somewhere out there, there were other people. But it didn't feel like that. We were all alone here in this place where the music wrapped us up and wove us together and *fuck*, I could stay here forever.

Safety. It was the sensation my mind was desperately trying to identify, and it was heady, strong, and addictive. Which was absurd. I was one of the most protected people in this city, and there was no time in my life I'd ever been unsafe.

I shoved aside the thoughts stubbornly pointing out there were different kinds of safety, and spun in Bennett's arms so we were face to face. He was so much taller than me, I had to crane my neck to see him. I wanted to look everywhere—examine the intricate details of his tattoos and find out if the body underneath this shirt was as perfect as the portions of it I could see. I wanted to see if his breath tasted as sweet as his scent.

Maybe other things tasted that sweet, too.

So many thoughts ran through my mind, I wasn't entirely sure how I suddenly ended up wrapping my arms around his neck, pressing my nose to his skin and inhaling like I was an addict needing a fix.

But here I was.

Reality slid into focus once more.

My knees were around his hips, and his hands were firmly—*firmly*—on my ass, keeping me in place. I pulled back so quickly I nearly knocked him into next week only find him smirking, green eyes sparkling with amusement and a darker shade of desire.

Oh, fuck.

I'd climbed the man.

I'd literally climbed him like a tree.

And beneath all of that, I realized the intensity of the scent surrounding us wasn't just him. It was me. I was *perfuming*. In a crowded room full of people, I was perfuming while practically humping an Alpha I didn't know. And there were photographers.

Mortification dropped through me so fast it left me dizzy and cold. I pushed away, and he set me gently on my feet, making sure I was steady on my heels before releasing me. He looked like he was about to say something, but I couldn't bear to think about what kind of remark he would make. My cheeks burned, and I turned, finding Eva through the crowd dancing with Dante. I pushed through the dancers to her, trying to ignore the smug looks and blatant stares.

I grabbed her arm. "Eva."

She startled, eyes going wide when she saw me. "Are you okay?"

"We need to go right now. Please? I need to go."

"Okay," she frowned but didn't argue. "Dante, can you take her over to the door? I need to find Jasmine."

"Sure." Dante was watching me warily too, searching the crowd behind me for the culprit of whoever he thought had upset me. But he didn't need to look behind me. It was me. *I* upset me.

I beelined for the door, slipping out of the curtains to wait near the elevators, Dante practically sprinting to keep up. "Woah, Esme. You're about to set the ground on fire you're moving so fast."

"I just needed to get out of there."

"What on earth hap—" He froze. Out here, where there weren't air filters purging everyone's scent and supplying dampeners, he could smell it. My perfume hung in the air, filling the small hallway, and I turned a thousand shades of red. "Is that why you want to leave?"

"Yes."

"But... why?"

It was too hard to explain. This didn't happen to me. I was the one no one wanted, and I'd never—*never*—perfumed for anyone. The only time I perfumed at all was during the occasional heat I couldn't avoid where I locked myself in my house until it was over. This wasn't heat perfume, but it didn't matter. It was too real.

How did I tell Dante I was too scared of what could be good? I wanted things too badly for them to fall apart, so it was easier not to have them in the first place. If I had to see one more Alpha suddenly look at me like I was broken or damaged because I wasn't what they expected, I would shatter. I couldn't take it.

And I especially couldn't take it from an Alpha who attracted me so much it overrode every bit of common sense I had. No, I needed to go home, wash off every bit of his scent, and pretend this never happened. If I was extremely lucky, there wouldn't be any pictures of me climbing him.

"Okay, I'm ready." Eva brushed out of the party entrance with Neil in tow and handed me my clutch. She stopped in her tracks, realizing exactly what Dante had only a minute ago. "You sure you want to go?"

"Yes," I said quietly.

She turned and quickly kissed Dante on both cheeks. "See you soon?"

"You bet," he grinned. "Hopefully you, too, Esme."

"Sure." My voice sounded strangled, like a dying cat, but I somehow managed a bit of a smile.

The paparazzi were still outside, but this time it was easy to ignore them. Security pushed us past the crowd into the car, and finally we were wrapped in glorious, blissful silence.

Eva pressed a button on the console. "Jeremy, please go to Esme's first."

"Of course, Miss Williams."

"Okay," she said when she released the button. "What the fuck was that?"

"What the fuck was what?"

She rolled her eyes. "One second you were dancing

45

with Bennett-fucking-Gray looking like you're in nine kinds of paradise, and the next you're begging me to leave like you're running from the law."

"Yeah." I wasn't going to explain it. She'd heard everything a million times and if she hadn't seen the climbing incident, as it was forevermore going to be referred to in my head, I wasn't going to enlighten her.

Eva sighed and looked out the window before looking back. "Did he hurt you? Did he try something?"

"No," I shook my head. "No, nothing like that. I just... I couldn't be there anymore."

We rode in silence, pools of light passing over us as we wove under streetlights away from downtown and into the older neighborhoods of the city. The further we got from the scene of my humiliation, the more relaxed I became.

"It's okay to perfume for someone, May-may."

"I know." I leaned my head back against the seat. Of course it was okay. It was everything that came after. "I just can't—" my breath hiccuped, and by some miracle, kept my voice even. "I just can't get my hopes up about something and then have them think I'm going to be you. Not when I reacted like that. I'm sorry."

"Esme." She slid across the seat and pulled me into a hug, and I let her. "I'm sorry."

"I know."

Despite all the ways her life made mine harder, there was no animosity between us as sisters. Eva only wanted the best for me, and she would be over the fucking moon to see me settled down and happy. It was everyone else who made it impossible when they looked at two people but only saw one. Like somehow the fact that we shared a womb and a face meant we shared everything down to preference, when we couldn't be more different.

Even our scents were opposites.

I leaned my head on her shoulder until the limo pulled up in front of my house and studio.

"You going to be okay tonight?"

"I'll be fine," I said with a sigh. I was always fine. "I'm done perfuming, and I'm going to take a shower and go to bed."

"Okay." She squeezed my hand. "Love you, May-may."

Stepping out of the car, I leaned back inside and smiled. "Love you, Va-va."

I watched until the limo turned the corner before I went inside, sadly and completely alone.

CHAPTER SIX

LUKE

*T*he design in front of me wouldn't fully resolve itself. I'd been staring at it for what felt like hours, searching for that intangible thing which made a tattoo sing. It was good I still had a week before the client needed to see it, because this wasn't working.

With a sigh, I clicked off the tablet I was sketching on and went to the kitchen to grab a beer from the fridge. It wasn't likely the beer was going to magically fix the design, but a man could hope.

The front door burst open and then closed again. Not quite a slam, but hard enough for me to pay attention. There were heavy sounds of equipment being dropped, followed by thumping, determined footsteps. Bennett strode into the kitchen looking absolutely wild and snagged the open beer from my hand. I hadn't even taken a sip yet.

"Why yes," I said sarcastically, "that was for you."

"Thanks." He tipped the bottle back, emptying half of it in one go.

"Fucking hell, Ben." I grabbed another beer and popped the cap off. "It was just a party. Couldn't have been that bad. And didn't they have alcohol there?"

The glass bottle hit the kitchen island, and he stared

at me. "Bad was the last thing it was. It was..." He ran both hands through his hair and huffed a breath. "I need you to smell me."

I chuckled. "Why?"

"Just do it," he said. "Now, before it fades."

Taking a sip of my beer, I circled the island and leaned in, doing as he asked. We'd done weirder things in our pack life.

It hit me all at once. Sweet floral fragrance lined with a deeper tartness. Powerful and heady—in no way should a scent be that strong when it was just a remnant. I blinked and inhaled again. It was there, a gorgeous thread which made my Alpha stand up tall and pay attention.

Omega.

"Holy fuck."

"Now you get it."

I'd never scented anything like that before. Omegas always smelled good, but *that*? That was something else entirely. A scent which told me it was *mine* and I needed to claim it. I needed to bury my nose in it and never stop breathing in.

"PACK ASSEMBLE," Bennett called, stripping the shirt off over his head.

I raised an eyebrow. "You couldn't have done that before you asked me to smell you?"

Bennett snorted. "I'm barely keeping my focus together long enough to talk to you all instead of finding her again right now, Luke."

I knew what he meant. If this was my secondhand

reaction, being in her presence must have been incredible. More than incredible. We walked to the living room, footsteps clunking from elsewhere in the house. "You going to tell us why her scent is all over you too?"

"Yes." He glared at me and tossed the shirt onto the coffee table. "I will."

Rylan came in, shirtless and mussed, clearly blinking sleep from his eyes. "Pack Assemble? What are we, superheroes?"

A growl rumbled from Bennett. "You might feel like it in a second."

"Probably not in the same way," I muttered. Rylan was a Beta. The only Beta in our pack. I didn't doubt the scent would be good for him, but it wouldn't have the same impact as it would on the rest of us.

I took another sip of beer in an attempt to keep myself from snatching Ben's t-shirt off the table again to inhale the scent which was already imprinted on my brain.

Kade and Avery entered together, looking at us expectantly.

"Is this where Bennett spills his feelings about being invited to a fancy party and how awful it was?" Kade asked. None of us really liked the party scene. At least not *that* party scene. But it was a good opportunity for Ben —for all of us—so he'd reluctantly agreed to go. Now I was fucking grateful he had.

"Smell the shirt," Ben said.

Avery raised an eyebrow. "What?"

"Do it," I nodded. "And be grateful he took it off for you first. Practically had my head in his armpit when he had me scent it."

Even as crazed as he was, Ben laughed once. "Asshole."

Kade leaned forward and snagged the black shirt. He didn't even get it all the way to his nose before I saw the change. He went rigid, suddenly inhaling deeply. When he looked up his eyes were dark, pupils wide and the same blank, wild look Bennett had on his face. "Who?"

"I'll get to that."

Avery stole the shirt and started to purr. "Holy shit."

"Okay, let me see." Rylan stole the fabric and scented it. His eyebrows rose. "Damn. Whoever's scent that is, it's incredible."

"She literally ran into me," Ben said. "I was tattooing Carson's wrist, and she crashed into me from behind." All of us cringed. "Luckily, I was reaching for ink when it happened."

"Thank fuck," I laughed.

"When I turned around, she was extremely upset I wasn't a cupcake."

All the air sucked out of the room at once. Bennett's scent was distinctly vanilla. Cupcake wasn't a far stretch, and if she scented him from across the room at a party where they sprayed industrial strength scent neutralizers...

"Holy shit," Rylan said.

"Now you're getting it," Ben said. "She was flustered and ran away. I finished Carson's wrist and packed up my equipment. By the time I'd done that, she was on the dance floor, which is how her scent is all over my shirt." He glanced at me. "It was... I don't know how to describe it. I was practically drunk on her scent, and she started perfuming."

My eyes widened. "Really?"

"Really. I think it freaked her out, because she left the party entirely."

"Seems like a theme," Kade said, eyes still on the shirt in Rylan's hands. I knew the feeling. "Who is she?"

"Her name is Esme Williams."

"The twin?" Rylan said with a grin.

Ben nodded in confirmation. "The twin."

I blinked. "Help me out here."

"Eva May Williams, the actress, is an Omega, and is bonded to that band Mindless Delirium," Rylan tossed the t-shirt back to Kade. "She has a twin sister who's also an Omega. The papers are pretty hard on her since she's not bonded and hasn't found a pack."

I frowned. That wasn't fair. Finding a pack was hard at the best of times for Omegas. Doing so in the public eye would be even harder.

"People know it too," Ben added. "Carson said as much. She also seems to think everyone prefers her sister to her. When I approached her on the dance floor I had to tell her I was there for *her* and not for Eva."

I took a step backward so I could lean against the wall. "What do we do about this?" I said. "If she ran away from you—"

"I don't think that was it," he said. "I think she... I

don't know. It seemed like she spooked herself. Both times. And frankly, I don't care if she's jumpy. I've never had this kind of reaction to a scent before. Have any of you?"

It wasn't even a question. We all knew we hadn't.

"I can't," Ben hauled in a breath and shook his head. "I can't walk away from that. If you'd been there, you'd feel the same. She's fucking beautiful, and her scent feels like you're inhaling fire in the best way. It *lights you up* under your skin. I want you all to meet her because I think she's ours."

My breath went short in my chest. It was a dream every pack had: to find *their* Omega and bond with them, creating the intangible bond you could always feel. Even Rylan could bond with an Omega if he was bitten. Right now we didn't have that, and we'd talked more than once about wanting it.

"How do we do it?" Avery asked. "If she spooks easy, the five of us aren't going to put her at ease."

"First, I need to know if you guys are with me on this." Ben looked around at each of us, and it was easy to say I'd never seen him like this. We'd all had flings at one time or another, but we'd never found an Omega who called to us, and my pack brother looked nearly haunted by the idea of losing this one.

"I want to meet her. Hell, I want to fucking bond her on scent alone."

"Agreed." Kade still held Ben's shirt, staring at it as if it would transform into the woman in question.

Avery smiled and said "Of course," at the same time Rylan was saying, "Hell yeah."

"But wanting to meet her still doesn't solve the problem of how," Avery pointed out.

Ben was smiling now. "For that? I have an idea."

CHAPTER SEVEN

ESME

I chunked more of the destroyed make-up palette onto the white marble slab in front of me before reaching for the bottle of linseed oil out of sight of the camera. I was out of binder and didn't feel like making more, so oil it was.

The color was gorgeous today, a peacock green which shimmered purple and blue when it moved in the light. As I picked up my smallest glass muller and slowly began to mix the paint, my shoulders started to relax. I hadn't left my house since the party, and that was just fine with me. A couple of days in the house wouldn't kill me. None of the world needed to see me right now.

Music blared through the speakers, and I was glad my face was never in these videos and that I always replaced the sound. It meant I could sing at the top of my lungs and no one gave a shit but me.

The paint I was making was going to be incredibly exclusive. Simply because there wasn't much of this pigment. Eva gave me all the make-up palettes she didn't want, and I used them sometimes when I didn't want to buy bigger pigment shipments. Or when I was bored.

Companies practically rained down gifts on her head, so I always had plenty of these to use. And people loved fighting over which ones they'd get when I put them up for sale.

I snorted, imagining what people would think if they knew they were buying watercolors from one of the most infamous Omegas on the planet.

I'd avoided everything on purpose the last couple of days. I wasn't interested in seeing a picture of me wrapped around Bennett Gray like I was a monkey. No matter that I couldn't get his vanilla cupcake scent out of my nose, and there were faint traces of it still on my skin because I hadn't bothered to shower it off.

Gross? Maybe. But no one was here to see me, and it wasn't like I was going to see him again.

And sure, I looked him up, since Eva seemed to know who he was. I think I lost several hours yesterday going down the rabbit hole of not only him, but his entire pack. They were all experts in their own right and owned a tattoo shop downtown. Nautilus.

Their work was *beautiful*. Once I was scrolling, I recognized some of their work. Particularly a tattoo of a statue Bennett had done on someone's arm. It was so realistic it felt like you could reach into their skin and feel the stone. It still popped up in my feeds now and again.

All of them had an impressive level of skill, and it seemed like they could do pretty much anything. I didn't have any tattoos, but scrolling through their work, which ranged from traditional to hyperrealism to watercolor, made me rethink it.

But I couldn't get a tattoo from them. Because if it were Bennett tattooing me, all the lines would get messed up because I'd probably end up climbing him again. And if his pack smelled anything close to as good as he did? I would keel over and perish.

Not to mention they were all hot. Let me spread frosting on you and lick it off just as an excuse hot.

Maybe...

The tiniest part of my mind held a spark of hope, but I dismissed it just as quickly. One delicious smelling Alpha and one dance didn't mean anything. Besides, they would know who I was because of how we met and the party. Either they wouldn't want to deal with the kind of attention that came with even speaking to me, or they'd be more interested in Eva and her connections.

I slowed down my movements. My thoughts were making me move too fast, and speed didn't make the best paint in my experience. For some pigments, maybe, but this was already fine and needed more mixing than crushing.

And there it was. I fought off the new wave of loneliness that washed over me, as they had every few hours since I came home. Fucking hell. Maybe I just needed to get laid.

Instantly, I recoiled.

Sex was fine. Great. But I'd learned through one too many encounters it was easier to stay home with a vibrator than risk either my date calling the paps, calling out Eva's name during orgasm, or any of the other ridiculous things which had happened. Few of which I'd ever told anyone.

I'd be fine.

I was always fine.

Grabbing my little plastic containers from the box I kept them in, I lined them up after adjusting the camera to a closer angle. I would only need about five for this batch. Slowly, I scraped the paint off the marble and gently dripped it into the boxes in equal measurement.

One of my favorite parts.

The jarring dissonance of my phone ringing against the music made me jump. Eva's name lit up the screen. I tapped off the music before I answered the call on speaker and went back to filling the paint pots. "Hello."

"Wow, you sound like shit."

I rolled my eyes. "And that kind of greeting is going to make me feel better?"

She laughed. "Fair point. I have the afternoon off. Want to have lunch?"

"I was actually planning on remaining in my house for the rest of history. I'm good."

She sighed. "Come on, May-may. We'll go to some-place tiny and dark with no room for photographers to follow us, and the whole thing will take two hours. Then I'll let you slip back into whatever hole you've dug for yourself."

I dabbed a glob of paint onto the top of one of my tiny boxes, creating the satisfying, *barely* overfilled bubble people always seemed to go nuts for in the videos. These would sell in about five seconds. But it was so pretty I kind of wanted to keep one just for me and use it on something new.

"You're going to keep making up new excuses or

ways to do things to get me out of the house, aren't you?" I asked my sister.

"Bet your ass."

Sighing, I glanced at what I had left. It wouldn't take long. "Fine, but I need to finish these so they can dry, and I'm not changing."

"Glad I didn't have to do more convincing," she said. "I'm letting myself in right now."

The line went dead, and I heard her steps as she moved through the house and finally ended up in my studio. "Remind me to take back your key."

"You want to cut off my thumb? That's harsh."

Security was obviously a big concern for us, so thumb-printed locks graced all of my doors with an alarm system which would make a museum's look tame.

Eva looked me up and down and shrugged. "You've looked worse."

"Gee, thanks."

"Oh, is this one of mine?" She leaned closer to the paint on the table.

I nodded. "Yeah. The palette is on the table behind me."

"Oh, I remember this one. Nice." I heard her move back toward my second studio—the one I used for my own paintings. I sold those under a fake name too. "Working on anything new?"

"No, but I am very tempted to keep some of this color and use it."

"Do it. Imagine the craze of only selling three pots."

I smirked. Eva was a fangirl of my paints in the way

only a sister could be. Putting the finishing touches on the last pot, I turned off the camera and rinsed my tools.

"Okay, let me grab my shoes and let's go."

My hair was in a high ponytail, so you couldn't really tell it was *that* greasy. Black leggings and an oversized pink hoodie were the rest of it. I grabbed a baseball hat and sunglasses too. No matter what Eva said, there was always the risk of photographers.

"Has it been bad?" I asked as I closed the door behind us and double-checked the lock.

"Has what been bad?"

I winced. "The press from the party. About me."

Neil was there opening the car door for us, but she paused, eyes wide. "What are you talking about?"

"I haven't looked, but I assumed there would be some sort of story about me and Bennett. How I climbed and practically licked him on the dance floor."

Following her into the car, she pulled out her phone and started texting. "There was nothing."

"Really?"

She nodded. "I don't think the photographer got any of you two tangled up, and even if he had, I would have made sure it was never used. That was a nice moment for you, and like hell would I let anyone ruin it."

My cheeks felt hot. "It was a nice moment. But that's all it was."

"Oh my god, Esme," she flopped backwards, letting her head loll on the seat. "You're going to tell me it meant nothing when you haven't showered and I can still smell vanilla on you?"

"Is it bad?"

She dropped her face in her hands. "No, it's not bad. But it tells me a lot about what actually happened. You know how long I refused to bathe after I met the guys because I couldn't *bear* the thought of washing the scent off me? It was *way* past gross, and half the reason I knew it was real was because they were just as reluctant to wash me off them. It means everything."

"His pack hasn't met me. There's no guarantee of anything." Nerves swam in my gut and I swallowed. Reasonably I knew I was being overly stubborn, but I had good fucking reason to be after everything I'd tried. If there were a choice between being potentially rejected by a pack and keeping a nice memory, I'd keep the memory, thanks.

"Esme," Eva leaned forward and looked at me. "Please tell me the truth. Do you like him?"

"I ran into him and danced with him. I have no idea if I like him." Sighing, I pushed my hands into the pocket of my hoodie. They still sparkled with remnants of the pigment from earlier. "But yes. I've never felt anything like that before. And it scares the shit out of me."

"Why?"

I couldn't put voice to the truth. Eva knew how bad it was, and yet she didn't. She didn't live in this skin and didn't understand how I butted up against her life in almost every way. Her life limited mine and formed the boundaries—it wasn't her fault or her choice, but it was the way it was.

"Don't make me beat it out of you."

A laugh burst out of me. Between the two of us, I was probably the one who would win, but I understood she was trying to make me laugh. "Everything you already know aside," I said. "The press already paints me as some kind of villain when I turn packs down. Imagine how hard they'd come after them if I was around this pack? Even if they *did* want me, that would put an end to it."

"Yeah, I'm going to need you to stop that."

"Stop what?"

"Shutting good things down before they have a chance to happen. Who gives a shit what the media says? Remember how badly they went after Mindless Delirium when we met? Was it rough? Yes. But it didn't matter in the end because I was happy and so were they. If you're truly happy, they can't touch you."

I slumped back against the leather seat, staring at the car ceiling. On the one hand, she was right, and on the other, I was a realist. The media loved Eva, and they were likely to forgive her more than they would me.

Eva had her phone out, texting someone. Probably Jasmine. Her schedule was so busy I was amazed she even had time to grab lunch. "So, where are we going again?"

"Almost there."

We were downtown now, the mix of slick high-rises mixed with older, more decorative buildings always an interesting thing to watch. When I was a little younger and I didn't have as much attention on me, I liked to come down here and draw the juxtaposition between the old and the new.

But this neighborhood wasn't where we'd find a hole-in-the-wall restaurant to eat.

The car pulled to the curb, and I saw the sign on the storefront we landed in front of. "No."

Nautilus.

There was a twisting spiral next to the word, evoking the image of the shell, but not completely. The studio where Bennett and his entire pack worked.

"Esme, it's going to be fine."

I looked at her, my heart already pounding. "Why would you bring me here when I look like this? When I still *smell like him*?"

Leaning across the car, she touched my knee. "Do you really think I would have let you out of the house to meet your future pack if I thought you looked bad? You look casual and adorable, and whether or not you believe it, smelling like him is only going to help you here."

I whined, anxiety welling up in my chest. "Why didn't you tell me? Why are we here?"

"Because I never would have gotten you out of the house *at all* if I had. Listen. If this is too much and you're genuinely terrified, I won't make you go in. But I hope you know I only want you to be happy, May-may."

Could I do this? Every part of me was terrified. But that tiny piece of me which had kept hope alive the past two days while I stalked all of them on social media perked her head up. The traitor.

"And we're here because I didn't lie. I've always wanted a tattoo by Bennett, and I think it's a good way to start to crack this goody-two-shoes image I have. There might even be a possibility to record the process. It could be a really great opportunity for everyone involved, so when they reached out I said yes right away."

I'd stopped listening after she mentioned her image. So this wasn't entirely about me. In a way, it was relieving. Eva was still talking, but I couldn't keep the words down. "They know I'm coming?"

"They do, and they were fucking ecstatic about it."

My stomach flipped. Neil opened the door, and Eva started to get out. "You coming?"

I wanted to say no and get a cab home. But that traitorous piece of my heart knew if I walked away now, I'd always wonder, and I didn't want to be left with questions forever.

Putting on my hat and sunglasses, I got out of the car.

CHAPTER EIGHT

ESME

*N*autilus was beautiful. Everything that made up a classic grungy tattoo shop, but elevated. Dark, clean cement floors and strong lines emphasized by square columns. A mirror all along the back wall which reflected the natural light. This building was lucky—having storefront windows on two sides, so the natural light felt fresh and clean.

There were doors to what looked like private rooms, and a few stations out in the open, only a couple of them full. Bennett was one of the ones tattooing, and he hadn't seen me yet. But I saw the others too. I knew their names now from stalking them on social media. Avery was finishing a tattoo on someone's shoulder, and one of the doors was open.

Grays with splashes of spring green decorated the space, with a lush waiting area and monochromatic prints on the walls. With one exception.

Behind the reception desk, over the metal sign which read *Nautilus*, there was a painting. The paint was chunky, thick, and layered like it had been put onto the canvas with a palette knife, radiating out in an abstract spiral. A deep blue-violet which reminded me of tanzanite and a metallic gold which winked in the light.

Streaks of black and white too, but it felt *alive* in this space.

It took my breath away.

I grabbed Eva's hand, and she gasped too. "See? I told you."

The other thing about this place was, it was like stepping into a candle store. Competing scents which were all so good, you didn't know which direction to walk in first. "I need you to tell me if it smells like the world's best perfume store in here, or if it's just me."

My sister laughed quietly. "That's just you, babe."

Fuck.

The receptionist—a petite woman with electric blue hair and every piercing imaginable looked up with a smile. "Hi there, welcome to Nautilus. How can I—" She faltered halfway through her sentence, eyes going wide as she realized who Eva was. "Oh, shit."

Eva laughed. "They know we're coming."

Bennett looked up then, and it was like our gazes had *snap-to-grid* turned on the way they locked in place. He grinned, pulled off his glove, and turned without hesitation to reach behind him where a box of six huge cupcakes sat. Vanilla cake, swirled white frosting, just like I'd imagined him to be at the party. He picked one up and bit into it, never looking away.

"Holy shit," Eva said, like she was inside my mind.

"What do I do?" I asked, breathless.

"Go talk to him, obviously."

Handing her my sunglasses, I took a breath.

I was incredibly aware of myself as I walked, and the

fact that Bennett was looking at me. Not only Bennett. Avery watched me, too. And Luke, who was sitting in a chair in the corner I hadn't noticed before. I stopped just before I bumped into him—hopefully I wouldn't make that mistake again.

This close, his warm vanilla cake and frosting scent wafted around me and holy *god*, it was just as good as the other night. "Hi."

He smiled and licked what remained of the frosting from his fingers. "Want a cupcake?"

"I don't know," I said honestly. My mind was still a wasteland of blankness and anxiety. All I knew was that I was here, and they were all here, and I didn't know what to do now. We never got this far, usually. The packs and I. They would have figured out the truth by now and I would have sent them on their way or they would have rescinded their application.

Bennett tugged on a new glove and leaned forward. "I'm glad you came. I have to finish this, and it won't take long. Would you be okay waiting in our office while Avery and I finish so we can all talk to you?"

It wasn't a dismissal. Nothing about the way he was looking at me was anything less than focused. But there was still a man lying face down on the tattoo bench, and I didn't think he would be pleased if his session was interrupted because I showed up.

"Okay."

"Rylan," Bennett called.

A blonde head popped out from one of the doors, and I recognized him too. Boyishly handsome face with a

69

smile that would knock the lights out of photographer's cameras.

"Can you take Esme to the office?" Bennett picked up the tattoo machine with one hand, and with the other, he touched me lightly on the arm. "Don't go anywhere."

I swallowed, trying to breathe evenly when the same impulse to force my nose into his neck was slowly taking over.

"Sure thing." Rylan gestured to me, and I made my way over to him, immediately warmed by the smile on his face and his scent. Summertime. A mix of fresh-cut grass and lemonade. Sweeter notes of fruit and jam. *Beta*.

"It's nice to meet you," Rylan said, pushing through a heavy door into a spacious room I hadn't expected.

There were a few desks and drafting tables, a kitchenette, and another set of huge windows looking onto the other side of the block, where there was a park across the street, and a door to a small parking lot.

The same color scheme ruled here, cool and comfortable. A big couch sat near the windows, and I knew that was where I'd end up.

"Why do all of you smell so good?" I blurted out, looking up at him. He was as tall as Bennett was, dimples in his cheeks showing when he grinned.

"I don't know, but I think it's a good sign, right?"

"Yeah."

He walked with me over to the couch. "We're going to try to not totally overwhelm you," he said. "That's why I'm in here with you and not one of the others.

But you should know we're all excited to meet you. Ben's shirt has taken up permanent residence in the kitchen."

I blinked and sat down on the couch. "His shirt?"

"The one he wore to the party," he clarified. "The one with your scent all over it."

My entire face turned bright red, and I was suddenly sweating in my hoodie. "He showed you that?"

"He did." Rylan now looked a little sheepish. "Not in a creepy way. In a 'my whole life is changed and I think it's going to be the same for all of us' way."

"Oh." The single word felt more than inadequate in comparison to his description, but it was all I had. I was so used to being on the defensive when it came to me and packs, and I had nothing here. Everything they said—every scent—so far had laid me open.

"I don't know how to do this," I told him. "And I'm... really fucking nervous."

Rylan sat down on the arm of the couch, close enough to lend me his comforting scent, but not close enough to crowd me. "It's okay. None of us have a clue what we're doing either. But we're going to try. Do you want something to drink?"

I shook my head. "I'm okay, thanks."

The scent hit me first. Vanilla and sugar. Bennett strode into the room, tossing his gloves into the trash can and putting the box of cupcakes on a desk as he came closer. It was his same uniform from the party—dark jeans which clung to his thighs in ways that made my mouth water and a dark t-shirt straining over his chest.

71

This one was navy blue. "Give us a second, Ry. Make sure everyone else is ready."

The Beta grinned. "Will do."

Grabbing a wheeled chair from one of the desks, Bennett rolled it in front of me, moving the coffee table away so there was room and trapping me between his knees. "First things first, what I should have done that night instead of letting you run away."

His hands came up around my face, one slipping behind my neck as he kissed me. It wasn't hesitant, and it wasn't out of control. It was just a perfect kiss, and my mind went blissfully blank. The same sense of safety I'd felt when we were dancing clicked into place, and I moaned softly, unable to help it.

I was perfuming again—frankly amazed I'd lasted this long without it—and at least we weren't in public.

He pulled back but didn't let me go. "The only reason I didn't come after you was because Eva told me she would help bring you when she called. Otherwise, I might have turned into a bit of a stalker just so I could scent you again. See you again."

"Really?"

A huffed laugh. "Esme, I've barely been able to think the last two days, and I'm not the only one. The others are barely letting me in here alone with you because they're so eager."

"Rylan told me about the shirt." I bit my lip.

"It has a place of honor." He leaned forward, inhaling deeply, the simple sound of it sending tingles through my entire body. The purr I'd only gotten the barest hint of at the party came to life, rich and deep. "Looks like I'm not the only one."

I colored pink all over again only for his hands to tighten. "Don't be embarrassed. I don't think you have any idea what you having my scent still on you is doing to me."

Every one of my senses was overloaded. It was entirely possible I would pass out. He'd kissed me, was purring for me, and I wanted more.

"Would you like to meet them?"

I nodded. "Yes, please."

"You feral beasts can come in now," he said, lifting his volume a little.

The door opened like they'd all been hanging on bated breath. Now it wasn't just my scent and Bennett's, it was all of them.

"Holy fuck," someone said under their breath. "The shirt was nothing compared to this."

I blushed, standing up to meet the four men who were filing into the room. "I might have done my own stalking," I told Bennett quietly.

His answering smile was wide. "Good. But introductions are still needed. This is Luke, our traditional specialist." It felt strange to shake hands with them like this was some kind of business transaction and not what it really was.

"Hi."

Luke's hand gripped mine, and he didn't let go. His build was lean, but he wasn't skinny. The henley he wore showed the power of his arms, as much as the pushed up sleeves did. Sandy brown hair and piercing blue eyes met mine, and unlike the rest of them, I didn't see any visible tattoos. "It's very nice to meet you, Esme, and if you're willing, I'd like to hug you more than just a handshake."

I blew out a breath in relief. "Yes, please."

He wrapped me up tightly, and I got the first real hit of his scent. It was rich and aquatic. Like the fresh scent after rain and the ocean on the wind. Somehow wild and steady at the same time.

The same reaction that I'd had to Bennett occurred. I wanted to inhale this man and explore him, my Omega brain recognizing him as *something*.

Deep down, I knew what it was, but I was still too nervous to let the thought surface completely.

Luke pulled away slowly, smiling at me. I knew from my stalking he was the oldest of their pack. Not that he looked it.

"You've already met Rylan," Bennett said.

The smiling blond held his arms out with a question on his face, and I nodded, unable to stop smiling back. His lighter Beta scent was just as delicious as the first time around, and his hug was *good*. The kind of hug you could breathe into and not want to let go.

But he had to.

"This is Kade, our piercer and chameleon. You come in and don't have an appointment or don't know what you want? Kade's your man."

The giant in front of me was covered in tattoos and piercings. A thick beard graced his face, dark as his hair.

74

When he looked at me, I felt like he saw all of me completely.

He had a ring in his lip and studs in one eyebrow. Gauges in his ears, too. His scent hit me before he even stepped close enough for me to decide whether to hug him. Oak and chestnut. Kettle corn. A wavering sweetness over deeper notes. A bonfire in wintertime. "It's good to meet you, Esme."

His voice was so deep it vibrated through me and *pulled* at something in my soul.

At first glance, he was the kind of guy you crossed the street at night to stay away from. But danger wasn't even close to the thing I felt from him. I let him pull me into a fierce embrace, scent washing over me in pure waves. A purr just as deep as his voice rumbled through both of us.

When he let me go, my hands were fisted in his shirt and I hadn't remembered doing it.

"And finally," Bennet said, "this is Avery. Our watercolorist."

The last of their pack was large. Red hair and full beard, he was burly. He somehow reminded me of a lumberjack and a teddy bear at the same time, and I wasn't complaining.

His scent was subtler than the others, but no less delicious. Spicy—that's what he was. Herbs like cardamom and cinnamon. Even sharper, like Anise. The closer I got, the more threads there were to follow in his scent.

I imagined spending all the time I needed breathing him in, just so I could trace down every little element of his spiciness.

Avery's hug was full and comfortable, enveloping me in warmth and softness. "I know we're a lot," he said quietly, "but I hope you know we're very glad you're here."

When he pulled away, I wasn't sure what to do. My scent permeated the room like it did only during my heats. I wasn't there yet, but with this many Alphas I responded to? I wouldn't be surprised if one came on soon.

Bennett pressed a hand to my lower back, guiding me back to the couch. But he didn't let me sit alone. He sat first, guiding me to sit between his legs, and I didn't protest. Being pressed up against him and surrounded by his scent along with everyone else's? I was pretty much in heaven.

One arm looped around my waist like he was afraid I might run again. Which was fair.

"Now that we've been introduced," he said, "let's talk."

CHAPTER NINE

KADE

I flexed my hands before crossing my arms. It seemed the easiest way to keep them under control.

The little Omega now sitting between Ben's legs was jumpy and skittish, just like he'd said. What he hadn't made clear was how absolutely fucking beautiful she was. Her scent was already everything, but the combination of the two nearly put me on the floor.

Jealousy flared at the fact she was sitting with him and not me, even though there was no room for that here. She knew him the best, and the last thing we wanted was for her to bolt. If I had my way, she'd be sitting with me plenty.

More than sitting.

Riding.

My face, my cock, and any other part of me she chose.

I was glad my dark jeans disguised how hard I was, because the second I walked into her cloud of perfume, I was gone.

Even her skittish nature called to me, imagining her running and being able to chase.

"I—" Her swallow was visible. "I'm sorry. I'm not good at this. But you probably already know that."

"Why would we?" I asked. Clearly, she was referencing what Ben had said, the media painting a picture of her. But I wasn't going to let her think we came in with negative expectations.

Her cheeks colored, and my imagination took the color and *ran*. What other parts of her small, curvy body could I turn pink? Pinker than the giant hoodie which swallowed her up.

"I just... quite a few packs have approached my family for something like this, and it never worked. They expected someone different." Her eyes were on the ground and then they snapped up to mine, rotating through the four of us she could see. "I'm not like her. You know that, right?"

"We do know that," Luke said.

Esme blinked. "Where is Eva?"

"She left," Rylan answered. "After I brought you back here. Said to call her if you needed. All our clients are gone too. The only one left is Daisy, our receptionist. She'll field anyone who comes in."

"Okay."

All at once, she dropped her face into her hands. "Fucking hell, I am so bad at this. I don't even know where to start except for the fact that your scents do things to me I've never experienced before—like climbing Bennett in the middle of the dance floor. And based on those hugs it would have been the same with any of you. Even you," she singled out Rylan.

He shrugged, grinning. Being the only Beta in the

pack had never bothered him. Not much bothered Rylan. He was eternally positive, which grated on my nerves sometimes, but he was the lightness our pack needed.

"And I don't know where to go from here."

Avery leaned forward, checking in with all of us silently one final time before speaking. We'd already decided, with the caveat we had to meet her first, but this little Omega was ours. I knew it. Deep down as far as I knew I was an Alpha, she belonged with me and this pack. Not everyone put stock in scent theory, that there was always a perfect match, a certain predestined *thing* which made people perfect for each other.

I'd been a skeptic until I put my nose in Ben's shirt and my entire world turned upside down.

Now I knew it was true.

Who knew if every Omega had a pack which would be their mates, but this one had one, and we weren't about to let her go. Not without trying first.

Avery cleared his throat. "We know it can be jarring, having something like this happen so quickly. But we're all in agreement—we'd like to court you, Esme. What you're feeling from our scents? It's just as powerful on our end. And I'm pretty sure Luke, Kade, and I are all feeling the jealousy of you sitting with Ben right now."

I nodded once.

Courting an Omega varied. There were different customs and different ways of going about it, but they all involved the same things—getting to know each other and spoiling the Omega absolutely rotten. I had no problem doing either of those things. There were no official rules, but given who she was, there might be more steps.

That being said, speed wasn't uncommon in situations like this. When you knew, you knew. We would court Esme as long as she needed, but I knew on scent alone she could say yes to being our Omega tomorrow and I'd be happier than I'd ever been in my life.

But that wasn't what struck me. It was her reaction. Her face was shocked and open, eyes glassy. "Really?" It didn't sound like she quite believed anyone would want to court her, and I suppressed the growl building in my chest from wanting to know who'd made her think she wasn't worthy of it.

"Yes," Avery said. "Absolutely."

"I've always wanted a pack," she said so softly we almost couldn't hear it. "After everything, I never really thought I'd have a chance."

We looked at each other in alarm. "Why?" I asked, the question coming out too roughly. Shifting my chair closer to her and Ben, I leaned in. Fuck, that floral scent was so good. It was layered with her sharper tea scent, which I could already tell was the note which shifted with her mood. Consciously, I gentled my voice. "What made you think you'd never have a pack?"

"It doesn't matter," she said too quickly. "Not right now, anyway."

It obviously did matter, but I couldn't push her

today. Not during this first meeting, even if my instincts were screaming at me to dig into why, so I could help her release the line of thought. I didn't care who the Omega was, male or female, no one deserved to truly believe they wouldn't have a pack.

"You mentioned your family," Luke said. "Do we need to approach them to make our courting you official?"

"Oh god please don't," Esme said with a laugh. "Then you'd have to deal with Katarina, and she's the worst. She would absolutely not approve of you, which is only a plus in my book." After a second, she remembered we had no idea who that was. "Katarina is a pack matchmaker my mother hired in a desperate attempt to find a pack for me. Because being a single Omega in my family isn't okay."

Luke chuckled. "What about your mother, then? I don't want us stepping on any toes."

She shook her head. "No. You won't be. Frankly, I hope Mom will be happy a pack is actually interested in me for *me* and not—" she cut herself off and cleared her throat. "She'll be happy. Maybe not at first," she glanced at me and I couldn't help but smile. I knew I wasn't the kind of Alpha you brought home to mother. I looked the part of the intimidating and scary, which had served me well in my life. "But she will be. My mother is an Omega too, but she didn't have a pack. Just one Alpha. And he died a couple of years ago."

"I'm sorry," I said.

While pack life was the norm, there were those who found a single person they wanted to partner with and were happy. Ben's sister was one such person. For myself, even with the frustrations and trials of pack life, I couldn't imagine myself without it.

"Thanks. But I think in the end she'll be happy to have me happy, and that will be the end of it."

"Does anyone have any more appointments left for the rest of the day?" Ben asked.

"No," I said. "I'm done."

Everyone else was the same. Knowing this might happen, we'd all kept our schedules light out of sheer hope.

"Would you like to come back to our house?" Ben gently pulled Esme back against his chest. "If you want to call Eva to come with you to make you more comfortable, you can do that. Or anyone."

I saw her think about it. Of course we knew we wouldn't do anything to hurt her, but I was glad she was taking it seriously. As much as I wanted to believe every pack in the world would cherish an Omega like her, I knew it wasn't true.

"I think Eva will distract me," she said. "But if it's okay with you, I'll ask if she can spare someone from her security team. Not that I think of you like that, I just—"

Holding out a hand, I stopped her from apologizing for it. "It's a good idea. We would all rather you both feel safe and be safe. I could, and do, swear on my life our pack won't hurt you, and I still think it's a good idea for the first time coming to our home."

She blushed again. "Thank you. What's the address? I'll call them now."

Ben stood with her, scribbling our address on a piece of paper as she stepped out of the room to make the call.

"Holy shit," Rylan said. "This is really happening."

I was still watching the door where she'd gone. "You were right, Ben. She's nervous as hell."

Luke nodded. "Loosening up a little, though."

Standing, Rylan stretched. "So what's the plan?"

"I'm thinking we show her the house, then pizza and a movie. My gut says Esme needs to know we're okay with her as she is. And as hard as it might be to *only* snuggle with her when she smells like that, I think she needs it." Avery said it with finality.

I couldn't agree more.

"Anyone need to sprint ahead to make us not look like complete shits when she sees the house?"

Rylan scratched the back of his head. "It's not bad, I swear."

We all laughed, and Esme came back into the room smiling. "Okay. Wes, one of Eva's security, will meet us at the house. She's very annoyed she's not allowed to come, by the way."

Avery laughed. "I'm sure she'll see it soon enough."

The briefest of shadows passed over her face. So there *was* something there with her sister. Something more complicated than we realized. Though it was clear she loved her sister based on what Ben said and her words in general.

"Let's get out of here," Ben said, gently turning her

toward the back door of the studio. "Start thinking of questions to grill us with."

She smiled, perfume still wafting away from her like a beacon to follow. A true, open smile with none of the shyness and nerves she'd shown before. "Don't worry. I will."

CHAPTER TEN

ESME

The house was *not* what I expected. Granted, I hadn't fully known what to expect, but the sprawling modern mansion on the edge of the city wasn't it.

"Holy shit." I stepped out of Luke's car and stared.

"Let me guess," Rylan said with a smirk. "You thought because we're tattoo artists we lived in a dark basement of some kind?"

I shook my head. "Not at all. I just wasn't expecting something this size."

Ben winked. "We do okay."

It made sense. Each of the guys were well known for what they did, and it was a fact people traveled from all over the world to have their ink done by one of the Nautilus men.

Wow.

A black car was already in the large gravel drive, and Wes stepped out as I approached, nodding. An older Alpha who'd been with Eva's security for years, I trusted him with my life. I didn't think anything bad was going to happen to me here, but the fact they'd encouraged me to bring a backup comfort person only made me feel better.

"I think I'm more nervous than I should be," I said quietly.

"Nerves are good," Kade said. "They keep you alert. And besides, would you be nervous if you didn't want to be here?"

He was right. I was nervous because I *did* want to be here and a brutal hope was blooming in my chest. Once we went into the house, I was terrified there would be something which would make this fall apart. And I didn't want it to fall apart.

The dream I'd always had of being loved and courted was so close it didn't feel real.

"Okay," I said, managing to take a breath. "Lead the way." I followed them up the steps and Wes fell in behind me. "How are you, Wes?"

"I'm doing well, Miss Williams. Happy to help."

"Thanks."

Luke held the door open, and we all passed through. One glance backward showed me Luke shaking hands with Wes, and my stomach flipped. I remembered the pack of businessmen from a year ago whose home I visited. The farthest I'd gotten up until now. I'd had security with me then too, and they were so offended I would bring him that it ended everything.

They felt insulted by the gesture. So seeing them not only encourage me to bring someone but *welcoming* them eased some of my nerves.

The inside of the house was both stark and comfortable, though those words didn't usually go hand in hand. But the clean lines mirrored the ones at Nautilus, combined with dark woods and plush white carpets which ran up the stairs. And here, in the entryway, was another painting.

More chunky paint, this one featuring an ombre gradient from a nearly neon yellow to a purple so deep it was basically black. "You have another one." The words slipped out before I could stop them.

"You know Elyse Taylor's work?" Luke stepped up beside me. "I'm a fan. We have a couple of other pieces, along with the one at the studio."

I flushed hot, suddenly wishing I had more than a bra on under my hoodie so I could take it off. "I do know her work," I said. "Very well. I can't believe you have so many of her pieces. It's..."

There were no words for it. And I couldn't lie to them if we were really doing this, so I finally looked at Luke. "Thank you."

The confusion crossed his face. "Thank you—" his eyes went wide. "Really?"

It wasn't incredulous, it was awed. I nodded.

"What did I just miss?" Rylan asked, looking between us.

Fidgeting with the cuffs on my hoodie, I looked at the painting again, and then back at Rylan. "I'm Elyse Taylor. Or rather, that's the name I sell my art under."

"Holy shit."

They were all looking at me now, but the way Luke looked at me made the floor drop a foot beneath my feet. Without warning, he reached out and pulled me to him, wrapping me fully in an embrace. This wasn't an introductory hug. It was more than that. I gave in to what I wanted to do with all of them and simply *breathed*. His scent was stronger right now, floating around me like the air off the sea, and I was perfuming.

I pulled back because we were only in the entryway, and there was a hell of a lot more to see. "If we're not careful, you'll never get my scent out of here," I said.

Bennett laughed. "You say that like it's something we want to get rid of."

My stomach swooped again. They were already so certain. I knew it too, down deep, but history had fucked me so many times, I couldn't bear to give in only to have my hopes shattered. Again.

"Come on," Avery said with a grin. "Let's show you the place."

The kitchen was first. Black marble floors and slick stainless steel made it look like one of those kitchens out of a design magazine, but still lived in. There was a kettle on the stove and mail on the counter. A tall bar with stools to sit on and a table next to a window which looked out over the backyard and the evening sky.

"Who designed this place?" I asked. "And the studio? 'Cause so far everything is beautiful."

"We did," Rylan said. "Together. The studio too. A designer helped it all come together, the logistics and stuff. But it took forever, and I'm pretty sure Kade and Avery got into about three fistfights over things like tiles."

I raised an eyebrow and Avery chuckled. "Not serious fights."

On the pale countertop there was a crumpled pile of black fabric. "The infamous shirt?"

"I'm tempted to have you put it on," Bennett said. "Another hit for when you have to leave."

"Remind me later," I said, smiling. Being here in their space was strange, but it would have to be for us to get past the awkwardness. "What's next?"

The house was *huge*. There was a living room with a TV practically the size of the wall and a couch which looked like I could get lost sinking into it, and another one of my paintings. This one was fiery sunset colors.

Because the house was set on a hill, there was more room downstairs, where there was a gym and a pool, along with a room that contained a bar and pool table, another huge television, and a bunch of video games. That didn't surprise me in the slightest.

"I think Rylan spends the most time down here," Luke said with a chuckle. "But all of us at some point."

"I think every pack probably needs a man cave," I pointed out. "But I'll kick any of your asses at pool."

"You sure about that?" Kade asked. "Ben and I don't play around."

"Reasonably," I looked between the two of them. "We'll see."

"Remind me to put it on the list of things to do," Bennett said under his breath.

Back upstairs on the second and third floors were all the bedrooms. Because of the size of the house, everyone had plenty of space, and most of them had some kind of mini studio or work area in their room. Luke had a large drafting table near the windows, Avery had an easel, and Rylan had a mix of musical instruments along with his art supplies.

Each room *felt* like them. Clearly, when they'd designed this place, they'd taken a lot of time to make sure they loved it. This was a home they didn't plan to leave.

"And, um..." Rylan cleared his throat. "Over here is the room we designed for our Omega. It's still a blank slate."

The 'room' was the entire right side of the house on the third floor. Rylan was correct—it was a blank slate. But it was beautiful all the same. Windows on the front wall, and an entrance to a bathroom I could already see was spacious. A walk-in closet. "There's so much room."

I was a little in awe. My house was lovely, but lay it all out flat and the entire thing was probably the size of this space.

"We wanted to make sure there was enough for whatever was needed."

One wall curved near the bathroom in the corner. Nerves curled in my gut. "Is that—"

"The nest?" Kade finished. "Yes. There's a connecting door through the bathroom, one from in here, and one from the hall."

We went through the door in this room, into a hall pressed against the back of the house. The entire side of the hallway was a big window, leading into a circular room which also had windows curving around it. The space arched overhead, every curved wall except the windows covered in white cushions. The floor too.

"Here," Luke said. At the entrance to the room, there was a panel of buttons. He touched one, and there was a soft whirring sound, a wall curving around into sight and blocking off the windows. It was covered in padded cushions as well. As soon as it settled into place, he flicked the lights on. They were dim and warm, and I immediately felt something *click*.

"The idea here," Luke said, "was to be able to decorate it the way you wanted as well. Colors. Fabrics. Whatever."

"This is amazing," my voice was quiet. "It's really beautiful. And you did it without knowing if you'd have an Omega."

Avery stepped closer. "We've wanted one. Not just any Omega, but the right one, and we would always rather be prepared than scrambling."

"Yeah." It was an inadequate word, but it was all I had. Because I couldn't stop staring at this soft, comfortable room and decorating it in my mind. It wouldn't stay white, that was for sure.

"Why don't you try it?" Rylan's voice was soft.

My heart ached, and I took a step back. "Thank you, and I want to. But it's not mine yet, and while I'm perfuming I don't think it's a good idea."

They'd have to rip out the cushions to get the scent out.

"Esme, may I touch you?" The question came from my left, where Avery stood.

I nodded before he reached out and tugged me closer, arranging my back against his chest as he held me so I could still see the nest. Warm spices wrapped around me with traces of warm comfort. Like apple cider and hot chocolate in the fall. "There's no right answer to this question, so you can't get it wrong. But what does courting look like for you?"

Opening my mouth to answer, I realized I didn't have one. When Eva's guys courted her, it was fast and mostly private. I'd never gotten far enough to know what I liked or what I wanted when it came to it. "I don't know. I've never had anyone interested enough to try."

A growl came from my left, and I looked over to see Kade's eyes on me, dark and direct.

"He's fine," Avery said. "Annoyed by the idea no one's seen you for what you are."

I didn't know what to do with that. It was something so deep and so painful I didn't want to think about it right now.

"Let me tell you what courting looks like for us."

"You talked about it?"

"Not just when I met you," Bennett grinned. "Long before that *and* after I met you. We have plenty of ideas."

Avery's arms tightened a fraction, and I startled, nearly forgetting he was holding me before I relaxed again into his warmth. It didn't feel strange for him to hold me like this, despite only meeting him today. "For us, courting is more than just giving you gifts and asking the basic questions, though we want that too. But we want you to feel what it would be like to be in our pack and belong to us the way we would belong to you."

Those words hit me in the gut, along with the same emotion I felt when they told me they wanted to court me in the first place. I closed my eyes so they couldn't see how much I wanted it because it felt too vulnerable.

"Stay here with us if you like. Make this place your own. There are more important things than paint and cushions. Hell, if you want to paint your room every week, we'll do it. But you don't have to worry about something not being yours yet."

I swore my perfume got stronger after hearing those words. This was all so fast, and it was too good to be true. It had to be, right?

"Just think about it," he said gently. "We're not going to force you. But know it's where we stand."

Glancing at the other pack members, I saw no signs of disagreement. "I'll think about it."

"Good," Avery said, releasing me and turning me around. "Now, are you a pizza girl? We were thinking pizza and a movie. Something we can talk over if we need to."

I laughed, appreciating the lighter topic. "Definitely a pizza girl. Meat lovers, cheese, whatever. No pineapple for me."

"Good to know."

I trailed behind them and looked back at the nest one more time before the lights flicked off. I'd never let myself imagine a nest. When my heats came I took the dampeners and holed up in my bedroom, just trying to get through them. Now I was afraid all I would see was the perfection of the nest behind me.

The guys were already halfway down the stairs, but Wes was with me. "What do you think?"

He looked surprised I asked, but Wes had been with my family for more than half my life. He knew me well, and his opinion mattered. "I think it's a beautiful house."

My heart started to sink, and then he continued.

"And I think even if these men lived in a dumpster I would have a hard time telling you to say no. You can't see the way they look at you, but I can."

"They don't know me."

He smiled gently. "It doesn't matter, Esme. I knew Christy was my Omega the second I scented her. Jacob and Trey did as well. We didn't need to get to know her to know that. And learning everything about her... not once did it make me question."

Wes was happily mated, and it shone through him. If he said it— "How do they look at me?"

He chuckled as we descended the stairs. "Like the sun shines out your ass."

I flushed, but smiled too. Having Wes say that made me steadier.

Avery was on his phone ordering the food, Rylan was flipping through movies on the giant television, and the others were missing, but I heard noises in the kitchen.

"What do you like to drink?" Luke asked when I entered.

"With pizza? I can do a beer. Or soda."

Bennett's head popped out from behind the refrigerator door. "We've got both."

"Soda then."

I didn't want any part of this to be clouded. I just wanted them. "Bennett—"

"Ben."

Blinking, I stared at him.

"Ben," he said again with a smile. "Calling me Bennett is going to get exhausting, I promise."

"Ben," I said, not realizing how close he'd gotten. Now I was staring up at him, just like I had on the dance floor. His cupcake smell was swirling around me, and just like the rest of them, I couldn't resist it. "You can't do that or I'm just going to climb you again."

He smirked. "Is that a promise?"

Kade placed a hand on my shoulder and guided me to the fridge. They had more than enough options to choose from. I grabbed one, still distracted by their scents. Would that ever get easier? Or would I always feel like their scents were perfection injected straight into my veins?

I needed to ask Eva.

Like I'd conjured her, I walked back into the living room and saw her face on the screen. The poster for one of her newer movies. "Feel like watching your twin?" Rylan asked.

"Umm..." I felt the divide in myself right now between the love for the woman who was my sister and the struggle with *who* she was. And watching her right now with the only pack who hadn't preferred her to me? I didn't think I could handle it. "No, thank you."

He shrugged, not questioning it and flipping away to something else. I breathed a sigh of relief and turned to find Kade watching me with eyes which saw too much. One corner of his mouth tipped up into a smile. "I won't ask you tonight," he said. "But I will ask."

I swallowed. "It's not that interesting."

"On the contrary, I think anything about you will be interesting."

Luke leaned against the doorframe and took a sip of his beer. "Elyse Taylor," he said. "It's like I knew what you were to us even through the paintings."

The fact that they liked my work before they liked me meant everything. Now I knew when they complimented it the words were real.

"Why sell them under a different name?"

"Elyse is my middle name," I told him. "And Taylor is my mother's maiden name."

"That's not why you do it, though."

I shrugged, moving to the couch and groaning as I sank into it just like I thought I would. "I want people to buy my paintings because they love them. Not because I'm a Williams sister or it's somehow related to Eva. I get enough attention as it is. I don't need more."

"How about this?" Rylan asked. It was a generic action movie. I think I'd seen it when it came out, and it had Dante in it, so I was sure it would be fun.

"Sounds good. Though I'll be honest, I'm not sure I'll be able to focus on the movie when you all *smell like this*."

Avery sat down on the couch next to me. "I'll take that as a compliment. Now, the first of many questions."

"Uh-oh," I laughed. "The interrogation begins."

His eyes sparkled with laughter. "Yes. But practical things first. Boundaries. Physical ones."

Oh. Right. Because they'd all already hugged me, but Avery had asked permission to touch me. Luke hadn't, but we'd both been so in the moment...

How much did I admit? It was embarrassing, but it wasn't like they wouldn't figure it out. "I'm pretty touch starved," I finally said. "So touching is fine. And—" the fact that Wes was sitting in a discreet corner of the living room hearing me say this was burned in my brain. Thankfully, I knew he'd already been through a lot of this with Eva. "Kissing is fine, too. Great. Excellent." None of the words sounded right and my mouth was suddenly dry. "Everything else let's play by ear."

"Perfect," Avery said, pulling me across the short distance between us on the couch so we were pressed together. "Because I'll say I know I'm not the only one having trouble keeping my hands off you."

Luke sat on my other side, and suddenly I was drowning in warmth and perfect scent. "It's a good thing I didn't take the beer," I whispered. "I'm going to be drunk on all of you in no time at all."

Avery leaned closer. "I hope so, baby girl."

My breath stilled in my chest, and I looked at him. I wasn't completely sure why my whole body tingled when he said that, but I also knew it wouldn't if it had been anyone else.

"It all right if I call you that?"

I nodded, unsure I could speak.

His eyes crinkled when he smiled, and I loved it. "If we're overwhelming you, you need to tell us, okay? We don't want you to run away from us because we came on too strong."

"I'm not sure I could come on any stronger than *literally* climbing Ben on a dance floor, so..."

They laughed, and Rylan clicked play on the movie but kept it on low so we could talk if we wanted. But I didn't want to talk right away. I leaned forward and put my drink on the table before cuddling down between the two of them.

It was like I'd run a marathon and was suddenly exhausted. Not sleepy, but tired in the way I just wanted to sit and feel that someone was touching me. Rylan was sitting on the floor in front of the couch, my legs brushing his shoulder. He curled one of his hands around my calf and squeezed, not stopping as he moved his hand up and down.

I couldn't remember the last person to touch me—before Ben at the party—who wasn't Eva or my mother.

Surrounded by them and their scents, my instincts were closer to the surface. I turned and slid my arms around Luke, laying my head on his chest. "I should ask you guys about boundaries too," I said quietly.

"Touch me however you like, Esme," Luke said. His lips brushed my forehead, and I whined. The sound was completely accidental.

Gently, Luke shifted us both so I was still holding

him, but I was leaning more against Avery now so he could see my face. Blue eyes. A soft blue that bordered gray. Like the sea before a storm. "I'm going to kiss you," Luke whispered. "Nothing more than that."

He did, and I almost opened my eyes to see if I'd fallen through the floor. His kiss was confident and firm. Demanding in a way I wanted to respond to. Tender and easy, but not hesitant. This was an Alpha who knew exactly what he wanted, and it was me.

The kiss ended far too soon, but it was a good thing. Every pack member was staring at me, breathing in my perfume, which had exploded the second Luke's lips hit mine. "I'm sorry."

"Don't apologize for that," Kade briefly dropped his head into his hands. "You smell—fuck you smell incredible."

"All right," Rylan said, standing and stretching. "Move over. Time for some calming Beta cuddles before every Alpha in the room goes full rut before you're ready."

I felt the reluctance in both Avery and Luke, but Rylan wasn't wrong. I was perfuming so much, it was a little shocking.

Avery moved to another seat and Luke slid away so he wasn't touching me, and I missed the warmth. It was replaced by Rylan leaning back on the couch and pulling me onto his chest. His Beta scent was just as delicious as the others, if not quite as potent. Right now he smelled sweet like strawberry jam, and I sighed, relaxing into him.

Things were quiet as the action played out on the

screen and my perfume calmed. Rylan's hand stroked up and down my back, and I found myself relaxing so much I almost *was* asleep.

"Some date I am," I mumbled. "Come over and fall asleep."

Rylan laughed softly, the sound musical beneath my ear. "If we have our way, we'll have plenty of time." He pulled me up higher so my face was tucked under his chin. "This was probably overwhelming, especially since you didn't know it was coming."

It was. I couldn't keep my eyes open now, fading down into comfort and Rylan's summery scent. Even asleep, I was vaguely aware of voices. All of them, and Wes.

Finally, when I woke up, I was being lifted. It was dark outside the windows, and Kade was carrying me through the entry to Wes's car.

"I fell asleep," I whispered.

A rumbling chuckle. "Yes, you did, and I'm glad."

"Why? You like boring?"

He set me gently on my feet next to the car, making sure I leaned against it and was steady. "No, because you felt safe enough with us to let yourself relax."

"I had Wes."

Kade inclined his head, his purr starting in his chest. The sound was heavy and loud, which had the effect of making me relaxed and drowsy again. "Yes, you did. But you still felt safe with *us*."

"Yeah."

"What I don't want you to do is go home and think

you disappointed us. You didn't. This is the first step. All of us want to get to know you and everyone in your life. When we say we're courting you, we mean it."

I looked down at the ground, and he lifted my gaze back to his. "Like I said, I'm not going to ask you now. But whatever made you think you don't deserve this is bullshit. Understand me?"

Out here in the nighttime darkness his eyes were black. Raw and hungry, and I couldn't breathe. I didn't quite believe it, because it had been too many times. "I'll try."

Leaning forward, he kissed my temple, and I leaned into it, savoring the rich scent of smoky oak. "Sleep well," he whispered. "And we'll see you very soon."

"Okay."

I was a little delirious as I slid into the back of the car, watching Kade as he watched me until we were out of sight.

"Thank you, Wes."

"My pleasure, Miss Williams," he said from up front. "They're a good pack."

"You think so?"

He smiled in the rearview mirror. "I do."

I snuggled down deeper in the back seat, warm and comfy and surrounded by their scents. Imagining that kind of life? It was exactly what I wanted, and I didn't ever want it to stop.

CHAPTER ELEVEN

RYLAN

I blew out a breath, watching Kade carry Esme out the front door. The last few hours had been glorious torture with her sprawled across me, sleeping like that. I wasn't an Alpha, but I wasn't immune to her scent, and I'd spent the better part of the evening singing obnoxious songs in my head so I didn't get so hard my dick was jabbing her in the stomach.

"Think we overwhelmed her?" Luke asked.

Avery laughed. "Yes. But I also get the feeling she would have been overwhelmed regardless of the pack."

"Overwhelmed, maybe," Ben said. "But she didn't freak out entirely. Hell, she *slept*. That has to count for something."

"It does." Avery nodded. "And the fact that she couldn't take her eyes off the nest. It feels like she wants this, even if it terrifies her."

"But *why* does it terrify her?" I finally voiced the question which had been nagging me all day. "She was shocked when we said we wanted to court her."

Kade stepped into the doorway and looked at me. "I have an idea about it, but I plan on asking her more about it when she's more comfortable."

"She's gone?"

"Yeah." Kade sank into his chair again. "Snuggled in the back seat."

"What's your idea about it?" I asked.

Kade sighed. "I don't want to dive too deep when we don't know the truth. But I feel like it's her sister. She made sure we knew she wasn't the same. Her family hired a pack matchmaker. She didn't want Eva to come with us or watch a movie with her in it. But I can tell she loves her sister. Which makes me think she gets lumped in with her a lot, and maybe the other packs she's met have had a... different view of who she is. If that's all that's ever happened? No wonder she's shocked a pack wants to court her for *her*."

"Fuck." I said the word under my breath.

"But like I said. I need to ask, and I've told her I'm going to later."

While she slept, we watched the movie, and Wes chatted with us. He seemed like a good guy. Happily mated, and happy to do his part to help Esme. But he was very close-lipped about our girl. Which frustrated me as much as I admired him for it. Esme needed people in her life who had her back.

I pinched the fabric of my shirt and lifted it to my nose. Her scent was still strong, but it was nothing compared to her in person. "Honestly, now I've scented her, the shirt isn't enough. Sorry, Ben. Your shirt might get booted from the place of honor."

He laughed. "If it can be replaced with Esme in this house and pack? I'll be more than happy to burn the shirt. Or frame it to remember the moment our lives changed."

Luke was staring at the painting on the wall. "I still can't believe it."

We all loved those paintings, but Luke had been the driving force behind them. Though he was the traditionalist in our studio, his taste in art varied, and he'd always loved their wild style. I couldn't believe she'd done them either. Just one more reason this was a small miracle.

I didn't know if we would have gone to a matchmaker to find someone, but we'd thought about it. That huge section of the house reserved for our Omega was like a bruise we were all aware of, bumping into it every time we remembered or passed the empty room. Now it might not be empty.

This weird mix of excitement and terror was going to make me sick.

"What do we do now?"

"We court her," Avery said, as if it were only that simple.

"Right, but *how*?"

Ben leaned forward. "I don't think we can let her rest too long. If she has that kind of doubt, she'll talk herself out of it."

"Do we have her phone number?" Avery asked. "I didn't think to ask."

"I'll reach out to Eva and see if she'll ask Esme if it's all right to get it from her," Ben grabbed his phone.

I stood and stretched. "Okay, but let's not make a

habit of going to Eva for things about Esme. All it's going to do is reinforce everything she's afraid of."

"Look at that," Kade said. "The Beta pup has some smarts."

As I passed I held up my middle finger toward him, and he laughed, a rumbling sound. At the doorway, I stopped. "Once we have her number, anyone have a good first courting move?"

"Honestly?" Luke shrugged. "I think Ben is right. We can't let her rest too long. But as far as courting, it has to move slowly. Another night like this, when she's not in complete shock from meeting us and seeing the house would be a good start."

Right. Her sister sprang meeting us on her, and I was glad it worked out. But I only wanted Esme to have positive memories of us.

"Tomorrow," I said. "Let's make sure to touch base with her tomorrow. She needs to know we're serious."

Ben quirked an eyebrow. "Sure you don't have an Alpha hiding under there somewhere?"

"Ha ha." I let the sarcasm drip. The guys gave me shit about being a Beta, but it didn't bother me. I was who I was, and though they gave me shit, they didn't treat me differently. I was an equal member of the pack, and that was that. "I just don't want anything to get in the way of this," I finally admitted. "Not when it's something we've all been waiting for."

There weren't any snarky comebacks to my statement. They all felt the same.

"See you all tomorrow?"

I didn't wait to hear them say goodnight. Sleep wasn't the main thing on my mind—it was a melody. One that popped into my head while Esme was sleeping on my chest. I needed to get it down while it was still fresh in my head.

Sitting down in the studio corner of my bedroom, I picked up my guitar.

CHAPTER TWELVE

ESME

My heart pounded as I slowed down, finishing the run near my front door. I pushed myself this morning, running all the way to my favorite place outside the city limits—Thompson Park, somewhere I usually drove to run—and back. I needed to get all the restless energy out of my system, and now I needed the biggest, longest shower of all time.

Even after the run, my mind wouldn't slow. Every moment of yesterday was playing over and over from Avery holding me in the nest to both Luke's and Ben's kisses, to Kade carrying me out the door and my snuggling with Rylan. It felt too good to be true. And now that I wasn't surrounded by all of their scents, I was afraid it *was* too good to be true.

I stayed under the warm spray until it began to go cold, relieved to feel clean and clear-headed after the amount of exercise. There were some videos I needed to film today, and paints to mix. I was even thinking about starting a new painting.

A pang of pain spiked through me, low in my belly, and I groaned. "No, please. Not now."

I should have seen this coming. It had crossed my mind, but I'd hoped otherwise. My heat hadn't come in a long time, and the amount of time in the presence of

Alphas... not just Alphas—Alphas my body *responded* to had woken up everything.

Heats weren't fun for me. A day of pain followed by hiding in my bedroom, desperately trying to keep myself from running out into the street and begging to be knotted by the nearest Alpha.

I was long overdue, but that didn't mean I was ready or grateful.

Fucking hell, I wasn't going to get any work done today. I only had a little time to get things ready, starting with taking the little purple pills which would help the pain of heat and maybe give me a little more time before the full onset so if I needed to run out and get some supplies I could.

I lowered the shades in my bedroom and grabbed the extra blankets from the closet. My room wasn't anywhere close to a nest, but I did the best I could. It was a far cry from the gorgeous nest at the pack's house. What did I call them as a group? Did they have a pack name? I needed to ask.

If they called.

Horror struck me. We hadn't exchanged information. I knew where they lived and worked, and they knew my name. That was it. I couldn't go down to Nautilus now.

I shook my head and grabbed the temporary suppressors. They didn't do much, but they took the edge off, and I felt myself relaxing as I fixed my bed with the blankets and pillows, grabbed water, and changed into the slouchiest, comfiest sweats I owned. Time to marathon bad romance movies and pretend the world didn't exist for the next few days.

The pain hit in earnest an hour later, and I wrapped myself around a body pillow, shuddering and waiting for the pills to really kick in. Once they did, it would be a dull, pulsing ache until the heat truly started.

My phone rang somewhere buried in the blankets, and I ignored it. It rang again, and I ignored it again. Finally, on the third call, I growled, scrambling for it in the blankets, fully prepared to throw it against the wall. Eva's name was on the screen, but the call ended. She could leave a message.

It rang again in my hand, and I slid my finger across the screen. "*What?*"

"Hello to you too."

Another wave of pain rolled through me, and I grit my teeth. "What do you need, Eva?"

"What do I need? Girl, I need *details*. Like every fucking one about you and your new pack? You know? The one who's courting you?"

I froze, unable to keep my eyes open and my voice steady at the same time. "How do you know about that?"

"Ben texted me last night after you left, absolutely mortified they hadn't gotten your phone number and asked *me* to ask *you* if I could give it to them."

"Oh." I took a deep, even breath in. "Yeah, that's fine. You can give it to them."

"Are you okay?"

The worst part about having a twin was they knew everything about you. Including what you sounded like when you were in pain and when you were lying. I tried anyway. "I'm fine. Why?"

"Because you don't sound fine, and based on Ben's text, I assumed you'd be over the moon. So why do you sound like you rolled over on the wrong side of a grave?"

"I'm fine." My voice was strangled, and I definitely did *not* sound fine. "Promise."

"Esme."

"I had a good time," I told her. "I'm having difficulty believing it happened at all, but it was great. I just can't talk about it right now." *Fuck.* I curled myself harder around the pillow.

A chime came from my phone, and I opened my eyes to a video request from my sister. Sighing, I accepted it. She wasn't going to leave it alone until she knew.

She was walking down a street somewhere downtown, bodyguards in tow. My little tiny square of camera was nearly black, with my face illuminated only by the brightness of her camera. I was shoved halfway into the pillow so my voice was muffled. "Hi."

"Holy shit. Esme, are you okay?"

"I told you I'm fine."

Her eyes went wide, and she leaned close to the screen. "You're going into heat?"

Nodding, I let my face fall the rest of the way into the pillow. "Hasn't happened in a while. Too much time with Alphas will do that."

"Okay." She snapped into what I called *Eva Action Mode.* "I'm on my way. I'll bring you all the things."

I sighed, squeezing my eyes shut against the newest wave. "I'm okay, Va-va."

"Sure you are. But I know what you like, *and* what you need. I'll be there soon. Oh, and I'm giving the guys your number."

She hung up, and I dropped the phone onto the bed. The sooner I gave in and let her take care of me, the sooner she'd leave me to my misery. Besides, in another hour the meds would kick in fully and it wouldn't be nearly this bad.

Instead, I just leaned into the pillows and breathed. I hadn't even gotten as far as turning the TV on, and that was okay. It was easier just to focus and breathe through pre-heat pain.

I wasn't watching the clock, so I wasn't sure how long it was before I heard my front door open faintly. The determined march of my sister's footsteps up the stairs, and a quiet knock on the door. "May-may?"

"Still alive," I said. "Meds should kick in soon. Hopefully."

"Well, I brought you your favorite cake from Oscar's. And another little surprise."

I looked up at her long enough to raise an eyebrow. "A surprise?"

"Your pack."

My eyes went wide. "No."

"Of course. I told you I knew what you needed, and what you really need is to be helped through your heat by a pack who cares about you and not locked in your bedroom going out of your mind."

Panic started to spiral through me, and I moved, pain slamming through me. "No, Eva, they can't see me like this. They won't want me."

She reached out and took my face in her hands, and she looked sad. "Esme, take a breath. You have a fever, and you're not thinking straight because of the pain. Once your meds kick in it will be fine. But they will absolutely want you. If you're a part of their pack did you think they wouldn't see you before a heat?"

It made sense, but I couldn't get past the horror of all of them seeing me in ratty clothes, sweating, and in pain.

"Who do you want to talk to?" She asked. "Let them say hello at least. Not all at once. Just one."

"No chance you'll tell them to leave?"

She snorted with laughter. "Even if I told them to, I don't think they'd go now that they know what's happening."

"Luke," I said, following my instinct. It was all I had to hold on to right now. "I'll talk to Luke."

"You got it."

"And just know I hate you."

Eva turned and winked before blowing me a kiss as she left.

A minute later, there were much slower steps on the staircase, and I was back sprawled on the bed again, unable to care about Luke's approach when the pain was getting worse.

"Esme?"

Calming, oceanic scent filled the space, and my mouth was dry with need. He smelled like a day at the beach. If I was around them when my heat fully hit, I was done for. They needed to be gone before then.

He was looking down at me, face full of concern. "This is because of us, isn't it." It wasn't a question.

"I guess," I said. "I haven't had a heat in a while. But you can't blame yourself for Omega biology."

He laughed once. "No, I guess not. Can I sit with you?"

A shrug was the best I could do.

Luke sat down on the bed and slowly stretched out beside me on the other side of my body pillow, covering my hand with his. Then he reached out and tucked my still damp hair behind my ear. His purr was strong and steady, just like him. It vibrated through the pillow and into me.

"I didn't want you to see me like this."

"Why?" His hand didn't move, gently stroking behind my ear.

"I'm a mess. Doesn't make a very good impression."

He smiled. "In case we didn't make it clear enough yesterday, the five of us could give a shit about impressions. We're courting you, Esme. That means we want you to be ours. In every way, which includes when you think you're a mess, even if you're not."

"Don't say nice things to me," I murmured. "I'll cry with heat hormones and it will be a whole thing."

Luke's lips twitched. "Not sure I can follow that order, sweetheart. I only have nice things to say."

The way he was stroking my hair felt nice, and slowly, as he did it, the meds began to kick in and the pulsing waves of pain dulled to something manageable. It felt like taking a full breath for the first time in hours. "Meds are taking effect," I told him. "I'll be okay now."

"Good."

"I'm glad Eva gave you guys my number. I'll see you in a few days when this is over."

His purr stopped, and he raised an eyebrow. "What?"

"When my heat is over."

"Hold that thought."

Rolling away from me, he went to the door. "Kade, get your ass up here."

The man took the stairs two at a time, based on the sound, and he smiled at the door. "Hey, beautiful."

I blushed.

Luke crossed his arms. "Esme told me she'll see us in a few days once her heat is over."

Laughing, Kade crossed to the bed, kneeling in front of it. "I don't think so."

I stared at him, finally able to sit up. Scooting so I was sitting cross-legged in front of him, I barely resisted the urge to sink my hands into his hair. His purr was far rougher than Luke's, and deeper. A different kind of comfort. "I'm not sure what else we would do?"

Taking my hand in his, Kade kissed the back of it. "We want to help you through your heat, baby."

My stomach dropped, and it wasn't entirely from fear. It was so soon, and I knew stranger things had happened, but it was still daunting. "What would that mean? For us?"

Luke sat down beside me. "Exactly what it sounds

like. We help you through your heat so you're not trapped in your house for days, and when it's over, we continue courting you. One heat doesn't have to mean anything more than that, though I won't pretend we won't want it to mean something. Plenty of Omegas have one-heat stands."

I laughed at the term, relieved the pain was receding enough that I *could* laugh.

"I know you're nervous about all of this," Luke said. "But I don't think you're nervous about sex."

He wasn't wrong. Sex was easy. Or easy enough, when I could find someone who wanted me and didn't end up calling out Eva's name. It was everything else *outside* of sex—the intimacy and vulnerability terrified me.

It was so nonsensical. I wanted all of it. I wanted that kind of closeness with a passion which made me shake, and yet it was also one of the things that scared me the most in this world.

"We can control ourselves," Kade said. "No bonding during this heat. Just pure, raw sex."

The way he grinned and the way his eyes sparkled told me he was looking forward to it. They wanted me. I gasped a little, the true knowledge of it sinking in like it hadn't yesterday when I was so overwhelmed with scent and everything else I was stuck inside my own head. They *wanted* me.

"You want me."

"Yes." Luke slipped an arm around my waist and tugged me sideways until I was nearly in his lap. "If anything, I hope spending your heat with us will show you *exactly* how much we want you, and let you believe it."

Kade rose up on his knees and kissed me. *Really* kissed me. Oh, fuck. "Esme, I wanted you the second Ben shoved that ratty-ass t-shirt in my face. The reason I didn't touch you more yesterday was because my cock was rock hard the whole time and I didn't want to make you nervous. I never believed in scent theory, and that single breath made me a believer. I don't care how long it takes for you to get to where we are. I'll wait as long as it takes. But please, let us take care of you. Don't ask us to walk away knowing you'll be in pain." His hand curled around the back of my neck and he pulled our foreheads together, gathering me into the scent of cool woods and a winter bonfire. "Please."

Being taken care of sounded nice. Staying in this room, aching and wanting more than I could have as I had during every other heat in my life wasn't appealing. Besides, this solution involved sex with men who made my mouth water, and would, in no way, be a hardship.

Still, it was hard to let go of the safety of the way things had always been. But they wanted me, and I needed to try. I was scared. Terrified. But I wanted them too.

My head was filled with visions of them walking away after my heat. Firmly, I closed my eyes and blocked out the voices which always seemed to tell me the worst outcome for everything. "Okay."

"Yeah?" Luke asked.

"Yeah. Doesn't mean I'm not nervous."

Kade stood and pulled me to my feet, purr growing louder as he held me against his chest, and I felt the echoes of what it would be when my heat fully arrived. I would be ravenous for these men. All of them. "Nervous we can work with."

"What about the studio? Your clients?"

Luke stepped in behind me. I was between them. Not quite a sandwich, but almost there, and when Luke started to purr too, I damn near passed out. "Daisy will reschedule them as soon as I give her a call. Not the first time someone has canceled something because of an unexpected heat. Besides, we have artists banging down the doors to do guest residencies. I'm sure we can find someone willing to do one on short notice, and they'll be fucking thrilled."

"Where's your suitcase?" Kade asked. "Grab only the things you need and don't stress about it. If you forget something, we'll get it for you."

"Um, it's in the closet out there by the landing."

"I'll get it."

Luke's arms slid in around me, keeping me in place and locked against his purr. He was hard against me, and his lips brushed my neck under my ear, causing every fucking cell in my body to perk up and say *hello!* My nipples were in the state of hardness that would fuel a million tabloid headlines, and I was wet. We weren't to slick stage yet, but *fuck* my body wanted to go there.

I still had some time, but once my heat perfume started? Man, I was in trouble. They already responded to my scent just as strongly as I did to them, and the perfume of heat was at least double in strength.

My body was a puddle under Luke's attention and the way he was lazily kissing my neck, moving down to where it met my shoulder. "You're distracting me so I don't second guess it, aren't you?"

"Partially," he admitted.

"What's the other part?" I gasped as his teeth grazed my skin, and my whole body flushed with *want*. How many times had I lost myself in an orgasm imagining I was being bitten and claimed? Pinned down and taken by someone who loved me and wasn't afraid to give me what I needed and take what they wanted.

I knew bonding was off the table during this heat, and that was good. But I wanted it more than I'd ever be able to tell them. Bonding was what I'd always wanted.

"I very much like touching you," he said quietly. "And tasting your skin might become my new favorite hobby."

My whine was loud and needy, and everything about Luke became more intense. He held me tighter, his purr stronger, and he kissed a path back to my ear, leaving tingles in his wake.

"And the final part," he said. "Is that we see you."

"What does that mean?"

He spun me in his arms so I was still pinned against him, but all of his handsome face was visible to me now. I wanted to run my hands through his sandy brown hair, trace the lines of his nose, and taste him, too.

"It means we can see you're scared. Someone did a

number on you, sweetheart. You're terrified you'll do one thing and suddenly we're not going to want you. That's not going to happen."

The terror he spoke about flowed through me, and I tried to pull away, but he held me fast. "You don't know that."

"I do, actually," he said. "Because if our courting doesn't work, it's because *everyone* agrees it doesn't work. Not because you did something we didn't like, made a bad impression, or fell asleep on one of us."

"He told you that?" Mortification crawled up my spine.

"We don't have secrets in our pack," Luke said gently. "Not like that. We all have our own space, and we're free to keep things to ourselves, but we trust each other enough not to need to."

I stared straight ahead through his chest, allowing all of that to sink in. "I'm sorry," I said quietly, raising my hands as much as I could the way he was holding me and clinging to his belt. "Because it won't be easy right away for me. But I do—" my breath hiccuped. "I do want to try. I like all of you, and for me? That's terrifying."

He smiled and released me just enough to slip a hand behind my neck and kiss me senseless. I was overwhelmed by the scent of the sea and the steadiness of his purr and god, I never wanted to leave this moment.

"It doesn't have to be easy. Good things usually aren't easy. Just promise me one thing."

"What's that?"

"If you're scared, talk to us. Don't run. You don't ever have to be afraid of us."

"Damn right." Kade stood in the doorway with the suitcase. He set it on the bed and opened it. "Let's get you out of here, all right?"

I nodded and pulled away from Luke. He let me go this time, and I already missed the feeling of him. I was so fucking screwed.

Kade caught me and whispered in my ear. "I heard what you said. Thank you for being brave, baby."

I smiled at him. "You realize you don't look like you should be saying things like that, right?"

He laughed. "I'm aware."

The man was *covered* in tattoos. I couldn't see much of his skin right now, but there were some climbing up his neck, and on his arms all the way down to his fingers. If he had that many, I guessed his chest was covered as well.

I guessed I was about to find out all about that very soon.

Kade laughed again like he'd followed my gaze and knew exactly what I was thinking. But I still looked at him. Messy hair gathered into a bun, rings in his ears, lip, and nose, beard that I wanted to feel the scratch of. He was scorchingly hot, just like the rest of them, and they were going to *help me* through the heat.

The thought got me moving. I grabbed clothes—though I didn't imagine I would be needing many—and my toothbrush. The other basics. But I tried to listen to him and not overthink it.

"Okay," I zipped the suitcase. "That's all I need. Just let me change."

Neither of them moved, and I flushed hot. I was going to be doing that more. Especially as my fever grew and heat settled.

Luke chuckled. "We'll take the suitcase downstairs. But if you're not down in five minutes, I'm coming to make sure you didn't bolt out the window."

"Trust me," I smiled, "I'm not that coordinated."

"We'll see."

They did go, and I changed. I just didn't want to go outside in the ratty sweats I had on. They would probably fall apart completely when exposed to sunlight. I opted for jeans and one of my favorite t-shirts. It slouched off the shoulder, and given what Luke had just done in that general area, I felt like leaving it available.

My first heat actually fucking through it... good thing I didn't have to worry about getting pregnant. I'd gotten the implant that locked shit down tight until I was ready. It was super-powered to make up for things like the heat.

Everyone was in the kitchen when I came downstairs, Eva laughing with them. The sight made me freeze for a second before I checked myself. They weren't here for her, they were here for me.

Ben looked over at me and grinned before he looked back at Eva. "We'll continue this later."

I cleared my throat. "Continue what later?"

"Eva had an idea for a TV show about the studio," Ben said, striding across the floor and lifting me off my feet enough to spin me around. "It could be interesting, so I told her we'd meet with her and her producers."

Relief flowed through my chest. "Oh. That will be fun."

Immediately shame came on the heels of the relief. Eva was happy with her pack, and she wouldn't do that to me. The fact it was even a possibility in my mind was fucked up.

But I was fucked up. I was self-aware enough to know.

"I'm glad you said yes," he whispered into my skin.

I was too, but I was still too nervous to say it.

Rylan stole me for a hug, and then Avery.

"I think I'm ready," I said, before stopping and looking at Eva. "Did the paps follow you?"

"Probably," she said, rolling her eyes.

I felt the blood drain from my face. "Did they get pictures of them coming inside?"

"We're not bothered if they did," Luke said.

That was good. "I know. I'd just rather have this courtship not be under the microscope when we all know it's going to be hard for me as it is."

"I'll leave first," Eva said. "Take them with me if I can. One of my guys can drive your car around back." She was looking at Avery. "He can find his own way from there."

"Are you sure?" I asked her.

"One-hundred percent. Come on. Walk me out."

I went with her, the guys staying behind. She took my hand. "I'm so happy for you," her voice was quiet.

"Really. And whatever you need to make it work, I've got you."

"Thank you." I held back the emotions which were at the surface. They were so much bolder around my heat.

"Do you want Wes to stay with you for the heat?"

"I don't think Wes wants to sit around while I get railed."

She raised an eyebrow. "He'd do it."

"It's going to sound stupid, but I feel safe with them. Wes said they were a good pack. But I don't want to be cavalier about it either."

"Let's do a call. Tell the guys since they'll have clearer heads than you will. Probably." She laughed. "Call me every night at seven."

"I'll try."

"If you don't, I'll send Wes and that will probably be worse."

I hugged her. "Thank you."

"Don't be scared. It's going to be great."

"I hope so."

"I know so. Have a fucking fantastic time, May-may." Eva pulled away and flounced out the door, making sure to turn and wave to me intentionally, so any cameras— both the ones standing outside and any who were hiding —simply saw two sisters visiting and not another potential pack for the Ice Queen to ruin.

I waited one more beat and then closed the door. Time to do this.

CHAPTER THIRTEEN

ESME

Eva's plan worked. The paps followed her and her driver, and Henry doubled around the block and dropped off any who decided to follow Avery's car before pulling into the alley behind my house.

The guys were ready anyway, getting me out of the house and into the car in a matter of seconds like we were on a spy mission.

"Thank you, Henry," I told him before he got out of the car. "Are you okay getting back? We could drive you."

He smiled. "I think that would defeat the purpose. I'll be fine, Miss Williams."

Avery switched places with him, and I snuggled down in the middle seat. It was a big car, and it was still cozy with six of us in here. Not to mention it was a fucking parade of scents with all of us in such a close space.

Tucked in between Ben and Rylan, I sighed and closed my eyes. Just being near them made me feel better and more settled. I tried to tell myself it was only the scents and what they did to me, but that wasn't entirely true, and I knew it.

"So what happened, exactly?" I asked. "It wasn't long between when Eva found out I was going into heat and you all showed up."

Avery glanced at me in the rearview mirror and smirked. "She called Ben and told us you were going into heat, and that you needed us even if you didn't think you did. I think we were packed up within ten minutes."

"Weren't you guys... working?"

"I was the only one with an appointment," Ben said. "Everyone else's were later, and it wasn't hard to tell the client there was an emergency."

I bit my lip. "You probably could have finished. It won't completely start until late tonight. Tomorrow if I get lucky." Pausing, I let myself smile. "Or at least I would consider it lucky if I had to be alone."

Ben kissed my hair, and suddenly the car was filled with purring.

We were pulling up to their house before long, and I was just as blown away as before. There were a few other cars in the large circular drive. Some had been here yesterday, but there was at least one I didn't recognize.

Luke turned around from the front passenger seat. "Were you expecting Addison and Claire?"

He shook his head before looking at me. "Addison is my sister. She's a Beta, and Claire is her Alpha partner."

"Oh."

"No, I wasn't expecting her, but I bet I can guess why she's here."

I hid my face in his shoulder. "Is it because of me?"

"I might have told my family we were courting someone, but I didn't tell them who. My sister," he laughed. "I think you'll like her. She isn't one to wait for the answer.

I told them I wasn't ready to say who it was. Because I didn't want you to be more exposed than you're prepared for."

"Thank you."

"I can go in first and get rid of them."

I gripped his arm. "No, don't do that. I know I've been really... jumpy about all this. I promise I'm not like this all the time. There's just been things that make me cautious. I want to meet your sister."

He pulled me as close as he could considering we were already squished together in the seat and breathed me in. "All right. But they're not staying. As much as I love my sister, she's not welcome for the heat."

A laugh bubbled out of me. "Oh, that reminds me. Rylan, Eva has instructed me, or rather you, to call her every night at seven to make sure I'm still alive, since I didn't want Wes lurking outside the nest and listening to," I swallowed, "everything."

Ben guided me out of the car, and Rylan followed. "You got it. We all know I'll be the only one with a clear head."

I looked at him, taking in every part of his tall frame. Warm brown eyes which reminded me of brownies and could match Ben's cupcake. Blond hair I wanted to run my fingers through, and a smile that made my belly swim with butterflies. "If you think you'll be less involved because you're a Beta, or that I want you less, you couldn't be more wrong."

There was a glint in his eyes which told me he hadn't

thought that, but at the same time he was grateful for the confirmation. "Good." He leaned closer so I was the only one who could hear him. "Because I plan on making you come so hard on my tongue you'll see stars in the middle of the day."

Every inch of my body turned pink, and the perfume of arousal flooded the space around us. Kade brought a hand down on Rylan's shoulder. "Stop teasing her, pup."

Rylan only smirked before heading toward the house.

I winced a little as I climbed the steps. The meds were in full effect, but aches still pulsed low in my stomach. It would come in waves until my body gave in to the full heat.

Kade was right behind me with the suitcase, a hand on my lower back. The tiny gesture put into perspective just how much larger than me he was, towering over me, and yet he wasn't crowding. Just making sure I knew he had me, and I liked it.

"Addison?" Ben called.

"In the kitchen!"

"Remember how we talked about calling first before using the door code? Which is for emergencies?"

I heard choked laughter. "It was an emergency. We were out of..." Lower. "What do I say we were out of? *Chips!* We were out of chips."

He groaned and strode into the kitchen. "And I suppose you also conveniently forgot there's a grocery store two blocks from your apartment?"

"I suppose I did."

I stepped into the doorway cautiously, and immediately, the woman I assumed was Addison looked at me. She froze with a chip halfway through her mouth. Addison looked a lot like her brother. Long, dark brown hair and a similar face and nose. Closer to my height, and undeniably beautiful.

A lithe redhead sat at the table behind her, lounging like this was her home. The comfortable way she sat made me think she would be comfortable no matter where she was and no matter the reason.

"You're courting Esme Williams?" Addison asked too loudly to be a whisper and too quietly to be aimed at me.

Ben scrubbed his hands over his face. "Yes. And she's right there, Addison. Don't be rude."

"Are you kidding?" She asked, dropping her chip back in the bowl and coming toward me. "This is badass."

Halfway across the room she stopped. Her eyes went wide, and she swung back to her brother. "You have an Omega in heat in this house and you don't have the nest ready?"

"It was unexpected," I said, fidgeting with my fingers. "I wasn't going to be here for it."

Addison's eyes were fiery, and in that moment, I decided I liked her. "If they bullied you into coming here—"

"No," I laughed. "That was my sister, actually."

"I'm Addison," she held out a hand, and I shook it. She smelled pleasantly like bubblegum. "And this is Claire, my bonded Alpha."

131

I smiled. "It's nice to meet you."

The woman returned the smile. "Are you comfortable with another Alpha approaching you?"

Nodding, she stood, and came over to me, graceful as all get out. Her scent was darker. Something like incense that I couldn't quite put a name to. "It's nice to meet you, Esme. The boys have needed someone like you for a long time. And the rest of you can stop hiding. We're not going to bite."

A snorted laugh came from behind me, but they were all in the entryway, staring in various directions. Addison turned to Ben once more. "Is the nest still blank?"

"Yes." His eyes were sad. "I'm sorry, Esme."

"It's fine. The fact that I'm here at all is amazing."

Addison scoffed. "It is very much not fine. You're in pre-heat?"

"I am."

"Are you in pain?"

I made a face. "Not really. It comes and goes in small waves. But nothing too bad."

She grinned. "Feel like going shopping? I know where we can get everything you need to nest."

"I—"

"Don't overwhelm her, Addison," Luke said, a gentle warning in his voice.

The way she looked at him made me both laugh and admire her. She told him exactly what she thought, and that it didn't involve him, all with a single look. "This is what I do, Ben. We'll be fast," she said. "Promise. But only if you're up to it."

I hesitated. They just got me here. Did they need attention? I'd never done this before, and I didn't know what the expectations were. Things for the nest would be nice, but every heat I'd ever had, I'd gotten by with what was on hand. I already knew the nest was beautiful. I didn't *need* anything else for it.

"Esme," Avery said. "Come here for a second."

I followed him across the hall into the living room, where he enveloped me in a hug. "I can see your mind going a million miles a minute, baby girl."

"Yeah."

"I'm proud of you for coming with us when you're already nervous. And I don't even have to ask them to know every one of our pack wants to make your heat perfect. If that means getting every little thing you want for it, then we'll do that. If it's too overwhelming and all you want is to curl up somewhere soft, we'll do that. Don't feel any pressure and don't worry about *anyone else* right now. Okay?"

It was easier said than done, but I inhaled the heady scent of spices and let my mind settle. "I think I'd like a few things," I said. "Not that the nest isn't beautiful. It is—"

"You don't have to justify it, Esme. I told you yesterday, we made the nest so our Omega could turn it into the place she wanted. And right now, for this heat? You *are* our Omega. Do whatever you want to it." He pulled me back far enough to look at my face. "Have you ever had a nest during a heat?"

I shook my head.

"Why not?"

Shrugging, I stepped back. "It seemed like it would be harder. It's already painful when you're alone. Why emphasize it by making a nest when you don't have anyone to share it with?"

"Then I want you to make it everything you've ever wanted. Do you have time before your heat settles?"

"I think so."

"And you want to do it?"

I pressed down my instinct to say it was fine and I didn't need it. "Yes."

"Go on then."

My breath was easier in my lungs as I went back into the hallway. "Okay, let's go."

Addison jumped once. "Hell yeah. This is going to be amazing."

"And a nightmare," Ben said sarcastically. "Esme, Addison is a designer. She helped us with the house and we could barely hold her back."

Suddenly her knowledge made sense.

"She won't have to hold me back," Addison said, and hugged Claire. "You have rehearsal?"

The tall Alpha kissed her gently. "I do. Have fun, and don't wait up."

Addison looped her arm through mine and pulled me toward the front door. "Oh, by the way," she called. "All of this is going on your credit cards."

I didn't know which of the men she was saying it to, and it didn't seem to matter. Laughter was the only thing behind me.

This place was *incredible*. Nesting Inc. was a place I'd never gone, because I was afraid of exactly what was happening in my brain right now. I was looking at everything around me and holy fuck I wanted *all of it*. Soft blankets and fuzzy pillows. Colored lights. Everything and anything you might need to create a nest. It was a three story warehouse divided by section, and then by color.

"Have I died and gone to heaven?"

Rylan laughed. "I hope not."

Addison stood beside me, and I looked over at her. "I have no idea where to start."

"I've designed plenty of nests before. Do you want me to go through the order I usually do? Or just walk through the store and point at what you like?"

"Order. Please." Another time if I needed more things I could come and browse, but I had a feeling it would be an all day thing, and even though my heat wasn't bearing down on me this second, I didn't have that kind of time.

She laced her fingers together and stretched her arms over her head, cracking her neck back and forth like she was about to run a marathon. "All right. Cushion covers first."

Setting off, I glanced at the pack behind me. Every single one of them was trying desperately not to laugh. Rylan was nearly in tears with it. Not at me, but at Addison's seriousness and determination.

The cushion cover section alone was incredible. The walls of the section kind of looked like the nest at the pack's house, with the cushions all the way up the walls in different colors and fabrics.

"So these all go over the ones you have at the house. They can be changed in and out easily for cleaning or if you decide you want something different. You can get as many as you like, any combination. The nest at the guy's house has... I think it was something like seventy cushions? So don't hold back."

Seventy? Wow. There were a ton of possibilities. But I couldn't only think about this like an artist. If I did, I would be here forever designing a pattern of fabric in my head. No, the Omega Instincts I always kept locked away needed to be what helped me here.

There was a screen and a rolling wheel of fabrics, so I walked over to it and started touching.

As soon as I started, it got easier. I *knew* what was wrong and what was right. Some fabrics were too scratchy, and others were too silky. Some were even too fuzzy. When I felt it, I stopped. Soft enough that I didn't want to stop stroking the sample piece of fabric, but not so much I'd get tired of it. It wasn't something to sink your fingers into like you would a blanket. It was a perfect base.

Tapping the button for it, the screen lit up a list of colors, and on the walls around us, tiny lights appeared next to the full-size samples. "This place is amazing," I said.

"I thought you might think so."

The guys were hanging back, but Luke stepped forward when I looked back at them. "You all right?"

"What do you guys like?"

He shook his head with a smile. "It doesn't matter."

"I don't want any of you to be uncomfortable while you're helping me."

"We won't be, sweetheart. The main thing which makes an Alpha uncomfortable is when the *Omega* is. It matters a hell of a lot more than the kind of fabric we're fucking on."

Warmth rose under my skin. I wasn't used to hearing things like that. But I better get the hell used to it, given why we were here. "Okay. But you guys don't have to stand over there like you're in exile."

He grinned. "We didn't want to influence you."

"Noted. But I'd rather have you closer."

"As you wish." Lifting the back of my hand so he could kiss it, he winked. "I'll tell them. Now keep picking things."

"And you're sure this is okay? I can pay for this."

Luke's eyes darkened, and I swore he grew taller. "Don't even think about it."

"You heard the man," Addison laughed.

137

My heart felt lighter. I was smiling now while I looked at the walls and thought about the shape of the nest. What felt right?

While the windows were visible, everything was open to that beautiful, natural view. What would it be like to sit in there in the dark and watch the stars? The entire image *clicked* in my head the same way I'd felt the instinct settled when they closed the wall and completed the nest. I knew what I needed.

Purples, blues, and blacks. Silver. Ombre and stars. Entire galaxies of possibility whirled open in my mind. There were pretty dusk blues in a line on the wall, and I saw the gradient I wanted and looked at Addison. "How many did you say?"

"Seventy."

That was an absurd number. But given the size of the cushions and how they rose up the walls, it made sense. "Okay. This is what I want."

I told her about the idea and started tapping colors on the screen from pale gray through blue and purple and all the way down to black. "I don't know how many to get to make that happen. Or if we even have enough time."

"I'll take care of it. The next thing on the list is blankets and extra pillows. That way." She pointed past the cushion covers to the next section. "I'll catch up."

This time the guys didn't stay back. They were with me. Kade stepped up beside me and took my hand, and my heart started to flutter, fever washing up and over me in a long wave.

God, this was going to be so different.

"Whoa." We'd turned the corner. I'd never seen so many blankets in my life.

"You say that like you've never been here before," Rylan said with a laugh.

I pressed my lips together and didn't tell him I hadn't. I was tired of being the saddest Omega alive today, and now that I was enjoying myself, I didn't want him to pity me. But I looked back in time to see Avery gently knock him on the back of the head, and that in itself made me smile. It was something brothers would do.

This place was like the biggest blanket fort in the world, with stacks and hanging pieces creating tunnels, and I couldn't stop running my fingers over everything, finding the softness.

"There's too many."

"You can never have too many blankets," Ben said. "Believe me."

Every color imaginable, and every type of fabric, just like the cushions. Soft silk ones, and ones where the fuzzy fur was so thick your hand disappeared into it.

Addison appeared a few minutes later. "Got it." Now she had a tablet in her hand. "I grabbed us this too."

"What is it?"

"I told the staff we're in a hurry. This will help us. As you want something, we'll mark it off and they're getting it ready so everything is packed and ready when we're leaving."

I gaped at her. "Do they do that for everyone?"

"No, they don't. But I know people. I'm here all the time shopping for clients."

"Wow."

Out of the corner of my eye, I realized Avery was missing. "Where did Avery go?"

"He'll be back," Rylan said. "Don't worry about it."

I tried not to, but a subtle thread of anxiety wove under my skin, and the thoughts which flooded my mind were because of the heat. They had to be.

He was *mine*, and I needed him close. I needed them all close. But he would be back. I swallowed and shoved the instinct down, focusing on the blankets.

"You're still holding yourself back, aren't you." That was Kade's voice, and it was a statement not a question.

"I'm not trying to," I said honestly. "There's just a lot here."

He reached out and covered my hand with his where it stroked a blanket of dark brown artificial fur. Sleek and smooth, and I couldn't help but wonder what it would feel like on naked skin.

"Do you like it?"

"Yes."

"Addison, mark it down."

I opened my mouth and closed it. "Okay, I get it."

"I hope so," he smirked. "Now go."

The words weren't a bark, but they were close. I found myself moving and telling Addison which things I wanted without questioning myself. It was too much—it was *way* too fucking much—but I gave myself over to my

Omega instincts and the vision which lingered in my mind.

Pillows were next, and I did the same. Silver and turquoise, sparkling things which seemed like stars. In my chest, there was a bright bubble of happiness that kept growing.

I noticed Avery came back and Luke left. When he came back, Kade slipped away. They all rotated, but I didn't ask. If they wanted to tell me, they would.

There were lightbulbs to choose from, or rather, lightbulbs which could be programmed to match the colors of the nest. And sparkling fairy lights to line the top of the nest and create a galaxy. There might have been some silky sheets and towels somewhere. By the time we reached the end of the store, I was completely overwhelmed and my pain was starting to come back.

It would only be a few hours now, and I was starting to feel both delirious and like a ticking time bomb.

"Esme?" Avery appeared in front of me and pressed the back of his hand to my forehead. "We need to get her back."

Addison waved a hand. "Go. I've got everything. We'll be right behind you. Just make sure the nest is accessible so we can get everything set."

"You got it," Ben called.

"I'm fine," I said. "Really."

Avery lifted me. "You're burning up, baby girl. Don't worry though, we're going to make you feel better."

Warmth was flowing under my skin now, pain rippling through my gut. This was usually the time when

I buried myself in blankets and felt miserable. But Avery's arms were anything but uncomfortable. "Really?"

"Really."

He carried me out of the store, and they were all with me. I didn't care if there were photos, and I didn't care if anyone saw. All I wanted to do was stay here, wrapped in their arms.

CHAPTER FOURTEEN

ESME

Fuck, it hurt. I was curled on my side, my head in Rylan's lap and my feet in Avery's. The pain was back in full force, which meant I didn't have long. It didn't usually kick back in so quickly, but being in the middle of these amazing scents and fading into my instincts brought things on quickly.

It wasn't here yet, but it was coming. I just wanted to hold on until the nest was ready. Because we'd gone to all the trouble for it, and I knew deep in my heart it wouldn't be the same now. My Omega had locked onto the image in my mind, and it was what I needed.

But all I felt was warmth and pain. When I was home, I didn't notice time passing or anything except the need for *more*. To be filled and taken and the desire for closeness I never had.

Avery had me in his arms again and he smelled like a chai latte with all the spices. I inhaled, turning into his chest and breathing him in. Every part of me he touched was on fire, and it was only growing worse. Or better, depending on how you looked at it.

"Addie is right behind us and she's going to fix everything up for you. What do you think about taking a bath? We can keep you cooler and talk a little."

I laughed, recognizing the sound as lighter and freer than normal. "What's there to talk about?"

He laughed too. "Would you like the bath?"

"Yes."

"Okay."

We were already moving up the stairs toward the nest. But we didn't go in that direction. We were in the big bathroom, and I knew why, but the soft whine still came out of me.

"You'll be okay, baby girl," Avery said, setting me on the counter. "They're fixing up your nest right now, and when it's ready, we'll go straight there. Yesterday we talked about boundaries. I know it's a bit different now. Other than not biting you, do you have anything you don't want us to do?"

"I don't like pain."

Anger flashed over his face, but he covered it quickly. "Trust me, we're not interested in hurting you."

"Like real pain. Something like spanking is fine, but more than that? No."

"Spanking," Avery looked both surprised and intrigued. "Not the direction I was thinking."

I flushed. "It's okay, I don't *need* that or anything. I just—"

Avery leaned forward and captured my lips with his. He hadn't kissed me yet, and *fuck* yes, I needed this. His kiss was impossibly all Alpha and all softness and warmth at the same time. I yanked him closer, wrapping myself around him and making sure we were touching in all the right places. Yes, yes, yes. *More.*

God, he tasted just as good as he smelled.

Placing his hands on either side of me on the counter, Avery pulled back and looked at me. I was noticing the way his shirt was tight across his shoulders and the freckles on his face.

Reaching out, I ran my hands through his hair, marveling at the red color and wishing I could have a paint exactly the same shade.

"We're all different," he said gently. "Some of us are more dominant than others, but none of us like causing pain. Spanking, however, is different. I know I'll gladly turn your ass pink if you want it. Roughness?"

It was a question about what I liked. My mind was slipping over itself, and I was having a hard time focusing when he was so close and he smelled so *good*. Why weren't we in the bath yet?

Avery smiled and went to turn the water on. I asked the question without realizing it. The bath was incredible. Probably big enough for ten people with jets and bubbles. With that kind of tub, they didn't really need the pool downstairs. "We'll be there soon. Lift your arms, baby girl."

My entire body shuddered at the term. I didn't know why him calling me that made me feel so good. Cherished. More like an Omega than I'd felt like in a long time.

He lifted my shirt over my head and tossed it aside so I was only in a bra, and his scent thickened as much as mine. One glance down at his zipper told me he had *incredible* self-control. More than I had right now.

"How rough do you like it?" He asked.

"I like it all," I finally blurted. "Gentle and rough. I can't even think straight about anything right now, Avery. You're wearing too many clothes."

He chuckled, stripping out of his shirt and giving me the first glimpse of his chest. My first impression of his body from yesterday was correct. Avery was built and burly, hair that matched the rest of him spreading across his chest. Smooth, slightly rounded stomach that was still firm with muscle. This man could probably lift a tree in one go.

A watercolor spiral flowed over one shoulder, spreading to a beautiful and abstract half-sleeve. "My mentor did it for me," he said when he caught me staring. "I have plans for more, but I always seem to be too busy tattooing other people."

On the other forearm, there was a sequence of sharp lines and shapes, like tangled geometry.

I couldn't stop staring at him, a beautiful dichotomy all together. Lumberjack and teddy bear. My teddy bear.

"Only a couple more questions," he said. "I'm about to get you naked. I know you know that, but I still have to ask."

"Please."

I helped him get my bra off, but he didn't pull back immediately just to look at me. He took his time, kissing my neck and shoulder before seeing my breasts, and I loved the look in his eyes.

Leaning down, he brushed his mouth over the top of one and then the other, groaning as my scent filled the room. It was heat perfume now, and my jeans were soaking wet with slick and arousal. The only thing which was keeping me from falling into the heat this very second was the bone deep knowledge the nest wasn't ready. Once it was? I was gone.

"Since there are five of us, how do you feel about double penetration?"

"Fuck," the word was a moan, mind filling with images of me pinned between Avery and someone else, knotted in *both* places. I was going to spontaneously combust before any of them were inside me. "Good. I feel good about it. Get me in the bath, Avery. I'm coherent enough to tell you if I don't like something, but if you don't put me in that water right now I'm going to explode."

"Yes, ma'am."

Lifting me off the counter, he stripped off my shoes, socks, jeans, and underwear with quick efficiency and lifted me into the water. I didn't even have time to think about the fact that I was naked with him, because he was stripping too, and I was staring at the rest of him.

His cock was just as hard as I'd imagined and oh, my, *fuck*, it was thick. The beginnings of a knot were forming at the base, and all I could see and feel was an inferno. The water in the bath was cool, and it was a damn good thing.

"What are you doing?" I asked as he stepped closer. Pain drove me towards the edge of the bath and toward him. I was so close. "If you get in here with me—"

"You're okay, baby girl. They're working fast." He

stepped into the water and sat down behind me, skin on skin, and I nearly fainted. He was warmer than the water, and I couldn't fucking breathe.

His cock was pressed against my back between us, and I wiggled for it. I need it in me. "Not yet." The order was firm. "I'm going to help you. And don't for one second think the others don't want to be in here. But you're seconds away from blazing like a phoenix, and one Alpha scent is about as much as you can handle right now."

"Doesn't it hurt?" I asked, aiming to make him take me. Every instinct needed this Alpha. "You could take me now. No one would mind, I'm sure. Knot me right here in the bath."

A low growl followed by a kiss on my shoulder. "I fully intend on knotting you many, *many* times over in the next few days, beautiful. But in your nest. Where your Omega feels safe. Now spread your legs." The term bark wasn't appropriate. It's what he used, but it wasn't rough. It was a tug in my gut which made me obey without question, spreading my legs beneath the water.

One final ripple of pain spread through my gut, and evaporated, leaving nothing behind but need and a spinning sensation of falling and warmth.

Avery's hand slid around my stomach, slowly tracing across my skin and distracting me. I moved, trying to turn so I could take him. I didn't need to wait. My instincts were lying. The bath was fine and I wanted him inside me *now*.

"Don't move, baby girl," he said, banding his other

arm across my chest, and falling again into the Alpha bark. "Understand? You will stay where I put you."

Gentle fingers descended between my legs, drawing a whine from me. Sheer pleasure was all his touch was. I was so sensitive and ready I nearly came from him brushing over my clit. Thrashing against him, I begged. "I'll present for you." My voice was barely recognizable. "I'll do whatever you want. Please, I need it. I need you. All of you."

I was burning. That's what was happening. Someone had tied me to a fiery stake and the only thing which would cool it off was getting a knot inside me.

"I want you to breathe in and hold it," he said. "Now."

Obeying, I did, unable to speak while I was holding my breath, and unable to think with the way he was steadily and firmly exploring me with his fingers.

"Breathe."

I gasped in air. "You lied," I told him. "You said none of you liked to cause pain. And this *hurts*."

"Close your eyes, Esme." Avery's voice was dark. "Focus on my fingers and nothing else."

They circled my clit with delicious pressure, drawing some of the fire away from my core and up to the surface. I was shaking in seconds, my arousal flooding into the bath. If I'd been out of it slick would be pouring down my legs but fuck it felt so good. "Please, Avery."

He kept his movement even, the exact rhythm which had made me shake and it was the same one making light flare behind my eyes. Pleasure exploded through me, bringing with it a raw inferno of desire I'd never felt in my fucking life.

"Oh *god*." I sagged against his chest, the pleasure fading through me quickly only to be replaced with true, feral need. I was in heat, and I was just realizing what I'd thought had been heats had been a poor comparison for the real thing.

"Good girl," he whispered in my ear. "You did so good, hanging on for me. And now you're in heat, baby."

"I can't wait anymore," I told him, turning with tears flooding my eyes. The emotion was so clear and strong it stole my breath. Nothing was the same and nothing was real. It felt like a fever dream far away from anything I'd ever experienced. "I need my nest."

"All right," he said. "We're going. I need you to stay here and sit while I get you a towel. Promise me you're not going to move."

I leaned my head on the cool porcelain edge of the tub and took a breath. Every single pull of air was a new line of heat. But away from Avery's skin, the coolness of the water helped.

Rationally, I knew pleasure was coming and I was going to get everything I needed with them. But I hated feeling this out of control and vulnerable. Anything could happen, and I closed my eyes, trying not to sink into that spiral, especially if I wouldn't be able to pull myself out of it. "Promise," I murmured.

Avery brushed the top of my head with his hand as he got out of the bath, and I heard the sound of water dripping as he moved and a door opening. "Hey."

Low voices floated through the crack in the door and hints of the other scents floated into the room.

Mine, mine, mine.

I needed the pack. Lust so sharp it nearly hurt cracked through me, along with a whine which was pure desperation. But I didn't move from where I was. I'd promised him.

"Get them out of there," Avery growled, and his steps were coming back to me. "Stand up, baby."

I did and was wrapped in a huge, fluffy towel which was warm and soft, and Avery lifted me into his arms. Just being held calmed me a little, pushing back the raging fire burning beneath my skin.

"You ready to see your nest?"

My nest. The word beat in my heart. It was mine. Even if it wasn't forever, right now it was mine, and it felt right. "Yes."

The door to the hallway was open, and the sunlight through the windows was too bright. Why was it so bright?

We stepped through the door to the nest, and their scents overwhelmed me. They'd all been in here while Avery had me in the bath, and the cool, dark silence of the space was perfect. And it looked entirely different.

It was perfect.

Every cushion which had been white was now colored. All the ones I'd picked. Lighter on the ceiling, fading through the colors and all the way down to black. The lights were cool-toned too, just like I'd picked, and all across the space were the pillows and blankets they'd helped me with. Even the twinkle lights flickered on the ceiling like stars, and I blinked away tears. "They did it so fast."

"We want it to be perfect."

"It is."

He set me down on the floor of the nest, and it was all softness. I reached for a blanket, not caring that there was still some water on my skin. I needed that blanket, and it needed to be over *there*.

They were all here with me. I saw them in the corners of my vision, carefully taking off their clothes and piling them at the edge of the nest, but I couldn't stop. This was my nest, and I was making it even more perfect. Because for the first time in my life, I was truly in heat.

CHAPTER FIFTEEN

ESME

I shoved the pillow into place and gasped, desire grabbing me like a vise and not letting go. The nest was perfect and they were all here and I still didn't know what to do. I'd always been alone.

That thought made me sadder than it usually did during my heats.

This was entirely different. I couldn't even really look at them and their bodies because my mind was moving too quickly, instincts reaching for things I couldn't explain.

"Please," I pulled one of the blankets closer to me. "Help me."

Ben was the first one to reach me, guiding me back onto the cushions and taking my mouth with his. His skin on mine was perfect, soothing the need and the craving I couldn't control. They just weren't allowed to stop.

It was the first time I got a true look at his tattoos—stars and galaxies drifting across his arms. A nebula. Words formed of stars I couldn't focus enough to read. I caught a glimpse of a wave on the curve of his shoulder and trees around his wrist, and that was all I could focus on, my mind drenched in need.

"I don't know how to do this," I managed to say.

"But you're helping me. We've talked about it. I don't want to ask anymore."

"You don't have to do anything," Ben told me. "We're going to take care of you."

The sound which came out of me was half whine and half sob as he kissed me again. He tasted like sugar and that incredible vanilla I'd been overwhelmed by at the party. "Going to show you exactly what I wanted to do the night I met you," he murmured against my lips before sinking lower, tracing kisses across my skin.

A new mouth, this one eager, covered mine. The scent of fresh grass and lemonade. I kissed Rylan back, winding my arms around his neck while Ben kept his journey downward toward my slick-soaked legs.

"Hi," Rylan whispered with a smile.

Avery's red hair was in the corner of my vision, and I was suddenly arching into his mouth as he covered one of my nipples and *sucked*. "Oh, fuck."

Ry laughed. "I think that's the idea."

Ben pushed my thighs apart and didn't hesitate. His tongue was all over me, licking over my clit and into me. "Fuck, Esme. You taste like heaven."

He pushed his tongue deep, fucking me with it, and it wasn't enough. Lazy, honeyed pleasure spread from his mouth. But it was slow, and I didn't need slow. I needed—

I didn't know what I needed. I needed fucking everything.

Avery grazed my nipple with his teeth, making it

harder than I ever thought it could be before moving his mouth to my other breast and starting over again.

Rylan's tongue was in my mouth, illustrating he knew exactly how to use it. I imagined him down there with Ben, both of them licking me together, and I gushed arousal onto Ben's waiting tongue. He groaned in response, drinking me like I was his favorite cocktail before rising up on his knees and yanking me toward him.

The movement broke me away from Rylan and put Avery's lips at my neck. And it let me see Ben kneeling there, my legs spread wide for him as his entire face shone with the remnants of *me*. His gaze was hungry, consuming every inch of my wanton pose, stroking his cock.

Ben was tall and built, and his cock matched him, thick and proportional. It was all I got to think before he pressed the head to my entrance and sank into my body.

Oh.

Fuck.

Me.

My mind went blank.

It had been a long time since I'd had something other than a vibrator, and the way Ben filled me had pleasure rising under my skin like a tsunami. My heat was too high and my pussy too needy for it to last long. Hell, Avery's touch had sent me over the edge in seconds.

Luke now stood behind Ben, looking down at all of us cock jutting out proudly as he watched Ben begin to fuck me.

"Look at the way she takes you," his voice was low and smooth as velvet. "Your entire cock disappearing just like that."

But Luke wasn't looking at the place our bodies were connected. His eyes were locked on mine, the barest hint of a smirk on his face. He was saying it for me, and only me. It lit the spark under my skin, orgasm racing upward and outward.

I couldn't make a sound. Pleasure twisted through me and I reached, finding skin and scent and the sense of absolute rightness. I was an Omega in heat, made to be taken and knotted and *worshipped* and this was just the start of it.

Ben didn't stop, thrusting slow and deep, all the way in and dragging himself out of me slow enough for me to moan before he slammed in to the hilt once again.

"More."

It was the only word I knew.

Rylan was still at my side, and he turned, dragging his hips higher. "Open."

The head of his cock pressed against my lips, and he slipped inside. He was so long he filled my mouth before I was even close to his base, and I heard him swear. A hand reached down and gripped my hair, guiding me deeper so he reached the beginning of my throat.

"Oh, fuck, Esme." His hips moved in shallow thrusts, fucking my mouth but desperately trying not to push too hard.

I wanted to tell him I could take him further and he didn't need to hold back, but I couldn't. He was already leaking, the flavor of him just like his scent, summery and fruity and so good I wanted to drink him just like Ben had me.

Avery's hand closed over my breast, squeezing before he slid it lower, finding my clit even as Ben was still moving, continuing the deep, rhythmic movement which was driving me towards another climax.

I couldn't focus on anything but the pleasure pulsing through me from every direction, giving myself fully over to the fever and need driving my hips to meet Ben's and my tongue to swirl around Rylan's cock.

Lips pressed just below my ear, leaving tingles behind. Avery's breath tickled my skin as he whispered directly in my ear. "Come for us, baby. Show us how badly you need to be knotted."

His finger matched his words, rubbing circles around my clit in time with Ben's thrusts, and my body was more than happy to oblige. I was blind with the fiery haze of bliss spreading through me, no longer in control of my body. My pussy squeezed down on Ben, and he cursed. "Get ready for my knot, Esme. I can't hold it back."

Rylan pulled free of my mouth, and I whined, wanting him back. "Don't worry," Avery whispered. "You'll get to taste him again. You're going to taste all of us like the good girl you are. Aren't you?"

"Yes. Yes. Yes." The orgasm still held me, and it only carried further as Ben took what he needed, harder and faster than before. I felt his knot against me, brushing with every thrust, and I wanted it. My body needed it, more slick appearing to help. Everything was bright and shining. The fairy lights were a mirage. I was floating in a galaxy made only of pleasure when Ben came, driving himself and his knot deep inside me, locking our bodies together.

In all my life, I'd never heard a hotter sound than Ben coming, the low grunts and groans I'd made him release. They shivered over my skin, heightening everything.

This wasn't like normal sex. I didn't need to catch my breath. I needed more *now*, but I also needed to wait until Ben's knot loosened and freed me.

Avery's mouth was still at my ear. "Such a good fucking girl."

My eyes nearly rolled back in my head with the sparkling, ethereal joy and happiness the words brought me. I didn't even protest when he moved away so Ben could cover my body with his and kiss me, my own flavor mixed with his on his lips and tongue.

"I think my knot was made for you," he whispered against my lips. "The way you're hugging it is going to kill me."

"No," I said, my mind not fully rational enough for the words. "Don't say that. I still need you for later."

He laughed softly, kissing along my jaw and my neck. "You'll have me. I'll never forget being your first knot of this heat." Slowly, he found my hands and wove our fingers together, pinning my hands to the soft cushions beneath us. "A couple more minutes and you'll be ready for the next one."

It was like his words struck a match. I nodded, unable to speak. All I was right now was pure instinct.

Ben kissed me again, softly. Up close, his green eyes were vibrant, and I imagined painting something like it in spirals of white and green surrounding a beautiful black void. Galaxies just like the tattoos on his arms.

He rocked into me, shooting off little flares of pleasure with each movement as his knot loosened enough for us to release. In the same way the heat made Omegas need everything more and faster, an Alpha's knot loosened faster too, their own instincts responding to the Omega's desire to be knotted again and again.

I shuddered as he pulled out of me, the need coming back in full force. Under my skin I was molten—a creature made of lava and fire which needed fuel to burn. They were the fuel.

As Ben pulled away I finally saw Kade in all his glory. I was right. His tattoos went *everywhere*. There was hardly any bare skin left on him. Tentacles curled over his shoulders and around his arms and ribs like there was a giant octopus on his back. They reached into a void of darkness and stars not so unlike what I'd tried to recreate here in the nest. I saw trees on his legs and there were more details too, but I couldn't focus because his scent was all around me, and his cock—his pierced cock—was hard and ready.

Studs lined the top of his shaft. It curved upward, thick and long, and his hand stroked it lazily as he looked at me. The possession in his eyes undid me. He hadn't even touched me and I felt like I was his. My perfume exploded along with brand new wetness on my thighs.

I was moving before he even said the words. "Present

for your Alpha." They were backed with a sound some-where between a growl and a purr.

My ass was already in the air and I clawed at the cush-ions, needing to beg and knowing he would do exactly what he wanted even if I did.

His hands came down hard on my hips and he sheathed himself in one brutal, delicious thrust. I nearly came then, my voice filling the nest. If there weren't so many soft things in here, my voice would have echoed.

Kade didn't hold back, fucking me hard and fast. I push up on my hands to move and press back into him, fuck him just as hard as he was driving into me. His hand slid up my spine, keeping my chest flush to the pillows. "Stay there, Omega."

Everything evaporated. His weight came down on that hand, holding me in place while he thrust deeper, the curve of his cock hitting and the piercings dragging against me in absolute. Fucking. Perfection.

A white-hot orgasm exploded, and somewhere far away I heard the sounds I was making. Raw, pure sounds of pleasure and pleading. Everything about this I loved— had dreamed about—and I needed more. "Please," I found the word somewhere in my brain. "Please, please, please."

Kade was still fucking me, working me with long, hard strokes. He'd never stopped, and I was shaking from the aftermath of pleasure and ready for the next round. It was so entirely different from the half-heats I'd put myself through and it was the beginning... I couldn't breathe. I was gone. Not in my right mind, and I didn't care.

Any concerns or shame I had were back at my house, abandoned.

"Please."

His body covered mine from behind, voice closer now as he moved. "Please what, baby?"

"Hold me down. I love it when you hold me down."

His answering growl sent me to the edge of bliss again. I was caught and tamed and pleasured and I needed this and so much more.

"Is that right?" Kade's hand fisted in my hair, turning my face to the side and pressing it harder into the softness of the nest. "Because I've already thought about chasing you when you run, baby. And if being held down is what you want, there's more where that came from."

He drove into me harder—feral and savage—the entire world turning golden. The orgasm built on the pleasure already in my body. All-consuming and never ending, I was limp with it. And he still didn't stop, fucking me with the force of a storm until he came, driving his knot into me.

Knots had never felt like this for me. I'd only had a few, and they hadn't made me ache and moan. Every cell was like a lightning rod channeling lust and need and *fire*.

His fingers tightened in my hair, body coming down on mine so I was surrounded by him. Drowning in the scent of campfire and earth. Darkness and deep woods. Everything was raw, and my Omega whined at the presence of the Alpha predator who held me even though I loved every fucking second.

I was impaled and knotted, trapped and frozen exactly where he wanted me.

"You feel good, little one." Kade's words rumbled through me. Shudders and shivers of pleasure echoed over my skin. "Mmm." He inhaled, running his nose up my neck, and a second later he licked over the point of my pulse. I jerked, the burst of heat and awareness of him telling me to run, and I couldn't. He held me fast with hands, body, and knot.

"We'll come back to this later." The promise in those words was so deep, I didn't doubt them for a second.

And somehow, as his knot loosened enough to release me, it still wasn't enough. Without him I felt *empty* and I couldn't bear it. Couldn't breathe.

They didn't make me ask.

Luke turned me over and he was already everywhere. Hands stroking down my arms and ribs, teasing my nipples until they ached. He was straddling my hips, cock laying on my stomach and that wasn't where I wanted it. Moving, I arched, trying to get him to move with me.

"No," he said, gazing down at me. There was only kindness and pleasure in those eyes, but there was also nothing which would yield. "Not yet."

"Luke, *please*."

"You'll get everything you need, little Omega," he promised. "But you'll get it when I give it to you and no sooner. I want you soaking wet when I fuck you."

162

I reached for him, curving my hands around his shoulders and pulling him down to me. "I already am."

"Not enough."

"*Luke—*"

His hand slipped around my throat, stilling me completely. I was the one who yielded. There was no pressure in his fingers. The gesture alone was enough to make me shudder and gasp, surrendering.

The brush of his lips and breath raised goosebumps all over my body. My nipples hardened even further and between my legs there was a flood of exactly what he wanted. Arousal and wetness, all slick and scent.

Luke's voice was calm and even, just like it always was, and his free hand skimmed down as he moved, reaching to tease my clit.

My hips arched into his hand. "I want you to feel so good, sweetheart." He circled my clit with agonizing slowness. "You're going to come. Hard."

"Yes."

"But I also want you to do everything I say. Can you do that for me?"

I nodded. My hands were still on his shoulders, and somewhere my logical brain was surprised Luke was one of the dominant ones, and the rest of me wasn't surprised at all. The rest of me *craved* it.

In the periphery, I could sense the rest of the pack, and I looked at them only for my face to be guided firmly back. "All of us are absolutely yours. But right now you're mine. You're only going to look at me."

Yes. I locked my eyes with his, struggling to keep

them open as his fingers still moved, teasing me and guiding me toward another impossible peak.

"Luke," my mouth found his skin, and I tasted him, licking wherever I could find. I loved the salt and flavor of him. Of all of them. I wasn't sure I was going to survive days of this. It was too good and too overwhelming. "I can't—I can't—" my words cut off and morphed into a moan stifled by my mouth on his shoulder.

All at once he moved over me again, sliding into me balls deep. I was too far gone. Dizzying pleasure spun around me as I came around his cock. I was so wet he was having trouble keeping his cock inside me, and I knew it was what he wanted.

He fucked me slow and hard, taking his time touching me. And I wanted to obey him and what he'd said desperately but I also couldn't wait. I couldn't take slow. I needed more of him. I needed faster and harder. I needed his knot.

"Later," I began to beg. "I'll do whatever you want later. Just take me, Luke. Make it feel better. I'm so empty without your knot, *please*."

Something in his eyes shifted, and he gave me everything I wanted. His hand returned to my throat, and he buried himself in me ruthlessly. Over and over again until I came, and came again. I was delirious, and overcome with sensation and need.

The third, or was it the fourth? Orgasm came over me, and I went limp. Bone-deep exhaustion took me, and I could barely keep my eyes open even as I felt the utter perfection of Luke's knot locking inside me.

My heat wasn't over—not by a long shot—but the first wave was. For the moment I was sated, and all I felt was happiness as Luke turned us on our sides and wrapped me in a blanket. The beautiful scent of the sea carried me down into sleep.

CHAPTER SIXTEEN

AVERY

J sat against the wall of the nest and watched Esme sink into sleep against Luke. "Hell," I said, scrubbing a hand over my face. "That was..."

"Intense?" Ben asked.

"Yes. And incredible."

None of us had ever been part of a heat before, so we were just as new to this as Esme was. We'd heard the stories, of course. But now I knew none of the stories remotely compared to what it was like to be in the same space as a perfuming Omega and hearing her beg for you. Or seeing how sweetly she submitted.

We all looked at each other blankly. This was the farthest thing from what I expected when I woke up this morning. I wasn't upset—I was fucking ecstatic—but I felt just as tired as Esme seemed to be from the whirlwind that was the last few hours.

She hadn't lied in the bathroom. It seemed like she liked it soft and gentle as much as she liked it rough. I looked forward to exploring every aspect of this with her.

"While she's sleeping," I said. "We need to make sure we order food. I don't think any of us are going to have the time or desire to cook, and we're not putting everything on Rylan because he's a Beta."

"I appreciate that," he said with a grin. "I do have to watch the time to make sure I call Eva for the check-in."

"Where did Addison put our gifts?" I directed the question at Ben. Since I'd been taking care of Esme while they fixed the nest, I hadn't seen where they ended up.

Esme had noticed we were leaving at the store one by one, but she didn't know we'd done that to choose our individual gifts for her heat, and the first of our courtship. Mine was an incredibly long pair of soft socks. On Esme, I estimated they'd reach her thighs and the image in my head of her in one of our shirts and those socks made my mouth water.

The nest was drenched in the scent of her heat perfume, which was her beautiful scent only more intense. Mouth watering and alluring, it made me want to bury my head between her thighs just like Ben had done and make her scream my name.

"Addie said she left them in the living room. I don't think she moved them. But I'm honestly not sure since things were so chaotic."

"Okay, I'll check. I'm going to go grab us some water and order food to be delivered. Anyone want anything in particular?"

Ben looked at Esme. "I wish we knew what her favorite food was."

"We can ask her when she wakes up," Kade said. "She'll be hungry."

I nodded, slipping into the hallway and into the bathroom where my clothes were. I found my phone in the pocket of my jeans and started ordering Chinese. A fucking mountain of it. None of us had eaten lunch in our hurry to get to Esme's house, and it was closing in on dinner time. Not to mention the ravenous appetite this amount of sex would bring.

Orange chicken, sesame chicken, fried rice, egg drop soup, steamed dumplings. I looked through their whole menu and ordered two of everything that looked remotely good. And I knew the guys' tastes well enough to know what they liked and what they didn't.

The kitchen was too quiet and still with everyone in the nest. There was an itch under my skin to get back to her, get back to her, *get back to her*, but this was helping Esme too, and she was resting comfortably with Luke.

We had water, but we were going to need more of everything. There was no way any of us would be willing to leave the house to go get groceries. So I scheduled a grocery delivery for the next day with everything we could need for the next week. I didn't know how long Esme's heat would last since this was her first real one.

Just the thought of her alone in her room, writhing in pain because she didn't have what she needed, made rage prickle under my skin. I was—we all were—going to make sure she had everything she needed regardless of whether she was in heat.

That was how quickly something could change. Barely two days since meeting her and I couldn't imagine her disappearing and never seeing her again. She was ours. We all knew it. Now we just had to convince her, and drive the knowledge so deep she would never question it.

Just like Ben said, our gifts were still in bags in the living room. I found my socks, a shade of dark gray I already knew would look incredible on her. I was tempted to put them on while she slept, but I didn't want to wake her. The heat would do that soon enough.

Grocery order submitted, I went back upstairs carrying the water bottles, unable to stay away from her and her scent for any longer.

Luke was no longer holding her. Rylan was now curled around the little Omega, and her head rested on his chest. She looked peaceful and content, the little lines of worry which seemed to always be there now completely gone.

I handed out the bottles, the last one to Luke. I set Rylan's at the edge of the nest—the small strip of bare floor which allowed the door to open.

"It doesn't seem real, does it?" Luke asked. "That she's here? That she exists at all?"

Kade was leaning against one of the cushioned walls. "I get what you mean. Almost like a fever dream."

I'd briefly told them her boundaries, few as they were, when I'd left her in the bath. But there was more to compatibility than simply being okay with the other's boundaries. And the moment she begged Kade to pin her down, the air in the room *changed*.

Not because of what she liked, but rather the way she fit. Kade was rough around the edges. He loved to chase and the more feral aspects of his Alpha nature. I hated to even think about anyone else but her, but over the years, all of us had a girlfriend or two, and we'd seen evidence of that in Kade.

Esme submitted to Luke too, and I already knew she liked being cared for in the way I loved. It was like she really *was* made for us. There was something beautiful about the idea that one person was always meant for you. Like you were going to find each other no matter what, and it was inevitable.

She moved a little, and all of us looked, turning at once like she was the magnet all of us were drawn to. She settled again, curling up tighter beneath the blanket.

"When the heat is over," I said, "I'd like to ask her to stay for the courtship."

"Stay here?" Ben asked. It wasn't a condemnation, but a clarification.

I nodded. "She's terrified. The heat is setting the feeling aside, but it will come back. If she's here with us, there's the chance to show her we're hers just as much as she's ours. Not to smother her, but I never want her to have questions. I just—" Shaking my head, I stopped speaking. There wasn't a way to articulate the feeling in my chest.

Luke finished drinking the water in his bottle. "I get what you're saying, and I agree. When I went upstairs at her house she was in so much pain, and all she could think about was that she didn't want us to see her like that."

Rylan reached down and stroked her hair. "That makes sense. Given the way she's watched with Eva and the media making her out to be some kind of cruel heartbreaker... not only, but her family. You know who her father was? Elias Williams."

My eyebrows rose into my hairline. Everyone knew who Elias Williams was. A businessman with a reputation for being ruthless yet fair, he'd helped make Slate City into the place it was today, and much of it for the better. But that kind of family, the money and the fame, it made sense her mother had hired a matchmaker. The stories about Esme in the press would only be considered a burden.

"Her whole life has been in one spotlight or another, and from the little clues she's given, not many people have bothered to look deeper than the surface. I'm not remotely surprised she chooses to sell her paintings under a fake name." Slowly, Rylan shifted Esme's head off his chest so he could roll closer to her on his side.

He was the youngest of us, and we often treated him like it. Not in a mean way, but the way I would treat my own younger brother if I had one. But the way he looked at Esme, and the insight he had, there was nothing boyish about him now.

"I agree," Kade finally said. "I want her to stay."

All of us agreed, as we often did on the important things. It was one of the reasons we were a good pack. We could fight, but in the end, we always found a way to come together.

Ben chuckled softly. "Avery, I think you and Rylan are up first for the next round. Make sure everyone gets a turn."

"No." I took a sip of my water bottle. "I mean, I'm

not going to say no, but this is her heat. She'll need who she needs, and I think she's going to need all of us in different ways."

My phone buzzed in my hand. The food was here. I set down her socks on the nest and downed the small rest of my water bottle. "Food's here. I need to grab some pants."

The nest was one thing, but I didn't need the food delivery guy traumatized. We were going to need more than one delivery.

CHAPTER SEVENTEEN

ESME

I woke slowly, the smell of something fucking delicious raising me out of the deepest sleep I'd had in a long time. The scent wasn't one of the pack, but I wasn't quite awake enough to figure out what it was.

Fever still raced under my skin, the need of the heat growing once again. But I had a few minutes.

Food.

My brain finally identified the smell. That was food, and suddenly my stomach needed it. It growled louder than Kade, and the soft conversation stopped.

I was curled on my side, a warm body pressed against mine. Summer jam and sweet tea. Soft skin. Rylan. Blinking open my eyes, I looked up at him, letting him come into focus in front of the twinkle lights on the ceiling of the nest. He smiled. "Hey, beautiful."

"Hi." I didn't move, very comfortable in the soft blanket and pressed up against a lot of his bare skin. "How long was I sleeping?"

"A few hours. We called Eva. She knows you're alive and well."

"That's good."

My stomach rumbled again, and I slowly sat up. I felt dizzy. Just the movement felt like it unlocked the fire under my skin, sparking need and more. But I was hungry.

They were all in the nest with me, an entire array of Chinese food containers on a big tray. And I wasn't entirely prepared for the sight of such hot men eating Chinese food naked.

"Want something to eat, baby girl?" Avery was the next closest to me.

"We weren't sure what your favorite food was. But if you tell us, we'll make sure to have it next time." Ben said between bites of rice.

I laughed, still a little hazy. "Most of the time I just like food."

Luke laughed too. "Good to know. But I'd still like a list of things you like after you tell us what you want."

My mouth was dry. That was the first thing. "Water."

A bottle appeared in front of me, and I drank all of it in one go. *Fuck* water was good. Why didn't I drink more water? My heat-clouded mind laughed.

"Here," Avery grabbed something soft and gray. "I got these while we were at the store. They'll help keep you warm."

Tugging a foot toward him, he started slipping the fabric over my toes. They were *socks*. Not just socks, soft ones that stretched all the way to the middle of my thighs. Every part of me stood up and paid attention to his fingers on my skin as he pulled them up.

"You bought them for me?"

"A heat gift," he said with a quiet smile. "We all have one, but I thought these might be helpful now."

I blushed, running my hands over the softness. "I love them. Thank you."

Leaning in, he kissed me briefly. I tried to make it last, but he pulled away with a chuckle. "You're welcome, baby girl. And the kissing can wait a couple minutes. You need to eat something."

A plate was passed my direction, and I saw it had a little sampling of everything on the big tray. I was *starving*. Instinctually, I knew I couldn't eat too much, because another wave was going to snap into focus, and I didn't want to be full to bursting when I was asking them to fuck me.

But it was so good. I picked up pieces of sesame chicken with my fingers and devoured them. When was the last time I ate? Oh, fuck, it was probably the pizza with them last night. That was forever ago. No wonder I was ravenous.

I downed the little cup of egg drop soup. *Yummm*. Chicken fried rice and a few potstickers later and the edge was taken off my hunger. "I love Chinese," I said. "But I also love Italian. And pad Thai. Burgers. I told you, I love food. I don't know if I could pick a favorite. Or at least I can't right now. I'll think about it. I run a lot, so I'm always hungry."

"Where do you run?" Kade asked, his eyes glinting with particular interest.

The way I'd begged him to hold me down came back in full force, and I flushed hot, food entirely forgotten. "It depends. Outside the city limits when I can. I like the peacefulness of it, and photographers usually think it's too much of a hassle to follow me. There are some nice places. Thompson Park."

My throat was suddenly dry again, and another water bottle found its way into my hands. I downed that one too, and it still didn't feel like enough. It was so *hot*, and I groaned.

I scented Rylan first, and arousal shocked through me. Wetness spread between my thighs, nipples hardening even as my skin flushed redder. "I think—"

They were ahead of me. Rylan pulled me back to him and spread me across the pillows. "You don't have to think, Esme. We've got you. Who do you want?"

"You," I whined. "I want you."

His smirk called more slick and my perfume swirled around the two of us. "It's so fast. I thought I had more time."

Lifting my legs, Rylan fit the head of his cock against me and eased in. And in. And in. Holy fuck he was so long it felt like he never ended. When his hips were flush with mine, I couldn't breathe. His hands were on my calves, pushing me open, and I heard the soft clatter of dishes as they got rid of the dinner spread.

"Hold her for me," Rylan said, and new hands touched my legs. One slid behind my knee, pulling it almost to my ear, and I looked over to find Kade there, holding me open for their Beta.

Avery held me on the other side, and I erupted. A very different way of being held down. I fucking loved this too. Open wide, unable to do a thing as Rylan drove himself into me with a force I hadn't expected. Oh, fuck.

Oh, fuck. Oh, fuck. I was saying the words out loud until Kade turned my head back to him and kissed me.

A raw kiss filled with biting and near clashing of our teeth. It bordered on pain but was the edge I needed more than anything. Half the people I'd ever been with wanted Eva, and the other half were afraid to do anything like this. They needed to be careful with the Williams sisters.

But I wasn't a pretty piece of glass that needed to be kept in a display case in case I got bumped the wrong way. I wanted to be shattered in all the *right* ways. And the way Rylan was bottoming out in my pussy was exactly the fucking right way.

Kade stretched my leg further, grabbing my ankle and pulling it back, causing Avery to do the same. I was practically bent in half as he fucked me, completely at their mercy, and it was perfect.

I trusted them enough to come here, and still I felt the shift. This moment right now, held by three, watched by two, and fucked by one when the deepest part of myself decided to *trust*. They were here, and they were with me, and this was more than helping me.

The emotion hit me in the chest and changed, carrying me straight into pleasure. More and more and more and Rylan growled in a way I didn't think a Beta could as his hands landed on my ankles too, helping pin me open as he moved like a machine, slamming through one climax and into the next.

My body tried to lock onto him desperately, wanting a knot he didn't have, and the look on his face was both devious and smug. He knew what I wanted and that he didn't have it. But at the same time, he was free to keep moving, keep fucking, and pinned as I was, I could only breathe and take it, shuddering into a third orgasm and he hadn't come yet.

Now I knew why Omegas looked the way they did at the end of their heats. Like they'd been put through the wringer and still the happiest they'd ever been. This pleasure might kill me, and I didn't think I'd be upset about it as long as I got to feel more.

Rylan shuddered, dropping his body onto mine as he came. Our mouths clashed together, tongues tangling, and he still stroked me through his orgasm, drawing shivers and sparkling aftershocks out of me.

And he'd only lit the blaze.

I didn't want to let him go, and yet I needed another knot. My vision swam, the fever even higher than it was before. How was this possible?

Avery pulled me to him, settling me over his thighs and pulling me down onto his cock like we'd done this a hundred times, and I nearly screamed. He wasn't long, not nearly as long as Rylan was, but like I'd already seen in the bathroom he was *thick*, stretching me before his knot had even swollen.

I braced myself on his chest. I couldn't breathe. Slow, rolling movements of his hips had me gasping. Avery held my face, making my eyes meet his. All I could see and feel was him. "That's right, baby girl. Relax and feel my cock. You're gonna feel so good."

I whined, trying to move faster, and he shook his

head. "You need to let us take care of you, Esme. We've got you."

Tears flooded my eyes. Half from the desperate need clawing through my veins and half from the tenderness in his voice.

He pulled me down and kissed me. "You remember what we talked about in the bathroom? What I asked you?"

"No." I shook my head. I did, and I didn't. It was all a hot haze. The only thing I really remembered was being sprawled over his body while he made me come.

He smiled, still moving, every hard inch of him stretching me as he moved. "I asked you if you wanted more than one of us at the same time."

White-hot arousal hit me, and I was wetter than I'd been this heat. "Oh, *fuck*."

"You said yes then, and I think I know your answer now."

"Yes yes yes *please*," I begged, forcing my hips to move, clawing at his shoulders. Now that he'd said it, I needed it now. "I want all of you."

The scent of vanilla blended with Avery's spices as Ben grabbed my hips. "We'll work up to that."

"Oh god," I dropped my face onto Avery's chest. I'd never had someone in my ass before, but it was my heat. It wouldn't be a problem. The Omega biology I regularly cursed was prepared for it, and I felt Ben *there*, pressing in.

"Relax, baby girl," Avery whispered. "You have to let him in and then we're going to fuck you so good you're going to come all over our cocks. Over and over again."

I was already a limp mess, slick drenching everything from his cock to my thighs, and even with Ben entering me, Avery still had that maddening slow roll which made me moan.

"There we go." Ben slipped in, and I froze. Two of them. I had two of them inside me. Stretched, full, and fucked. "Ready, Avery?"

"Ready."

No more slow.

They both plunged into me, one and then the other and back again. The thrusts which lined up together sent me over the edge. I was made of nothing but pleasure and light and I couldn't get enough. My eyes were closed and my mouth was open. I think I was speaking or moaning or something, but I was so lost in the whirlwind of pleasure I couldn't have told you anything other than *fuck yes*.

Hands and the scent of water lifted me, pushing me against Ben's chest so I was still upright and being fucked. A hand around my throat, firm enough to make my stomach drop before Luke whispered in my ear. "They're going to fuck you until they *both* knot you, Esme. Do you want that?"

"Yes."

"Good girl. And if I give you a third knot?"

Just the word knot made my entire body shake and my vision flash white. I leaned my face away from him, baring my neck under his hold, the instinct to let him claim me so strong I couldn't stop it.

"Mmm." Luke inhaled the scent of my pulse. "I'm not going to bite this pretty throat, Esme. But I *am* going to fill it with my cock. And you're going to take all of it. Every last inch while they fuck you."

The orgasm dropped on me like an anvil, making me blind. I didn't know I would like this so much—being informed what was about to happen instead of choosing. God, I was so tired of trying to choose. Letting them decide, when I knew without a shadow of a doubt they would stop if I asked. And it was fucking liberating.

Luke wasn't finished. "And then I'm going to come so deep you won't even have a chance to taste it."

My whine was so loud it drowned out every other sound. "Ben, take her hands."

He did, holding them behind my back and using them as leverage to sink deeper and harder into my ass. Luke's hands were still on me, and I felt more than saw him turn my head. "Open."

The head of his cock pressed against my lips, and I let him in. He wasn't gentle, and I didn't want him to be. Long inches of his cock filled my mouth, stretching me wide, and when he'd reached the back of my mouth there was still more of him.

His hand sank into my hair, angling exactly how he needed to slip the rest of his shaft into my throat. All the way down, every inch, until my nose touched his stomach, lips stretched around his base.

"Holy gods, Esme." Ben let out the words, half a groan.

And they all fucked me. I let everything go, falling into what felt like an infinite storm of pleasure. When Luke let me breathe, I breathed, and when he was fucking my throat, the lack of air made everything deliciously sharp and focused.

I lost track of the times I came. It didn't matter anymore. I was a creature in heat and I would take everything they gave me and more. Beneath me, Avery fucked faster before sinking deep with his knot, our bodies together so tightly I could barely move. And the motion of Ben's cock in me pressing against the knot—

A scream tried to come out of me and it turned into nothing, my throat too full to make a sound.

Luke held me harder, his other hand curving under my chin. "Scream all you want. It feels amazing."

He let me breathe just in time for Ben to shout his release, burying himself in my ass, his knot there pressing against Avery's, and I nearly fainted. "I can't—" I hauled in breath. "I can't." There was no way I could come anymore. Everything was too heightened and too bright. I was as high as I could go.

"You can," Luke said. "Open, sweetheart."

This time he didn't slide in again, instead turning my face toward Kade and Rylan. Their cocks were in their hands, and Rylan's face was hard with concentration. I couldn't focus. My body pulsed around the knots in my pussy and ass. Avery was teasing my nipples, and Luke still had a hand in my hair.

He leaned down and kissed me hard, not bothered at all by the fact he'd just been fucking me there, the taste of him still on my tongue. "You're going to swallow their cum, too, before I make your throat mine again. Then you'll have all of us, just like you wanted."

My eyes fluttered closed. It was too much. It was all too much. And it was *exactly* what I needed. The taste of them all over me and inside me. Everywhere. I needed to be coated in them until I couldn't smell anything else. Until they were mine.

Rylan stepped forward and Luke held my head still. Cum splashed across my tongue, tasting like sweet strawberries and sharp lemons, and I moaned. It wasn't fair for them to taste so good—how would I ever get enough?

I swallowed, reveling in the raw, dirty feeling of cum dripping off my tongue.

Kade's eyes locked on mine, and he didn't look away, even when he bit his lip and stroked himself, thumb swirling around his head until he erupted into my mouth, the dark flavor of him taking me over the edge again. I had to swallow more than once.

He smirked when he was done, reaching down to wipe a drop from my lip and push it across my tongue. "Missed some, princess."

Holy fuck, I couldn't breathe. I was burning up. Could Omegas spontaneously combust? Cause I was almost there.

"Take a breath," Luke said. "You won't get another one."

I did before he worked himself into my throat once

more, all the way down to the hilt. He held me against him, thrusting into my mouth and letting go of the control he'd held himself back with. "Oh, fuck."

Just like he'd told me he would, I felt him orgasm, holding himself deep while cum spilled down my throat without me even getting to taste it. I whined, wanting the flavor and also dazzled by the incredible possessiveness in his gaze.

His knot swelled, and I nearly panicked. It was locked behind my teeth. He was *knotted* in my mouth and I couldn't breathe.

Luke held my face in his hands. "Breathe through your nose. Slowly. You can."

I tried, and somehow I could, the air sliding around him and his cock. My whole body relaxed, comforted and satisfied, suddenly realizing I had three knots in me. Holy fuck. I couldn't move. Any way I wiggled, I was stuck, and when I did, echoes of orgasms rippled through me.

Wholly and entirely taken.

Avery pressed his thumb over my clit. "So swollen, baby girl." I could hear his smile even though I couldn't see it. "We're not too much for you, are we?"

He circled, my whole body shaking in response. I couldn't help it. Everything they did, every movement triggered more heat. More slick. More pleasure. And more need.

Luke moved, his knot easing just enough to release my jaw. He smiled, stroking a hand over my hair. "You did so good."

Those words made me shudder.

"Let's get you some water," he said. "I have a feeling you're not even close to done, are you."

It wasn't a question, and I shook my head. This wave still had me, and I let them care for me before we started all over again.

CHAPTER EIGHTEEN

―――――――

ESME

I dropped my mouth onto Avery's cock, savoring the spice and the sweetness. I'd woken with a craving for the taste of him, even though they were all asleep. It was the third day, or maybe the fourth? I couldn't remember. It was a fog of sex and pleasure and wanting them more than I could remember wanting anything in my life.

Avery hardened in my mouth, a soft moan coming from him as he woke. "Baby girl, what are you doing?"

"I thought that was obvious."

Moving, I licked down his shaft all the way to his balls, and I savored those too. He was a fucking lollipop. They all were. I was more familiar with all of their tastes now. The subtle variations.

"Come here." Avery pulled me off his cock and up next to him, cuddling me in next to his side. "Is a wave coming?"

With a sigh, I nodded, not a little put out he was depriving me of his taste. But I was exhausted. We were all exhausted. As wonderful as it was, I wanted to sleep for twelve hours and not move. "I'm sorry."

"Why?"

"I know you guys are as tired as I am."

He laughed softly, nuzzling his mouth into the crook

of my neck. "I don't mind being tired because I'm fucking you. Believe me, if I'm going to be tired I'd rather it be from too much sex than anything else."

"Okay."

My back was cradled against his chest, and he moved enough to stroke his hand up under my hair and along my scalp. I sighed, relaxing into the feeling.

"And it's okay to be tired and want it to be over." He kept stroking through my hair. "None of us are wondering whether you're enjoying yourself. We know you are. But you still you don't have a choice about being in heat."

"I'm finding I like not having choices," I mumbled, making him laugh again. This entire heat had woken up a different side of me. A softer side than the one I showed to the world. I'd already known I wasn't the ice queen, ball-busting heartbreaker the paparazzi made me seem like, but I *hadn't* known how deeply opposite my instincts were. That I loved having no control at all in situations like these.

I wondered what the headlines would say to that if they ever found out. They'd probably spin it into something awful too—*Esme Williams A Total Pushover? The Ice Queen Melted and Now She's Nothing!*

Curling in on myself, I tried to push out all those thoughts. I knew they didn't have a place in my head, but it was still impossible to stop them once they got going. Maybe the fact that they were coming back at all was a sign my heat was finally ending. It wasn't over—I still felt it lurking beneath my skin, but we were reaching the end.

190

Avery kept stroking my hair until I dozed once more, taking the opportunity to rest while I could. It wouldn't last forever, and it didn't.

Painful need speared through my gut, and I hissed. *Knot.*

I pressed my face down into the cushions, which smelled like all of us now. "Avery."

His hand was already stroking down my body and over my hip, sliding between my legs where I was newly wet. "Hmm, I wonder if I should get a taste before everyone wakes up?" The question wasn't really directed at me. It was soft enough to just be an errant thought, but my thighs pressed together over his hand in response.

"That feels like a yes."

"I—"

He smacked my ass lightly. Just enough to sting, and I gasped. With shocking clarity, I remembered we'd talked about spanking before my heat fully started. None of them had done that yet, and it did nothing to cool the temperature rising within me.

"Were you about to tell me I didn't have to eat you out?" I hesitated, and his hand landed on my ass again, harder this time. "Don't even think about lying, Esme."

"Yes, I was."

Another slap which had me arching into his hand and not away from it. Oh, god. This was a side of Avery which had been hovering at the edges but I hadn't seen yet. He was the one who made sure I was taken care of. Eating. Drinking water. But there was a delight in this, too.

"First," he said, rolling me fully onto my stomach and smacking the other side of my ass, "don't ever lie to me. We don't have secrets in this pack, or lies. Second, if you don't want me to go down on you because you don't feel like it, or anything else, that's fine."

Smack!

I yelped at that one, but his hand brushed over the heated skin and it transformed into rosy pleasure. "But if you say no because you think you're not worth it, or I'm only doing it out of obligation? That's not acceptable. I can choose what I want, and what I want is to taste this pretty pussy. And if I decide I want to eat your pussy for breakfast, lunch, and dinner, you will accept it's what *I* want. Understood?"

I nodded, and his hand came down four more times, twice on both cheeks, and I was wriggling, trying to get away, but he wouldn't let me, and I wasn't really trying.

"Up on your hands and knees, baby girl."

Now I obeyed, but he still spanked me again. "Dripping just for me. That spanking didn't make you more wet, did it?" I felt his smile against my skin before his tongue plunged deep inside me, and I cried out, unable to form an answer to the question.

Avery wasn't kidding. He *consumed* me, tasting every part of me from my clit to spearing his tongue so far inside me I thought it might disappear. There were more spanks too, until I could feel how red my ass was, warmth radiating from my skin.

Abruptly, he rolled me to my back and spread my legs, continuing the incredibly thorough meal he was making out of my pussy. And yet I hadn't yet been pushed into an orgasm, and I wanted it. The heat was starting to drive me again. Lifting my hips into his mouth, Avery slapped the inside of my thigh.

The sting burned and eased into the rest of the fiery yearning. "Please?"

"I like the sound of you asking nicely," he said, licking beneath my clit while he looked up at me. "But I think you need one more lesson."

He sealed his mouth over me and sucked so hard I arched off the pillows. I didn't know what the lesson was, but if it was coming on his tongue, then that was definitely, *definitely* going to happen.

Pleasure spiraled up from deep below. Closing my eyes, I focused on it, every pull of his mouth making it sharper and bringing it into focus. "Yes. Yes, *yes.*" I was so close and just when I was about to orgasm in a blaze of glory, he pulled away. "Wait—"

Avery's hand came down on my pussy. The stinging sound was loud in the nest, fiery pain morphing into pleasure I couldn't hold back. I screamed, body bowing toward the ceiling as I came. Another stinging blow directly on my clit, and another one before he licked me again, soothing away the pain and drowning me in fresh, golden bliss.

I was shaking when he pulled back and looked at me with an eyebrow raised, beard shining with my slick. "What was the lesson?"

"Don't lie and don't question if you want to eat me."

Lifting my legs in one hand, he spanked me again,

right at the place my legs met my ass. "That's fucking right, baby girl. Never question it. If I tell you I want my tongue buried in your pussy, you believe it. If I tell you I want you impaled on my cock, believe it. Now come for me again."

I wasn't ready for the searing heat following the next slap on my clit. My body, already prepared to come, obeyed his words and his hands, throwing me down into pleasure so quickly I screamed again. My throat was raw with it after four days of begging them to take me over and over again.

Collapsing back onto the cushions, my breath was ragged. Avery was stroking my legs and hips in soothing motions. "Good girl. You took that so well. Was that too much pain? Or was it all right? You mentioned you liked spanking."

"No, that was good." My voice was ragged. "Really good. Really really good."

He laughed, and Kade's rough voice entered the mix. "That was the hottest thing I've seen in a long time."

I looked over at him, meeting his dark eyes where he was watching me, now wide awake and stroking his cock. From here the silver studs of his piercings glimmered in the dim light, and my mouth watered. I'd tasted them all by now—multiple times—but Avery had pulled me off his cock, and I was craving one in my mouth, and Kade looked delicious.

His face pulled into a smirk. "What's that look in your eye, baby?"

"I want you in my mouth."

"I won't say no to that." He rolled toward me, rising up on his knees. I met him halfway, licking the broad head of his cock and savoring the flavor already leaking from him in anticipation.

Sealing my mouth against the side of his shaft, I worked my tongue against his piercings and down to the base of him. "I love your dirty mouth," he muttered, and I proved to him exactly how dirty my mouth was, dropping down and sucking his balls between my lips.

Kade cursed, and if my mouth weren't full of him I would have smiled. I liked it when they came undone just as much as they liked it when they made me scream.

A hand stroked down my spine. "Want more, sweetheart?" Luke's voice was rough with sleep. All of us had barely left the nest. For food and the bathroom. On day two I had a shower I desperately needed and even then I ended up fucked twice against the shower wall, my voice echoing off the tiles.

"Yes," I moaned the word against Kade's growing knot. I couldn't take him all the way I could with Luke between the curve of his cock and the piercings, but I was going to take what I could.

"*Fuck*," the word was long and drawn out as Luke slid into me. It didn't seem possible that after so much sex it could still feel this impossibly good, but it did. I was soaking for him, body silently begging for more. I arched my back, tilting my reddened ass up for him, and he took the bait, massaging with his palms.

It hurt, and it felt so good I nearly lost my focus on the delicious cock in front of me. I slipped my mouth over him, savoring the woodsy flavor of the wetness gathered at the tip, and he sank both hands into my hair.

"I feel left out," Rylan said. I couldn't see him, but I *felt* him suddenly underneath me, tongue teasing my clit even while Luke was beginning to fuck me.

Oh god. The slide and swirl around my clit rendered me helpless to do anything but feel, caught between the sensations echoing back and forth between tongue and cock.

Kade chuckled, tightening his hands in my hair. "Let me take it from here, baby. You just enjoy."

I was doing that. Oh, I was so fucking doing that.

"You have the right idea, Ry," Ben said, and I heard a smirk in the words seconds before I felt a hand on my ribs and his mouth close over one nipple.

And the scratch of Avery's beard was at the other one. The whine which ripped out of me had all the Alphas purring in response. But I still couldn't move. Couldn't breathe. Every combination I couldn't think of had happened in this nest, but nothing with all five of them.

I was a live wire waiting to explode, and it was so much sensation from so many directions, my brain short-circuited and shut off.

Kade's hand curled under my throat, holding me so he could fuck deeper into my mouth, matching stroke for stroke with Luke, driving into my pussy. The three mouths beneath me, licking and sucking, grazing me with their teeth, I erupted.

There wasn't one place the orgasm started—it felt

like it came from everywhere and didn't stop. I screamed around Kade's cock, and the sound made every single one of them intensify. I came apart under lips, teeth, tongue, and cock. It didn't stop.

This felt like the grand finale of a firework show, where everything was exploding at once and it was so fucking beautiful but you also couldn't tell what was what.

Kade moaned, the sound setting me off again, another ripple of all that pleasure while my mouth filled with the hot richness of his cum. He wasn't knotted, but he didn't pull away, the presence of his cock forcing me to swallow, and god I wanted it.

My body shuddered, hands and legs shaking and weak from all the pleasure. Luke drove himself hard and deep, coming with a shout and knotting himself so deep I wasn't sure he'd ever get out. Waves upon waves upon waves, and I couldn't hold myself upright anymore.

Avery moved out of the way so I could collapse, Luke coming with me and holding me to his chest. There was still pleasure, but there was also sudden, sharp clarity and a cooling in my mind.

It had been the grand finale—the orgasm to end all orgasms, and the one to end the heat. It was over. Emotion rushed up so quickly I could barely hold it back. "Can I have a blanket, please?"

Kade handed me one, and I buried my face in it before the tears came. Deep, wracking sobs I couldn't stop and couldn't control. But it wasn't entirely out of the ordinary for the comedown to affect me this way, even when I struggled through my heats by myself.

"Esme?" Luke asked.

I shook my head. "I'm fine."

"That doesn't sound fine."

Wiping my eyes, I pillowed my face on the blanket. "I promise, it's okay. It always happens when it's over. The release of all the hormones and stuff. Almost like withdrawal."

"It's over?" Ben asked.

"Yeah. It is." Those words made more tears come even though I really *did* feel fine and crying in front of them felt silly now. I was no longer an Omega in heat and I didn't have the excuses. "And I'm okay. I'm a little sad it's over, but it's good. You guys can go back to your normal lives."

"And courting you," Avery said. "Don't forget about that part."

"Yeah." My voice was quiet.

Luke's knot loosened, and he slid out of me, turning me on my back and covering my body with his. "I hear doubts."

"Welcome to life with Esme Williams. Fucked up and broken."

His eyebrows rose, and I heard soft growls to my left. "You're coming down pretty hard, but you're going to be okay. The rest of the things we bought you were for right now, after you finished your heat, and we also have something to ask you."

"What is it?" My stomach tightened, and I closed my

eyes, wishing for once I could not anticipate the worst.

"While we're courting you, and while we're all learning more about each other, we'd like you to move in here. This is your nest. This can be your room. Until you decide whether you want to stay."

I blinked up at him, not fully comprehending. "You want me to live here?"

"Until you decide if you want to stay," he repeated quietly.

"That makes it sound like you already know you want me to stay," I said.

He smiled, leaning down to kiss the corner of my mouth. "You hadn't realized that already?"

"But you don't even know me."

The warm, steady sound of his purr filled my ears. Vibrated through my chest. He moved his mouth so it was pressed to my ear and only I could hear his words. "I'll tell you as many times as you need until you believe it, but we're not courting you hoping to send you away, little Omega. We're courting you because our *deepest* instincts have already told us you're ours. And yours are telling you too, and I want to string up every person who's made you believe you're not worth it."

My whole body relaxed underneath the words and the purr. They wanted me to stay, and just the thought of packing up and going back to my house alone had tears pricking my eyes again.

I knew I would struggle, and I knew they were right. Everything had done a number on me. But just like the beginning of the heat, I wanted to try. I said they didn't know me. But they did now. They knew me inside and out, just like I knew them. I knew the taste of their skin and the quiet sounds of their pleasure.

But I didn't think they'd ever really know how much I wanted to stay.

I was just afraid.

It would take patience, but for the first time in forever, I felt hope I might have found a pack willing to work through it. Who saw me for me.

Finally, I smiled up at him. "I'll stay."

Not one of them held back, burying me in hugs and kisses until I was drowning in pleasure and purrs.

CHAPTER NINETEEN

ESME

The shower was something I actually got to appreciate this time around. It was big enough to fit all of us, with heads coming from every direction, including straight down. I didn't really want to wash all of them off me, but the hot water felt good on my exhausted muscles. And right now I was so covered in them the only way I was going to *not* have their scent on me would be to use scent cancellers.

Yeah. No fucking chance.

I washed my hair with one of my gifts. The basket was still on the counter in the bathroom. From Rylan, it was filled with everything from shampoo and body wash to bath bombs in a whole rainbow of colors. Lotions, too. It wasn't lost on me that the scents he'd chosen resembled everyone in the pack.

The shampoo I chose smelled like strawberries enough to remind me of him, and I chose it for that reason.

The socks Avery bought me were in the laundry. They'd had to be after surviving a few rounds of the heat, but I wanted them back. They were soft and comfortable.

The others hadn't quite given me their gifts yet, and my stomach flipped. I wanted to say I didn't want them or didn't deserve them, but I did want them. I wasn't a person who needed things to be happy—it wasn't about that—it was that they'd thought about *me* and what might make me happy.

I rinsed out my hair and wrapped it up in a towel before finally turning off the water. It felt like I'd pushed myself too hard on a run, but for five days straight, and in a way I had. My pseudo-heats weren't nearly as exhausting even though they were way more painful.

There was a soft knock on the door from the hallway as I dried myself off. No sense in being modest with them now. "Come in?"

Luke poked his head in and smiled. His own hair was damp, but he was wearing clothes, and there was a small part of me disappointed by that. Still, the sweatpants and t-shirt he had on showed me everything I needed to see.

He had one hand behind his back. "Have a good shower?"

"Yeah. My body feels like I've run three marathons."

"Ours too." He stepped in and shut the door behind him. "Time for my gift."

"What is it?"

He shook his head slowly. "Close your eyes."

I did, startling when he pulled my towel away. "This seems like a different kind of gift than I thought."

"Such a sassy little Omega. Don't tempt me. I'm perfectly willing to bend you over this sink and take you again."

But he didn't. Instead, I felt fluffy softness over one

arm, and then the other. It completely enveloped me. "You can open."

I did, and took in the robe I was now wrapped in, a beautiful shade of violet. "This feels so nice."

"I thought so." Luke took the sides of the robe and closed it and tied the belt all while his arms were around me, and when he was finished he didn't remove them.

"This was at the nesting store?"

"Mhmm. There's a whole section devoted to pampering Omegas. We would have taken you down there, but you didn't have that kind of time. We'll go back next time."

He rested his chin on my shoulder. He had to lean down to do it, but I liked it, especially the way he was meeting my eyes in the mirror, just holding me like it was natural.

"The way you were in the heat..." I looked away. "I didn't see that coming."

"Is that a bad thing?" The words were careful.

"No. Not at all. But when Avery said some of you were more dominant than others, I just didn't think it would be you. Kade, I figured. And Avery. I wasn't sure how you'd be."

Luke turned me around and lifted me to sit on the sink so he could stand between my legs. "I'm glad you don't mind."

No, I didn't 'mind.' That was the most mild description I could think of to describe the way I'd reacted. "How far does it go?"

"How do you mean?" His hands were on the counter

beside my hips and he was leaning into me. I could feel him between my legs, our bodies separated only by the thin fabric of his sweatpants.

Swallowing, I had to remind myself I wasn't in heat for a second because the urge to reach down into his pants was so strong. "I mean, is there a secret dungeon in the mansion I don't know about? Am I going to be in your bedroom and find whips and chains?" I laughed. "Not that it's a deal breaker, I'm just curious. I think it's probably something we would have talked about if my heat hadn't come on so quickly."

"Yes, it is something we would have talked about. And no," he chuckled. "I don't have a dungeon or whips or chains. Well, that's not strictly true. I do have some handcuffs and rope. I can't remember the last time I used them, though. Does it bother you?"

"Nope. In case it wasn't exquisitely clear, I loved it. It wasn't just the heat. I've just never done anything like that."

Lifting a hand, he tugged the towel off my hair and ran his fingers through the damp strands. "I love being able to create a space safe enough to let go and trust. And just to reassure you, I haven't done it often."

My cheeks flushed. He answered my worries before I could even voice them. I didn't want him to stop, and I felt silly for worrying about anyone else after they spent four days locked in a room while I begged them to fuck me. "I'm sorry I'm so..." I sighed. "Whatever the hell you want to call it."

He kissed me, catching my mouth with his. Fresh

mint mixed with his ocean-like scent. "I don't want to call it anything, sweetheart. There's nothing wrong with you, and certainly nothing you need to apologize for."

I turned my head to lean on his shoulder. "Okay."

Wrapping his arms around me fully, he held me quietly for a few minutes. It was nice to just rest, wrapped in his scent and the softest robe on planet earth.

"If you ever want to tell me about it," he said softly. "I'm happy to hear it."

"Not yet."

"Fair enough." A hand stroked down my spine. "As for the other thing. I like to be in control, but it doesn't have to be anything you don't want it to be. It's not a requirement."

I shook my head against his shoulder. "I like it. It's hard for me to stop thinking sometimes, and I like not having to worry."

Luke laughed once. "You do worry a lot, little Omega." He pulled back and pressed his thumb to the crease between my eyes, smoothing out the worry line there. "But I'd like to explore it with you. If there's ever anything I do—hell, that any of us do—that makes you uncomfortable, tell us. This is about finding what works for all of us."

Because they were courting me and wanted to keep me. "It doesn't feel real," I admitted.

"We're very real, and no matter if we make light of it, we've been waiting a long time for you. I don't say that to put pressure on you. I say it to tell you how serious we are about this courtship. It's not a fling, and it's not all of us liking your scent and figuring we'd have a go."

My eyes slid away from his instinctually. Luke didn't let me get away with it. He curled his fingers into my hair and firmly guided my gaze back to his. "I know talk like this makes you uncomfortable because you're so used to thinking no one wants you, but I need you to hear me and believe it. If you understand, tell me 'Yes, Alpha.'"

The command in his tone was just shy of a bark. Not compelling me, but offering the dominance we'd spoken of as a lifeline. Let him lead me to where I needed to be and start the journey of getting my head around them and what was happening between all of us. "Yes, Alpha."

Luke's eyes crinkled at the corners when he smiled. "Good girl."

My stomach *swooped*, and I groaned. "I shouldn't like it when you guys say that. But, *fuck me*, I do."

"Why shouldn't you?"

"I—" Luke looked at me expectantly, and I tried to find the right way to explain it. "Because I'm a woman, not a girl? People would turn it into something it's not meant to be. They always find a way to make it look bad."

He nodded. "I agree. You are an incredible woman. But in this house with us, there's no one else to make it seem like what it's not. I'll stop if you want me to, but I like the look in your eyes when I tell you you're my good girl."

The words brought out a soft whine, and he laughed. "Should I take that as you wanting me to keep saying it?"

"Yes, please."

Luke winked. "Good girl. Now let's get you some food."

He lifted me off the counter and held me in his arms, pushing the door open with his foot. We made our way slowly downstairs, and already I could smell something amazing.

"Just not in public," I said. "I can't—I don't want them to know."

"Esme, look at me." Luke's face was serious. "No one in this pack has any interest in making your life anything but perfect, and we certainly don't want to make it harder by giving the idiots with cameras who exploit you to make a living more ammunition." He lowered his voice. "You're *my* good girl, and maybe I'll share you with the pack. But you're no one else's."

I was pretty sure my whole body turned pink with pleasure.

Everyone was in the kitchen, and the smell of Italian made my mouth water. Ben was at the stove minding a boiling pot of water, and Rylan was with him stirring sauce. The oven was on, too. "Is that garlic bread?"

"Yes ma'am."

"Kade, take over for a second," Ben said, grinning at me. No one batted an eye that I was naked, in a robe, and in Luke's arms. "Can I borrow her for a minute?"

Luke passed me over and I squeaked. "I can use my own legs."

"You can," Ben said, sitting with me at the table. "But I don't find it necessary at the moment. Now, this isn't my heat gift, but it's something you and I both need."

"Oh?"

From behind me, he pulled a cupcake out of nowhere. "As far as I remember, you still haven't had your cupcake."

My eyes went wide. "No, I never got one."

Maneuvering me so he could use both arms, he peeled the paper off. "Open."

"Ben, you don't have to feed me the cupcake."

"Oh, I think I do." His voice was a low purr.

I opened my mouth and took a giant bite of the cupcake in his hand and moaned. He was right, something about finally getting the hit of both cake and sugar after wanting it for *days* was so fucking satisfying.

"That's really good."

"Bet your ass they are." He fed me another bite, and the lust in his eyes was enough to send me into a second heat. He kissed me on the last bite, stealing some of the frosting with his tongue. One hand cradled my face, keeping me where he could kiss me, and I faded into the true scent of vanilla.

"There are more, right?" I asked when he released me.

"Yes."

Avery pointed at the two of us. "But maybe some real food first, considering we're all running on fumes?"

He had a point, but damn if I didn't want another cupcake.

"You need your strength," Avery said, looking pointedly at me. "For tomorrow."

"What's happening tomorrow?"

Rylan turned. "Shopping. This time for your room."

My mouth popped open. "You guys don't have, like, an air mattress or something?"

They all burst out laughing, and Ben started purring, nuzzling into my hair. "Our Omega isn't going to sleep on an air mattress."

"Okay, but hear me out," I said, sitting up straighter. "I don't know how much money you spent on the nest, but I know that stuff isn't cheap. Furnishing a bedroom so large is like an entire apartment. You don't need to spend that kind of money. I've got money."

I had plenty. My paintings sold well and when my father died, both Eva and I received *extremely* generous inheritances. When my mother passed, we'd get more. I didn't need them to go broke for me.

Kade looked at me. "Absolutely not."

"Let me make you feel better," Ben whispered. "There's not one person in this room whose talent doesn't bill out for four figures an hour. And on top of that, I come from a family like yours. I consider it the pack's money, but we're not wanting for it."

"You're sure?"

"Yes."

I pressed my lips together. "Okay, fine. Because you guys aren't going to let me protest. But—"

"No buts." Avery cut me off. "We know there aren't any official rules to courtship. This is one of ours. We

209

fully intend to spoil you. So when we go tomorrow, you won't be looking at prices. The only thing you need to think about is what you want."

Instinctually, I nodded, my Omega responding to the Alpha's command. I did feel spoiled. I had five men who were bending their lives to fit me into it. Hell, they'd already made space for me and were begging for me to fill it in.

Another thought froze me. "What if we're followed?"

"By photographers?"

"Yeah."

Kade looked at me. "We'll call the store and see if they can give us a discreet entrance. But we can't guarantee we won't be seen forever, baby. They're going to find out sometime."

That was true, as much as I didn't want it to be. "It's not that I'm ashamed to be seen with you, I promise."

"No one was thinking that," Ben said.

"I just don't want to share you yet." But there wasn't a way to get around it. The paps were hungry for more of the ice queen, and even with a discreet entrance wherever they were taking me, it wouldn't be long until someone called them.

"Whatever they write about you, I'm sorry. It probably won't be nice. Or it might be fine about you. I don't know what they'll think."

"Nor does it matter." Luke settled in the chair across the table. "The whole world doesn't know our names, but we've had our fair share of press. It's never fair, never flattering, and never actually about you."

The oven door opened and I was hit with the *amazing* smell of garlic bread. Suddenly, my mouth was watering and I was ravenous. We'd eaten during the heat, but I could still consume an entire restaurant by myself.

"Food's ready," Rylan called.

Ben finally set me beside him on my own chair, kissing me on the cheek before he let me go.

Kade brought the pot of pasta, Rylan brought the sauce, and Avery was the bearer of the garlic bread which currently had a hold on my soul.

"Let's eat," Kade said, but looked at me. "Don't worry, Esme. We've got you, no matter if there are photographers. We knew who you were before we started this, and some photos or bad headlines aren't enough to make us change our mind."

The way he said it, so matter of fact, flattened any remaining worry in my chest. They'd decided, and that's the way it was. Just like when I'd told Luke I liked to let go, it didn't have to be sex. This blissful, worry-free space I was existing in was new, but I loved it.

So I took a breath, put all the thoughts about tomorrow aside, and we ate.

CHAPTER TWENTY

BENNETT

*B*ergman's was wild.

The nine-story department store had been around forever, almost taking up an entire city block. It also had a reputation for being exclusive and for the wealthy. All five of us knew Esme would be perfectly happy going somewhere else for the things we needed, but this trip wasn't only about furnishing her bedroom.

It was about showing her she was worth everything,

We had more than enough money. I hadn't lied to her. My family was nearly as wealthy as hers, and both Addison and I had healthy trust funds on top of our inheritance. We were lucky. When my parents passed I inherited a disgusting amount of money, which we'd used for the house, and continued to ensure all five of us could continue our careers without any pressure.

But even without that, we'd worked hard to get to where we were. Nautilus was a world renowned studio, and people traveled from everywhere to be tattooed by us. We were well aware of our status, though we tried to keep our lives as normal as we could.

Thankfully, being a tattoo artist didn't come with the level of scrutiny Esme was used to.

But regardless, I agreed with Avery's rule. Our little Omega wasn't allowed to look at prices, and she wasn't allowed to ask how much we'd spent at the end of it. It wasn't about the number. We were taking care of her, and it didn't matter what the cost was.

Bergman's had agreed to usher us in the back, which would help a little. But the truth was the world would know about the courtship by the end of the day. The staff would do their best to head off any photographers, but they weren't perfect, and it wasn't really their job.

I tugged on Esme's ponytail, currently woven through the back of her baseball cap she wore with sunglasses. She was still recognizable, but I recognized her need for armor.

She looked back at me and smiled before holding up her wrist. My heat gift was there. A simple bracelet with five beads which looked like nothing but silver. But they were little scent pods. All five of us had input our scent into one, so if she needed comfort or anything else, she could have our scent near her.

When I picked it up at Nest Inc. I wasn't sure she'd like it. I was proven wrong when I gave it to her before we left the house. Her eyes turned glassy, and she jumped in an attempt to get her arms around my neck. The rest of them had found us making out against the front door.

Kade's gift had been silky pajamas she wore last night in the nest since her bed wasn't ready, and all of us slept in there with her. None of us were quite ready to let it go.

There was a service at the house right now cleaning the nest and the cushions from the heat without completely removing the scent marking on all the fabric.

Esme was fidgeting, her fingers tapping back and

forth on her leg. So I scooped her hand up in mine and kissed the back of it. "You're okay."

"I know." She didn't sound like she did.

Kade looked over his shoulder. "Should have called Addison. She's going to be furious we did this without her."

I snorted. "She can be pissed all she likes. This isn't about her."

Esme squeezed my hand. "I like your sister."

"I *love* my sister. But this is about the six of us. I'm sure she'll corner you into another shopping trip soon enough."

"So, where do we start?" Rylan asked. "This place is huge."

Luke swiped on his phone. "Paint seems like a good place to start."

"They have paint here?" Esme asked. "House paint?"

"We have everything here." An imperious voice sounded in front of us, and a man in a suit appeared. "You must be Miss Williams."

"That's me."

"I'm Mr. Syme, the manager. I spoke to your pack on the phone earlier."

Luke stepped forward and offered a hand. Mr. Syme shook it. "Thank you for helping with discretion."

The man nodded. "I can't guarantee anything more."

"We know." I held out a hand. "But we still appreciate it. We'd also appreciate someone to take note of what we purchase. Especially while we're in the furniture department. We expect to be purchasing quite a lot."

He glanced between all of us, eyes lingering on Kade. "I'll see what I can do."

I gave Esme's hand to Avery. "Why don't you guys go to paint and get started? I want to arrange the delivery with Mr. Syme."

Kade was smirking as they left, and Esme was looking back at me, worried as always.

The manager straightened after they disappeared. "You're not our usual clientele," he said. "I'm not sure I can justify excusing someone from their duties to tend you simply because your Omega has some fame."

"That's not why you'll do it," I said mildly, pulling out my wallet. The slick black card for the pack account got things done when everything else couldn't. You couldn't get one of these without... well, a lot.

"When I said we intend to spend a lot today, this is what I mean." I held out the card to him and watched his eyes go wide. "Not only will we be furnishing our Omega's suite, we will want immediate delivery, and people to paint the room when we leave here today. I'm sure you can make that happen, right?"

He nodded. "Absolutely, I can. Mr.?"

"Mr. Gray." I handed him the card and let him see it. "Do you need anything else to give us the service we need?"

"Ah, no. Thank you." He handed the card back to me. "And my apologies."

"Accepted. With a note that perhaps you shouldn't judge your clients based on appearance."

He looked appropriately chastised, and I smothered

my smile as I walked past him to go after my pack. I turned back to him at the last second. "Oh, and Mr. Syme?" He was already typing on his phone. "Yes, Mr. Gray?"

"Miss Williams is not to be told the cost of anything, nor the total of what we spend here today. Even if she asks. Is that clear?"

"It is."

"Good. We'll be in the paint department."

I almost wished I'd had Esme stay to see it because it was so satisfying, but humiliating the guy wasn't going to get him on our good side. As it was, he was embarrassed enough and would probably spend the day making sure we had a good experience. Nothing else was necessary.

"Is wallpaper weird now?" Esme asked no one as I entered the small section of the floor dedicated to paints and decorations. "Because this is pretty."

Her fingers were on a pale gray wallpaper covered in metallic silver trees. I touched her on the shoulder to let her know I was back. "It's very pretty. And no, I don't think it's weird."

"There are too many colors here," she said. "I'll never be able to choose. We'll be in this section for hours."

"Okay," Luke said. "Forget looking at what's here. If you could do whatever you wanted in the room, what would you do?"

Esme thought, biting her lip. I loved that little movement. It was entirely unconscious and told me she was actually considering his question. "Hold that thought."

She pulled a sample of the metallic tree wallpaper and

put it on the island in the center of the space and then went hunting. She pulled swatches from the gradient color racks and came back to us, spreading them alongside the wallpaper. The pale gray she'd chosen matched the paper almost exactly, and then the gradient faded through to a blue so deep it was almost purple. "Ignoring reality," she said, "one wall would be this." She touched the silver trees. "Like maybe the wall with the doors to the bathroom and the nest hallway. And then the rest of the walls—ceiling too— would be a really smooth gradient all the way down to this."

"That would be beautiful," Avery said.

"I'd probably paint clouds or stars on the dark end."

Luke picked up all the swatches and looked at them. "This is what you would pick? For sure?"

"It's the first thing I thought of," she said. "Always wanted to do a gradient in a room, but it seemed tedious. I didn't want to spend that much time with a giant airbrush."

I laughed. "I don't blame you."

"All right," Luke said. "Done. Next department."

"Wait," Esme reached for the swatches which he kept away. "You can't do that—it's not even practical."

Luke caught her around the waist and held her against him even as he held all the swatches up out of reach. "Do you really want it?"

She bit her lip again. "Yes."

He kissed her forehead. "Then it's all you have to say. Go."

Esme's cheeks turned pink, and she stared at Luke for

long seconds, judging if he was being serious. And he was. We all knew it.

Finally, she leaned in and laid her head on his chest, eyes closed. It was both concession and submission, and my heart ached at the sight of it. Esme was a woman who had her own business, survived on her own under the brutal scrutiny of the press, and knew what she wanted even if she didn't have practice asking for it. Watching her let us in and accept the help and love she'd never had was beautiful.

"Go pick out your furniture," Luke whispered. "And keep this in mind."

She looked up at him and accepted another kiss on the forehead. "Thank you."

"You're welcome, sweetheart."

I stole her away, knowing Luke would take care of everything. Especially now that the manager was on our side. Walking slowly with her out of the department, I wrapped her up and paused. "Do me a favor?"

"I can try."

"I give you permission to enjoy yourself, Esme. The same way you liked picking things out for your nest. Please, for me, try to stop feeling guilty. Trust us to enforce our own boundaries the same way we respect yours, and vice versa. If there's something we can't do or don't want to do, we'll tell you."

She sighed and relaxed into me. "Okay, but on one condition."

"Name it."

"I get to pay for dinner for everyone tonight so I can feel like I'm contributing something."

My instinct was to tell her she was contributing simply by being herself, but she wasn't ready to hear it. And if this day could be a hundred times better by letting her pay for dinner? "You got it. Now let's go pick some furniture."

CHAPTER TWENTY-ONE

ESME

I was creating a fairytale. The paint for my room and the giant bed with posts which looked like the trees in the wallpaper. Dark furnishings with beautiful carvings, a big cabinet in a peacock green with the same bird on the front. It had so much space, I could keep some of my personal art supplies in it. All my big stuff would stay at my studio.

The thought froze me, and I set it aside, not ready to actually let it surface.

We went into the chairs and couches section, and everyone sat on everything, even Luke when he came back from working whatever magic he had.

"I don't need a couch in my room," I said, lounging on a gray velvet one which would look beautiful with the color scheme. "That's not me being stubborn. I just don't see why I need a couch when there's a living room."

"I don't know," Kade said. "We all have couches and chairs in our rooms. It's convenient."

They did. I'd forgotten. Running my hands over the one I sat on, I loved it. The arms curled over in swirls in an older style, and the matching chairs were perfect.

An entertainment center which could hide the giant TV they insisted on buying and a plush purple rug later, and I was starting to slow down. It was a lot of decisions, and I didn't usually make them this quickly.

Twisting Ben's gift on my wrist, I lifted the beads to my nose. It was like getting a hit of all their scents at once, mixing into an indescribable cocktail that calmed me and energized me all at once.

Kade reached over and pulled me into his chest. "You can have the real thing right here."

I laughed as he rubbed his face on the side of mine, beard tickling my skin. "And it's amazing. But serious question, is there anything else on the list? I'm exhausted."

Besides, there was the woman who'd been following us for the last few hours, marking everything down. She had to be tired, too.

Luke checked his phone, where it seemed he did have a list of necessities. "There are a few things, but they're less important. We can order them online or come back another day. Like curtains and pillows."

"But there is one more stop we need to make," Rylan smirked. "Promise you'll like this one. You don't have to choose anything. It's all on us."

Click!

I whirled, searching for the sound.

Click! Click!

The blood drained out of my face. "Kade, where are they?"

He curved himself around me as I pulled my glasses and hat out of my purse and put them back on. Still, it was done. Whoever had found us now had pictures of

Kade touching me. Or Rylan smiling and me laughing. They'd be all over the internet in hours.

I tried not to worry about it.

"Let's get upstairs," Avery said quietly. "The manager will stall them, so they'll have to find us again."

We took the elevator, and sure enough, Mr. Syme stepped in the photographer's path as the door closed. That was a relief. We whizzed up to the seventh floor, which looked like clothes when the doors opened.

I laughed. "I have clothes. We just have to go get them."

"Yes." Rylan slung an arm around my shoulder. "We do need to go get those. But we thought we might get you something more fun."

"Like—"

In front of us was the biggest, frothiest lingerie section I'd ever seen. Every color of silk and lace. There were feathers in there too. It was an explosion of all things sexy, and now I was blushing bright red.

"Is this okay?" Rylan asked. "If it's weird, that's okay."

I took the time to think about it. He said the choices were theirs. Which meant they wanted to pick stuff for me to wear with them, and the thought of being in something they picked because they thought it would look sexy on me? "No, it's not weird."

Fuck, I was glad I wasn't going into heat anymore. I was already perfuming as it was. There wasn't a second around these men when I wasn't. But there was no mistaking that it just got stronger.

"You pick something too, baby girl," Avery said quietly.

I could pick something only for sleeping. Or sexy. There were too many options, but the guys split off without hesitation.

"You all already thought of what you wanted, did you?"

"Bet your ass, baby girl."

Smiling, I wandered through the displays, looking for anything that caught my eye. There was a black strappy thing which looked badass and reminded me of my conversation with Luke. A couple of babydoll style nightgowns which were cute and seemed comfortable.

Silky shorts and lacy tops. God, at this rate I was going to have more lingerie than regular clothes.

I snuck up behind Luke, or I *thought* I had when he turned and smiled. "No peeking."

"I don't even get to see?"

He sighed, but he was still smiling. "When you look at me like that, you do."

The rack in front of him was covered in the same style of babydoll dresses in various colors. Some revealed more than others. "Any preferences?"

"I hate wearing orange and yellow. Brown too. Anything else is fine, color wise."

"Good to know. In style?"

"I—" Clearing my throat, I resettled the selections I had over my arm. "I don't really wear lingerie. Or I haven't."

His tone was gentle and his eyes were sparkling, but I

still sensed the seriousness underneath. "Are you going to run away if I ask you why?"

I shrugged. "Just haven't. Not a lot of opportunity."

He tilted my face up and kissed me, pulling me in and turning it into a kiss that would fuel a million headlines if the photographer saw it. And yet, I couldn't bring myself to care as long as he kept kissing me. "You'll have all the opportunities you want with us," he said. "The fact that we've been able to—mostly—keep our hands off you in the store is a miracle."

Rylan pulled me backwards before I could respond, kissing my cheek as he leaned over my shoulder. "How do you feel about feathers?"

"Pretty, but I really don't like being tickled."

"Noted. But they're not off the table?"

"Nope."

He paused, pressing his nose to my hair and inhaling deeply. "Excellent."

"The feathers or the way I smell."

I jumped as he nipped my ear before walking away and asking. "Why can't it be both?"

"I think I'm done," Luke said, lifting my selections out of my hands and adding them to his own. "I'll get the others and we can check out and head home. Stay here. You're still not allowed to see the total."

I sighed, but smiled. "Fine."

The house sounded nice. I'd order food for everyone and then curl up on the couch or something. I wasn't fully recovered from the heat. Normally a day like this wouldn't have me feeling exhausted.

You've never had five men paying attention to you like this either.

Kade led the way out of the section. I got a glimpse of what they were carrying, and now I was blushing at the amount of lingerie the guys were now shamelessly carrying to the cashier.

But I stopped in front of a mannequin, taking in the dress on it. It could have been a gown meant for the red carpet, but it wasn't. Pale blue silk dropped down in a long wave, pooling around the mannequin's feet. The neckline was straight and low, held up by strings of pearls which draped over the shoulders and continued around the back where the silk dipped to expose miles of skin.

I couldn't explain why I was drawn to it.

"You like it?"

Avery's voice made me jump. He was standing close behind me, now the scent of spices wrapping around me a second before his arms did.

"It seems very impractical," I said. "If it's just for sleeping."

His low laugh rumbled through me. "Very little of what we're buying today is practical, baby girl." That was true. "But saying it's impractical doesn't tell me if you like it."

Nerves seized my gut. I did like it. I loved it. So why was I having a hard time saying so? Today had been all about what I wanted and *only* what I wanted. What was different about this?

Because it wasn't me. Or rather, it wasn't what anyone thought was me. Of the pair of twins, I was the one with the harder edge. Something like this flew in the face of everything anyone thought about me, and I wasn't going to wear something only to be laughed at.

They'd made clear they didn't care about any of what the press said, but nerves were swirling in my gut in a way they hadn't with anything else. With a bedroom, it was something private. Only they would see it. This was clothing. No one but them would see it either, but it hit me differently.

It was all right. I could deal with whatever the hell this was later.

"I like it," I hedged. "But I don't need it."

Avery turned me, guiding me back against the nearby wall. We were in the very corner of the store, so no one could see us. "Try that again, please," he said gently. "This time without lying."

"How the fuck do you *do* that?" I snapped. "You just *know* I'm lying and it's annoying." In the last bit of the heat he'd sensed it too.

Avery raised one eyebrow, and I sighed, relaxing back against the wall. "Sorry."

"Hit a nerve, did I?" I glared at him, and he chuckled. "Tell me why."

Those same nerves jangled along my skin. I didn't want to lie to them—of course I didn't—but I wasn't used to anyone caring whether I did. Especially when it usually made things easier. I wanted to be here with them, but it was still soon. A heat and a few days wasn't enough time for me to let go of all this.

If I ever really could.

I swallowed and looked into the center of his chest, where the green fabric of his shirt stretched to accommodate his size. My voice was barely a whisper. "I don't want anyone to think I'm silly for wearing something like that. Or for wanting it. So it's okay, we can just go."

His purr started, so strong it practically rattled the wall behind us. One hand slipped behind my neck and tilted my head back so I was looking at him. He stared at me in silence for a minute before speaking. "You're still waiting for us not to want you."

It wasn't a question, just a steady, solid observation.

And that statement had me collapsing, curling in on myself with shame and pain. I didn't want to feel like this —I didn't constantly want to feel like I was just a replacement. But at the same time, it was all I'd ever known, and I didn't know how to break out of the thoughts.

Avery let out a long sigh as he pulled me to his chest. Not a sigh of disappointment, but of realization. I wanted to apologize for the thoughts, but I knew better.

With one hand, he fished his phone out of his pocket and dialed. "One of you come back. We've got one more thing." He paused. "Yes, I'm aware."

Ending the call and pulling back, he looked at me. "Don't move. I want you standing right here when I get back."

"Okay." I leaned against the wall, pressing my lips together and trying to resist the urge to run. It was so much easier to just get out of a situation than to sit in the awkwardness. But I owed Avery more than that. All of them more than that.

Through the racks of clothes I saw Luke appear, looking for me, and I saw Avery hand him the pile of blue silk and pearls. Luke didn't blink at the garment in his hands. All he did was look for me, and I pressed myself further back into the wall behind a display of bras.

Avery took his place in front of me when he returned, using his body to pin me to the wall, ensuring my chance of running was now completely gone. And the way he was looking at me brought all my fear back.

Not because I was afraid of him, but because all these men saw through the shell I'd carefully carved to protect myself, and they were asking me to leave that shell behind.

"Now," he said. "The others are buying everything, and they're going to meet us at home. But you and I need to talk a little about this."

"Do we have to?"

"Yes." There was enough Alpha power in the word to make me shudder.

I swallowed. "Okay, but do we have to still be in the middle of all the underwear to do it?"

"No," he chuckled. "I think we can work on that."

We walked through the department store, Avery leading me, holding my hand firmly until we reached the nesting section. "Choose a place to sit."

"We can't use these," I said. "They're for everyone."

"Everyone includes you, baby girl. And I'm sure people sit in them to try them out. I'm not going to fuck you in one, but you need a place that's safe."

I looked at the various fabrics and colors, looking for

something that looked and felt like my nest. Nothing even came close to what they'd let me do with mine, but there were a bunch of dark blue velvet pillows calling to me. I went and sat in the middle of them, pulling one of them into my lap so I could feel the texture.

Avery went a step further. He laid down in the pillows and patted the one beside him. Fuck it. If the employees had a problem, I would let him handle it. I scooted over to him and laid where he told me to, tucking one pillow under my head.

He rolled me gently to my side so I faced him, and I didn't meet his eyes. There was no part of me which wanted to have this conversation, just like I knew there was no part of him which would let it slip by.

"Before I ask you anything, I need you to know I'm not angry with you."

"I know," I said. If I'd sensed any anger in him, I knew myself well enough to know I'd already be gone.

"Good. So tell me why you think we would think you're silly for wanting to wear something as pretty as that nightdress?"

I ran my finger over the pillow squished between us, savoring the softness of the fabric and trying to distract myself. "It's just not what I usually wear."

"And?"

"I don't know."

"Don't lie to me, Esme. You already tried it once, don't do it again."

Squeezing my eyes shut, I curled around the pillow. I wasn't lying. Not completely. I didn't know which single thing made *this* hard. It was too many things to figure out, all tangled up in my life as a shadow girl.

Avery's scent wrapped around me, and his purr started. I couldn't help but relax when I heard that sound, but it wasn't enough to make me let go of the pillow which was anchoring me to the earth.

"Baby girl," he said, sliding a hand over my side. Just soothing, but not trapping me. "Talk to me."

"It's too much. There's not just one thing, it's *everything*." Memories flashed through my mind I thought I'd buried completely. Being forced to change because I needed to look different, and Eva's image was the more important one. Being instructed on how to make sure I didn't do anything to damage her brand as the wholesome girl. I had freedom, but only as long as I did it in a different way from Eva. I was the comparison others measured her by. To them, I wasn't a person, only a reflection.

"A few years ago, an Alpha asked me on a date. My family knew his, so I said yes. We went to Aurelia's, so we were seen, and I wore what I wanted." I still remembered the outfit. A magenta dress which slipped off the shoulders, and flared out at the knees. It was pretty and frothy, and Eva helped me do my make-up. "When we sat down, he told me I should leave the pretty dresses to my sister. He laughed and said it was her job to look pretty and smile, and it was my job to make her look better in comparison.

"Everyone wanted her, but since they couldn't have her, they would settle for me, the knock-off version. So I

231

should play up what everyone really wanted me to be and own being the dirty one. The slutty one. Everyone's fantasy fuck. He tried to touch me under the table." I took a breath, feeling the stillness which now clung to Avery. "I left, and I know he was an asshole, but it turned out he was right. I love Eva so much, and it's not her fault, but they all want her. She's the face of everything sweet, good, and wholesome, and I'm the edgy, bitchy sister everyone wants as a replacement. So they can pretend they have her." The words tasted bitter on my tongue. "There's a reason I asked if you all knew I was different."

He didn't say anything, still stroking up and down my side, waiting for me to get it all out.

"So I can't wear things like that. Because—and I know you wouldn't. I promise I know—but all I can think about is how it would feel to see laughter in Ben's eyes when I put it on. Or Luke's, or yours. Any of you. And... I'm not sure I would come back from that."

He did pull me in now, enveloping me in strong arms and a purr so loud it blocked out everyone and everything else. One hand stroked up my back, finally cradling the back of my head, and it just felt... complete. Complete comfort and complete safety.

"Eva is a lovely person," he said. "But you are not your sister, and we know that. And I hope *you* know, not for one second have I wanted you for anything else than being you."

I nodded where my face was buried in his chest.

"How long has it been since you've been able to be yourself, Es? Really?"

One hiccuped laugh burst out of me. Had I ever been able to do that? "Only when I'm alone in my studio where no one can see me."

"This pack is a bunch of misfits," he said. "We know a little about being on the outside of things. Even now, not everyone approves of what we do. They think it's shady or dirty, that marking someone's skin somehow makes them lesser. You saw how the manager first reacted to us. We haven't faced it on the same scale, but we know. Which is why we're so close. We can be ourselves with each other, and it's always going to be okay."

I'd seen what he said in action, and it was true.

"So if you want to dress like a princess, then dress like a princess, baby girl. There's nothing wrong with you for wanting soft, pretty things. It's okay to like hard and dirty things, too. It's safe to be yourself with us, even if the world wants to tell you that you can't."

I closed my eyes so the tears blurring my vision didn't spill over. Of course I knew, but knowing it and feeling it were two different things. "I'm still scared."

"I know, and that's okay. As much as anyone might wish it, you can't just ignore a lifetime full of pain overnight."

A *click* sounded in the distance, and I groaned. Couldn't they leave me alone for one fucking second? There was nothing wrong with this. Nothing bad or ugly. We were simply cuddling in a nest, but it would still be picked apart by everyone and everything. "I want to go home now."

"I couldn't agree more."

My hat and glasses were on before we walked out of the store. The photographers were at least more discreet here than they were at events, or when they were dealing with Eva. With me they tried to be stealthy because they wanted to catch me in the act of something.

But there were more outside, and everyone saw us getting into the cab together, shutters snapping wildly. The news was out, and there was nothing I could do about it now.

CHAPTER TWENTY-TWO

ESME

*T*here was a truck in front of the house, and a veritable army of people moving things inside. All the stuff I'd picked.

"That was fast."

"Mr. Syme felt... particularly motivated to make a good impression after Ben talked to him. And Luke called Addison to coordinate the rest."

"Is she here?"

Avery shook his head. "No. But I'm sure you'll see her soon. She likes you."

I liked her, too. But Ben's sister wasn't the thing weighing most on my mind. "Do I have to tell the others? About what we talked about?"

"I think it's important for them to know." Avery took my hand and made sure I didn't get hit in the head with one of my new bedposts. "But if you want me to tell them the basics so you don't have to, I can, with your permission. No one is going to think less of you."

Something in my chest eased. I didn't think I could look at all of them and go through the memories again. Especially since I already knew they'd be upset *for* me. "Yeah, that's fine with me."

They were in the kitchen, and Rylan was face deep in one of my cupcakes.

"What do you guys want for dinner?" I pulled out my phone. "Ben promised me I could buy it since I'm sure you just spent a fucking fortune on me." Kade opened his mouth and I pointed at him. "Nope. I'm doing it."

He smirked. "I suppose I'll let you get away with it. *Once*, Omega."

The way his voice rasped over the word *Omega* had chills running over my skin.

"How do you feel about Thai?"

"I theel gooth aboud it," Rylan managed, the last of the cupcake in his mouth. Luke rolled his eyes, and I saw him kick Rylan in the leg.

They all agreed, so I pulled up the app for my favorite Thai place in the city. Pad Thai had been on my mind for days, and I desperately needed some.

A man stepped into the doorway. "It's all unloaded. We'll be back tomorrow with Miss Gray for the rest of it."

"Thanks." Ben lifted a hand.

I kept adding food to the cart. "Do I even dare ask what 'the rest of it' means?"

"Oh, they're going to paint the room tomorrow," Luke said. "We need to go back to the studio. Do you have any plans?"

"No." I shook my head. It was the weekend, but that was when tattoo studios were the busiest. It was right that they needed to get back. "But I'll probably go to my house and catch up on paints. The heat set me behind schedule. I've been ignoring the notifications."

I'd been posting on the Elyse Taylor paint account nearly every day for years. People were asking if I was okay, and I hadn't wanted to dive into everything. But I did have to get back to some kind of real life. "Am I sleeping in the nest? Since the bed isn't ready?"

"If you want to. You can sleep wherever you want. But if you're in the nest," Rylan said, "I'll be in there with you."

None of them contradicted him. Especially since they would all likely do the same. I wasn't going to argue. I'd always hated sleeping alone.

I pressed order on the food. "Okay. A literal mountain of Thai food is on the way."

Ben crossed his arms and leaned on the kitchen island. "Happy?"

"Very. If I'm a part of this pack, I fully expect to pay for some things."

Someone grumbled, but I couldn't pinpoint who it was.

Avery stepped closer. "They put all the bags of lingerie in your bathroom. I'd like you to try it on."

All the blood drained from my face. "Now?"

"Right now. I'll talk to them about our conversation, and when you're ready, you come down."

Terror built in my chest—all the fear I didn't know what to do with.

"Give us a chance to change that image in your head, baby girl. Please."

I closed my eyes. It was a choice I had to make. I either trusted them enough to show them all of me, or I needed to walk away. Because I couldn't be a part of a pack that wouldn't accept every piece of me, and they didn't want any walls between us. "Okay."

He smiled. "Good girl. We'll be in the living room."

They didn't start talking until I was halfway up the stairs, and I was glad I couldn't hear what they were saying.

There were *way* too many bags in the bathroom. All filled with lacy fabric and crisp tissue paper sticking out of the top. I peeked into the main room, but it was a mess of boxes and unassembled furniture all clustered in the middle so the walls could still be accessed.

Okay. You can do this.

I splashed cool water on my face and took my hair out of my ponytail. Fast. I needed to do this fast or I would lose my nerve.

Digging through the bags, and doing my best not to spoil the surprise of the other things they bought, I finally found it. The tags on it were gone. Those sneaky bastards. I was sure all the tags were already gone so I couldn't see the prices.

I undressed and tossed my clothes on the sink before lifting the dress and bringing it over my head.

The blue silk fell around me in a smooth, satiny wave. The pearls were cool on my skin and rolled into place smoothly. In the mirror, I blushed. It was so *pretty*. The softness on my bare skin and the way my hair fell around my face, I looked beautiful.

It wasn't a thought I had often. Not because I had any illusions about what I looked like, but because of what I'd talked about with Avery. I rarely, if ever, wore what I really wanted. Even the night I met Ben, it had been a dress of Eva's. It looked great on me, but it wasn't what I would have chosen for myself.

Running my hands down the fabric, I loved all of it, but the thought of going downstairs was still like walking straight into my funeral. There wasn't a way to conquer this fear without facing it. And yet, I wanted to stay locked in here forever, just me in the dress. If I was by myself, there was no one to laugh at me.

My stomach flipped with nerves. Someone would come looking for me when I didn't come down. By now Avery would have told them enough. I didn't want them to suddenly feel like they had to walk on eggshells around me because I was afraid of them. I wasn't afraid of *them*. It was the cruelty of my own mind.

I *hated* that I was so fucking broken I couldn't even walk into a room with a pack who was on my side without ending up a mess. It was that thought which finally drove me from the room and down the stairs.

The dress had a train on it, dragging behind me down the stairs, and for a brief, fleeting moment, I felt like I was in a different time, descending the stairs to a ball filled with suitors waiting for me.

In the living room the television was on, low in the background while they talked. What was I going to do, sweep in there and yell 'ta-da'? I stopped just outside the door, terror sinking through me all over again. Under my skin, the urge to run was building. My entire body shook.

Conversation stopped in the room.

Luke's voice. "Esme?"

I didn't answer him.

"We can scent you, sweetheart. Are you going to come out?"

"No," I mumbled. But I took a deep breath, curled my hands into fists, and walked out into view. My spine was so straight it could snap.

They were all staring at me, and no one spoke. All the air was gone. There was nothing to breathe, and they were still in complete silence. I couldn't stay here, not while they stared and decided what they thought of this version of me.

I turned and took one step.

"No you don't," Kade's voice froze me in my tracks, all Alpha bark. He was already halfway across the room to me, eyes roving over me and this confection of a dress.

He took me in his arms, purring while one hand wove solidly into my hair to make sure I didn't look away. "If anyone, *anyone*, makes you feel like you're less because you want to wear something that makes you feel beautiful, they'll have to deal with me."

I shuddered, blinking back tears of relief.

"There's nothing funny about this. You are stunning. That's the reason we didn't say anything, because there are no words for how beautiful you look."

There was no holding back the tears now. They came even though I didn't want them to. The fear in my gut was finally starting to ease. One moment wouldn't make it go away, but they hadn't laughed at me. They still wanted me. It felt foolish to *need* to know that, but I did.

Kade leaned in, voice a deep growl in contrast to the sensual purr coming from him. "I'm going to kiss you now, and I want you to tell me you understand I'm kissing you for *you*. Not because of a dress, even if you look like a goddamn queen. Not because of anyone else. I'm kissing you because I want you, Esme Williams." His voice lowered even further. "You're *my* Omega."

"I understand." The words were barely understandable through my tears, but I did, and I believed him.

Kade's mouth crashed down on mine, arms hauling me even tighter against his chest. The heat of his hands sank through the silk of the dress, and he touched me everywhere. His mouth moved to my neck where he breathed in my scent.

He didn't let me go, pulling me to the couch and settling me beside him. Ben was on my other side, and an anonymous hand held out a tissue. "I'm sorry," I said quietly.

"Why?" It was Rylan's voice. "It's a real question."

"Because it feels like a silly thing to be afraid of."

Ben took one of my hands. "We're not born with fears. Fear comes because we learn it. Because something forced it into us and taught our minds it wasn't safe, even if we're not fully conscious of it. There are no silly fears."

Curling into Kade's chest, I laid my head where I could hear the now softer sound of his purr. "I can't promise it will be easy. I've had... a lot of practice being terrified."

"But you still did it," Luke pointed out. "That's all that matters."

Avery had the remote. "I'd originally planned to barrage you with first date questions, but I think tonight calls for something more low-key. How do you feel about soccer?"

I raised an eyebrow. "I feel like if you guys aren't fans of the Slate City Scoundrels, this will be a difficult courtship."

Luke sipped the beer in his hand. "I knew I liked her for a reason. We're all fans, but Ry practically has a shrine in his room."

"We've been through this. It is a signed jersey, not a shrine."

Avery chuckled. "Whatever you say."

The game turned on, and we were down by a goal. Not great, but the team had come back from worse odds. But while I watched, soccer wasn't the thing filling my thoughts.

I was sitting here with a pack who wanted me—who was doing everything in their power to treasure me—in a frothy dress I couldn't wear anywhere else. It was perfect.

"What are you thinking, baby?" Kade's voice was a whisper only I could hear.

"Why?"

"Because my Omega just sighed and snuggled down like I'm a nest."

I hadn't even realized, but I was snuggled as close as I could be. Closer than was reasonable, and I didn't care. "I'm just happy."

His smile warmed my forehead. "I'm glad."

The doorbell rang for the food, and Avery went to

get it. The Thai was *delicious*, and I managed not to spill anything on the nightgown. That would have been a tragedy.

Unfortunately, the Scoundrels lost, but it didn't feel that way. Not between the food and conversation and the endless rotation of arms holding me. Tomorrow, I needed to call Eva. She hadn't heard from me since the heat started, and I had questions. Besides—

Oh.

"Has anyone looked at anything online? I haven't had my phone since I ordered the food. Are they there?"

Ben nodded. "They are. So far it's nothing bad. The photos are innocent. You, Kade, and Rylan. Then you and Avery cuddling after we left. The two of you getting into the cab to come home. They could try to make something out of the second photo, I guess, but it's honestly a nice picture."

I swallowed. We knew it was going to happen, but that didn't make it easier. "Do they know who you are?"

"Yes."

Wincing, I sat up straight. "They'll probably be at the studio tomorrow. I'm sorry."

"Like we said, Esme," Kade ran a hand through his hair. "We didn't go into this blind. We knew exactly who you were and what came with it. But while we're at the studio, if you go home or anywhere else, do us a favor and call Wes or one of the other security guards? They're going to be looking for you more than they're looking for us."

I sighed, but nodded. It was a good idea.

"Are the headlines okay?"

Ben shrugged. "Average. Not all of them are flattering, but they don't know anything more than they saw us all together at a department store. There's only so much they can make out of those details."

"What if they're here tomorrow morning? You don't have a gate. They'll be hounding you and trying to see into the windows. Oh, god, I didn't even think about that. All your privacy will be gone. I—"

In the middle of my words, Luke crossed to me and knelt in front of the couch. His eyes had the quiet power in them I now recognized. "Take a breath, Omega."

I did.

"Another one."

Yes.

"Now, is it your fault if paparazzi show up on our doorstep?"

"I know you want me to say no, but of course it is."

"Why?" He asked. "Are you going to call them?"

I huffed out a breath in frustration. "The five of you are so fucking *reasonable*."

Luke was still trying to be serious, but an amused smile tugged at his lips. "Esme, we'll deal with the press. If we have to put up a fence, then we'll put up a fence. But someone trying to take my picture is *not* enough to stop me from wanting to court you. And anyone who thought that, in my opinion, is a punk-ass little bitch."

Rylan snorted, nearly choking on his drink. "Is that you trying to use hip language? Because if it is, we need to revisit your training, old man."

I burst out laughing, and everyone else followed, even Luke. Though he wasn't even close to being old. He was still looking at me. "Have any of the headlines about you ever been true?"

"No."

"So why does it matter?"

My hands began to fidget. "It's such an inconvenience."

Luke shrugged. "An inconvenience which can be solved with a solid pair of sunglasses and making sure we post a sign in the studio window not allowing any press. Hell, we'll even spring for a 'no trespassing' sign in the driveway. Then we can have them thrown off the property anytime we like."

"Basically," I said. "It doesn't matter what kind of chaos I bring into your life, you're going to pretend it doesn't mean anything?"

"Not pretend," he said with a smile. "It really doesn't mean anything. But I'm glad you're getting the idea."

Standing, he pulled me with him. "Now, I think it's time the Omega got some sleep, and maybe a distraction or two."

I'd never seen a room clear so fast. The food was put away, the TV and lights off in less than a minute, with them guiding me back up to the nest.

I tripped over the long skirt of the gown, and Avery caught me. We were a little behind the rest of them now. "I'm proud of you," he said. "For earlier."

"Thanks."

"All you have to do is be here, baby girl. It might be

hard sometimes, but we've got you. And we'll do whatever we have to in order to prove it."

The same contentment and happiness rested in my chest. I didn't have any lingering doubts. They were telling me what they wanted, and for the first time, I believed it.

CHAPTER TWENTY-THREE

KADE

The blaring sound brought a groan out of me, and I turned over. That was the shrillest alarm sound I'd ever heard, and it had to be Esme's phone. None of the pack's phones sounded like that.

Her phone ended up on the floor at the edge of the nest. I grabbed it and swiped the alarm off, too late realizing it wasn't an alarm at all, but a phone call.

Fuck.

"Hello?"

"Who is this? Put Esme on the phone *right. Now.*"

I blinked, still not fully awake. "Hold on." Muting the call, I rolled back toward the center of the nest where Esme was sleeping, laid out in her silk nightgown like a fairytale princess who needed to be woken with a kiss.

So I did just that. I stepped over Rylan and Luke before kneeling beside her and kissing her. "Time to wake up, baby." She moaned and curled toward me. "Not yet."

"Someone's on the phone for you, and sounded... insistent."

Her eyes opened, looking at me as I held out the phone. "I thought it was an alarm and accidentally answered it."

One look at the screen had her rolling her eyes. She unmuted the call and put it on speaker. "Hello?"

"ESME ELYSE WILLIAMS."

I picked Esme up and turned her so she could sit across my lap. "Mom, if I wanted screaming as a good morning I'd live on a farm. With roosters."

"You think this is time for a smart mouth? What the hell is going on?"

I felt her wince. "So you saw the pictures?"

"Everyone in the world has seen the pictures. Is there a reason I found out you're consorting with a pack from everyone else but you?"

The word 'consorting' made me chuckle. I buried the sound in Esme's shoulder.

"It wasn't planned. I promise I can explain." She pressed a hand to her forehead. "It's Saturday, right? We're supposed to have lunch, anyway."

Over the line there was a frustrated sigh. "Yes. Be at Aurelia's by noon, and for god's sake take the back entrance. They're already going to be all over you. And make sure you're camera ready."

The call went dead, and Esme dropped the phone. "Good morning to me."

"I'm so sorry," I said. "I wouldn't have answered it."

"No, it's not your fault. She would have kept calling until I answered either way. We just got it out of the way faster."

Luke pushed up from where he was lying on his stomach. "I now understand your fear of judgment with regard to clothing."

Esme stiffened. "My mom's not a bad person. I promise."

"Sweetheart, that's not what I meant, and I think you know it."

"Yeah."

My little Omega leaned harder into my body. It did nothing for the state of my cock, already hard simply because it was the morning and she was close and smelled like a fucking treat.

"It's just the world she's from. I'm from. It was so important when Eva was younger, trying to cultivate a brand which could be successful and not harm her career or my dad's. It matters less now, but it's still the way she is." Then more quietly. "That little bit of control in her life is all she has left."

I banded my arm around her chest, keeping her fully against me. "It's good to understand where it comes from, even if she doesn't mean any harm. It's affected you."

Esme shrieked as Ben pulled her away by the ankles until he had room to settle over her. Much like last night when our Omega was given every distraction she needed with our mouths between her thighs, showing her exactly how much we loved the dress.

"When you go meet your mom, wear what you want to wear. I don't want you thinking about how the pictures of you will reflect on us, on your mom or Eva, or even on you. They're just pictures, and people will forget about them. I would one thousand percent rather you be happy and comfortable with a few 'bad,'" he used his fingers as quotes, "pictures than to keep feeling like you can't be who you are. Okay?"

"She's already pissed at me. You want me to poke the bear?"

Avery sat up. "If poking the bear is what it takes for Momma Williams to understand who you are, that you're an adult and your own person, and your personal image isn't going to shatter the family? Then yes."

Rylan stretched. "Bonus points if you wear some of our lingerie underneath it, knowing we chose something for you. So scandalous, wearing something sexy under your clothes."

She flushed, and Ben kissed her before he let her up. "I guess it's time to get back to a regular schedule. Not gonna lie, I enjoyed the break. My tattoo ass is going to be out of practice from lounging in this nest."

He wasn't wrong. It was time to get back to the studio. Our clients had been good about pushing off appointments, and the guest artists who'd agreed to fill in during our absence were hits, so we were told. But we were behind schedule now. I would put it off forever to be with Esme, but she had a life and a career too. We needed to settle into a more natural pattern with her now that we were courting, her heat was over, and she'd agreed to move in.

"I'll bring more clothes back tonight," Esme said. "Pretty sure everything I have here needs to be washed."

I picked her up off the soft floor of the nest. "I wish I had time to take a shower with you."

"Yeah, well, we both know that would take longer than we have."

"Damn straight it would."

But I loved that she was teasing me and taking it as a given I would fuck her senseless in the shower. Because I absolutely would. But my first appointment was early, and I hated being late.

"You're not going to get home and want to stay there, are you?" I set her down in front of the bathroom door. "Because I have no problem tossing you over my shoulder and bringing you back here."

"No," she shook her head. "I'm coming back here. If only because I need to see what the hell Addison does with the room."

"*Your* room. It's your room, Esme. You can say it."

She swallowed. "My room."

"Not so hard, was it?" I winked and kissed her before jogging away. Five more seconds and I would have pushed her in the bathroom and into the shower. I needed a cold one myself.

My room was at the front of the house, and I took a look outside the windows, given we were now the new stars of what was sure to be a tabloid whirlwind. Sure enough, there were cameras outside. Most of them were hanging back further down the driveway, partially hidden by trees. But they were there, waiting to ambush.

The cameras didn't bother me. Like we'd told Esme, we knew who she was and what we were getting into, and she was *more* than worth it. But we needed to be careful too. Too much exposure for her would hurt her, and the last thing I wanted was my little Omega hurting, unless it was her ass under my palm.

I flew through my shower and jogged down the stairs

to grab a cup of coffee. I would need it to get through the day. The heat and furnishment of Esme's room had taken a lot out of us. Not to mention the adrenaline and energy of a new relationship. We were all going to be dragging for a while.

Rylan was already lounging in the kitchen. "You see outside?"

His room was on the other side of the house on the front. "Yeah, I did."

"What's outside?" Luke asked.

"Cameras. Waiting for us, or Esme."

He swore softly. "She's going to hate that."

"She'll be fine," I said. "But I don't want her leaving without security. They went after her enough when she was alone. Now they'll be ravenous."

Her scent floated into the kitchen before I saw her. "Who's ravenous?"

"Me," I said immediately. "For you."

The shade of pink she turned was a fucking miracle.

Luke was the more pragmatic one. He turned to her. "Just like you thought, there are paparazzi outside."

Esme's eyes went wide, and I saw the immediate panic, but Luke had it handled before I could take a single step.

"We're fine. Everything is fine and there's nothing to worry about. But I need you to do something for me, and I'm not going to take no for an answer."

"What?"

"Don't leave this house without Wes or another security guard."

Esme wrinkled her nose. "I need to call them, anyway. I don't have my car. But I guess my run is off the table. All of them will be until they stop actively following me."

"'Fraid so," I told her. "You can run on the property here. But I know it's not the same." The back of the house had a fence high enough to keep her safe, but our land—large as it was—didn't compare to the woods and parks outside the city where she was used to going. I was familiar with the area. It was stunning.

"I need to go to my house before lunch with my mom, and I'll go back afterwards to do some work and grab my clothes. But I probably won't stay too late. I've gotten used to having company."

The words startled me, and I had to turn away and take a sip of my coffee. The stark, brutal knot in my stomach at her words. Fuck, why hadn't I even thought about it?

No wonder Esme was skittish. Not only did everyone she'd tried to love want her to be a version of herself that didn't exist, she was *alone*.

Her house was lovely, but she was still by herself in it. Watching her sister have a bonded pack, and watching the people she hoped might love her pass her off as nothing, and going back to her house afterward. Alone.

I had a visceral image of her in her bed, face ragged with the aftermath of pain, just as I'd seen her that day. She would have been by herself for days, whining, trying to bear the brutal need an Omega's instinct for an Alpha's knot.

Fuck me.

When you realized that, it was amazing she was staying with us at all. It made sense she was terrified, because every sign told me this was what she wanted. She wanted to be loved. Spoiled. Cherished. Everything which came with being an Omega. And she was scared it was going to disappear, just like it had every time before.

"Baby, come here for a second?"

Her soft footsteps circled the island until she was in front of me, and I wrapped myself around her until she was lifted off the floor. I inhaled her and reveled in the scent of sun-brewed tea and the sharp sweetness of lilacs. Just the one breath made my mouth *water*.

"What's this for?" She asked.

I allowed her feet to touch the ground. "I just realized something, and it made a lot of things click into place."

"About me?" Her voice shook a little.

"Yeah," I said gently. "About you."

She swallowed. "Do I want to know?"

Letting her stand, I tugged her back so I could see her face and tilted her chin up. "We've told you a lot of things, but I don't think we've said this, and I think it's something you need to hear. You don't have to be alone anymore, baby. Okay? You never have to be alone."

Her eyes went glassy, and she blinked away the reactionary tears. "You're right. I did need to hear that."

"You're going to have a great day, and after it's over, come home to us and have a great night."

"Okay."

Ben and Avery came down the stairs, and Ben called us. "Ready to face the music?"

I kissed Esme, taking the time to taste her lips. Just the one small taste had to last me the whole day. "I'm ready."

Luke looked at her. "Call Wes."

"I will."

She followed us into the entry, and the others kissed her too before she fell back. Pictures were fine, but giving them *easy* pictures was silly. Esme stayed out of sight as we opened the door, and just like I'd thought, they converged from every direction.

The flashes were blinding and the questions overlapping so quickly I couldn't make all of them out. What I did hear made me clench my fists, and I forced myself into the car before I made an ass of myself for punching a photographer in the face.

"Now I know why she wears sunglasses," Avery said.

I tried to unclench my jaw. "I'm going to need some. Did you hear the asshole ask how good it felt to knot her?"

"Yes," Luke said darkly. "But it's going to be like this until they lose interest."

They would. Eventually. When they saw Esme was actually fucking happy. They preyed on weakness, exploiting the cracks in her armor. I planned on making that armor stronger.

They were at the studio too. It was actually a bigger crowd. We parked behind the building. "Should we go in the back?" Rylan asked.

"No." Ben stretched. "If we give them some of what they're after, they might fade out after a while. But if we sneak in the back, they'll be waiting and trying to photograph us through the windows all day."

The man had a point. Ben was the most visible of us, having a large following on social media for the incredible hyper-realism he had the ability to create. I'd known him for years and it was still fucking impressive.

"All right," I said. "Let's get in the door first and make a plan after."

We did. They swarmed us as soon as we turned the corner.

How does it feel to fuck the ice queen? Did you thaw her out at all?

Did you pick her because she was a challenge? Are you seeking fame by taming the ice bitch?

Everyone wants to know how good she is. Come on, give us a clue.

I somehow managed to keep my face blank through the barrage of questions and let them roll off my shoulders. They were assholes, and were being assholes *on purpose*. But yet again, I suddenly understood Esme more. These questions weren't even about me. They were about her. If they'd say these things about her to us, what kind of questions had they asked her to her face?

Everything I was learning made me want to bundle her up in the nest and never let her out. Just make her feel *safe* for once in her fucking life.

The barrage of yelling quieted when the door shut, but they were still peering in, trying to get images of us.

"Daisy, you okay?" I asked our receptionist, who was watching the window warily.

"I'm good. They're not interested in me."

I nodded. "Can you make some signs for the door? No unsolicited photographs, and no one not seeking a tattoo appointment or without prior permission can enter."

"You got it. But first... I swear I'm not trying to pry, but I'm like so *fucking* happy for you guys. You don't have to tell me anything, but I hope it's going well."

"It is going well," Luke said. "Very well. And I think we'll be more inclined to talk about it once all this dies down. You'll definitely be getting to know Esme more."

She clapped her hands, beaming. "Seriously, that's awesome."

"You're the one who's awesome," Ben told her. "Thank you for keeping the place going while we were out."

Daisy did a dramatic flip of her wild blue hair over her shoulder. "It was a breeze. And yes, I am awesome."

Picking up clipboards from the desk, she handed out the consults we had. I knew I had a couple of piercing appointments, and I was likely going to be tattooing my ass off with walk-ins trying to rub off on the fame. But we wouldn't give them much.

"Once we make those signs, if even one of them tries to come in here, make it clear we'll call the cops if we have to."

"What happens if one of the photographers makes an appointment?" Ry asked, looking at the windows.

Avery swore under his breath. They would do it, too.

"We'll cross that bridge when we come to it," Luke tucked the clipboard under his arm. "The most important thing is to keep everything as normal and boring as possible. If there's anything the paparazzi hate, it's boring."

I couldn't agree more. So we all broke apart like it was nothing but an ordinary day, and I hoped it would go quickly. Not even an hour and I was already missing my Omega.

CHAPTER TWENTY-FOUR

ESME

Eva picked up on the third ring. "Nice to hear from my wayward sister."

I laughed. "I know. I should have called before. I've been exhausted."

"I bet you have." There was laughter in her voice. "Are you okay? With the news breaking?"

"I'm fine. I mean, I wish it hadn't, but there's nothing I can do about it. Mom, however, woke me up this morning by *literally* screaming my name through the phone."

"Ouch."

"Yeah. Any chance you're free for lunch? I'm going to need massive back-up."

"I am actually. Getting ready to leave, so I'm not doing much."

"On location? Did I know about that?"

She laughed. "I'm pretty sure I told you. Like four times."

"Fuck me." I'd completely forgotten.

"From the sounds of things that happened a lot."

"Ha ha. I just forgot about it."

Running water filtered through the phone, and a clatter like Eva was rinsing dishes. "Well, now you remember. Is lunch at Aurelia's?"

"Yeah, but I have another thing to ask. I've been instructed not to leave the house without Wes or one of the other guys. And I think it's pretty clear this is going to be... visible for a while. Do you mind if I borrow Wes and Henry for the time being? I can pay for replacements."

Eva snorted. "I don't need you to pay for replacements. It's actually perfect timing. Since I'll be on location, I'll need less of my own security. I'll send them over now and see you in a bit!"

She hung up before I could say anything else, but that was fine. Neither of us loved the phone. We used it when we had to, but especially being twins, in person was always better.

Now I just had to wait for my expensive bullet-proof chariot.

Instead of going anywhere else, I sat on the stairs, arms around my knees, and just breathed. Kade struck a nerve this morning, just like he had last night. I was alone at this moment, but I wasn't *alone*. They would be back tonight, and so would I.

There was excitement lurking in my gut, but right now it felt more like relief than anything else. Just to have people to come back to.

My phone buzzed a while later. Wes. "Hello?"

"I'm outside at the door. They're out here, but Henry and I are ready."

"Be right there."

Putting on my trusty hat and glasses, I took a breath

and went outside. The door locked behind me, and I was slammed with sound and light.

Esme, have you finally tricked a pack into putting up with your shit? Have you finally been knotted enough to thaw out? Are you slumming it because none of the high-class packs want you? What would your father think?

I tried to shut out the words and let Henry and Wes help me through the crowd and to the back of the car. They were just words. They didn't matter. I kept the mantra strong in my head. Just words. Only trying to get a response.

"Thank you for coming," I said.

"Of course. Eva told us we're with you for the fore-seeable future."

I let my head flop back against the seat. "Yeah. Because I'm once again the center of attention."

"Where are we going?" Henry asked from the front.

"My house. I need to change, and then lunch at Aurelia's with Mom. Depending on how long that takes, I need to do some work at home before coming back here. I'll be staying here for the courtship, at the pack's request."

I caught Wes's quickly hidden smile.

"It's okay, you can be happy."

"I am, Miss Williams. It's good to see you find a pack who knows your worth."

There wasn't much I could say to that. It was the truth. It was nice, even if everything in me was terrified it would collapse like a house of cards. I fluctuated between being scared and elated.

It didn't take long to reach my house, and there were paps there too, but the words barely reached me this time. "I won't be long."

Under my clothes, I'd taken Rylan's idea to heart, putting on some of the sexy lingerie they'd bought. The lacy bra and underwear set were dark grey, and I had no idea who had chosen them. All I knew was I hadn't seen this set in Luke's selections.

But for my actual lunch outfit? I didn't know. Without the guys, I would have put on nice pants and a blazer over some kind of t-shirt. Nice, but edgy enough to fit the role which had been cast for me. I liked being edgy sometimes, but I liked softness more. Had Eva been given freedom to choose her persona, we would have been entirely reversed. She would have been the one with edge, and I would have been the one in floral dresses.

Pushing aside my normal clothes, I went to the back of my closet, where I kept things I loved but hadn't had a chance to wear.

Immediately, I saw what I wanted. It was a perfect crossover between what was expected of me and what I wanted. It was a black dress. Lacy and off the shoulder, it somehow managed to be feminine and edgy at once. I distinctly remember how I felt when I bought it, and the disappointment when Eva's media team told me I couldn't wear it.

It had been a long time since I had been told I couldn't wear something. But it was more because I'd stopped trying to break out of the mold than that they'd left me alone.

I rarely wore dresses other than when I accompanied Eva to parties like the one where I'd met Ben. So fine. The paps wanted pictures of me? I would give them good ones. The fear in my gut was still real, but I was going to hold on to the courage the pack gave me.

My pack?

This morning Kade had made me say *my room* instead of *the room*. My pack instead of the pack.

I slipped the dress over my head and found matching shoes. This might be considered over-dressed, but it was Aurelia's. I needed the armor. The same restaurant where I'd been humiliated, and still one of my mother's favorite places to go.

She didn't know about what happened. No one did —not even Eva. I hadn't told her because it wasn't her fault, and there was nothing she could have done.

Make-up, jewelry, and dry shampoo later, I was ready to go. It was a touch early, but I'd rather be early than late.

"Ready, Wes."

This time I only had my sunglasses. My mother would kill me if I wore a baseball cap with this dress.

I winced, remembering this morning. It didn't matter. I knew it didn't, but the voice in my head was so used to it. Truthfully, I hadn't even noticed until they pointed it out. My mother's voice was as strong as my own in my head.

What made it worse was that she didn't mean any harm, and I loved her. But at some point, it needed to stop.

Esme, why the black dress? Ready for another funeral? Why try dressing up? Everyone knows you're the edgy twin. Trying to fancy up the fact that you're slumming it?

I pressed the heels of my hands into my eyes when the car door shut, breathing deep. Those questions cut deeper, and I was seeing Aaron's face as he told me I should embrace being the slutty sister everyone wanted to fuck but no one wanted to love.

"Are you all right?"

"No," I said with a sigh. "But I will be. I might have to stay inside for the rest of the courtship if it's going to be like this, Wes. I'm not sure I can handle this kind of shit being thrown at me every day. I know it's just headlines and I know they don't matter—"

"But it doesn't make people screaming your worst fears at you any easier."

I looked at him, the question in my eyes.

"It's different with Eva," he said quietly. "Different questions, but they still manage to pick at the things which bother her. I don't know how they manage it. They're a bunch of industrious psychopaths."

A laugh burst out of me. "That's the best description of paparazzi I've ever heard."

"If you want to stay at the pack's home until you decide, we can certainly help you move your studio equipment to their house if it's easier."

"That's nice of you."

He chuckled. "It might be overstepping, Miss Williams, but I've known you a long time. You're probably not surprised how much we know and have seen, and you have good reasons for every hesitation. But though it might not be my place to care about you, I do. We all do. And I would hate to see industrious psychopaths derail the best thing to ever happen to you."

"Thank you, Wes."

I didn't think about it a lot, but Wes had been with us for the better part of my life, working for my father before he switched to Eva's—and occasionally my —security.

We pulled up at Aurelia's, and blissfully there were no paps because they didn't know I was here yet. I was sure there would be a swarm by the time I left, given Eva and I would be in the same place at the same time. Since the way was clear, there was no point in using the back entrance like Mom asked.

"Think about it," he said as he ushered me inside. "If you need to move things, we'll help you."

"I will think about it."

On the one hand, having my studio at the pack's house sounded nice. And on the other hand, I felt it was important to keep my own space. Not as a reservation in case things went wrong, but just for some distance if I needed it. I'd been single and alone for twenty-eight years. Almost twenty-nine. I was sure I would need time-outs now and then.

But then, there wasn't anything saying I couldn't go back to my house as a studio once everything was settled one way or another.

"Name?" The maître d' asked without looking up.

"Esme Williams. I'm meeting my mother, but I doubt she's arrived yet."

She looked up in shock, and the smile replaced it just as quickly. "Of course, Miss Williams. My apologies. Right this way."

She led me through the restaurant. There were plenty of patrons even though it was barely noon. Slate City's elite, most of whom had few things better to do than go to lunch. I caught a few stares, but not nearly as many. Some of these people I recognized, and some were friends of my parents. But my presence wasn't startling to them.

"Here you are."

The table was in the center of the room, and incredibly visible. Naturally. But there were only two places set. "Please bring a third place setting. My sister will be joining us."

"Oh!" The woman perked up, clearly delighted to have *Eva* Williams in her restaurant. "Right away."

I sat, and the production began. Aurelia's never let any customer want for anything. A menu was in my hand and a glass of water poured in seconds.

The room was wall-to-wall shades of white. Table-cloths, pearly wallpaper, chandeliers painted white, and plush carpet. It had the look of a giant wedding cake. Frothy and beautiful. I wished it had better memories.

In contrast, I looked like a dark stain. Black on white.

My mother entered the restaurant, brushing by the maître d' with a wave. She didn't need directions. This was her favorite place, and was here at least twice a week. Usually at this exact table.

She wore a subdued pant-suit in pale pink. It suited her, even though I knew she despised the color pink. All a part of the image she presented. Why?

As I stood, she looked me up and down. I clocked the look of surprise and faint disapproval at the dress, and it was hard to ignore the pang in my stomach. Feeling like a disappointment was the worst—especially when I tried so hard. But still, she smiled when she saw me.

"Esme." She pulled me into a hug. "You look different."

"Thought I'd try wearing something I actually enjoy."

Her eyebrows rose, and we sat down. She didn't say anything as the waiters converged with her menu and water and the third place setting before disappearing once more. "You look... nice. Not what I expected, but I wasn't expecting a lot of things this morning."

"*Hi!* Sorry I'm late." Eva breezed up to the table and kissed Mom on the cheek before she got up. "That is a killer dress, May-may."

"Thanks. Mom's not a fan."

Mom sighed. "Esme. It's a perfectly fine dress. But it's different from your usual style, and given everything that's... happening," she couldn't even say I was courting a pack. "I'm not sure right now is the best time to change your image. We've all learned the lesson not to change too many things at once. It confuses the press. And it is much closer to Eva's current style."

She told the truth. My sister was in a red maxi dress

which flowed around her and set off her blonde bob perfectly, along with matching lipstick. But frustration burned in my chest. I was more than tired of my life revolving around the media. We would have been characters in it regardless of Eva's career because of who dad was, but it was exhausting no matter what, and I didn't want this to be my life. I didn't want to be her, wearing a color I hated at her age because the media thought it was my personality. So, wrapping the confidence from this morning around me, I looked calmly at my mother.

"Eva and I are nearly twenty-nine. The public knows who we are and why we're different. I think it's time I'm allowed whatever the hell I want to wear without it being approved by a committee. Especially since the style everyone wants to give us is the polar opposite to our personalities."

"*Language*," my mother hissed.

"Oh my god, Esme." Eva was beaming. "Hell yes. I totally agree. Let's trade."

"Stop it. Both of you. This is not the time or place to talk about a different media strategy. We'll come back to that. Please explain to me why I woke up with my phone ringing off the hook, asking why my daughter was all over the papers with a pack of tattoo artists? Not to mention Katarina calling me, frantically asking if she was fired?"

All of this was happening in hushed tones since we were in the middle of the restaurant, which was fine with me. If we'd been at Mom's house it probably would have been much louder. If everyone remained calm, it was easier to keep my head and be rational.

Eva snorted and took a sip of her water. She also held up a hand to keep our waiter from approaching. "I hope you told her yes. That woman is a bitch and has no place helping Esme when her advice is to *pick a pack who's good enough and make it work*."

Our mother pressed her lips together, but notably, she also didn't disagree. "How did you meet this pack?"

"First, I want to say my life is not a media strategy, nor do I want it to be one." Putting my hands in my lap, I clenched them together to keep myself from shaking. "I don't want to live a curated life. I want to live a real one. So I won't be talking about a different media strategy. Not here, not ever. Not once have I ever done something to warrant the press's hatred of me, and I'm not planning to. All I want is to be myself and live my life. If the press and the public can't handle that, I'm sorry, Mom, but it's not my problem."

Beneath the table, Eva reached over and squeezed my hand. I squeezed back, grateful for the support, and equally grateful for her silence in this moment.

Mom, however, was staring at me with a mixture of incredulity and shock. I continued. "I met one Alpha at the studio party I went to with Eva. He's a world-renowned tattoo artist who was invited to do tattoos on whoever wanted them. Our scents—" I took a breath. "Given the amount of scent cancellers in the room, the strength of his scent was notable. The rest of the pack are also renowned artists, and when I met them, they asked to court me. Shortly after, because of the presence of so many... impactful Alphas, my heat started.

They helped me through it, and now I'm courting them.

"I wasn't hiding it from you intentionally. I was going to tell you, it was a little impossible given the timing and the flow of events. I'm sorry you found out from the pictures—I did my best to keep out of the eye of the press. For my own sake."

"Let's not keep the staff waiting." She waved the waiter over, and we ordered. I didn't order much, uninterested in food. But Mom got her glass of white wine and waited until the waiter retreated. "While I am happy you've found a pack who's interested in you, this looks bad, Esme."

Shame coiled in my gut, though I knew it didn't belong there. "Why?"

"You might not care about the appearances, and I wish they didn't matter. Truly, I do. But our family is well known, and whether or not you like it, people are paying attention. I'm sorry it's not the life you wanted, but it's the way it is. We have a legacy now, and it needs to be protected. It's why I hired Katarina, to help you find a *suitable* pack. One who could support you in a life like this one. Maybe you think I'm blind, but I am plenty aware lives lived in plain sight like ours aren't easy. But it is the way it is, and your father—"

"Mom." Eva's voice was sharp as a slap. "If the next words out of your mouth aren't 'your father would be incredibly proud of and happy for you,' then I don't even know what to say."

Another sip of wine, and Mom sighed. "You know very well they weren't."

"I don't see why not. This is hypocritical, even for you. I love you, but how do you not see what's happening here?"

I stared down at the plate in front of me, frustrated that any strength I had was gone. The force and simple logic of her words made sense.

Of course they did, since it was the thought process fed to me my entire life. Why was it so hard to break away from something I *knew* I didn't want when it was laid out in front of me like this? And why couldn't I seem to open my mouth and defend myself after I'd been the one to start this?

"Do enlighten me on my hypocrisy."

Eva huffed out a breath and tossed her napkin on her plate. "I'm mated to a *rock band*. Not exactly the high end of society by your standards, and trust me when I say every member of my pack did a lot of shit you wouldn't approve of before we met. Certainly more than Esme's pack of tattoo artists. Who, as she said, are *world-renowned* artists. Just because their art doesn't hang in galleries doesn't mean the quality is any less, and I can prove it in about ten seconds. You didn't bat an eye when I met my pack. You were over the moon, and weren't worried about the appearance of it. So why is this different?"

"You couldn't help yourself," my mother said. "You were clearly scent-sympathetic. It would have done

271

nothing but brought you pain if I disapproved. And the story played well."

"What, the story of the wholesome ingenue swept away by the reformed rockers who changed their ways, charmed by my innocence?"

I looked up at Eva and found her eyes *burning* with anger on my behalf. I was grateful for her silence earlier. Now I was grateful for her ability to speak.

"And what exactly do you think is happening here with Esme? She told you in the gentlest of terms she was scent-sympathetic with Ben at the party, but I promise you, there was nothing gentle about that connection. I was there. It was exactly the same as me, except my career and what Esme has had to deal with because of it made her doubt it was real.

"You haven't even met them, and you're judging them. I have met them, and let me tell you, if Dad was alive to meet them he would be *thrilled*. You've sat through all those pack interviews and seen all the assholes trying to make her into an Eva Williams clone, and you aren't even willing to consider it? I'm so disappointed in you."

My head snapped to my sister. That was the last thing I expected to come out of her mouth.

Mom was staring at her too, and slowly, she looked at me. The good daughter in me wanted to comfort her and tell her everything was okay. But this had been coming for a long time, and there wasn't anything Eva said which was untrue.

I knew Mom loved me, and I knew in her own way

she wanted what was best for me. But her vision of what was best and mine were entirely different.

She didn't say anything, and we simply stared at each other. There wasn't an apology coming right now. I knew that. But I couldn't leave it like this. "Will you at least meet them?"

"I'll consider it."

"Great," Eva said, tossing back her glass of wine. "So glad you're going to consider meeting the men who are head over heels in love with your daughter. Let's go, May-may. I don't feel like salad with a side of snobbery today."

She was already halfway to the door when I stood to follow her, giving my mom a sad and apologetic smile. But that was the only apology she was going to get from me. We stopped before we left, waiting for Wes and her bodyguard. "You didn't have to do that, Eva."

"Yes, I absolutely did. Because it's been years, and I'm sick of it. I know you are too. You think she's going to be angry at me because I just made a scene in the middle of the restaurant? No. She'll still find a way to blame you. And I'm happy to be the one to do it. Even though you would never say it, all of this is my fault."

I sighed. "No, it's not."

"You're right. It's not *directly* my fault. But it is because of me."

Eva's car pulled up, but I had to ask her. "It's gotten worse since dad died, right?"

"Yes. It has."

When my father was alive, it was the same. I was still placed in a box for the sake of Eva's career, but it wasn't nearly so obvious. And the matchmaking didn't start until after his funeral. The whole thing with Aaron happened while he was alive, but it got worse after he passed.

It was something I needed to think about. Without thinking too much about Dad.

"Want to go to Oscar's? I am in desperate need of some cake with a side of greasy fries."

"Yes, please. Maybe it will make me feel less guilty."

She tugged me outside, and the press converged. We didn't speak until we were inside her car. "You have no reason to feel guilty, Esme. And believe me when I tell you it's not easy. My heart is still racing. I've had years of practice standing up to assholes in the industry and you haven't. But I hope you can tell Mom how you feel—how you really feel—at some point."

It was a nice thought. But most of all, I wanted her to see I was happy, and I wanted her to be happy, too.

Hopefully, there would be something for both of us.

CHAPTER TWENTY-FIVE

ESME

I tossed a scoop of dark blue shimmer onto the table along with the iridescent white and purple I already had. It was going to mix into a gorgeous, pale lavender when I was finished.

This was the calmest I'd felt in a really long time, and it took coming back to the studio and starting to realize my mind wasn't racing in the way it normally did.

Eva and I spent time at Oscar's, dodging the photographers who followed us. No doubt they'd known from the restaurant what time we got there and what time we left, and there would be questions about why we left our mother sitting there. Thankfully, Jasmine was already on it, and was going to put out a statement saying our exit was planned. We were touching base with Mom before going on our own excursion.

Anyone who said they saw us arguing would be ignored. Because that was how the game was played.

And I was done playing.

I wasn't going to pretend it would always be easy or that I wouldn't fall back into old patterns or behaviors, but I felt *better*. Just a bit of freedom and it was like a band around my chest had been snapped. The paps were still going to haunt me and I was still going to avoid them like the plague, but I was also going to do my best to not care about the pictures and the questions.

My life *was not theirs*.

I couldn't wipe the smile off my face, and I sang along with the music in the studio as I mixed the powder under the camera, getting enough shots for a new video. It was simple to edit it and post it, with an apology and explanation for my brief and sudden absence from posting.

It was strange having people care about Elyse Taylor. The way the followers of my art and paint cared about me was completely different from the way the ravenous press did. Sure, there were still some people who tried to cross lines, but a lot of them were simply art enthusiasts or people who enjoyed the videos and found them soothing.

While I was gone, I genuinely scared some of them with my sudden disappearance, and while I was vague in my explanation, I knew it would be a celebration if I announced Elyse Taylor had found a pack.

I glanced up at the clock. The mixing of this batch needed to wait. It was getting late and I needed to pack. In my haze of worry this morning, I hadn't thought to bring my suitcase with me from the pack's house. That was okay. I would be going back and forth at least a few more times.

Wes's offer to move my studio to the pack's house lurked in my mind. It was a nice idea, but it would be a lot of work, and I still wasn't sure. It would make things easier, for sure. But I didn't even know where the studio things would go at the house, and if I was trying this new don't care about the paparazzi thing, then did it matter?

I would talk to them about it. I was sure their reaction would be to say yes and figure out a way to get my studio into the house immediately. But I was also sure they would listen to my concerns and think about it as a whole once I pointed out the issues, and it was nice to know they would.

One more reason I felt like my lungs had so much more room today.

I grabbed one of my empty running bags and filled it with clothes. A mixture of everything I might need. Plus a few of the wild things from the unworn section of my closet. Minus underwear. I was pretty sure I had enough lingerie and underwear at their house to last me a month.

Most of the paps had gotten bored after I spent hours in my house with no sign of leaving. One photographer was still hanging on, but he got the tamest picture imaginable–me on the way out of my house in leggings and a t-shirt with what looked like a gym bag over my shoulder.

We pulled up to the house, and there were people clustered around the door. Not press, but a couple of men in maintenance uniforms, and Addison.

"What time would you like us here tomorrow, Miss Williams?"

I blinked. Right. They were my security detail for the foreseeable future. "I'm not sure. I might not go anywhere. But I can text you?"

"We're on call for you. Even if you need us to stand outside and keep the idiots away from the door."

I smirked. "Thanks."

He walked me up the steps, and Addison saw me coming. "Just the girl I wanted to see!" She threw her arms around me in a fierce hug, painting the air around us with the sweet fragrance of bubblegum. "I'm glad you're still putting up with the pack, and that room is a fucking masterpiece, if I do say so myself."

"It's done? Already? That feels impossible."

She grinned. "I only work with the best. It might still smell like paint for a bit, but the windows are open, so it's only a matter of time before it airs out."

"You're a miracle worker."

"I know."

"What's happening here?"

She glanced over at the two men–betas by their scents–working on both sides of the front door. "New security. A thumbprint lock, like Ben told me you have at your house. They're having me look into gates and fences too."

My stomach twisted and leapt at once. "Really?"

"Yes. And honestly, it's something they should have done a while ago, regardless of the press hounding you. It's not like they're inconspicuous. They're just cocky and have gotten lucky not to have someone figure out where they live and come try to trade *something* for a tattoo, if you know what I mean."

I laughed. Given the way every single member of the

pack looked, I was kind of shocked it hadn't happened yet.

"How did you get rid of the press so they didn't run over you into the house?"

She grinned. "I threatened to cut every one of their dicks off with a circular saw. Turns out I had one handy."

"Oh my god."

Even Wes laughed. "If you ever decide to change careers, Addison, let me know. We could use you."

"Noted."

I looked at the mechanics installing the lock, and all I felt was relief. I hadn't even asked them to up their security, they just did it. But this, and the fence, it was so *much*. It was an internal battle, loving every second and every gesture they made for me. And yet I was so aware of the cost, and I was just one person.

What if it was all for nothing?

I closed my eyes, trying to banish the voice from my head. It didn't work.

"If you're thinking it's too much, it's not," Addison said. "They're not here, so I can talk about them however I want, and I get the big sister privileges over Ben, even if he is an Alpha."

"Remind me to come get embarrassing stories from you when I need ammo."

"I've got plenty of that," she said with a laugh, pulling me inside the door so I could put my bag down. "Seriously though. I don't know how cool they're playing it with you, but this pack has *always* wanted an Omega, even if they didn't fully voice it. I've designed and decorated houses for plenty of them, and not one pack put the care and thought into designing an Omega wing the way they did. And before you think they would take any Omega just because she was there, that's not true either. I've never seen any of them act this way before. It's you, Esme."

"Thank you."

I hated needing reassurance from someone outside the pack, but it was an added measure of relief.

"Done over here."

She smiled and pulled me to the door. "Ready to program?"

"You bet," the man said.

"Great. Wait until they find out you're the only one with access to the house. You could lock their asses out here and leave them with the paparazzi if you wanted."

"I would never do that!"

She tapped a few buttons on the keypad. "It would be fun, though. Okay, go ahead and scan. Right thumb first."

I was used to this. Both thumbs scanned, plus a numeric code as a backup. The code would come later. I wasn't picking the door code for a house that didn't belong to me.

The mechanics had packed up and gone before we'd finished the programming. "They're just gone?"

"I'm the best for more than one reason," she said with a shrug. "I work with a lot of clients like you, who have privacy issues or need security. I only hire loyal people and pay them enough to keep them disinterested. You're all set."

Wes nodded to me. "In that case, let me know if we're needed, Miss Williams."

"Thank you, Wes."

Addison closed the door and locked us in the house. It was so quiet without all of them here. "Go on up and take a look."

"Without you?"

She laughed. "I know what it looks like. I've spent all day in there. It's your space, and I've learned from enough clients it's better to give them a chance to absorb it without any expectant eyes on them. Go on."

I looked at the floor, hesitating only for a second before I stepped in and hugged her again. "You're all so nice to me."

"Well," she said mildly. "I don't want to put any pressure on you, but it's kind of looking like you're going to be my sister-in-law. Also, Esme, basic human decency isn't being nice. It's the bare fucking minimum."

"Still. Thank you." My smile was hesitant. "I'll come back in a minute."

My fingers were nearly white I was gripping the strap of my bag so hard. I wasn't nervous about the room. Not really. More because of what the room meant. And walking into a place that had the potential to be your new home was nerve-wracking. Or at least I hoped I wasn't the only person who would find that nerve-wracking.

The door was ajar, and it did smell like paint, but I pushed open the door into a miracle.

Ombre walls which did exactly what I'd asked–dark near the windows so it didn't feel stifling, and the beautiful, delicate silver trees along the inside wall. The bed on the darker side of the room and the velvet couch on the lighter, facing the entertainment system. Even the closet was incorporated, the walk-in walls painted with the same shade of the ombre.

Things I hadn't ordered but were perfect—gray velvet curtains for the windows and a dark rug at the end of my bed. There was plenty of room for me to hang art, and even without all my personal possessions, it was stunning.

I allowed myself to think about what it would be like to live here. Have this be my home and come back to it all the time. It was a beautiful image, even if it wasn't real yet. Regardless, this space soothed my soul deep down in a way I hadn't experienced in years.

Setting my bag down inside the closet, I went to the bed, ran a hand over the comforter, and felt the softness. It was perfect. Beautiful. The colors on the walls were seamless, and I couldn't wait to grab my paints and create constellations on the ceiling.

"Knock, knock." Ben's voice was at the door.

I hadn't heard them arrive, but the third floor was a long way from the first. "Can I come in?"

"Of course."

He came straight to me, enveloping me in a hug and kissing me soundly. "I missed you."

With everything that happened today, I missed them, too. I hadn't realized how much until exactly this moment.

"You okay?" He asked the question quietly, sensing my own solemness.

"I'm fine. Things didn't... go well today. With my mom."

"You know what? That makes a lot of sense."

I pulled back to look up at him. "Why?"

"Because the paparazzi are assholes trying to get information about you through us, and they asked about her." Kade's scratchy voice pulled my attention, and my stomach twisted.

That probably meant they were outside. Pushing myself backwards from Ken, I rolled across the bed, aiming to close the windows Addison had left open. The curtains too. I wanted to enjoy my newfound resolve without being spied on.

I came up off the bed and was caught by Kade. "Where do you think you're going?"

"To close the–"

The softest growl came from his chest. He yanked me into his arms and suddenly his teeth were at my throat, biting just hard enough to make me go limp, my Omega falling into instant submission. He licked over the point of my pulse when he released me, dragging his nose up to my ear, taking his time and making no secret of the fact he was enjoying my scent.

Prey.

I was prey, and this close to an Alpha I couldn't

breathe. Instant, thick perfume swirled around us. I needed to run, and I needed him to fucking *chase* me.

"You're so fucking tempting," he murmured. "But I need you to breathe. Ben will close the windows and the curtains."

"Okay."

I heard the sounds of it happening. "Did they bother you a lot?"

"No more than expected. And as much as I'd like to punch a couple of them in the dick for the things they think they're allowed to say, they're not going to get anything. From any of us. Right?"

Four voices answered in the positive.

Twisting, I saw the rest of them had entered and were looking around the new space.

"How do you like your room, baby?"

I couldn't contain my smile. "I love it. And I love that you changed the lock without me even asking."

Rylan bounced on the bed, pulling me down onto my back to kiss me. "Why would you have to ask?"

"Because she's used to having to ask for everything which should be a given," Avery said. "And I'm determined to break the habit."

My face flushed, and Rylan kissed me again, long and slow. When we pulled apart, they were closer. Ben had a hand on my leg. "Tell us what happened?"

Not a command, but a request. I didn't want to, because it would mean admitting Mom didn't want to give them a chance in the same way the store manager had judged them. But they didn't have secrets, and not telling them wouldn't save them from the truth of it. That would only delay the process, so I told them.

"Sorry."

Luke chuckled. "Your mom isn't the only one who's made the wrong judgment on sight. We get that a lot and you've already seen it. We'll be fine. As long as *you're* happy, your mother's approval isn't the one I'm looking for."

"I do want her to meet you, because I think she'll change her mind. But it will take time."

"We have plenty of that," Rylan said with a grin.

"Wes asked if I wanted to move my studio stuff over here to avoid the paparazzi, but I don't think I'll say yes. Not because I don't think you guys would be okay with it," I clarified. "I already know if I wanted to you would say yes and find a way to do it faster than I could blink."

"Glad you're getting the idea," Avery said with a laugh.

"It's just that everything's already settled and how I like it. I'm sure you guys understand. Switching my studio just feels wrong. And I don't mind having a separate space for it."

Ben nodded. "I definitely understand wanting your space the way you've developed it *and* wanting your own. It's healthy. That being said, you're right. We would move your studio here in a heartbeat if you needed it."

Avery settled on the end of the bed. "You told us about your day. Now we get to tell you what we decided during ours."

I raised an eyebrow. "Am I going to like this?"

"I hope so." He held out a hand and I put mine in it. "It's important we get to know each other as a group, and we'll continue to do that. But it's also important you get to know us one on one. Or a couple at a time. So, we decided to take turns doing things with you in between everything. If you're up for it."

Sitting up, I laughed. "Yes, I'm up for that. Who's first?"

"I am," Ben said. "Because I met you first I made the argument I should have the first date."

"Are you sure it doesn't mean you should have the last date, Mr. Cupcake?"

"Very sure." The words accompanied the rumble of a purr.

"Okay, so when are we going on this date?"

Ben shrugged. "We can go tonight if you want."

I thought about it. More often than not I was a homebody. I created spaces I enjoyed being in and staying there because I was so used to avoiding the public eye. But today, the public had already gotten an eyeful of me, and I was feeling daring. Plus, being here, with them, the same happiness settled over me like a blanket, washing away the anxieties which managed to creep back in.

"Okay, where are we going?"

He grinned at the rest of them. "Don't kill me."

"Why would I want to kill you?"

Leaning in, he brushed his lips across mine. "Because we never got to finish our dance, and this time I'm not going to let you run away."

CHAPTER TWENTY-SIX

ESME

I was glad I followed my instincts when I packed earlier. Whatever possessed me to grab the scandalously short electric blue flapper dress, that angel was looking out for me. Covered in layers of sparkling fringe, I looked like a deranged disco ball, and it was perfect.

I'd thrown a few random things in my bag like that. Clothes from my closet I'd bought and never had a chance to wear, but today had made me determined.

That being said, I was still nervous about facing the cameras. I hoped after today, there would be too much to cover for *Esme Williams* and they would have to pick their options between the rogue daughter and the club seductress.

But coming down the stairs and seeing Ben's face made me forget all of it.

As soon as I came into view, his jaw went slack, eyes went wide, and his gaze traveled from my head to my toes and back again. Strappy silver shoes completed the look, and a tiny bag for my phone, money, and ID, small enough I could slip it into the side of my bra if I wanted to.

"I honestly didn't think anything could top that gold dress I met you in, but I was wrong."

"You liked the gold dress?"

He swept an arm behind me and pulled me against his body. "Did I *like* the gold dress? I think that's an understatement. Your scent hit me first, and the dress hit me second. And while your scent was the first thing I missed when you walked away—both times—it wasn't the only thing. I think I'm going to miss this one more."

I laughed, enjoying the way I could sink into his scent and let it wrap around me. "It's not going anywhere."

He kissed my cheek. "It is when I tear it off you later."

"You're so sure that's going to happen?"

"I'll make sure to earn it."

"Are they still outside?"

It wasn't late, but I was still hopeful.

"A few of them are, yeah. I say fuck them, and own how fucking hot you look in this dress."

I pressed my lips together. "I'm trying very hard not to care what they think."

"I know." There was no doubt in his eyes. "But no matter what, it's not going to be just you. It's you and me together. And I fully intend to lose them."

"Then let's do this."

Ben himself was dressed in dark jeans and a button-down rolled to the elbows, showing off his gorgeous tattoos. Silhouetted trees around one wrist and rain swirling the other. All Ben's tattoos were of nature, and there were words hidden inside them, if you knew where to look.

My heart sped up at the thought of dancing with him

again. The first time had been... I wasn't sure I was allowed to call it a transcendent experience, but it had certainly felt that way.

Wes had answered on the first ring and didn't seem to mind when I told him the plan. He was waiting outside now, with Henry. I needed to ask him what his days off were, and what his normal schedule was. I wasn't Eva, and he had his own pack. But tonight, he'd seemed happy to come back and escort us.

I laced our fingers together before we opened the door, and in the falling darkness, it was a galaxy for flashing stars. Wes cleared a path for us to the car—not our normal one. This was a longer one, the kind that divided driver and passenger and made people look as you drove past. I ignored the shouted questions and the flashes, but I didn't look away. I held onto Ben, looked up at him, and smiled.

The door closed behind us, and he grinned. "Well done."

"I'm just looking forward to when they get bored."

"For your sake, I hope it's true, but I happen to know you're not boring. So I don't know if it will happen." The kiss he laid on me was far from appropriate, and it took Wes clearing his throat for me to realize it because I was so swept up in everything that was Bennett Gray.

"Sorry, Wes."

He laughed. "Nothing I haven't seen before, Miss Williams."

"Still." I leaned my head on Ben's shoulder. "Where are we going?"

"Surprise."

I made a face. "That's no fun."

"On the contrary, I think you're going to have to learn to love surprises."

"And you *all* will have to learn there are only so many surprises I can take."

"Noted, little Omega."

Henry drove us downtown, and in the newly budding darkness, Slate City was beautiful. We crossed the bridge over the river, and I watched more and more lights flick on, reflected in the water like a murky second world.

Ten minutes later we pulled up to a block filled with people. The line went into the distance around the corner, and there was music, lights, and dancing all the way down.

Next to us, building-sized crimson curtains billowed in the wind, an impressive vision.

Scratch that, it looked like the line was more than one block, and I knew why. "The Pavilion?"

"Yeah," Ben squeezed my hand. "Inspired by the night we met. Is that okay?"

"I mean yeah." The Pavilion was a relatively new club, and had made a splash for being avant garde and over the top. Case in point, with the building being draped in shimmering fabric like a circus tent. "But I've never gone. I heard about the line."

People turned the line itself into a party because the chances of getting into the club were so slim. That, and in general I wasn't a club person for all the same reasons.

"You didn't think you could get in?"

"Oh, I know I could have. But clubbing? Alone? A recipe for disaster."

A low growl emanated from his chest—a sound I now associated with their frustration whenever I was mistreated. It probably shouldn't make me as happy as it did. "Well, you're not alone now."

Wes opened the door and got out, holding it for the two of us. "How are we getting in?" I asked.

Ben shrugged. "I know the owner. He has a killer sleeve I did for him. If we run into him, I'll have to show you." He was still holding my hand, and I squeezed his.

It was the little things that mattered—like not using my name as an excuse to pass go and collect two-hundred dollars.

The front of the line eyed us as we approached the bouncer. An Alpha who easily matched Ben for height and strength. He looked us up and down with a skeptical eye.

"Bennett Gray." Ben said before the man could ask why the hell we were trying to skip three city blocks' worth of line.

The bouncer blinked. "Of course, Mr. Gray. Welcome to the Pavilion."

Ben nodded to Wes behind us. "This is my Omega's bodyguard."

"Not a problem."

My whole body flushed with pleasure at the way he said *my Omega*. Utter possessiveness and no room for doubt.

A predictable groan came from the line as we stepped through. I gave them a sympathetic look and heard a gasp. "Oh my god, that's Esme Williams."

Ben's hand landed on my lower back and he ushered me inside. The small entryway was relatively quiet compared with the dull roar of the crowd outside and the pulsing bass notes I felt from within.

Ben turned. "Wes, I hope you know I'm not insulting your manhood when I ask you to hold Esme's bag?"

Wes smirked. "Not at all."

I handed him my small purse and followed Ben into another circus.

It was immediately clear the Wellbridge Studio party had tried to imitate this vibe and failed. What they'd tried to create with a temporary space, the Pavilion was able to build and keep.

A giant circus tent flowed from the ceiling and down the walls. Rich crimson trimmed in gold. The air was murky with fog, making things hazy and mysterious. Aerialists spun to the music, which managed to be ethereal and electronic at the same time. Colored lights flowed across the crowd, and random acts performed on pedestals among the dancers. A burst of fire from a man's mouth and a woman juggling what looked like balls of iridescent glass. A contortionist, ribbon dancer, and gymnast working with both hoops and balls rounded out the acts I could see.

Ben wrapped his arms around me from behind, enveloping me in sugary vanilla. My mouth watered, connecting the atmosphere to the night I met him.

"Tonight you're not Esme Williams and I'm not Bennett Gray. You're an Omega and I'm an Alpha, and I want to dance with you, however that presents itself. If you end up climbing me again and I have my hands on your gorgeous ass, then that's what happens. I don't want you to think about anything else."

I bit my lip. "Okay."

"Okay."

We didn't bother with drinks. Who needed a drink when just smelling him felt like getting high?

He spun me into him, pulling my back against his chest and easing us into the crowd.

Unlike the first time we danced, Ben's hands roamed across my body, possessive and powerful. He tilted my neck to the side and kissed me—that was all it took to make me let go.

Him and me.

No one else mattered, and no one here cared. My arms were around his neck, and I sank into the song of his scent just like the first time.

The lights and the smoke, the way we moved together, it was like going back in time to when he first saw me at the party and met me at the dance floor.

I came for you.

Under the music, I felt the strength of his purr. Ben's scent curled around me in a bubble. The creamy top notes of his vanilla and the sharp pureness of it, and beneath it, the sweetness that made my mouth water.

His hands weren't the only ones wandering as I touched him, felt his body under his clothes and marveled that this was somehow mine. I *wanted* to climb him again. Hell, I almost wanted to leave now and go home just so I could have him all to myself.

We lost ourselves in the music, reduced to nothing but rhythm and instinct. He was right. We weren't anybody but dancers. I didn't care that I was perfuming like crazy in front of strangers or that photographers were probably already here. All I could think about was Ben touching me and the way his hips slid into mine.

His fingers bunched in the fringe on my dress as he locked my body to his. The darkness in his eyes told me he was just as gone as I was. I wasn't sure how long it had been since we got here.

We were both sweating, and my feet ached. The time with him slipped away so easily. When I caught the time on a nearby phone, it had been nearly three hours dancing. Ben had my body on fire. Every place he touched me felt like I was fully back in heat, and I was so wet between my thighs there was no way he didn't scent it.

"You're pushing against my control, Esme," he whispered.

"What if I'm doing it on purpose?" I rolled my body into his, intentionally grinding our hips so I could feel his cock. It had been hard all night, and now was no exception.

Ben tugged me through the crowd of dancers toward the back of the club, only stopping when we reached the dark hallway that led to the bathrooms. I was up against the wall in seconds, his mouth on mine.

"Your scent will drive me to madness."

"Maybe we need a little madness," I managed.

A growl rumbled through his chest before he kissed me again, one hand in my hair, the other sliding down to cup my ass.

God, I wanted him to fuck me against this wall. It was a terrible idea, and we both knew it, but I was feral enough that I didn't care.

One strap of my dress slipped off my shoulder and Ben's mouth followed it. "The second you ran into me that night, you were all I could think about. You're still all I think about. Every fucking second my lips aren't on your skin I feel like I can't breathe."

"Ben—"

The kiss stole words and breath and everything else. I needed him closer, and that was impossible because the only way for him to be closer was for him to be inside me. The moan in my throat told him everything he needed to know.

A flash brighter than the sun broke us apart, blinking. A man with a camera stood there, smiling like he'd just won the fucking lottery, and he had. That photo would make him money.

I heaved in breath, leaning against the wall. No part of me was processing what just happened. I was still drunk on the scent of Alpha, and I still wanted to pull him to me until we were merged.

But Ben? The fury on his face was like thunder, and it was fucking beautiful. He turned on the photographer, seeming to grow another foot. "Did you just take a picture of my Omega without her consent?"

The man was a Beta, and even in the colored lights, I saw him pale. But he stood his ground. "There are no laws against taking pictures, Benjamin."

Ben took a step forward. "The owner of this club is a friend of mine. I'm going to make sure you never set foot in this building again. And I have a message for you and all your friends." Another step. The man was almost backing into the dancers. "Esme Williams is off limits. To you. To anyone. That's the last photo you get of her. And if it's not?"

All Ben did was smile, and it was not a kind smile.

"You can't stop me."

"I protect what's *mine*," Ben growled.

The photographer lifted his camera and snapped another photo of the two of us together. I jumped and grabbed Ben's arm at the same time he lunged for the photographer.

Everything he said...

I didn't care about the photos anymore. All I wanted was for him not to get arrested for assault. Spending the night in jail was not on the agenda.

"Ben!" I yelled over the music.

He turned to me, and his eyes roved over me, pupils wide, searching for where I was hurt. Full protective Alpha mode, and I loved every fucking second. "He's not worth it."

My Alpha hauled me against his body so my feet were off the ground and kissed me. There were more pictures. I heard them clicking in the background, but I didn't care. All I needed was him.

"Take me home," I whispered in his ear. "Take me home and then take *me*."

He put me down and grabbed my hand. I only stopped for a second to look at the photographer. "His name is Bennett, asshole."

Wes met us halfway across the dance floor, and his face was equally angry. "I didn't see any cameras."

"It's not your fault, Wes. Your job is to keep me safe, not to keep me out of sight."

"Still—"

I held out a hand. "I promise, I'm okay. But I need you to sit up front."

One look at Ben, and he nodded.

The car was pulling up as we stepped out into the cool night air, and Ben's hand was gripping mine. He was on the verge of rut. I could tell. Us diving into our instincts and sensing a danger to me? He was close.

Wes opened the door, and I got in first. Ben was inches behind me, and as soon as the door slammed, he was on me. Pulling me to him and kissing me. Pinning me to the seat and inhaling.

"I'm all right," I breathed. "I promise. You were amazing. Thank you for doing that."

The sound he made was somewhere between a growl and a purr. This car was big enough for him to sink to his knees in front of me, pushing my legs apart and shoving my dress up my thighs.

"Ben." My voice was breathy. "When we get home."

"You'll come long before we get there."

The words were followed by his tongue stroking up

the lace of my thong, tasting the arousal already there from our dancing. Already, I was seeing stars because it was him and it was me and I'd already been halfway to coming when he kissed me in the club.

He didn't even bother taking the thong off, just pulled it aside so he could consume me. Long, deep strokes of his tongue, thrusting into me before circling my clit, and sucking like his life depended on it before starting all over again.

My legs were over his shoulders, my heels digging into his back, and he didn't care. He only pushed deeper, fucking me with his tongue until I couldn't breathe. Pleasure spiked through me, making me gasp.

Fuck, I was trying to keep myself quiet enough the guys up front couldn't hear me, but if he kept licking me like that? All bets were off.

Sliding his hands under me, he pulled me to the edge of the seat and devoured me like I was his last meal, and my vision went white. The orgasm hit me hard and fast. I shook and twisted, squeezing him with my thighs. He didn't miss a beat.

I just barely managed to keep myself from making enough sound for the entirety of Slate City to hear, and Ben kept moving, tongue driving into me. Tasting, licking, and claiming all at once. I lost my grip on reality because he had my hips in his hands and wouldn't let me go.

The only reason I knew we were home was because the car stopped, and for a second I wasn't sure Ben was going to realize. But he pulled away, yanking my dress down and pushing out of the car. There was determination in his body. I barely managed to grab my bag from Wes as Ben was pulling me toward the door. "I'll call you, Wes. Thank you."

I heard laughter before the front door shut behind us, all the photographers blissfully gone.

Luke stepped out of the kitchen with something in a bowl. "I didn't expect you back so—"

Ben turned and scooped me up, heading for the stairs and ignoring Luke completely.

"Is everything okay?"

"It's fine," I waved over his shoulder. "Tell you later."

Ben's room was on the second floor, and he didn't stop until we were inside, and I was alone with my Alpha.

CHAPTER TWENTY-SEVEN

BENNETT

*A*ll I could see was her. The scent of lilacs filled my nose along with the richness of tea on a winter afternoon. The play between electric blue and the perfect creaminess of her skin was taunting me, and her orgasm still coated my tongue.

I needed her. To be inside her. To knot her and know she was safe and here with me.

Protect what's mine.

I didn't even set her down, just shifted my hold and pressed her back to the wall. The fucking dress she wore was so short it rode up her hips, nearly exposing all of that perfect, soaking pussy to me.

The fabric of her thong shredded under my hands, and somehow I managed to get my belt undone.

"Ben," she said my name, and I liked hearing it in her voice.

I was out of control and I knew it. My Alpha side had never risen like this, and it wasn't going to fade until it was satisfied with *her*.

The words felt like rocks in my chest. "If you need me to stop—"

Esme arched her body into mine and kissed me. More than a kiss. A meeting of two people so far out of our own minds for each other nothing else could replace it. "Don't you dare fucking stop."

The growl unleashed in my chest felt good. Powerful. The way Esme's body shuddered against me. "Take the dress off if you don't want it ripped."

My fingers gripped her ass, supporting her as she wiggled out of the concoction of a dress which had been driving me to distraction and had me hard all night.

"*Fuck*, Esme."

She wasn't wearing a bra. Which meant she was naked in my arms except for the shoes whose heels were digging into my back. And she was absolutely fucking everything. Her lithe body was all softness, and all *mine*.

The urge to bite her rose. In my head, I saw myself biting down on her shoulder and completing the bond that already sang between us.

Instead, I thrust my cock into her, and she let go. Everything she'd been holding on to in the car. She cursed, and I cursed with her. I was sheathed in heat made to take me. Every stroke of my cock was enough pleasure to make me see stars.

I wanted to drown in it.

And every move we made together soothed the feral heat and drove me into comfort and bliss.

Esme gripped my face, eyes wild. "I need your knot, Ben. Please."

Pressing her harder into the wall, I fucked her. Grinding into her clit and rolling my hips in the way I already knew she liked from her heat. I wanted her to come apart on my cock before I came. The deepest Alpha part of me needed to feel her yield and accept it. "You'll get it. After you come."

She shook her head, lips pressed together. "I can't. It's too much."

I pinned her to the wall with my cock, finding her wrists and pinning them to the wall too. My Omega liked it when she was vulnerable. It made her fall into the place where she didn't question what we felt for her and could take all the pleasure we wanted to give her.

Slowing my motion, I eased into her with aching slowness, drawing it out for the both of us. "No," she moaned. "Don't stop."

"I didn't." I moved on purpose to show her, savoring the whine she gave me. "Come for me, Esme." Leaning forward, I whispered the words against her lips. "Beg for my knot."

"*Fuck.*" The word was strangled. "Please, Alpha. *Please.*"

I unleashed myself, slamming to the hilt. Esme screamed and neither of us stopped. She came, pussy squeezing down on my cock like a vise, and it was the best damn thing I'd ever felt.

"Yes, yes, yes, yes, *yes.*" The single word was chanted and moaned, dragged out of her every time I fucked.

There. I felt the moment she completely let go, her Omega fully surrendering to my Alpha, and it blazed through me. A meteor and burning star of pride and pleasure and the knowledge I'd done my duty to take care of who and what was mine. Keep her safe, make her scream, and give her my knot.

It swelled at the base of my cock seconds before I came, slamming deep and holding myself there as our bodies locked into place. Esme's voice was raw. "Oh my god. Oh my god, Ben. Yes."

Her body hugged my knot so tightly I felt blind. I wasn't going to be able to keep us upright anymore.

Stumbling away from the wall, I managed to get us both to the bed, laying her out underneath me. This wasn't a heat knot, quickly released so she could take the next one. My body was more than happy to keep her here for a while.

But my mind was clearer.

Her hair spread out across my comforter, skin shining with sweat from the club and sex, heels from those glorious shoes still pressing into me.

Esme reached up and ran her fingers through my hair before tracing them down my cheek. "You're back."

"I'm back."

She smiled. "I thought I might have lost you to rut for a second there."

I laughed. "Would that be so bad?"

"Not at all." There was only truth in her words. "But I like you being here with me. My cupcake Alpha."

"If I wasn't knotted in you I'd go get what's left of those cupcakes in the kitchen and spread it all over you just so I could lick it off."

I watched her pupils dilate with new need. "We'll have to try that sometime."

"We *will* try that sometime," I corrected her. "And more."

"More?"

The image came so sharply into my head, I had to say it. "One day I'm going to borrow Luke's handcuffs and put you on your knees. And I'll watch you suck my cock with these lips I can't get enough of until I'm about to explode. *Then,*" I paused for effect. "I'll grab a cupcake and come all over it. Until it's dripping." Lowering my mouth to hers, I teased her mouth with mine. "And then I'm going to feed it to you, and watch you swallow all that frosting laced with my cum, knowing you love every single drop."

Esme's pussy clenched down on my knot, making me blind for long seconds. She moaned her words. "What are you doing to me?"

I laughed. "Hopefully fucking you again."

It wasn't what she meant, but it was still the right answer.

Reaching back, I gently took her shoes off before peeling off my shirt so we were both more comfortable. My pants would be too difficult.

"If I overstepped a boundary with my Alpha—"

"You didn't," Esme said. "I promise. It was... well, it was incredible. The man had some balls provoking you like that. I just didn't want you to get arrested when we could be doing this."

She squeezed me, on purpose this time, and I swore glitter exploded across my vision. "Fuck, you don't know how it feels when you do that."

"Good?" She did it again, smirking. On the contrary, she knew exactly what she was doing.

"If you don't want me to turn you over and knot you again as soon as this one releases you, you can't do that."

"Who says I don't want that?"

I kissed her. She tasted like sweet tea in the middle of summer. "I'm going to do what I said, by the way. Jason won't have a problem banning the guy from the club. And for the other thing?"

"There's no way they'll listen. I loved that you did it, but this is my life. Our life. They're not going to stop taking pictures."

"I know," I admitted. "But I'm hoping this gets them to take a step back. They take pictures of you because it makes them money. If they leave you alone and interest fades, you'll be less worth it to them, as crude and cruel as it sounds."

"I know what you mean. But I'm not sure they'll listen, given the photo he got."

My heart faltered. "I'm so sorry, Esme. I should have been more in control of myself. I put you in this position."

"No," she grabbed my shoulders and pulled me down so we were skin on skin. I slid my hands underneath her so I was holding all of her. Knotted inside and cradling her body, my purr started without me even thinking about it. Her body relaxed even further, and I purred louder.

An Alpha's purr would always comfort an Omega. But the kind of trust it took for them to completely unconsciously relax? I wouldn't take it for granted.

"You didn't force me to make out with you, Ben. I

wanted to. And the way you tried to fix it..." Her eyes went glassy and she blinked it away. "I don't care if I have pictures with you. *You* help me not to care."

I understood what she was trying to say. Before, when it was only her, every photograph was an assault she couldn't stop. She was alone, wading through everyone else's thoughts about her. With us, it was just her being with us. We didn't care about the photos, as we'd made it clear, and we would protect her against the people trying to use her.

"But," she said, snuggling down underneath me, "since this is supposed to be a date, and we have some time. You need to tell me something I don't know about you."

"Hmm. Well, you've already met Addison. Sorry about that, again."

Esme grinned. "I like your sister."

"That's good, because she loves you and I'm sure is going to kidnap you for shopping trips. I went to art school before my parents died. It's where I got some of the skills I use in my tattoos. But I didn't figure out I loved tattooing until I was getting one after they died."

"I'm sorry." She rubbed her fingers over my arms. "You got these for them?"

"It started that way," I admitted. "But it evolved into more. My dad loved astronomy and was always dragging Addie and me out at night to look through the telescope. It was fun, but I didn't appreciate it as much as I should have. The other nature stuff is for my mom. Or it started for her. She was a photographer, and she loved landscapes. Some of the places are her favorites, and some of them are mine."

"That's really beautiful, Ben."

"Thank you. I can't help but see you don't have any tattoos." There was something singularly tempting about virgin skin to a tattoo artist. The craving to be the first one to make a mark. But if any one of our pack would be the one to do it, I would be happy.

"I thought about it. I did—do—want to get one for my dad. But I've just been a chicken. I already told Avery I don't like pain."

Normally, as a tattoo artist, I rolled my eyes when people said that. But it wasn't always easy, and the idea of my girl and pain made my gut twist in a way I *hated*. "Well, if you decide you want to, I happen to know some world-class tattoo artists."

"Oh really? Where? I don't see any."

I moved my hand and smacked her ass. She yelped, but she was smiling. This felt comfortable and easy. Anyone who'd looked at this woman and thought she should be something different was out of their mind.

Her lips called to me, and I spoke in between kissing the ever-loving fuck out of her. "Rapid fire. My favorite color is blue, though I've become very partial to a shade of brown resembling a certain Omega's eyes. Italian is my favorite food, and I'd rather lift weights all day than go running. I do traditional art in my spare time. I can kick anyone's ass at pool, no matter what they tell you. And my Alpha knew you were mine the second it scented you."

Her small gasp tugged at my heart.

She finally found her words. "I'm glad you weren't a cupcake."

A laugh burst out of me, and she collapsed into giggles. By the time we were done, my knot had loosened and we were sprawled next to each other. "I'm glad you taste like a cupcake, though. I will suck a dick all day if it tastes like a cupcake."

After the fantasy I spun for her, the image of her between my legs, looking up at me as I came to the sound of her moaning had my dick entirely hard once more. "I'm going to keep that in mind." Grabbing her around the waist, I rolled her over and pushed into her from behind. "But for now, I'm not done being inside you."

Esme let out a breathy moan that sent all my remaining blood south. I gently bit her shoulder, fantasizing about the day I could break the skin and feel everything she was feeling, too.

"Alpha." The single word was filled with need.

"Hold on, Omega. I'm about to fuck you breathless." Wrapping myself around her so all she could feel was me and my cock, I did.

CHAPTER TWENTY-EIGHT

ESME

The photo was everywhere.

I waited for the dread to hit me, followed by the shame, but it didn't come. My only wish was that it had been a consensual photo, because it was hot. My dress was mussed, strap scandalously off my shoulder. Ben's hand in my hair, his hand on my ass pulling my leg around his hip, and us kissing each other like we needed the other's lips to breathe.

Even the headlines weren't bad. Some of them were a bit snarky, commenting about how the ice queen had thawed out. But on the whole, the press was positive. The only negative thing was Mom, who had about ten missed calls on my phone with matching voicemails. I hadn't listened to any of them.

The photo came out after I left the pack's house, so I hadn't had a chance to talk to any of them about it yet. But I was walking up the stairs, Wes retreating behind me. No press was waiting today, and there hadn't been. It was too much to hope they heeded Ben's warning. Tomorrow things would surely be back to normal.

"Hey, beautiful." Rylan was waiting for me on the stairs. Casually dressed in a t-shirt and sweats. He put his phone away. "You okay?"

"Surprisingly, yes. It's actually a really good picture."

"It is. I think we should get a high-res copy and print it. Put it in your bedroom or Ben's. Maybe downstairs in the game room."

I laughed. "You want a picture of us making out at a club in the game room?"

"Hell yes. It's fucking hot. Come to think of it, we should do a series. One with each of us."

It was a statement which assumed this would work out. *Why not?* The idea of a photoshoot like that? On purpose? It lifted heat under my skin in a way I wasn't prepared for. Rylan knew it, the smirk on his face sliding into place like he could read my thoughts.

"Where is everyone?"

"They all had late appointments, so I claimed my night with you."

"Oh," I grinned. "We're all alone?"

He laughed. "Scared?"

"No. I'm not scared of any of you."

"Good." Holding out a hand, he stood. "I have something to show you."

His room was next to Ben's, and he went straight to the portion of his room crowded with musical instruments. His room felt like him. Light and bright and playful with an understated elegance running beneath it. Rylan was a jokester, and it was fine with me, but he was so much more than that.

Picking up a guitar, he sat with it. "Someday I want this to have words. But I wrote this the night you first came over to the house. When you fell asleep on me." His grin was shameless.

"You wrote me a song?"

"It just came into my head, and I couldn't stop until I got it down."

He started to play, and I sat on the floor in front of him, listening. It started with a simple strumming melody, and Rylan hummed over top of it, showing the path the lyrics eventually take.

Watching him, I absorbed the intense focus on his body and the way his forearm flexed as he played. All the skin from his wrist to his elbow was black—one single, daring tattoo. It matched the thick black rings he had around his thighs and the interlocking circles which ran down his spine.

I closed my eyes, listening, unbelieving someone wrote a song for me.

The melody lifted and turned, becoming joyous and large, filling the room and echoing back on itself. Rylan's eyes were closed in concentration, and I watched him as the song scaled itself back to the first melody again, this time with a small shift in key. Both melancholy and hopeful, it ended with a questioning note.

We both knew what the question was, but neither of us said it.

I stood up. "That's incredible, Ry."

"I like it when you call me Ry." He smiled. "It makes me think you've already chosen us."

He put the guitar down just before I pulled him into a hug. His face pressed into my stomach, and he held me there between his legs. "I'm sorry."

"Why?" He laughed once. "I know this isn't easy.

313

Especially for you. But I'm not going to pretend I don't want you to stay, Esme. I'm not afraid to tell you that.

"You can tell me it hasn't been long enough to be sure or that I don't know you well enough, and every excuse you give me, I'll call bullshit. I'm not even an Alpha, and every instinct I have is telling me you're pack. You're meant to be here with us. There's nothing—" he broke off and pulled back to look at me. "There's nothing I could learn about you that would make me change my mind."

I swallowed, both awe and terror clinging to my chest. The good kind of terror. Like when you were standing on a diving board knowing you would be okay, but stepping off still made your insides scream. "Not even murder?"

"Not even murder," he whispered.

We stayed there, staring at each other for a long minute. His eyes were a warm brown which reminded me of brownies, and his blond hair just long enough for me to sink my fingers through. He had a little stubble on his face which scratched deliciously.

"What should we do tonight?" He asked.

"I don't know."

Rylan stood without letting me go, so now he towered over me and I was still in his arms. "There are plenty of things we can do that are *things*, but also, we can do nothing. Of all the rest of them, I'm the movie guy. I'll always be happy chilling with a movie and cuddling." Slowly, he ran his palms down my spine. "And whatever happens after that? Happens."

"You mean where you fuck me?"

One corner of his mouth quirked up into a smile. "Maybe. My point being, there's time to do things. I don't want you to feel pressure to make everything a *date*. We can just hang out, like we will once you're bonded."

I saw the hope in his eyes, and I breathed it in. "That sounds nice, actually." After going out last night, a quiet evening with a movie and—probably—sex was exactly what the doctor ordered. "Seems like you have quite the set-up."

Ry had a television even bigger than the one in my bedroom, and a comfy-looking couch in front of it. "It's a nice place to watch things. Any preference?"

"I'm not much of a movie person," I told him. "Except for when I would lock myself in my room and marathon romcoms. So you pick something you like."

Plus there was every chance we wouldn't make it through the entire movie.

It wasn't what I expected. A quieter movie about a man on a journey. Darker fantasy with beautiful visuals and a gorgeous soundtrack. There were images in there I wanted to paint.

"Are you one of those people who cares if people talk in movies?"

"Sometimes. But more if it's something I haven't seen before."

"Will you tell me how you ended up with the pack?"

"Sure." He tucked an arm around my waist and let me lean against him. "But it's not really that exciting.

Everyone thought I would be an Alpha, and it was a surprise when I never broke out of being a Beta. I don't mind," he said quickly. "You of all people know there's more to life than your designation. But it ended up being a blessing in disguise. My family, the business—construction and contracting—is run by Alphas. Always been that way, and I don't think they wanted to break the tradition, even for me. So I ended up going to school for art, and it's where I met Ben and Avery."

On screen, the knight started fighting. A battle with a sword where the blades were moving so quickly you could barely see them. "How did you know you were meant to be a pack?"

"Hmm." He turned his head so his lips were brushing my forehead. "It's hard to explain because it's not tangible. You just know. There's no friction or questioning. You feel a pull. Like it makes more *sense* to do life together than apart."

"That sounds nice."

He laughed softly, the sound vibrating under my ear. "None of us had really chosen tattooing, and then Ben found it, and we all kind of dove in head first. We found Kade while looking for studio space. We walked into a place that was going under, met him, and he never went back to work there."

"Oh wow." I'd never asked any of this, and it was good to know how they'd found each other. "What about Luke?"

"Another chance meeting. When we started Nautilus, years ago now, before we had the house or the current studio and we were a hole in the wall on the other side of town, we knew we needed a traditional specialist. So we put out a call and set up tests. Luke wasn't even on the schedule. He'd heard about it and walked in. The rest was history. We grew together, the studio grew, we all got better, and now we're here."

I bunched my fingers in his t-shirt. "I'm sure that's a huge simplification."

"It is. But the rest isn't that interesting. We worked our asses off to get where we are and have the freedom to do what we want with our careers. Including spoiling an Omega."

They were spoiling me, and I loved every second.

"I will tell you, though, when we were naming the studio, we had to overrule Avery. He wanted to spell Nautilus with a K."

"What? Oh my god. Knot-ilus." I laughed. "That's funny."

"It is. We just wanted to be taken more seriously than that."

Breathing him in, I couldn't help turning my nose into his shirt and getting a more direct hit of his scent. "Why the name?"

"Nautilus? It has some nice symbolism. The perfect precision and geometry, the way it wastes nothing in its growth but also *continues* to grow no matter what. Some people consider it a symbol of perfection and beauty, too."

What a lovely thought. To grow with nothing

wasted. I hoped it would be me. Or me and them together.

Sliding down, I laid my head in Rylan's lap, thoroughly enjoying the way he ran his fingers through my hair. Long, luxurious strokes which had me relaxing, and nearly falling asleep surrounded by the scent of summer. Shades of freshly cut grass, lemonade, and strawberry jam.

My mouth watered. God, why was my entire pack so *edible*? I made a mental note to ask Eva how she felt about that. The craving was so sudden and so strong, I needed it. Right this second. I wanted the taste of him, and I wasn't going to be able to breathe until I did.

Turning, I grabbed the waistband of his sweats and yanked. "Down."

"Es, you don't—"

"I swear to God, Rylan, if I don't taste you this second I'm going to combust."

He lifted his hips, letting me slide the sweats down his legs. His cock sprung free, hardening already, and I dropped my mouth onto him. Pleasure spun through me along with cold, sharp relief.

My Omega soothed at the taste of him and the feeling of his skin. I didn't question the impulse—fighting my Omega had only caused me trouble.

Rylan was all sweetness and tart flavor. He moaned, and it was the hottest sound I'd ever heard in my life as I took him deeper into my mouth. He had the longest cock in the pack and the urge to take all of him overcame me. I didn't know if I could, but after taking Luke, I wanted to try.

During the heat was one thing, but this was another. I'd given a few blowjobs in my time, and I liked it. I loved the idea of something so selfless and giving someone this kind of pleasure, but I also wanted it to be what they wanted. What they craved as much as I was craving doing it.

"Show me," I said, releasing him long enough to swirl my tongue around the head of his cock like a lollipop.

"What you're doing is great."

I looked up at him, intentionally locking eyes just as I ducked my head and ran my tongue up the side of his shaft. Ry's cock bobbed, and I grinned. "Thank you for the compliment. But I want to know exactly what you like. And I want you to show me." I sucked the tip into my mouth and loved the sight of his eyes rolling back in his head.

"Fuck me."

"I'm trying."

Rylan looked down at me, eyes ablaze with fire and lust. A tiny smirk played on his lips. The touch of arrogance in this moment set me ablaze, making heat gather in my chest and arousal shudder through me. He leaned back, spreading his arms along the back of the couch. "Keep going. Suck my cock, Esme. I'll take over when I'm ready."

If I was ready to combust before, his words set me on fire. Taking him in my mouth again, his head fell back with a groan. I would have smiled if I could. Savoring the flavor already leaking from him, I closed my eyes and focused on the feel of him. The slick hardness of him against my tongue, the way it felt to suck him deeper.

"*Yes*," he breathed.

Ry slid down the couch a little, and his hands came to my head, suddenly holding me still. And suddenly I wasn't the one in control. He thrust up into my mouth casually—almost lazily—keeping me exactly where he wanted me as he took what he wanted.

I'd asked him to show me, and he was. The rhythm and speed, thrusting all the way into my mouth. "Deep," he said, and shifted my head, changing the angle and guiding me down onto him.

His cock slipped into my throat, and I moaned. Holding me there, his hand slid under my chin, feeling himself inside me as he pumped deeper and making sure I was taking him deep enough.

My eyes watered when he released me, gasping in breath. And at the same time every cell in my body was tingling with need. He still had me where he wanted me, thrusting up into my mouth again with that perfect rhythm. I squirmed, trying to give the ache between my thighs some relief, and there was nothing.

Part of me loved that.

"Again."

Down into my throat, he guided me down all the way until my lips were pressed against his balls. "Right there," he moaned. "Fuck, that's good."

His hips still moved, pushing deeper and holding me

there until I needed to breathe.

Ry pulled me off his cock and lifted me. "Get up here and ride me."

He didn't have to tell me twice. I shed my clothes, and he got rid of the rest of his by the time I straddled him, sinking down onto his cock.

"Oh, fuck," I murmured.

"You can take me all the way to the root in two holes," he pointed out. "Now all I have to do is see if the third will take all of me as well."

I barely remembered every position they'd put me in during the heat. They'd all fucked me almost everywhere, but Rylan hadn't taken my ass. I remembered that now.

But memories were washed away in the wake of him fucking me. Steadily and deeply, using his hands to angle my hips just like he'd angled my head. Suddenly, light flared through my body, and I shook. "You're all so good at this."

He laughed, low and dark. "Esme, we had four days of learning, in detail, every way you like to be fucked. The way you come. What you respond to on a level you don't even realize. I'm sure there's more to learn. But it's not us just being good at sex. It's us knowing what you *love*."

As if to prove his point, he rolled his hips slowly while pulling me down onto him, making sure my clit brushed against him so both inside and outside were suddenly struck with electric shocks of sensation.

"What else do I like?" I challenged him.

There was a gleam in his eye, and he flipped us

together so I was under him on the couch as he fucked me. Both my wrists were in one of his hands as he held them over my head. I wasn't sure how they got there, and the response was immediate. Three more strokes and I was coming all over him. Soaking him and the couch beneath us, gasping for breath.

"That isn't fair," I finally found the words. "You have a roadmap for everything I like, and I don't have the same for you."

"Learning takes time, and we have time." His jaw was clenched, and he drove himself deeper, closing his eyes. He moaned with each thrust, releasing the frenzy he needed to find release, and I matched him, body shuddering with delicious aftershocks.

Pushing my hands into the couch, he came. I felt him jerk inside me, slowing his rhythm so he could look down at where we were connected. Ry pulled back, keeping only the tip of his cock inside me. I watched his abs flex and ease as the orgasm washed over him and felt the warmth of his cum seeping around his shaft and out of me.

When his eyes opened, they burned. That same mix of lust and awe. But playfulness too. Sharp and dangerous. Rylan was a wildcard. I wasn't ever sure what side of him I was going to see, and I loved it. I knew no matter how long I was around him, I would never be bored.

"Why did you start sucking my cock?"

I blinked, still in a daze of warmth and the shimmering remnants of orgasm. "What?"

"Why? It was so sudden."

"I don't know. I just had to—like a craving."

He smiled. "For the taste of me?"

"Yes."

My wrists were still held under his hands. Between our bodies, he pulled the rest of the way out of me, allowing the flood of his cum to rush out. But his other hand was there to catch it. Oh, *fuck.*

"I didn't give you what you needed." He lifted his hand, dripping with both him and me. "Taste me, then."

Rylan's fingers slid over my lips and tongue, feeding me pure sugar. Pleasure spiked through me along with the heady taste of strawberries. The nearly too-sharp taste of lemons. The deeper flavor of him that represented the grassy shine of summer. I loved all of it, and the craving I had eased.

Not before another orgasm broke over me. Deep, quaking, and all consuming. The relief of getting *exactly* what you wanted and needed.

Once more he dipped his fingers inside me, collecting more of his cum and letting it fall between my lips. *Yes.* One final time, he covered himself in cum, this time with his cock. Dragging himself along my entrance and coating himself before moving up, still keeping my hands prisoner, and allowing me to clean him.

I savored the last drops, both of us easing as the feral need went out of me, and he released my hands and his normal, playful grin appeared. "That was fun."

"I think I ruined your couch."

"Couches can be cleaned," he said with a shrug. "I

will gladly trade what just happened for a couple of couch cushions."

"I don't know what happened. It was so sudden, I needed it."

Ry pulled me up and settled me so I straddled his lap again. This time he wasn't inside me. "Are you embarrassed?"

"A little." My hands were on his shoulders, and I didn't think I'd ever get tired of touching them. They were all different, and each of them fit me in a different way. I couldn't picture what we just did happening with Ben or even Luke, but with Rylan it made sense. Still, I wasn't used to giving my Omega what she wanted. Was this even normal?

"Why?"

"I'm not sure it's entirely normal to crave the taste of cum, Ry."

"But wouldn't life be more interesting if it were normal?" He was grinning, clearly joking. "The important thing is whether you enjoyed it."

"Yes." My body convulsed in memory. "Yes, I did."

"Then it doesn't matter if it's normal. 'Normal,' is a setting on a washing machine. Watching you eat my cum off my fingers? Fuck, Esme, I'm never going to forget it. And I will happily feed that craving until you're addicted."

He pulled my face closer and kissed me. I still tasted him on my tongue, and he didn't care, invading my mouth with his own.

"I'm not an Alpha," Rylan whispered. "But I know

what I like, and I have no problem showing you. I have no problem giving you what you need either. There's nothing to be embarrassed about here."

Pressing our foreheads together, I breathed him in, an echo of the flavor I still savored. "Okay."

"Should we take a shower?"

I raised an eyebrow. "Just a shower?"

"Well, this was going to be *just a movie*, and we saw how that turned out. So who knows?" He shrugged.

Laughing, I stood, enjoying his gaze on my skin from head to toe. "I guess we'll see, won't we?"

He reached for me, but I was already out of range. There was only laughter as he chased me to the bathroom to turn on the shower.

CHAPTER TWENTY-NINE

ESME

"*W*hat?"

I flushed bright red and Eva laughed.

"No, I'm sorry, say it again?"

"Does it happen with your guys? It doesn't hit me the same way it does you, obviously. But I know they smell good. And last night—I just... their scents always make me crave things. Rylan smells like strawberry jam and lemonade, and I feel like whenever I'm around them, fucking any of them, I just want to taste the scent. More than the scent, it's them. Is it like that for you? I got a *craving* like if I didn't have the taste of *him*, if you know what I mean, then I was going to lose it. I didn't think it was normal."

Eva nodded, picking up a French fry and eating it. "Yes. Yes, it is like that. And it is normal, from what I've gathered. But only with scent-sympathetic packs. Cravings and all. Dylan smells like chocolate, and that takes *all* forms. And yes, he tastes like chocolate. He's very happy about that for... reasons."

I snorted. "Yeah, because no one knows what that means."

"It's totally normal," she said. "Even Liam. He smells floral, and not exactly traditionally edible. But that doesn't mean I don't crave the taste of him every day. And the others too. My knees had bruises the first couple of weeks we were together."

Another blush rushed over me. "Okay, I'm not that bad."

"You would be if you let yourself," Eva said. "Trust me."

"What do you mean?"

"I mean you're doing the smarter thing and taking it slow. We didn't. The second we met, we were fucking, and we didn't stop. Jasmine had to move my schedule around because I *couldn't* leave them. It's better now. But still get these cravings that can't be stopped. It's part of being an Omega with your pack."

Anxiety shivered under my skin. I hadn't had all of that yet. The craving yes with Rylan, and it had been the first time outside heat, but the frenzy? No. Maybe the frenzy had been replaced by the heat? Did that mean something was wrong?

"Stop it," Eva said, leaning across the table and covering my hand with hers. "You will have that. But for you, I think it will be after you bond. Because you need to know things are one-hundred percent. No going back."

"Am I so obvious?"

"May-may, you say that like it's a bad thing. After the shit everyone's put you through, I'd much rather you be careful and take your time than get hurt."

I bit my lip, unable to stop the question. "Do you think I am going to get hurt?"

She shrugged. "Anything can happen. Do I think they're out to hurt you? No. Not at all. And I think they're good for you. But you're the only one who knows it all. As soon as you choose, I'll be either cheering for you or helping you through it."

That didn't exactly calm all the anxiety in my chest, but she was right. This was my call, my choice, and I was going at my speed. Eva had always been the 'faster' of the two of us. She dove headlong into things without thinking about it, while I tended to take my time. Neither was wrong, it was simply who we were.

"Well, at least I'm not losing my mind with the craving. Out of nowhere it just smacked me in the face."

"And how'd that go?"

I took a long sip of the chocolate milkshake in front of me. "Good." Amazing. Spectacular. Mind-blowing. I was looking forward to both more cravings and more showers.

Rylan took me from behind, and being caught between the cold, slick tile and the heat of his body was delicious torment.

Eva smirked at me. "Why do I feel like 'good' isn't an accurate description?"

"Smart-ass."

She grinned, but then paused. "Have you talked to Mom?"

"No. I haven't listened to any of the voicemails, and I haven't called her. I don't want the lecture. It's a picture, and I'm not a public figure. Has it caused any problems for you?"

Eva snorted in a way her publicist would murder her for. "No. And it won't. Things are different than they used to be. Oh, before I forget. I'm planning a session with Ben for a tattoo consultation since we never got to do it. Are you okay with that?"

"Yeah, of course. I hate that you have to ask."

"I don't. Even if we know something, it always feels better to know. If you were doing something with the guys and didn't tell me, I wouldn't worry, but I'd also feel weird if I didn't know."

She had a point.

"Though you would feel their shock through the bond."

Eva grinned. "True."

I tamped down the jealousy I had. Bonding sounded... incredible. Some day I would feel it too.

Her phone chimed, and she sighed. "Okay. I have to go. I'll be out of town for a week, but you can call me. Try not to kill Mom while I'm gone, okay?"

"That's not the plan."

She laughed and stood, pulling me into a hug. Eva always smelled like familiar comfort. Roses and coffee. If there was anything I could count on, it was that we'd always be all right.

"Don't work too hard."

"Oh, I am going to," she said with a grin. "The harder I work, the faster I can get back here to fulfill those cravings. Now you understand them."

She waved and left the diner where we were eating. Her security peeled away with her, leaving Wes behind. I lifted my scent bracelet to my nose and chills ran across my skin. The blend of all of them had my hair standing on end.

It was getting later. Dinner with Eva was last minute before she left to go on location. By the time I'd woken up in Rylan's bed, he was kissing me goodbye, and I hadn't seen any of the other guys in what felt like forever.

I didn't have Wes make any stops, and I didn't talk. All the courting and dates and lunches, it wasn't the norm for me, and I was tired. I could probably use a few days simply to sleep, but I didn't want to do that either. Not when there were more fun things I could do.

"Bye, Wes. Thanks."

There were no photographers, and it had been a nice change. Ben's word had spread, and he texted me telling me his friend Jason had gone a step further and banned all press from the club without prior permission. That must have scared them, because I hadn't even heard the quiet click of stealth photographs the last few days. It was amazing.

I opened the door with my thumbprint and sighed. The scent of the mansion was a comfortable blend of the pack and my own scent, and I was getting used to it now. It was comforting, like coming home. A thought which was both incredible and terrifying at the same time.

With a start, I realized I *had* started thinking of this as home. When I went to my house, I thought of it as going to the studio and not going home. And when I was there, it felt like my workspace and not where I lived. Not anymore.

I shouldn't be scared anymore. None of these men —*my* men—had given me a second's pause about wanting me or courting me. As far as they were concerned, even with the short amount of time, I was already pack though we hadn't officially talked about it. Still, the permanence of it was terrifying even with the way I longed for the bonding and true acceptance of a pack.

"Hello?"

There weren't the normal telltale signs of life in the house. I didn't hear anything. No TV, no cooking, not even the faint sounds of video games from the basement. It was... eerily silent.

Then I saw the nerf gun on the console table beneath my painting, and a piece of paper with it.

Esme—

Come and find us. We're hiding everywhere. Every bullet which hits is a minute of shooter's choice. You know what we mean.

You hit us? We're out.

If anyone lands three hits on you, they win the next date.

. . .

Oh, shit.

I looked at the gun they'd given me. It was loaded with six sticky darts, so I assumed they had the same ones.

Dropping my bag on the floor, I picked up mine. Five vs. one was hardly fair, but did I want it to be fair? Still, they were going to be surprised.

One of my father's favorite things when Eva and I were little was laser tag. And I won every single time. Granted, that was on a closed course I had memorized. A house this size had any number of hiding places. So I need to clear it methodically.

I peeked into the living room, and didn't see anything immediately. But there was still behind the couch. The darts were loaded, and I turned sharply into the line of fire behind the couches.

No one. The living room was clear. It didn't mean they couldn't move in there, but for now I had a safe zone.

The kitchen was clear too. They didn't want to hide anywhere too obvious. There were too many places upstairs for me to do yet. I went down instead toward the pool and the game room.

A tiny creak gave it away. Below me, as soon as I turned on the landing. Clever. But I was ready.

I moved, spinning into view, ducking and firing at the same time Rylan jumped out and sent a dart flying toward me. His went over my head, and mine hit him in the chest.

"Damn, woman."

Smirking, I let him lift me down the remaining steps and kiss me. "You guys chose the wrong game. Meet Esme Williams, laser tag champion and expert marksman."

"Sure about that?"

"Wha—"

The sound of a dart firing cut me off, and the soft impact landed in the middle of my back.

I glared at Rylan. "You traitor."

"I'm out," he shrugged innocently. "Can't help it if I want to help my pack score."

Turning, I found Kade with his gun raised. "All is fair in love and darts. I'm going to win, baby."

"So confident."

Rylan only released me when Kade was there, hauling me against him. "I am. And now I have sixty seconds to do whatever I want to you."

"Okay."

His mouth came down on mine, hard and quick. "And for my *first* sixty seconds, I want you to talk to me. Don't stop talking. Tell me about what you want when I chase you."

"When?"

A slow, rumbling purr. "When, princess. Talk."

"I don't even know," I said quickly. Kade kept me pressed against his body and there was no escape. "But when you're near me, sometimes I feel like prey, and I want that. I want the adrenaline and the chase. And I want you to—"

"Hold you down?" He finished the sentence for me.

"Yes." We both remembered the moment I begged for it in the heat.

"Is there anywhere I can't fuck you?"

I shook my head. "No. I just don't want pain."

Kade's eyes flashed. "If I'm chasing you and holding you down, there might be some pain. But I'm not going to do it on purpose. Believe me, *hurting* you isn't the goal."

"What's the goal?" I bit my lip.

"Catching you," he said with a smirk. "And then making you scream like you *are* in pain. But it's all pleasure."

Releasing me, he took a step back. "Better go hunting. I can't hit you again for five minutes."

I looked behind him inside the game room, but there wasn't anywhere to hide. The gym was equally open. The pool and sauna looked empty, but you couldn't be too careful. The sauna was clear, but it didn't feel right.

The sliding door to outside caught me off-guard. Avery was already firing, and I fired on instinct, nearly losing my balance and falling into the pool.

"I hit you," I said. "You're out."

"I am. But my dart hit first, so I'm taking my sixty seconds." He pulled me down onto one of the chaise lounges around the pool, rearranging me across his lap, face down. Like he was going to—

"Hey!"

Avery yanked down my pants to bare my ass, and the sound of his purr and the stroking fingers over my skin instantly settled me. "You can say no, baby girl. You can *always* say no. Understand?"

"I understand." And I thought about it. But he smoothed over my skin again and my traitorous body arched into his hand.

The last time Avery spanked me it had taken me by surprise, and it had also been one of the hardest orgasms of my life. It wasn't the kind of pain I was talking about when I told them I didn't like it. The sting was gone so quickly, and in its place was heat I couldn't get enough of.

It wasn't even about the sensation of the spanking— it was everything that came with it.

I didn't tell him no. His hand came down on my ass, one cheek and then the other. "Guess I get to punish you for getting caught." The smile was obvious in his voice, as was the arousal beneath me where I was sprawled over his lap.

The sound of his hand echoed loudly in the room, and it felt like an eternity instead of sixty seconds. How were we even counting those seconds? But when he pulled my pants back over my ass it burned with warmth, and I was wetter than if I'd actually fallen in the pool.

"Better find the rest of them."

"Any hints?"

I needed to take more of them out if I was actually going to survive the evening. Because I already knew they were going to tease me until I couldn't take it.

"Nope."

Of course not.

I glanced into the game room on my way out. They would all be upstairs now.

Another dart hit me in the back, and I turned to find Kade. "That was just sloppy, baby. You didn't even check your corners."

Pressing my lips together, I glared at him. "Five on one is a little unfair, don't you think?"

He just smiled. "Not at all. Better get used to it. Because we all have the same goal, and it's not going to change."

"What goal?"

"Hands on the pool table, Omega."

"What's the goal?"

Kade stepped close behind me, scent washing over me in a wave. All darkness and heat. "Hands on the table. I'll tell you the goal when I'm finished with you."

My whole body shook under the power in his voice. I placed my gun on the pool table and spread my hands out flat.

One of Kade's arms snaked around me, hand sliding up to circle my throat. The other dove into the danger zone, into my pants and underwear, finding me soaked. "You're going to count out our minute," he said. "If you stop, I stop."

"Stop what? Ooh."

He slid his middle finger inside me, the heel of his palm over my clit. I was already aroused enough, it wouldn't take me long to reach where I wanted to go. But sixty seconds?

"*Count*, Omega."

He moved his hand, and I gasped. "One, two, three, four," it wasn't easy to keep my voice and counting steady when he was moving, circling his palm over my clit and brushing against my G-spot because his fingers were long enough to reach.

The hand around my throat wasn't doing anything but keeping me still, but I was still aware of it. Frozen where he'd placed me, under his word. It would be so much *more* when he chased me, whenever that happened.

"Twenty-one, twenty-two, twenty-three, *fuck*." I stopped to breathe, and he stopped moving instantly. My whine came out, and he just laughed. "You stop, I stop, baby. Keep counting."

I did, my words slurring a little as I tried to remember where I was and also soak in the feeling of his fingers teasing me. He could take me all the way there.

"Forty. Please, Kade. Forty-one."

He didn't move any faster or harder, keeping the same delicious, maddening rhythm. I was rocking into his hand, trying to make it to the peak which was just out of reach. "Fifty-nine, sixty," I gasped the words, and he stopped, pulling his hand out of my jeans and releasing me.

"No, wait."

"Those are the rules," Kade said, licking me from his fingers. "We only get a minute. If I break the rules and keep going, I'm not likely to stop. How is that fair to the others?"

The smirk on his face told me he knew exactly how frustrated my body was, and was loving it. "Not fair to my orgasm," I muttered. "What's the goal?"

"To make you scream. Obviously."

Risking rolling my eyes at the feral Alpha, I turned and left the room before I jumped him, grabbing the dart gun on the way. No more surprises on the stairs, and I heard both Avery and Rylan talking in the kitchen. That must be out of bounds.

Making my steps as quiet as possible, I kept going up the stairs, skipping the second floor entirely. Ben gave himself away. The tip of his shoe was visible behind the open door. That counted, right?

I took aim and landed a perfect shot, the dart sticking to the top of his sneaker.

"Fuck," he said with a laugh. "You got me."

"Three down, two to go."

He kissed me on the forehead as he passed, and a gentle glow of happiness gathered in my chest. There was no animosity or anger that I'd taken him out early. Just enjoyment of the game.

Kade was somewhere below me. That I knew, but Luke? He was a mystery. I had no idea where he would hide.

In the end, it was easy to find him. He was in his bedroom, across from mine in the front, sitting on his couch. The dart gun sat beside him untouched, and he was sketching on a pad. I raised my gun and shot him in the chest before he could make a move.

Luke smiled, and his voice was filled with over the top emotion. "Oh, no. You got me! I'm so sad about it."

"You didn't want to play?"

"On the contrary, sweetheart. I love this game, and next time I'm determined to win."

I raised an eyebrow and sat down beside him, looking at the stylistic swallow he was designing. "But?"

"But I already have my plans for you, and I know someone else wanted to win more this time."

That had me intrigued. "What are your plans for me?"

"I'm going to feed you, maybe give you a massage so you're as relaxed as possible, and then you and I are going to play and we'll see how far down the control rabbit hole you want to go."

I shivered. "And you didn't want to win so you could do that?"

"I made a deal not to."

"What kind of deal?"

Setting aside the sketchpad, he tugged me closer by the shirt and kissed me. "You're too trusting, sweetheart. I'm the bait."

I jumped back, but he already had a hold on me, pulling me down onto his lap and spinning me to face the door where Kade stepped in, a grin on his face. "Told you I would win."

The last dart hit me in the stomach, but Luke didn't

let me go, holding me fast. "Isn't making a deal to win cheating?"

"That depends," Kade said. "There weren't any rules against it."

I struggled in Luke's arms, only getting a chuckle and a kiss on the back of my neck. Finally, I stopped trying to pull away. It was clear he wasn't going to let me go yet. "I would like to be consulted on the rules next time."

"That can happen," Kade said, kneeling in front of me and Luke. "But next time."

"I lied just a little, Esme," Luke said. "We're going to start right now."

My stomach flipped, every part of my body standing up and paying attention. "What are we doing?"

"Kade is going to claim his prize, and you're going to be a good girl and let him."

Kade's hands were already at the waistband of my pants, tugging them down, and not stopping until they were gone. My thong followed, and Luke widened his legs so I was entirely on display. He still held me fast.

"Luke."

"Shh. Close your eyes, sweetheart."

I obeyed, moaning as Kade's tongue met my skin. The arousal he'd teased me with before raced back to the surface in full force.

Strong hands on my thighs, pushing them further apart, and the scratch of his beard as he ate my pussy for his prize.

"Mmm." The sound nearly made me come. My hips

jerked toward him, and he pushed my legs back. "Remind me Luke, not to go so long between meals."

"Noted."

He hadn't tasted me since the heat. It hadn't been that long. Kade licked into me, curling his tongue inside me and sealing his mouth over me to suck.

"Don't hold back, Esme," Luke said. "We're not edging you now."

My eyes still closed, I released the breathless tension in my body, and fell into bliss. The climax shattered through me faster than the next dart could hit me, and I moaned. It was one of those deep orgasms that shook you inside and out, pulling you down and holding you close.

When I opened my eyes, Kade was licking his lips and my chest was heaving. "You both planned it?"

"Sort of. Didn't know it would happen like that, but we knew it would happen." Luke released me slowly. "Hope you don't mind."

How could I mind when they made me feel like this? And Kade...

I looked at him, and his already dark eyes looked nearly black. "You're mine, baby. Tomorrow night."

"Tomorrow?"

"Our Saturday."

The studio was open on weekends, since most people didn't have time during the week to get tattoos. They closed on Tuesday and Wednesday instead.

"What do I need to do?"

"Wear clothes you don't mind getting ruined," he said. "And be ready. That's all."

My heart skipped a beat. I would be ready. That was for damn sure.

Leaving them to get dressed again, I loved how settled I felt. How easy and right it had been to play games with them. I was ready. Not just for the chase, for everything.

And deep down, I felt like I'd been ready my entire life for this.

CHAPTER THIRTY

LUKE

I watched Esme's perfect ass walk out of my door and adjusted myself in my pants.

"You owe me one," I said.

"You're right, I do. Will you be my backup?"

Looking over at him, I gauged what he was asking for. "If you're worried about something, don't do it."

He shook his head. "I'm not worried about that part. It's just a safeguard in case something happens I *haven't* thought of."

"Sure." I could sketch in the car as easily as I could sitting here. "Have you ever done this before?"

"Not like this. And I'm glad. I want the first time with her. It feels... it feels right."

"Everything with her feels right," I said. "If she doesn't—"

I couldn't bring myself to say the words. She was ours, and we were hers. There was no questioning it, and I was sure by now she knew it, too. But the world had been cruel to our Omega, and chipping away at fears took time. But I already knew if she walked away, it wasn't something I'd recover from.

"I know." Kade stood and grabbed the dart guns. All three of them now on the couch. "Hey, did Ben talk to you about the producer thing?"

"Yeah. Sounds like we have to wait until Eva gets back into town."

"All right. Sounds like it could be cool."

I agreed. It would be cool. When we were at Esme's house picking her up for the heat, Eva had shot out an idea. She wanted a piece from Ben and was practically salivating to change her image from the wholesome one she had into something edgier. She pitched the idea of a show following celebrities getting tattoos from us. Or just a show about the studio in general.

It wasn't a fully formed idea, but it was something they wanted to talk about.

Nautilus was already well known, but having something like that connected to the studio would only benefit us. I had only one hesitation. "If it makes things harder for Esme, I don't want to do it."

"Yeah," Kade nodded, looking more than a little ridiculous with the pile of nerf guns in his arms. "She knows, right?"

"Ben said Eva told her, and she walked into the kitchen when they were talking about it, but I'll make sure."

He took the guns and went downstairs. To put them in the game room where they belonged, no doubt.

I flipped my pad closed and went across the hall. Esme's door was open, and she was in her closet changing. Nothing but leggings and a bra at the moment, and I took her in. It was more than just her scent I was falling in love with, it was her.

These instincts we had weren't always easy. I didn't

know anyone who found scent-sympathy the way we had where it hadn't worked out—if you defined working out as being a pack—but happiness wasn't a guarantee. I knew it well. All I wanted was for Esme to be as happy with us as we were with her, and I thought she was getting there, but I still craved the assurance more than anything. "Can I come in?"

She glanced over at me and smiled. "Of course."

"Did Eva mention to you she had an idea for a tv show involving the studio?"

Esme frowned. "I think she did. What's going on?"

I sat on the edge of her bed. "Nothing yet. I just wanted to make sure you knew in case it was mentioned."

"Eva's already meeting with Ben about a tattoo. I know that much."

"This might be part of that. A way for her to break out of the image she has."

Esme laughed. "Yeah, she does want a change. Both of our lives would be easier if we could just switch our public perception."

Tossing on an oversize t-shirt, she came over to me, and I loved the sight of her so comfortable. She might not even realize she was doing it, but she was making herself at home. "Rylan told me how you guys found each other last night."

"I got lucky."

"Yeah."

I leaned back, lying down, and she followed, curling on her side toward me. Unable to help myself, I tucked a strand of her hair behind her ear like the last time we'd lain like this, when she was in pain and trying to send us away.

"All of us are happy you're here. You know that, right?"

She nodded slowly. "I'm happy I'm here too."

"Even when I give you up to Kade?"

"Even then." The way she bit her lip made me want to taste it. "I'm still curious about how you found them. I know you went in for an interview, but before that?"

Settling my hand over her hip, I moved us closer together. "That's not really a happy story, sweetheart."

"Oh, I'm sorry."

"You have nothing to be sorry for. The short version is, I didn't come from the same world you do. Or Ben and Rylan. Kade's a little closer. Avery is somewhere in between."

Slate City was a sprawling metropolis, and like any city, there were the glittering parts which shone in the sun, and the depths that lived in shadow. Where people were just scraping to get by and were lucky if they could break out.

I was one of the lucky ones. Luck, and putting everything into my art, because I knew it would save me. "I've been tattooing since I was twelve," I said quietly. "Where I come from it's really the only art that means anything, and certainly the only one you could learn. If I'd tried to go to art school, I would have been jumped for saying it out loud, let alone try to find a way to pay for it. But I knew I could find a way out with tattoos."

"You don't have any," she pointed out.

"No. Back then, I didn't want tattoos to be a barrier against the world I wanted to reach. Now I just haven't found the right tattoo yet."

"Oh." Esme reached out and smoothed the crease between my eyes with her fingers. "I'm sorry you went through that."

"I'm not. What would the point be? It's my life. If I'd had a different one, I wouldn't be who I am now. Just like if you'd lived a different life you might not be here next to me."

I caught the slight widening of her eyes—the realization all of the pain and fear she kept locked up inside her had a purpose, even if it didn't feel like it.

"Would you ever get one now?" She asked. "A tattoo. Nothing could be a barrier for you now."

"I might," I said. "It would have to be the right one."

I already knew what the right one would be, but I didn't want to tell her yet.

"Maybe I'll get one," she said softly. She was examining the shimmering comforter, dragging a finger across it. "I've always been nervous about it."

"When you know, you'll be sure."

"Really?"

"Yes."

That finger pushed deeper into the fabric. "How do you know?"

"Because I've been doing this a long time." We weren't only talking about tattoos now. "And I can't count the number of times someone has come in and said they'd been going back and forth, but when they knew, they knew. And after, they always say they'd known for a long time, and they wished they'd done it sooner."

Her eyes lifted to mine, filled with hope.

"Come here, sweetheart."

She curled closer, and I slid an arm underneath her. Having her this close satisfied me both as an Alpha and as a man. Her scent was so sweet now, the lilacs overlaying the sweetness of her tea, which turned darker and more bitter if she was afraid or sad. Right now she was all sugar.

"When I was a kid," I told her, shoving down the nerves about telling this story, "there was an Omega who lived on our block. She was sweet, and she babysat me sometimes. Her name was Mira. She had a pack, and I knew enough about them to know they were like us. Their scents brought them together. But her Alphas—"

I huffed out a breath and held Esme to my chest, cradling her head, as if being here with me could protect her from the words I was about to say.

"They didn't treat her well." It was an understatement. "Because they belonged together, they took advantage of her. There were always bruises on her she tried to hide, and because I was so young I didn't know what it meant. It wasn't until far later I understood, and I'm sure it was far worse than I knew."

Esme's fingers clung to the back of my shirt, and she tucked her head under my chin.

"I swore if I was ever lucky enough to have an

Omega, she would be my entire world. Nothing would be more precious. And I had been pretty close to giving up, until Ben walked in with your scent all over him, and it was like every piece of my soul was pointed toward you."

There was a small sniffle. "I don't think I'm ever going to get used to hearing things like that."

"I hope you do, sweetheart. Because if you get used to them, it means you finally believe them."

I pried her away from my chest and tilted her face up to mine, taking her lips. She was the most precious thing, and she had no idea.

"All right, time to break up the make-out session," Rylan called from the door. "Kade said something *interesting* happened on the pool table, and I think we need to show Esme how it's done."

Quickly swiping her eyes, she sat up. "What makes you think I don't know how to play pool?"

Ry smirked. "Spend a lot of time in dive bars, Miss Williams?"

"Enough to beat you."

I grinned at him. My sassy Omega was showing her colors, and I was going to have a hard time keeping my dick in my pants. Especially knowing the same sassiness melted away when I took her under command. Our date was going to ruin us both in the best way.

"Don't worry," Rylan said. "I'll be happy to show you how it's done."

"We'll be right there," I said, sitting up with her and watching Rylan disappear. "You okay?"

She laughed, twisting her hands together. "I feel... perfect. And that's scary."

"I know." Of all the people in the house, I understood what it meant to be afraid of a good thing. When you were so used to it disappearing, suddenly having everything you ever wanted felt like one big lie. But we were going to show her it was real, and the truth. "Ready to get your ass kicked at pool?"

She rolled her eyes. "In your dreams."

Following her out of the room, I admired the view, and I agreed with her.

I felt perfect.

CHAPTER THIRTY-ONE

ESME

My phone buzzed on the bedside table, and I almost ignored it when I saw mom's name, but I didn't. Something caught my eye.

Please call me, Esme. Please.

With a sigh, I dialed her number, putting it on speaker.

"Esme?"

"Hi, Mom."

She took a hitching breath, and I covered my face with my hands at the shame which hit me. "I thought you weren't going to speak to me anymore."

"Of course not. I just needed some time. And I didn't want to talk to you about the photo."

"Yes, well, I may not agree with what you're doing, but I understand it's what you feel you need to do. You're an adult, you can make your own choices."

"You're right," I said with a sigh. "And I'm not making those choices to hurt you."

"I know. And I want to try. Can you bring your... I'm not sure what to call them, over for dinner tomorrow?"

Tomorrow would work perfectly in the schedule, as far as things went. But I wasn't going to sign them up to meet my mother without at least talking to them first. "I'll ask them, but I'm sure it will be fine."

"Excellent. I'm looking forward to it."

"You are?"

She sighed. "Esme, I'm trying. Do I love that you're being courted by a pack of tattoo artists? No. I don't like it any more than I liked Eva being courted by a rock band. But there wasn't much I could do about it then, and it seems like this is the same. So I will meet them, but it's all I can promise."

Pressing my lips together, I tried not to beg or ask for more. I'd already hurt her. Without dad, Eva and I were all Mom had left, and she felt like she was losing us. Change was hard for her, and though the change was necessary, it didn't make it easy.

"I'll ask them about dinner and text you."

"Thank you. Hopefully I'll see you tomorrow."

The line went dead and I groaned. "What's the matter?" Avery asked. He stood in the doorway to my bedroom, a soda in one hand.

"My mother wants you to come over for dinner tomorrow so she can meet you."

He shrugged. "Done."

"I have to ask everyone first! I can't just throw everyone to the big bad wolf without preparation."

"Sure you can. We knew we'd have to meet your family at some point, and we have the night off, so we'll meet her."

"You realize she's only inviting you over so she can find out what's wrong with you?"

"No worse than anyone else has done." He took a sip of soda. "We'll be fine, baby girl. Promise."

I left my phone on the bed and went into my closet. I'd brought over more and more things whenever I went to my house to work, so most of my clothes were here now. Kade had said ones I didn't mind ruining. So I grabbed a pair of old leggings which were hanging on by a thread and a t-shirt I was pretty sure I'd had since high school and was so faded you couldn't even make out what the image was.

Avery stepped into the closet with me. "I'm guessing wearing underwear beneath these is probably pointless?"

He laughed. "Unless you want to lose them, commando is the way to go."

"Got it."

I started to change, not at all bothered Avery was still in here with me. He was the first one of them to see me naked, and though we hadn't had our date in the rotation yet, I was looking forward to it.

"Baby girl, you need to warn an Alpha before you start stripping."

"Do I?" I raised an eyebrow.

He smirked. "Careful, or you won't make it to Kade's plans."

I shivered in response. Kade had told me nothing except for what time to be ready, and we were almost there. The sun was already setting, and we were going out of the city. That was all I knew. That, and Luke was coming with us just as a back-up.

"It's okay to be nervous, right?"

"As long as there's excitement."

Prey.

Just the thought of Kade at my back, invisible and chasing me, ready to pin me down and have his way with me...

"Yup. You could say that."

"Don't have to tell me, baby girl. You just let out enough perfume to get everyone's engines running. You'll be just fine."

I pulled on the leggings and let the t-shirt fall over my head. "You'll tell everyone about dinner?"

"Yes."

"Thanks." I sent a text to Mom telling her dinner was on before dropping the phone back on the bed. I wouldn't need it tonight. The only thing I would need tonight was speed.

I grabbed the cheap shoes I'd picked up earlier today. I didn't have any running shoes I wanted to ruin, and running barefoot the whole time wasn't a good idea. It would probably end up that way, but I didn't know for sure. This was all new to me.

"Don't be late," Avery said gently.

"We can't have that." I shoved my heel into the second shoe. "See you later?"

"Depends on how long you run."

My breath picked up in my chest. He had a point. I didn't know how long this would last.

"Okay. Well. I'm gonna go."

"Good luck." His tone told me I would need it.

I couldn't believe I was doing this. At the same time, it was absolutely everything. It felt like my whole body was electrified.

Kade waited near the front door, and he looked me up and down when I approached. "Ready?"

"I think so." I reached out for him, and he held me. His arms were comforting and warm around me. Later they wouldn't be, and I loved the dichotomy. "I don't really know what I'm doing."

"I have a couple of questions and then I'll tell you."

All my attention zeroed in on his voice. "I'm listening."

"How far do you want to go, baby? How rough? How deep are we going?"

Shaking my head, I looked up at him. "I'm not sure. Doesn't mean I want to pull back, it just means I've never done it before and I don't know. But I imagine you chasing me, ready to take what you want and I—" I swallowed and took a breath. "I like that."

"Okay, first, I need you to pick a word. One you won't forget in case you need to stop. And it can't be 'stop.'"

I thought about it. What did I want to stop most? For most of my life, it was the press. "Camera."

A small growl, and he pulled me closer. "That makes sense. And now, baby, I'll tell you what I have planned. If it's too much, *you tell me*. This isn't about scaring you. It's supposed to be fun for both of us."

"Okay."

One hand behind my neck, he leaned down so his lips brushed the shell of my ear, raising goosebumps on my entire body. "When you're ready, I'm going to blindfold you. And tie your hands behind your back. I'm going to carry you out of this house and put you in the trunk. You're not going to know where you're going. And when we get there, I'll let you out. Free your hands and take the blindfold. Then I'm going to drive away."

I gasped, and he grabbed my wrist, wrapping something around it. "The watch has GPS. You won't be lost for a second. I'll always know where you are, but it's just in case. Because I'm going to hunt you, baby. You're not going to know where I am."

There was no denying the hot, honeyed arousal which flowed through me, making me wet and releasing a cloud of perfume around the two of us.

"But I'll find you. Run all you want, but I'll find you, and when I do..."

Kade let the words hang in the air, tantalizing. And nothing more. "I'll let you think about what happens when I do."

I'd already told him there was nowhere he couldn't fuck me, and he'd warned me about ruining my clothes.

"But you say 'Camera,' everything stops. And I need you to hear me, princess. I will *not* be disappointed if that happens."

I nodded. There wasn't a situation I could imagine being afraid of him enough to tell him to stop, but it was good we had a way to do it. Just in case.

"Does any of it sound like too much?"

"No."

He smiled, and it had an edge. "Then let's do this." He kissed me and lifted a piece of black cloth I hadn't noticed before. It blocked any light that might have gotten through my closed lids, and there was no moving it. It was solid.

I sucked in a breath when he took my hands, pulling them behind my back and wrapping more fabric around them. They wouldn't move apart, and my heart started to pound, adrenaline already kicking in.

It was disorienting to be picked up when you were blindfolded. I heard the door close behind us, and the gravel of the drive under his feet before he laid me down. I was in the trunk of a car. *The trunk.*

"See you soon, baby."

The lid closed, and the car started.

Oh god, we were really doing this. There was no trying to figure out where we were going. I was already turned around being on my side. Instead I curled around myself and calmed my breathing. I would need it.

How long had we been driving? Time seemed to stretch. It could have been twenty minutes, or it could have been an hour. There was no way to know.

Finally, the car slowed. I faintly heard twigs snapping under the tires and the crunch of dirt. The passenger door slammed, and heavy footsteps circled the car. The lid opened, and I smelled him. Darkness and oaky smoke deeper than the woods we were in.

Heaving me out of the trunk, he set me on my feet,

and the blade of a knife sliced through the fabric binding my hands. I rubbed them, warming them back up.

Kade's hand fisted in my ponytail, and he groaned, licking up the side of my neck. "Your scent is already making me hard."

The blindfold came off, and for a second it felt like there wasn't any difference. The woods were nearly pitch black.

"Run, baby."

Footsteps retreating, and the door slamming again. The car left me, and I didn't move until I could no longer hear it. I didn't look to see where it went. I stayed frozen as a statue, committing to what we'd agreed until I was entirely alone.

My eyes adjusted to the darkness, picking out the faint glow of the moon that let me distinguish between the black trees and navy sky. There was nothing else I could do to get ready.

I took a deep breath, and ran.

CHAPTER THIRTY-TWO

KADE

*E*sme's scent was heavy in my nose. I could already taste her on my tongue and all my senses were sharpening.

"You have a boundary?" Luke asked.

I nodded as we got further away from where I'd left her. "River on one side, seven-foot fence on two other sides. There's plenty of room, woods and fields."

As soon as she'd given the indication, it was something she wanted, I started looking. This wasn't precisely where she ran when she left the city, but it was close enough she wouldn't be out of her element. The watch on her wrist would let us find her anytime we needed to.

I'd also checked to make sure this section of land wasn't frequented by anyone in particular. The couple of times I'd come to evaluate it, I also removed some of the bigger, more dangerous obstacles. A big bush covered in thorns, a sudden, brief ditch she could fall into in the dark. Some low-hanging branches.

Luke pulled the car to the spot I told him and killed the engine. He pulled out his phone, and I saw the dot on the screen showing where Esme was, and tried not to mark the location. "She's moving?"

"She is."

I pushed out of the car, pocketing my own phone. One of us needed to have one.

"Happy hunting," Luke called.

Walking away from the car, it didn't take long for me to be absorbed in the darkness. The sounds of night creatures, and the scent of earthy, fresh air. No sign of my Omega's scent yet, but it didn't matter. I would find her.

The thrill of the chase had always been something I was attracted to. The idea of letting your feral side free to act on these instincts we held inside of us? Beautiful. But it wasn't for everyone, which was why I hadn't truly done this until now.

Adrenaline sang in my veins, and I headed back to where I'd left Esme standing in the trees. From there, her scent would be a beacon to me. I knew my Omega wouldn't make it easy, but there was nowhere she could hide. She was *mine*.

A possessive growl built in my chest, and I forced it to quiet. My thoughts needed to empty. This wasn't the time for self-examination or anger about what she'd gone through. This was only about the two of us.

I let my Alpha rise, the strength of that side of me suddenly making my stride longer and my steps quieter. Long buried instincts showed themselves, and my senses sharpened. The woods no longer seemed as dark, lit by the sliver of the moon in the sky.

A cool breeze shivered between the trees, all the leaves rustling like a cascade of rain. The faint hoot of an owl overhead, and creaking of too-heavy branches.

There.

A trace of lilacs touched my nose, every sense focusing on the tiny trace of scent. I was close to where I'd left her. The mouthwatering flavor of her grew stronger. The tea under the flowers was bitter with anticipation, nerves, and the barest hint of fear.

I loved the sharpness of it, knowing my little Omega wasn't afraid of me. She knew exactly what was going to happen and had every way to stop it if she wished. And that gave us both the freedom for *anything*.

The place where I'd left her was soaked with her scent. She'd stood here, waiting to get her bearings or for the car to disappear. Something. The pause was long enough to create a ghost of her, like a flare for my nose.

She'd headed straight away from the drop point, and the scent was fleeting in the wind, and because she'd obeyed. She was *running*.

I couldn't control the hardening of my cock. She'd obeyed my order to run, and that alone was enough to make my body respond. The kind of trust it took for her to do this?

My baby was going to have the time of her life.

I followed the snatches of lilacs and brewed-too-long tea like they were shreds of fabric that had ripped off her clothes and left a trail. They wove back and forth— Esme's attempt to mislead me.

All the way to the fence she wouldn't be able to climb and back into the woods. At one point she led me in a circle, and I laughed, not caring if she heard.

Clever little Omega.

But the bursts of scent were growing stronger as she

slowed down, unable to run forever. Rushing water was a low sound humming under everything now, blocking out the smaller sounds of the woods. I didn't have to be as quiet, but neither did she.

I finally gave in to the urge to run, jogging along her twisting path toward the water. Her scent slammed into me—another flare. She'd stopped here by this tree on the edge of the woods before the open space between the safety of cover and the water. Imagining her looking for me, seeing if I'd already made it here, knowing she was *wet* with nerves and excitement.

It was all there in her scent, the deeper, richer layers of her arousal. Perfume she couldn't control. Poor Omega, giving herself away with her need. My cock was rock hard now, aching to fulfill that need.

She wasn't in sight, but the trail led toward the river. I stepped out from the edge of the woods and followed it to the edge of the water, where it disappeared entirely.

It wasn't far across. A couple of rocks and a jump had me on the other side, and there was nothing. She hadn't crossed the river. No, she'd used it to mask her scent.

The watch she was wearing was waterproof, but the river was freezing even in the middle of summer. It would slow her down. But I had no idea where she was now.

In the darkness, I smiled.

The hunt was on.

CHAPTER THIRTY-THREE

_____

ESME

I couldn't stop shaking. My clothes clung to my skin and my breath was thin in my lungs from the cold water. It was worth it to break the trail, swimming up the river away from where I'd entered it, as far as I could stand before becoming too cold.

I'd even gotten out quickly on the other side to give him a false trail before pushing on. But it was only going to last a certain amount of time. Kade would find me.

I was in the woods again, weaving through the trees. But I needed to stop. Find a place to hide and wait. Catch my breath. If he found me and I was entirely exhausted, I wouldn't be able to run.

By now, he was hunting me. I had no idea how much of a head start he gave, but it had been long enough.

Ahead of me at the top of the hill there was a tree larger than the others—thick enough to hide behind and not be seen. It would be good enough. For now.

I could see in the dim moonlight I'd nearly reached the other side of the woods. They ended and broke out into an open field filled with tall grasses. On the one hand, there was no real cover, and on the other, ducking down in the grass would be a decent hiding place.

If my perfume wouldn't lead him straight to me.

I shivered with both cold and anticipation.

The water had been freezing, but my core was *hot*. It was pulsing with need, my deepest instincts dying to be fucked, taken, and knotted. It felt like I was on the verge of heat, though this wasn't the same. My Omega simply knew.

Pressing myself to the bark of the huge tree, I slowed my breathing. I leaned so I could let my muscles rest and tried not to give in to the shivers. They wouldn't last forever.

But mostly, I *listened*.

There were natural sounds, but they were easy to tune out. The unnatural ones were the sounds I was after, the huff of his breath or the scrape of his shoes on the dirt. A misstep on something that cracked.

I listened for the Alpha hunting me.

And there was nothing.

It was like I was alone out here in the woods, but I knew I wasn't. I knew he was here, even if my senses were trying to trick me.

My entire body went still, instincts reacting before I processed them. Was that a scuff on the dirt? Another slow sound turned me to stone and made me hold my breath. He was close. I wasn't sure where, but he was coming.

The sound felt like it was coming from the right, so I moved with painful, aching slowness to the left, not making any sound as I circled the tree. I didn't see any moving shapes in the darkness. Everything was still and silent except for the wind. Another small sound in front of me made me jump, but it was just one branch brushing against another.

I blew out a breath in relief. It was me. I was being jumpy. It hadn't been enough time for him to find me.

"Hey, baby."

Kade stepped out of the shadows behind me and I ran without thinking, back toward the river, downhill. The low words pulsed in my mind. Soft and sensual, dark and determined.

He wasn't hiding his presence now, steps crashing as he chased. I felt his hand move in the air behind me when I whipped to the right, grabbing a tree and using it to propel me in the opposite direction.

Kade cursed and turned to follow. He was fast. So much faster than I was. He hadn't run to begin with, and I was already tired.

Prey.

My mind was sinking into a base place of both reaction and acceptance. I was going to fight like hell, and I also knew my capture was inevitable, along with everything which came after it.

I dodged him one more time with a sharp turn, but this time he was ready, catching the back of my shirt and tugging me off balance. I stumbled, but caught myself, pushing up to run. There was a crashing sound behind me and a curse a second before a hand circled my ankle.

The dirt and leaves were loose—they gave me nothing to hold on to as I clawed at the ground, trying to stop my momentum backward. Kade was pulling me, dragging me underneath him.

I spun, kicking out only to meet his hand. He was so fucking big and so fucking fast. I was halfway into trying to get up when he pounced, knees landing on either side of my body.

Screaming at him, I clawed, trying to get away. It only made him smile deeper. Dirt streaked his face, hair having come loose in the chase just like mine, and he looked like a monster. An animal. One who wanted to eat me and I wanted to let him.

But I wasn't going to.

"I caught you." The words were pure growl.

"Anyone can catch someone. Can you follow through, *Alpha*?"

Taunting him was foolish, and I didn't fucking care.

"Not going to give me my prize, Omega?"

I spat at his face and missed. "Never."

His growl ripped through me. "You'll pay for that."

"You're going to have to take everything," I told him. "Every inch you want, I'm going to fight you."

Kade laughed, the sound sinister in the darkness. "Good."

I threw a punch, and he caught my wrist, pinning it to the dirt. Trying to use my hips, I bucked underneath him, trying to get him off me, but he was too heavy. There was nothing I could do. I was trying to pry his hand off mine when he took the other one, pinning it too.

"How does it feel?" The words were soft as velvet. "Fighting me, and knowing every second you're going to lose?"

"I won't lose."

"You will, baby." He moved upward, sliding his hips so they rested just beneath my breasts. "You've already lost. Keep fighting all you want. It's not going to change a thing. You're getting fucked in every hole you have tonight, and you're going to swallow every drop of cum I give you because it's a fucking gift."

Heat crashed over me like a wave, perfume exploding in my arousal, and still I fought him like a cat, because this was the game. He'd caught me, but he still had to take me, and me giving in wasn't what either of us wanted.

I kicked high, trying to reach him since my hips were free.

"Mmm." The sound was long and slow. "Since you won't stay still, guess I need to help you."

It was impossible. He squeezed my body with his thighs, lifting one knee at a time and dragging my arm beneath them so I was still pinned like a fucking butterfly and now his hands were free.

He lifted my wet shirt, pulling the extra fabric over my head and leaving it there. I couldn't see him, and the wet, heavy fabric made it harder to breathe.

"That's what I want." His hands covered my breasts, rolling my nipples between his fingers to the point of pain. "Look how hard they are. Mmm." Delicious, wet heat enveloped one of them and a moan escaped me. It didn't mean I stopped fighting him, but it was hard to fight him when all I wanted to do was submit.

Teeth scraped my skin, and a sharp, stinging slap to

the side of my breast, and then the other one. The sound of his belt coming undone drove me to movement. I yanked on my arms, but his weight was too much.

Even pushing with my legs and arching my hips had no effect. He simply *had* me. Like I was a toy and his plaything.

"Such a considerate Omega, getting these tits wet for me so I don't have to."

"Wha—Ohh,"

Kade pushed my breasts together, and the solid heat of his cock slid between them. The studs of his piercings dragged against my skin, and *fuck me* this shouldn't be this hot. I was pinned to the ground, faceless, while he slowly fucked my tits, and I was almost wet enough to feel like slick.

"I've wanted to fuck these since the first time I saw them," he growled. "Nothing you can do to stop me, huh?"

I tried, but there was no move I could make. Every twisting movement only made each thrust feel like *more*. A desperate whine broke free. I wasn't sure what I was asking for, but I needed more. I needed Kade to give me everything.

"*Quiet.*" One big hand held my breasts together, and the other covered my nose and mouth, pressing the wet fabric down so there was no air.

Oh god.

I was a creature made of molten metal. Too hot to the touch. I was burning and melting with need, the hunger digging down into my center and unleashing itself.

I fought. I screamed until my lungs were empty, and he didn't release me, just fucked harder, grunting with every thrust.

The edges of the world faded, and my mind opened. A new level of acceptance and obedience. Kade was in control, and he knew. There was nothing to be afraid of.

Fire burned in my throat as my lungs heaved in air. Kade took the fabric away from my face, brushing my hair away and searching me. His eyes were still hard, and he was still the predator, but I saw the truth there too.

He took my shirt in his hands and pulled, yelling with the effort. The fabric ripped, and he kept going, tearing it open all the way to the neck so it was nothing but tatters.

"Can't hide from me now, Omega. Even if you escape, I can see all of you, and you're *mine*. Now open."

He shifted, pushing up on his knees so his cock was there, brushing my lips. And further. He stroked lazily while grasping my jaw with one hand. "I said *open*. I already know how much you like these in your mouth."

Kade's fingers pressed, forcing my mouth open, and immediately it was filled with his balls. Full to bursting. They tasted like him, and my eyes fluttered closed. He was right—I loved the taste of them. And I couldn't admit it now. I couldn't give him victory this easily.

Fighting every instinct I had to surrender, I spat them out.

Fire burned in what I could see of Kade's face, and a

challenge. Towering above me, his eyes glittered in the darkness. "You'll fight me for every inch?" With a laugh, he fisted his hand in my hair. "Go ahead."

The tip of his cock speared between my lips, and I couldn't fight it. His piercings slid in, one by one, until he was as deep as he could go at this angle.

Still in my throat. Still nearly all of him. Still so much of his cock my mouth stretched.

His free hand closed around my throat, holding me down even more, and I sank into bliss. I was supposed to fight this? He tasted like roasted chestnuts over a bonfire, sweet like kettle corn, and the darker, intangible taste of the night sky.

Kade took my mouth like only he could. He fucked, working his hips and holding me exactly where he needed to drive himself in to the hilt. The sounds of his pleasure echoed off the trees. Raw, savage sounds. Where I was, I was floating in a space of perfect contentment.

Somewhere outside of my own mind I realized how strange that sounded, having my throat fucked in the middle of the woods after being hunted down like an animal.

But *fuck*, I loved it.

And it wasn't over. Kade had won this round, but he'd said every hole, which meant there were two more rounds, and I could still win.

"Fuck," he moaned the word, thrusting faster. "You lose one drop and we do this all over again, understand?"

There wasn't time to do anything but swallow. Cum splashed across my tongue, rich and hot and salty, the very essence of his flavor, and I didn't want to fight this. I drank him down, like I would every one of them every single time.

The raw, haunted look in his eyes made me feel powerful. Kade was on top of me, yet I was the one who'd just made him come and swallowed every drop. Arching up underneath him, I licked my lips. My voice rasped from the way he'd used my throat. "Is that all you got?"

Kade moved so fast it stole my breath, ripping my hands free and rolling me face down in the dirt. Now I fought back, scrambling away from him as best I could. I didn't get far, but every foot was a fucking victory.

He fell on me, pinning me to the ground and we wrestled for my hands. The remnants of my t-shirt were in his hands where he'd grabbed it while I was getting away, and he was too strong for me. I screamed again, twisting to bite him, but he already had my hands tied. One push, and my face was in the dirt, hands outstretched and useless.

"Oh, baby, you don't have any idea how much more I've got." Fabric ripped, and my ass suddenly felt the air, followed by his tongue, right there.

A hand was in my hair again, turning my face and pressing it harder into the dirt. Déjà vu swam in my head. The heat, when he'd done exactly this, but not in my ass.

It was so much more there. And he took me without mercy.

The thickness of his curve, filling me an inch at a time, I came, seeing stars that weren't there and tasting dirt on my lips. Pushing up with my knees, I bucked up, trying to tilt him off me.

"I don't think so, baby." Another deeper thrust. "Fight me. Go ahead. But I'm gonna be all the way in this ass, and you're going to take it."

"Fuck you."

His dark laughter rippled over my skin. "That's my line."

One final thrust buried him to the hilt, the edge of his knot threatening to push inside, and I screamed a different kind of scream. The way he curved, the metal on his shaft, everything hurt and in the best way possible. I always said I didn't like pain, but this moment was about to make me change my mind.

Kade's mouth was at my ear, whole body pinning me down. He growled in time with his thrusts, not slowing and not stopping. "*Mine.*"

I was.

In this moment I was.

He took what he wanted, fucking my ass so deeply I would never forget the feeling. My body was imprinting the feeling of his cock, and I wondered if I'd ever feel whole again once he let me go.

"Right there," he snarled. "Right, fucking, there."

He punctuated the words with deep rolls of his hips before pulling back and coming all over my ass. The heat of it dripped down my thighs, soaking into the ripped leggings and mixing with my own wetness.

I yelped when he smacked my ass. Again, and again, and again before ripping the leggings further. "Your body belongs to me, Omega. I want to see every inch of it.

He split the fabric along the seams, tearing down one leg and then the other so I was naked except for my shoes. It was when he tried to pull off one sneaker, I saw my chance.

Heaving off the ground, I shoved my foot into his chest and pushed off him, stumbling to my feet and *running*. My hands were still bound, hair wild, and I sprinted, not saving any energy. I gave it all to my flight, knowing it was the last chance I had.

Kade roared behind me. Branches snapped and his steps thundered. I pushed myself, cresting the hill and down the incline on the other side, flinging myself out of the trees and into the tall grasses.

He was only seconds behind me. If that. The grass stung against my legs, whipping past my skin. It was a little brighter out here without the cover of trees, but not much.

A snarl was my only warning.

The arm that curled around my waist yanked me down and against Kade's body as we crashed together. He'd jumped—tackled me. And we were still moving. My hands were tied by the t-shirt, and I had nothing left to fight him with. My strength and energy were gone, my limbs shaking with the remnants of adrenaline.

There was no sky, only him. Pinning me down, holding me by the throat and shoving my thighs apart to drive himself home. I moved, and the growl that met me was different.

Somewhere along the way his shirt had gotten lost, and all his beautiful tattoos were inky stains in the night. Even more a monster taking the maiden. He melded in with the darkness. A shadow creature appearing to hold me down.

His hand tightened on my throat. Not enough to frighten me, but I understood the warning. "*Mine,*" he said again. But the word was different. It wasn't conscious. Pure, ruthless, claiming instinct.

"Kade," I breathed, and he growled, sinking his cock —and his swollen knot—all the way into me. "Oh, fuck."

The eyes locked on mine weren't those of my conscious Alpha. They were Kade, but stripped back to the barest hint of humanity. He was in rut.

I stopped fighting.

There was no part of me afraid of him, but I also knew better than to fight back against an Alpha in rut. He wasn't toward the surface enough to play the game.

Kade would never hurt me. Not on purpose. And even now the way he was fucking me, I was going to shatter into a million pieces of glowing glass and melt back together with the second wave of pleasure.

I looped my bound wrists around his neck and pulled him closer. He was already knotted, and it wasn't coming out now.

No, he was thrusting deeper, knot pushing against all the delicious places inside me, and sparks were flying behind my eyes. "Kade. Please. *Yes.*"

His answering snarl wasn't remotely human, and the

376

next plunge sent me over the edge. I tipped my head back and let go, finally, fully surrendering. The orgasm took me in a wave, breaking me apart so thoroughly I couldn't even say his name.

I shook, and writhed, tried to lift my hips to meet his only to be held down again.

His hand was still at my throat, and the other was flat between my breasts making sure I went absolutely fucking nowhere. And I wasn't.

I lost all sense of time and space except the motion of Kade above me and inside me. I lost count of the number of times new pleasure crashed over me or carried me upward like I had wings only to drop me into free fall. My Alpha came and then came again. Another time. Between my legs, I was coated in it where he kept fucking, causing his cum to spill onto my skin and the grass.

"Kade," I said.

"*Mine.*" He leaned down, mouth covering the skin where my neck met my shoulder. His teeth were there, holding onto me, but he didn't bite.

The vibrations between us were somewhere between a growl and a purr. A final orgasm shuddered through him, and his hips finally stopped moving. His mouth stayed where it was, holding onto my neck without fully claiming me. Another place he was holding onto me. Keeping me his.

Kade was still in rut, but we couldn't stay here until he came out of it. I didn't know how many hours it might be.

"Kade," I whispered. "You don't have to let me go."

He growled.

"You don't have to let me go, but you do have to take me to the car. We'll go home, and you can have me all to yourself in your bed, okay?"

It took long seconds for him to move, lifting me off the ground and keeping me on his knotted cock. I wrapped my legs around him and held on. His teeth stayed where they were. They didn't move an inch.

Before long, I heard the car door. "Kade? What's going on?"

Kade's growl splintered the air, and I pulled him as close as I could given his hold. "That's Luke. Luke is going to drive us home. Don't worry, Luke isn't going to touch me."

It was enough to get Kade moving toward the car, and Luke caught on. He got to the back door and opened it. "He's in rut," I whispered as Kade maneuvered us into the back seat. "Everything is fine."

"You're okay?" Luke asked, eyes roving over the two of us.

I realized what I must look like, naked with sneakers, covered in dirt and cum, but I was perfect. "Yeah, I'm okay." I smiled before he shut the door, easing myself down to lean on Kade's chest for the ride home.

CHAPTER THIRTY-FOUR

ESME

I opened my eyes to morning light, aching. Like I'd had the worst and best week at the gym in my entire life. "Fuck," I rolled over and came face to face with Kade, who was already awake, and looking at me like he was unsure. It was just him now.

When we'd gotten back to the house he'd brought me straight here and fucked me again. Twice. I'd fallen asleep from exhaustion still knotted. But he wasn't inside me now. "Morning."

"Hey." He reached out to touch me hesitantly. "Are you all right?"

"A little sore, but I kind of expected that. You don't volunteer to have some feral chase sex without getting bruises."

"Right." He cleared his throat. "I'm sorry, Esme."

I frowned. "Why?"

"I lost control. When you ran, the rut snapped into me, and I couldn't break it."

"Kade." I slid across the sheets to him. We were both still covered in dirt and sweat. "You didn't hurt me. You listened to me, even while you were in rut. I'm fine, and I'm very happy."

He searched my face, looking for any sign of the lie

that wasn't there. Finally, he closed his eyes and reached for me. "God, you're perfect."

"You were worried?"

A kiss warmed my forehead. "You haven't seen your bruises. And I remember what happened after the rut kicked in, but it's different. Like it was a dream. Yes, I was worried."

"Don't be. It was incredible."

He held me close, and I took the time to breathe him in. This was the real Kade. The one who was soft and loving. Letting the beast inside him out was just a small fraction of this man.

"It's your turn," I told him.

"My turn for what?"

"I'm hearing everyone's stories about how they came to the pack, and now I want to hear yours."

A soft purr rose in his chest. "It's a pretty average story, baby. I'm a kid from the suburbs. Normal, nice family. Rebellious teen decided to get a tattoo and fell in love with it. I dropped out my senior year and never looked back. Worked my way from studio to studio getting better until Ben and the others walked in, and it clicked."

"That quickly, huh?"

"That quickly."

Slowly, I sat up, wincing. "I'm sure there are details there you're not telling me. I'll get them out of you, eventually."

"All right, little one. You can try. But I promise it's boring as shit."

I made a face telling him I didn't believe it even for a second. "Take a shower with me? I still have *you* all over me. And dirt."

"If we have to." His purr got louder as he grinned. "Can't say I mind you being covered in my scent."

Rolling my eyes, I headed to his bathroom. "Given we're having dinner with my mom tonight, maybe I shouldn't smell this intense."

"Fair point."

Kade took care of turning on the water, and I looked at myself in the mirror. He wasn't wrong. There were darkening bruises on my arms and stomach. There was even one on my neck, likely from his hands. He turned me to see my back, where there was a black and blue splotch growing. "Okay," I admitted. "I see why you were worried. But I promise I'm good. I like my battle scars."

He dropped a kiss on my shoulder and wrapped his arms around me, sneaking his fingers between my legs. "And here?"

I gasped, going up on my toes. "Funnily enough, it's one of the few places *not* sore. Ass, too."

Fucking Omega biology. Even when we weren't in heat our bodies were ready to go, prepared to take knots and all. Rut was a part of life as much as heat. If rutting behavior harmed the Omega, it would be monumentally shitty.

"I'm glad," Kade said.

Stepping under the spray of water, I let him take care of me. He washed my hair and body, and I didn't interrupt him, because I knew he needed it. But when he was finished, I kissed him. "Thank you for chasing me."

"I'll chase you anytime, baby. I loved every fucking second. Just seeing you banged up is harder than I expected."

After he washed himself, we stood under the water until it started to go cold. And then he carried me up to my bedroom where there were clean sheets so we could sleep some more before we had to face the collective horror which was dinner with my mother.

I found a shirt that covered almost all the bruises. If I was going to do this, I wasn't going to have my mom wondering why I was covered in them, and I certainly wasn't going to tell her it was because I got ruthlessly fucked in the woods.

The one visible bruise was on my wrist, and I could say I got it because I fell down while running.

Which wasn't exactly a lie.

I was keeping it casual, but all the guys looked nice. Not suits, but button-downs or henleys, almost all of them wearing dark jeans. They weren't a tuxedo wearing pack, and we weren't going to pretend they were simply for my mother.

We were pulling up to her house, and though I wished Eva were here as a buffer between me and her, it was my saving grace no photographers were waiting outside the gate.

"Baby girl, you are going to chew through your lip at this rate."

Avery took my hand in his and laced our fingers together. I hadn't even realized I'd been biting it. "I'm nervous."

"We know," Luke said with a laugh. "And it's going to be okay. No matter what your mother thinks of us, it's not going to change what we think of you."

"It might," I muttered.

"Stop," Avery commanded.

Ben met my eyes in the rear-view mirror. "I think I might be able to smooth some feathers with who my parents were. It shouldn't have to come to that, but we've got that in our back pocket just in case."

The gate closed behind us and he parked the car. "We can still get out of it," I said as Avery was pulling me out of the car. "We can say I got food poisoning."

"Food poisoning never works," Rylan said. "Trust me."

I raised my eyebrows. "What's the story there?"

"I'll tell you once we get through tonight."

He laughed when I cursed under my breath. "Let's get this over with."

Kade caught my arm and Luke stepped in, back and front, just like they had before my heat. Overwhelming and Alpha. It wasn't fair, the way the sudden purrs and scents made me calm against my will.

"That's a dirty trick."

"Is it?" Luke asked. "Or do Alphas have the ability for a reason?"

Kade's hands were on my hips, gently squeezing and massaging, soothing me with his hands while he wasn't with words.

Luke tilted my chin up. "Tell me why you're so nervous."

It wasn't a request.

I blinked back emotion unexpectedly. "I just really want her to like you, and I don't know if she will."

"Are you still going to love your mom even if she doesn't like us?"

"Yes." Of course I would. Though I wasn't going to pretend it would make our relationship easier.

His eyes crinkled with a smile. "Are you going to stop courting us if she doesn't like us?"

"No."

"Then you have nothing to worry about, because no matter how dinner goes, nothing is going to change."

"So fucking *reasonable*," I said quietly, and Kade burst out with a laugh.

"All right, fine. Let's go."

They let me free, and I led the way up the stairs to the door. I wasn't even at the top of the stairs when the door opened and Mom stood there. She out dressed all of us in a deep blue pantsuit, but I knew she loved this color, and it felt like a nod to me. Wearing something she loved.

A tiny peace offering, just between us.

She was looking behind me, but her eyes finally landed on mine, and she gave me a strained smile.

"Hi, Mom."

CHAPTER THIRTY-FIVE

AVERY

*M*y first impression of Esme's mother was that they didn't look much alike. While Esme's wavy brown hair was wild, and sometimes untamable, her mother was blond, with her hair pulled back in a slick style suited to who she was. But even their features were different. I'd seen pictures of Esme's father, and it was clear both she and Eva resembled him far more.

"Hi, Mom."

"Hi, sweetie."

I spotted the tension in the hug, and the relief in both of them when they relaxed. No matter what fights you had with your parents, something about hugging them could always bring you back to center.

At least that was the way it was with my family. I couldn't wait for Esme to meet them.

"This is the," Esme hesitated, and her face turned to panic. We'd never talked about our pack name, and she didn't want to look like she didn't know the most basic thing about us.

"The Nautilus Pack," Ben filled in smoothly, stepping up to shake her mother's hand. "We're honored to meet you."

She didn't look so sure, but she shook Ben's hand

politely. "Eleanor Williams," she said. "Please call me Eleanor."

"I'm Bennett Gray," he said. "But most people call me Ben."

Esme reached out and took his hand, pulling him inside, but kept watching the introductions. "Rylan McBride," he said. "We've been really excited about this. Thank you for inviting us."

"Of course," she murmured.

I couldn't help but feel like we were in a receiving line at a formal function. It was already clear Eleanor was far more reserved than her daughters. Or at least she was that way with us.

"Kade Porter."

Her mother flinched and tried to hide it. Kade was used to it, but I was still grateful Esme was behind her and hadn't seen the reaction. Even knowing we were fine with any outcome, my little Omega was a bundle of nerves. She was wound so tight I thought her spine would snap.

"Luke Holloway," Luke said. "Thank you for the invitation. You have a beautiful home."

She looked him up and down and smiled. "I've heard rumors you have one as well."

"I don't know if it's on the same level at this place, but it's home."

Finally, Eleanor's eyes fell on me. I smiled at her. "Avery Quinn, at your service."

She shook my hand lightly, and I passed her into the house. The doors closed behind us and she dusted her hands off like she wasn't quite used to touching things like doors. "Now that the slight awkwardness is finished, dinner is served."

"Oh," Esme said. "Sure."

Maybe there was normally a different protocol? Drinks and cocktails first? I wasn't sure. But she was clinging to Ben's hand hard enough her knuckles were white. All I wanted to do was wrap her in a hug and tell her it would all be fine.

That part would have to come later.

The dining room was gorgeous. Something out of a decorating magazine. Hell, if Addison was let loose in this house she would have a fucking field day.

White walls with old style molding in rectangles which gave texture without being intrusive. A couple of beautiful landscape oil paintings, and a set of large French doors which led out onto a slate patio over-looking a lush garden.

The table itself was beautiful too, set with food and drinks. I couldn't tell immediately what the meal was, but it smelled amazing.

"Where is everyone?" Esme asked. "Where's Arnold?"

Eleanor waved a hand. "After Alicia finished cooking and everything was laid out, I sent everyone home. Since it's just us, I didn't think a lot of ceremony was needed."

"That's kind of you," Luke said, pulling out Esme's chair. But I was watching her face, and she went pale after her mother said it.

There were landmines here we weren't fucking aware

of. We were going to do our best, but tonight, Esme was going to be in my bed. My instinct to protect her was out of control, and the only thing keeping me from walking around the table and having her sit in my lap was the thought of having her near me later.

"Please help yourselves," Eleanor said. "Would you like some wine?"

"Wine sounds great," Rylan said. "Would you like me to pour? I can."

She looked surprised. "That would be lovely. It's behind you."

Rylan was up on his feet, and I smothered a smile. He uncorked the wine with ease, and Eleanor watched, stunned, as he poured her a perfect glass. He smiled at her and moved around the table. "I was a waiter through school. At *Troisgros*. I don't think I'll ever forget how to pour wine."

"My, I haven't been there in a while. It's a lovely place."

"Yes, it is."

Which was a fucking understatement. *Troisgros* was one of the finest restaurants in Slate City. The kind of place with a months-long reservation list and people who traveled simply to eat there.

Rylan had waited tables because the money was good, and he wanted to do as much as he could to minimize his debt. But right now? All he was thinking about was making it easier for Esme.

Kade reached forward and pulled the top off the first

dish, unleashing a wave of delicious aroma. "It smells incredible, Eleanor," I said. "Thank you."

She took a sip of wine and smiled. "My cook, Alicia, is the best there is. I never eat poorly. One of the indulgences I allow myself."

Esme was looking down at her plate, and I recognized the posture from when we'd first met her. She was locked up, unable to get out of her own head with nerves.

"So tell me about yourselves," Eleanor said. "Esme told me you are tattoo artists."

"Yes," I said. "We are. Ben, Rylan, and myself began as classically trained artists and moved into the field, while Kade and Luke started out in the trade."

"Interesting. And what made you leave the traditional field?"

Ben took the dish from Kade and served Esme before serving himself. "That's mainly my doing. We formed our pack at school, and after my parents passed, I got one in their honor. I fell in love with it and these guys followed me."

"I'm sorry to hear they've passed." Eleanor inclined her head.

"You might know them? Roy and Kelly Gray. I know my father was a huge fan of your late husband's work, Mrs. Williams."

She looked stunned for a moment. "Yes. I did know them. You're their son? My, it's been long enough I forgot they had children. A sister too?"

"Correct."

Rylan finished his circuit of the table with the wine,

and the food gradually made its way around. But no one spoke for a minute, and the silence was painful.

"Besides our occupation," Kade finally broke the silence, "is there anything else you'd like to know about us? We're incredibly happy to be courting your daughter, and we're equally happy to answer any questions."

Esme's mother didn't touch her food, but she took another sip of wine. "My other daughter, Eva, says you're well known. Is it true?"

Kade nodded. "Yes, it's true. I could be humble about it, but I won't be now. Success is partly luck, but it's also talent and hard work. The five of us are some of the best in the business, and just like *Troisgros*, our waiting list is months long."

"I think it's actually closer to a year now," Luke said. "We might consider bringing in an artist who isn't pack to help stem the tide. But it might not get better. Eva has an interesting idea for a possible show involving the studio, and we're eager to see where it goes."

"*My* Eva?"

Esme cleared her throat. "Yeah. Eva wants a tattoo from Ben. It's how she tricked me into going to the studio to meet them. Set up an excuse to go get a consultation and shoved me in the door."

Luke chuckled. "I don't remember the shoving."

"It was a mental shove."

Her mother stared at her. "You had to be *tricked* into meeting them? I thought you were scent-sympathetic."

"We are." Esme's words were careful. "But I was...

nervous. For obvious reasons. You know exactly why, Mom. Don't pretend you don't."

Ben cleared his throat. "When I met your daughter, it was clear we were compatible. I immediately showed her scent to the rest of the pack, and we agreed it was something we needed to pursue. It was instant and strong. We would have pursued her sooner, but we didn't have her contact information."

Eleanor looked around the table. "Might I ask why you didn't think to come to me first?"

I looked at Esme, whose wine glass was halfway to her lips, her eyes closed in exasperation. "Because the way most packs court is by asking the Omega, Mom. Not jumping through hoops of a matchmaker. And they asked me. When they told me they wanted to court me they asked me if there was anything special they needed to do, and I told them no. So if anyone's to blame, it's me."

"I'm not blaming anyone," Eleanor said.

"Mrs. Williams," I said, drawing her eyes to me. "I'm unfamiliar with the interview process you must have been doing for other packs, but we're happy to do what you need us to."

She stood and walked out of the room abruptly. We all froze, but she was back in a few seconds with some file folders in her hands. "No need. I had my matchmaker produce files for each of you with the information she could find. I hadn't looked at them yet, because I didn't want to give myself unnecessary bias." She glanced at Ben. "Otherwise I would have known whose son you were. I'll look through them and let you know my decision."

Esme's mouth dropped open, and she looked at all of us. This was about to spin very badly, and we only had a few seconds to pull it back.

Luke cleared his throat. "My apologies, Mrs. Williams. I want to clarify one thing about what Avery said. We're willing to do what you need us to in terms of getting to know us. We have nothing to hide. But what we aren't doing is asking your permission to court Esme."

The words fell heavily into the silence.

"I see." She smiled, but it wasn't entirely real. "In that case, tell me about yourselves. Beyond your job description. I'm sure it will be more interesting than reading it."

Esme breathed, body relaxing, and the atmosphere eased too. Not nearly enough, but it felt like there was air in the room again.

In the time we'd known her, I'd never noticed Esme's scent turn *bitter*. The rich scent of tea was like a cup had been brewing all day and it was so dark all the good flavor was gone. Of course, we could scent her far more deeply and with more nuance than others, but how could her mother not sense the change? Surely she could tell the difference.

Everyone had a note which shifted with their mood. It was both a blessing and a curse. You could tell when someone was having a bad day, but you also couldn't hide it.

A horrifying thought struck me as Rylan started talking, telling Esme's mother about himself.

Did her mother not notice because this was always the way she smelled in her presence? Filled with anxiety bordering on pain?

Esme loved her mother. It was crystal clear. But loving someone didn't make a relationship easy. Sometimes it made it that much harder.

I needed to ask her.

We went around the table and gave our basic history. The styles of tattoo we specialized in. A little about our families.

Eleanor listened and smiled, nodding the entire time. I was sure to most people it seemed warm and welcoming. But I wasn't judging based on her actions. I was watching Esme's reactions, and my little Omega was... cautious. Very clearly not comfortable, though not wound quite as tight as she had been.

Finally, Eleanor turned to Esme. "And work is going well?"

"It is. I've got a few new paintings I'm working on, and everyone loves the exclusive paints. They can't get enough of them."

"I'm glad you're happy," Eleanor said, rubbing her fingers along the stem of her wine glass. "And you know—"

"Yes," Esme said quickly. "I know. Thank you."

The rest of us shared discreet looks, not having any idea what she was talking about.

Downing the little left in her glass, Esme stood. "This

is the guys' Sunday night, so we should let them get some sleep before they tackle their long waiting list."

"Of course."

We all made our way to the door, and I couldn't help but feel like we were walking on glass that was already cracked and just waiting for us to fall through it.

We shook hands with Mrs. Williams. I would have hugged her if I thought she would accept it, but her handshake was warm, regardless. "It was very nice to meet you."

"You too. I'm sure we'll be seeing more of each other."

She just smiled.

It was starting rain, and the rest of us stepped back to let mother and daughter have a moment. I heard snatches of the conversation—something about lunch next week, and maybe about Eva, but nothing more.

Esme's eyes were focused on the ground all the way to the car, and inside it, she didn't say anything. Beside me, she looked out the window as we started to drive.

"Your mom is nice, Esme," Ry said quietly.

"Yes," she choked out. "She's nice."

Then, under her breath, she said. "She's always nice. Always so fucking nice."

CHAPTER THIRTY-SIX

ESME

My mind was blank. Not because I didn't have thoughts, but because I was holding them all back. If I let them out, I wasn't quite sure what would happen, and I didn't want it to be in the fucking car.

The guys seemed to sense it too, and didn't say much, or said it quietly.

I hadn't expected it to go well, but I hadn't expected it to be like *that* either.

As soon as we were inside, I pushed for the stairs.

"Esme." Avery's voice was all Alpha command. "Living room, please."

My body turned and went, though my mind didn't want to be there. I didn't want to rehash how awful dinner was, or why I was somehow unable to use my fucking voice when it mattered. I just wanted to curl up —preferably in my nest—and sleep for a million years.

Rylan sat in one of the big, comfy rockers and held out his arms. Yes. I folded myself in beside him.

"All things considered," Kade said, "I don't think it went too badly."

I laughed, but it was the furthest thing from funny. "I suppose it could have been worse, but not much."

"Why?"

It was a genuine question, and I didn't want to tell them all the ways my mother thoroughly snubbed them, but they needed to know. "She sent the staff home. Which means she didn't want any of you to be seen in the house. That right there says plenty about what she thinks, but you not asking for permission is another strike. Plus, you're corrupting Eva." I rolled my eyes and looked at Ben. "Trust me, the fact that Eva wants a tattoo from you is your fault entirely. And just... she expected you to fall in line, and you didn't. I'm happy you didn't, but you got the 'nice' version of mom. The one she puts on when she doesn't want to be somewhere and is only passing the time until it's over.

"She's used to it. She's done it for years, because she hosted dinner parties for my dad, and now the charity work she does. Her image is always perfect, and doesn't crack. But it's not real."

I leaned on Rylan's shoulder, and his fingers drew patterns on my hip where he was holding me.

"She was about to ask a question and you cut her off. Why?" Ben was leaning forward on his knees, totally focused on me.

"Because it's a fight we've had plenty of times before. She would rather me be a part of her charity work or start a non-profit. Anything other than what I'm doing with my art."

He frowned. "But Eva is an artist. An actor."

"Yeah, but that was never her choice. It was a chance thing that happened when we were little. Some guy approached my parents and wanted to use us as models

398

for some clothing thing. Eva was amazing at it, and I wasn't. She wanted to keep doing it, and they let her. By the time my mom wanted her to pull back, it was already too late. The career ball was rolling.

"It was the same with Eva's pack. Her courtship happened quickly and publicly, so Mom couldn't say anything. She's grown to like them because she's had to, but she never would have wanted Eva to choose a rock band." I sighed. "Mom just had very different dreams for her daughters than we ended up having, and I'm the one whose life she can still influence, so she tries. Pretty much done letting her do that, but I still understand it."

Avery cleared his throat. "What would her ideal life for you look like?"

"She comes from that world," I said. "From old money, where everything is decided for you before you're born and that's the end of it. For her, she always knew she would marry a high-society Alpha and be his right-hand woman. Do charitable work and be one of the benevolent public figures talked about in those circles. She thought we'd be the same. She doesn't understand why we don't want it... and it makes me sad."

The words kept pouring out of me like someone left a faucet—I couldn't stop them.

"She and my dad. I mean, Mom always knew the kind of Alpha she would marry, but Dad still took her by surprise. He was amazing. They were so in love, and I think Mom was happier than she imagined she would be. So when he died—" I cleared my throat. "She feels like she doesn't have much left, except for us. I know she wants me to be happy. We just have very different ideas of how to get there."

Luke smiled and stood, coming over to where Rylan and I sat. "Well, I hope one day we'll be able to win her over. If she got used to the guys in Mindless Delirium, she'll get used to us."

"I hope so."

A small intake of breath, I didn't know from whom. It was as close as I'd come to saying I'd decided. I knew what I wanted, but I didn't know how to say it yet. And tonight wasn't the night to make that kind of declaration, especially when I was still reeling from Mom's reaction.

"I can't believe she had files made on you guys."

"Baby, there's nothing for her to find. Promise." Kade winked.

"Oh, I'm not worried about that. I just can't believe she did it. Though I would pay money to see what Katarina's face looked like when she asked. You guys aren't in her *normal* clientele. Thank fuck."

Rylan laughed. "Yeah, we're pretty glad about that, too."

Avery stood and stretched. "I was about this close the entire night from pulling you into my lap to make sure you were okay. So I'd like to spend the night with you, Esme, if that's all right."

I startled. "Why wouldn't it be all right?"

He chuckled. "I'm just checking to make sure you didn't have other plans."

"No. Before you ordered me in here I was going to go bury myself in my nest and wallow."

Luke leaned in and kissed my temple. "No wallowing allowed. Relationships with parents are hard, and just like we told you, nothing's changed."

I leaned into the kiss, enjoying the feeling and trying to let go of my shell-shocked anxiety. Avery came across the room and pulled me up from Rylan. "Go wait in the nest for me."

"So you can talk about me?" I raised an eyebrow.

Reaching around, he smacked me lightly on the ass. "No, baby girl. So I can grab a couple things."

"Okay." My lips were pressing together and the same anxiety was bubbling up again. I didn't quite believe they weren't going to talk about what happened, but there wasn't much I could do about it either way.

Going up to the nest, I peeled off my shirt and jeans at the door. I needed the softness of all the pillows and blankets on my skin. The nest had been cleaned. Not enough to get rid of all of our scents, but to clean up all the mess from the heat. Still, the mixture of all of us was comforting. I pushed my way under one of the fuzzy blankets and finally breathed.

The dark, soft space soothed something in me, and my muscles relaxed. All the aches I had from last night were still there, but at least I didn't feel like I was going to snap in two.

Avery's soft footsteps entered the nest. I heard the faint shuffling of fabric, and the movement of him across the cushions before he laid down with me, not bothering to unearth me from the blankets before pulling me tight to his body.

"You okay, baby girl?"

It seemed like such a simple question, and yet it wasn't. Was I okay? Yes. I was fine and happy to be here in my nest with him, relieved to be out of that horrendous and awkward dinner, and yet my chest ached.

"Kind of."

Now he peeled the blankets back so he could see my face, and I watched the twinkle lights flicker above us. "What's going through your head?"

"I think I wanted her to like you more than I realized. Like I knew, but I didn't know how much, and it hurts."

He moved, stripping back the blankets and grabbing one foot. It took me a second to realize he'd brought my socks—his gift from the heat—and was pulling them on. They came halfway up my thighs, and I loved how cozy they made me feel. "I need more pairs of these."

"I'll buy you as many as you want," he said. "They're damn hot, and I love how you relax in them."

The blanket was tucked over both of us when he finished. "I brought chocolate too."

"What kind?"

"Filled with caramel." He kissed me on the nose.

I closed my eyes. "That's perfect."

Reaching out of sight, he brought back a piece for me to unwrap. "It's okay to be disappointed about your mom's reaction. Don't think because we're telling you it's fine that you're not allowed feel it. We just want to make sure you know it doesn't affect anything for us."

"Yeah." I turned toward him, burrowing into his warmth. He was naked under the blanket with me, which was a good distraction along with the dissolving sugar in my mouth. "And I am. But I think I'm going to have to get used to it. Because I'm doing my own thing and not trying to make her happy at the same time, I'm going to feel it more."

Avery's scent grew stronger, spicy and amazing. Like being enveloped by a chai latte, or gingerbread cookies. Savory spices too, like oregano and basil. I breathed him in and let him hold me.

"You like taking care of me," I said quietly, barely even aware I said it.

"Yes, I do."

"Why?"

I felt him shrug. "Why does Kade like chasing? Or Luke like to be in control? It's who I am. Nothing makes me happier than making sure someone is safe, fed, and happy. Even if that last part takes a while."

I laughed into his chest. "It's like having a mood ring. However I feel, there's always someone to satisfy the craving."

The rumble of his laughter moved through me, and I let myself settle and drift, nearly drowsy. "I didn't know that about you, from dinner. I'd planned on asking, but I didn't know."

When it was Avery's turn to speak about himself, he revealed his upbringing wasn't all sunshine and roses. He started out in foster care and bounced around, saw some terrible shit before he landed with his parents and they adopted him and changed his life. They let him pursue his passion for painting, and the rest was history once he met Ben and Rylan.

"I want to meet your parents," I said. "They sound nice."

"They are, and I promise they'll love you."

"Have you told them about me?" I instantly regretted the question, because I wasn't sure which answer I wanted.

He tilted my face up to his and kissed me, deepening it slowly, bearing me back onto the cushions and weighing me down with his body. My Alpha teddy bear was also a weighted blanket. I could get used to this.

"I didn't, because I didn't want them to celebrate early. But they know now." He was grinning. "Your picture with Ben took care of that."

"Oh my god, I'm sorry."

Avery looked at me in that way he had, stripping everything back to the core. "Did I say I was upset about it?"

"No."

"I'm not. And you should know we *are* getting a copy of that photo printed for the house. It was shitty the way it happened, but it's hot as fuck."

I flushed red. "We can't just have that where everyone can see it."

"Everyone's already seen it, baby girl. Not much you can do about it."

"Fair point."

The way he was lying on me, his arousal was clear,

but his movements were still slow and deliberate, peppering me with kisses and dragging his hands down my skin. "When I ask this Esme, I expect an honest answer."

"Uh-oh."

He smiled. "Are you too sore from last night? If you are, I have no problem making this a night of cuddles and different kinds of pleasure."

"I'm not," I said. "Honestly. That's not what's sore."

"Oh really?" A hand drifted down my stomach, fingers slipping beneath the elastic of my underwear. "Spread your legs, baby girl."

I shuddered. His commands weren't any less powerful than Kade's or Luke's, but they hit differently with their sweetness. Obedience wasn't a question. I parted my thighs and let him between them.

"I think you need some soft and slow."

I whined, arching into his hand. "What does that mean?"

He kissed me instead of answering. His fingers circled my clit with gentle, steady pressure. Enough to make me wet, but not enough to take it anywhere. A little harder, and I gasped into his kiss when he circled and there was a sharp surge of pleasure. "Right there, baby girl? Okay. We can do right there."

Focusing on the single spot on my clit, he teased it, pulling wetness up to make it slicker.

"Soft and slow means I'm going to take my time. My pace, my pressure. No matter how long it takes for you to come. You can beg me to go faster if you want to, but it's not going to make me speed up. I want you to enjoy the journey and not just the climax. Help me." He lifted his hand up to my mouth and offered his fingers.

I tasted myself on his skin while I wet his fingers, pressing my hips up to meet his hand once more. "So you want to torture me?"

"Oh, I don't think it's going to be torture."

He was moving again, and it was *maddeningly* slow. And yet, I couldn't argue with him on the torture. It felt incredible, every brush of his finger letting pleasure seep into me slowly.

It was like falling into a haze where there were only his fingers and his lips. The feeling of his breath and his scent. That haze was pleasure and it built slowly. So slowly you almost didn't notice until it suffused everything around us.

I needed more. Writhing, I begged him without words. My teeth bit into my lip, trying not to speak and ask uselessly.

"You're doing so good, baby girl," he whispered. "Feel it. Enjoy how good my fingers feel on your clit, and knowing nothing you do is going to make them move faster."

"*Fuck.*" My voice was a strangled mess. "Avery, please."

"Mmm." He kissed the space below my ear. "I like the sound of you begging me."

The pleasure inside of me was like a lighter trying to start. Every pass over that one fucking spot was a spark trying to catch, and failing. It sank into me, tunneling deeper, until the entire inside of my body was filled with the *deep*, sharp feeling of bliss which came just before an orgasm.

I was hovering on the edge, somehow impossibly not quite there. There was no way to keep still. I reached for the cushions—blankets, anything to anchor me—and Avery didn't stop. Just like he'd said, the same pressure and the same speed, my body straining for the one little extra spark to drop me over the cliff.

"You can take it," Avery whispered, kissing me breathless. "Every inch of you is soaked in it. I can scent the way you want it, baby girl. Let go."

How could I let go even further than I already was?

My mind spun back to last night when Kade was in rut and I'd simply... surrendered. I thought I already had, but there it was. That one final little place deep inside, grappling for control even though I knew I needed to be without it.

But choosing it here felt like so much more than last night. Here was opening my soul up to vulnerability and hurt, and it was absolutely terrifying.

The image of a rope appeared, holding down the final sail in the boat of my mind. The sea was crashing, and I had a choice here. Every part of me was shaking, but I grabbed the rope and untied it, letting the last fraction of me fly free.

Pleasure slammed into me as I dropped over the cliff into a sea of pure sensation. My body wasn't mine, possessed by the waves rippling through me. And through it all, Avery's voice. "There we go, baby girl. Come all over my hand. I've got you."

I strained upward, arching until I was taut, orgasm ripping its exquisite claws through me one final time before I collapsed back onto the pillows.

Avery purred, still caressing my clit, even softer now, sending glittering aftershocks racing over my skin. "Good girl. You did so fucking good, baby. Thank you for trusting me."

"That was—that was—"

"The first of many." Avery moved slowly and steadily, removing my underwear before settling between my legs, easing his cock into me. I forgot how fucking *good* he felt. Not quite as long as some of the others, but he was the thickest of my pack. Not even all the way inside me and I was stretched.

All the way in, until it felt like I couldn't breathe from the thickness. He lowered himself on top of me, at once stealing my breath and short-circuiting my brain. Weighted blanket indeed.

"Ready, baby girl?"

"I don't know if I'll survive that again."

He chuckled. "Let's find where this pretty pussy loves to be fucked."

I didn't have a chance to ask him what he meant. He rocked deeper into me, and I moaned. "I think it loves it all."

"Bet your ass it does, baby girl. But I want the spot that makes you go blind."

Pace and rhythm were even, slow and smooth, just

like he'd promised, and I couldn't even be angry because I was still so steeped in my own orgasm it all felt amazing. Avery shifted as he rocked, changing the angle slightly every time, and it all felt good.

His lips were on mine, dragging me down further into the delicious haze he was creating around us, more than his scent and my perfume. He was putting pleasure into the air. It coated my skin and made me feel high.

"Oh *shit*."

He laughed, the smile on his face absolutely perfectly happy. The one fraction of an inch he'd moved suddenly felt like every slow thrust was a lightning bolt inside me. "How are you doing that?"

"Close your eyes." They fell closed, and he fucked me. Slowly, steadily, and hard enough every time he pushed forward, I felt unsteady in the best way.

"I like the way your pussy takes my cock, baby girl." Avery's voice was strained, like he was having just as much trouble as I was not going faster. "You fit me just right."

"Harder, please." I bit my lip, keeping my eyes closed. "Please, I know you want to, too."

"No."

The simple answer lit me on fire. Lightning built under my skin until I was trying to move, trying to pull myself closer to bridge the gap which once again seemed impossible. But the way Avery held me to the ground with his weight prevented it entirely. All I could do was feel every stroke and savor the sensation of being alight with pleasure.

I didn't know how long it was until I broke. "Oh my god. Oh, *fuck*. Avery—" I was shaking, trembling like I was ice cold, but nothing about this was cold. Sheer, overwhelming bliss soaking every inch of my body, mind, and soul.

"That's my good girl," he brushed the words across my lips. "Coming all over my cock, taking what your Alpha gives you."

The words triggered a second wave, light bursting behind my eyes. I forced my head to the side, baring my neck out of pure instinct. He could bond me right now and I wouldn't care as long as he didn't stop moving.

Avery kissed the point of my pulse. "Not yet, baby girl. But fuck, seeing you beg for it ruins me." The ragged words turned into a groan as he came inside me, knot swelling, firmly locking us together.

True calm washed over me. I would never understand Omega biology, the way being knotted soothed every worry, whether it was in our minds or under the surface. But it did. My mind was quiet, and I loved the feeling.

"I can get behind soft and slow," I murmured.

He dragged his lips along the line of my jaw. "I thought you might say that."

"When your knot releases, maybe—"

"Baby girl, this knot isn't coming out of you."

I froze. "What do you mean?"

"I mean you're mine for the night. When I feel it softening, I'm going to take you again. And again. And again. Every time will be soft and slow, and every time I fuck you, those orgasms are going to get deeper. I fully plan on being knotted in this perfect pussy in the morning, and having you be wrecked from the orgasms."

In response, my body squeezed his cock. There was no hiding I loved the idea. Not with my perfume filling the nest and my pussy already begging for more.

"If you're a very good girl, I'll take you from behind and spank you as I do."

"I thought you said you didn't want to torture me."

"This is torture?"

"Yes. Absolutely. Torture of the worst kind."

He smiled. "Then yes, I want to torture you. Give me those tears of pleasure, baby girl. Scream my name and try to get me to go faster. But unless you tell me you don't want more, my cock owns your pussy until morning. Do you understand?"

I was covered in goosebumps and about to come all over again from his words, but yes. "I understand."

"Good." Avery raised himself on his elbows and reached between us, finding my swollen, sensitive clit. "I think you need to come again just to make sure."

"I can't. Not yet."

"You can. Tell me yes, Alpha."

His fingers moved, and there was no fucking air. I had to gasp it, trying to fill my lungs between the pleasure of his fingers and the magnificent pressure of his knot. "Yes, Alpha."

"Good girl."

Avery slowly circled my clit just like the first time, infinite patience in his eyes.

It was going to be a very long, incredible night.

CHAPTER THIRTY-SEVEN

ESME

*A*very did wreck me. I was wrung out of pleasure when his cock finally slipped out of me. Blissfully exhausted. The rest of the day I spent in bed, answering comments on my phone on my business account and making notes about ideas I had for paintings.

Between the sex, the chase, and dinner with my mother, I was already fading by the time the pack came home, and falling asleep before dinner. Someone carried me to bed and tucked me in. I wasn't awake enough to remember who.

I woke again in the morning with far more clarity. My bruises were fading, I had energy, and I didn't want to waste it. Today was going to be a fucking amazing day.

Wes showed up thirty minutes after I texted him, and I spent the day at my house. I mixed six different paint colors and set them into containers to harden, and I spent time working on a new piece. One I had started shortly after I met the pack.

It was chunky and three dimensional, like most of my work, but this was an outward explosion of color from a central point. I mixed some of the pigments I had left to harness the iridescent quality, and it was coming along nicely. I hadn't found the *thing* yet, but it was close.

Eva told me I needed a better name than the *thing*, but I didn't have one. The thing was what made the piece work. Sometimes it was just a clicking in my brain showing me what needed to happen. Other times I would see something and envision how it needed to change. I'd even had times where I made a mistake on the canvas, but the mistake was what I needed to reveal where the piece really wanted to go.

I knew my art wasn't sentient, but man, it felt like it sometimes.

My phone buzzing made me look up. Somehow it was already three o'clock. I hadn't even noticed it getting so late. I grabbed it with paint-stained hands and saw a text from Rylan.

So you don't get blindsided. Just in case, sorry. (And exciting news to tell you at home!)

The first part was ominous.

I clicked the link, and my stomach plummeted to the floor. No wonder he sent it to me. The article was pictures of both Eva and I. Me, my most recent photo with Ben at the club, and Eva a picture from when she'd met her pack. A photographer snapped a photo of them when they were still in the phase where they couldn't get enough of each other. She was pinned against a wall, kissing Liam while Tyler's mouth was on her neck. The other two weren't even there.

And the headline:

WHAT WOULD ELIAS WILLIAMS THINK OF HIS DAUGHTERS?

Fuck me, Eva was going to lose her shit. I texted the article to Jasmine before flipping back to it. It wasn't a piece of any substance. All flash and mirrors. They were trying to be provocative, and the most damning thing was in the headline, but it was still a shitty thing to do.

I thought about what Eva said at lunch. Would he be over the moon about the Nautilus pack? Everything in me was desperate for the answer to be yes, but it wasn't like I could ask him.

Well...

I could, but it meant doing something I'd avoided. But maybe it was time I faced it.

I cleaned my brushes and found Wes sitting in the kitchen with a cup of coffee. "Wes?"

He looked up.

"Can you take me to the cemetery?"

Wes studied me carefully, in the Alpha way I now knew well. "Are you sure?"

"Yeah. I am."

He nodded slowly. "Let's go."

I understood the hesitation. Eva went regularly to visit our dad's grave, and I didn't. It was too hard seeing his name carved out like that. He'd been so full of life, and a white marble headstone felt too stark and cold to have anything to do with the father I knew.

It was easier to let him live in my memories. But I felt like I needed to see him right now, despite my resistance to touching my grief.

The cemetery where he was buried wasn't far from Mom's house. They'd planned it that way on purpose, in case either one of them passed, the other wouldn't have far to go.

I didn't know how often my mom visited, but I hoped the closeness at least gave her some peace.

"Do you want me to come with you?" Wes asked.

"No, thank you, Wes."

This was something I needed to do alone.

Dad's grave was in the corner beneath a willow tree, backed by the tall wrought-iron fences. There was space next to him for when Mom passed, and a bench under the tree.

A fading bouquet of flowers rested against the pale stone. Tiger lilies, like he always bought for my mom. I looked away briefly, blinking away the tears.

It felt like an eternity, but he hadn't been gone that long, and every day I ignored the hole he left. Right now it was a jagged, gaping wound.

The bench didn't feel right. I sat down on the grass right in front of the stone and traced his name with my fingers.

He wasn't here—I knew that. But I needed the relief of speaking out loud. "Hi, Dad."

I pulled my knees up to my chest and wrapped my

arms around them. "It's been a while. I hope you don't mind."

There was no way for me to keep it together. I pressed my face in between my knees and let the tears come. "I'm sorry I can't come here as often. It feels like it's harder for me than everyone else. Just like everything."

A breeze picked up, stirring the branches of the willow surrounding me. It smelled fresh and green, so far away from Dad's scent, but it was still comforting. I missed the rich smell of leather that always surrounded him.

"I met a pack, dad. You're probably rolling your eyes and saying 'finally.' But... I really like them." It was more than that, but those words were stuck in my throat. "Mom doesn't, but I think you would. I hope you would. Honestly, just everything. I hope you'd like what Eva and I have done since you've been gone, and I hope you'd be proud of us. Of me."

My voice cracked on the last word.

I never let this pain in. Never thought about it or even let it surface because it was too much, and if it was this bad for me, I couldn't even imagine how hard it was for mom.

"I really fucking miss you."

It all came crashing in then, and I let it. A wash of grief and everything I'd pushed away the last two years. More than the grief for my father, and more than my mother's disappointment. It was everything. Every moment of desolation and loneliness. Of pain. Of everything I'd let hold me back. The feeling of being replace-able and invisible. The utter worthlessness that slithered in my mind every time someone mistook me for Eva or told me I needed to be her.

And of course, this.

I'd never planned on doing all of this without him, and I was furious. At him and at the fucking heart attack that took him from me.

Our parents loved both of us, but Mom was Eva's, and Dad was mine. It had always felt that way, and neither of us questioned it.

"I'm so angry at you for not being here," I whispered. "I can't even fit it all in my body because I'm so angry. And it hurts so much I can't *breathe*. That's why I can't let myself think about it. Because I turn into this mess, and everyone already thinks I am one."

I took a shaky breath and swiped at my eyes. "I don't know how to do any of this without you."

My phone vibrated on the grass beside me and I ignored it. There was nothing to take the place of this moment, when I was finally here.

The tears wouldn't stop coming, hot and fast, and I stopped trying to wipe them away, letting them blur my dad's name in front of me.

Elias Williams
Beloved husband and father.

. . .

"Please come back," I whispered.

There was nothing but silence and the sound of the breeze in the branches, and there never would be. But I needed to say it. "Please come back. I wasn't ready."

My phone vibrated again, and I turned it over on the grass so I couldn't see the screen. Whoever it was could wait.

"I love you," I finally said, letting the true pain of everything wash over me. "And I'll try to come back more. I promise."

I sat with him, my words spent and tears flowing, rocking myself back and forth, listening to the rustling leaves and trying to find the words and voice I desperately wanted to hear.

The sky was darkening when I heard the soft sounds of footsteps on grass. I didn't move, though I knew who it was. Their scents were on the wind.

Luke sat down next to me, and I tilted my head over to lean on his shoulder. "Hey, sweetheart."

I didn't say anything.

"You had us worried. Wes told us when we called."

"Sorry." What little was left of my voice was a rasping whisper.

Gentle hands on my shoulders. "You okay, baby?" Kade kissed the top of my head.

"No, I'm not." Rylan was on my other side, picking up one of my hands and weaving our fingers together, and I scented Avery somewhere behind me. "Where's Ben?"

"His parents are buried here, too. He's paying his respects."

It caused a whole new flood of tears, and I tried unsuccessfully to blink them back. "It was the article," I told them. "I needed to see him. Not that he can hear me, but I needed to do it. I didn't expect it to be this hard."

Rylan squeezed my hand. "When you feel like you can, I'd love to hear about him."

"Okay."

Kade's arms came around my chest. "Come home, baby."

I nodded, and he lifted me to my feet and then into his arms. Ben joined us, and we didn't need to say anything to each other to understand the twin pain we felt.

One of them held me all the way home, all the way up the stairs, and all the way into my nest. No words were needed, just the warmth of their presence and the sound of their purrs.

CHAPTER THIRTY-EIGHT

ESME

"I feel like I haven't seen you in days," Luke breathed into my neck.

"You haven't, really," I pointed out.

The exciting news Rylan teased me with was a screen test. Eva had been putting things together behind the scenes, and the test was scheduled for right after she was back so producers could get an idea of how everyone interacted, and if the energy they brought was something they were interested in filming.

The five of them had been distracted for the last week getting ready. Everything revolved around it, getting the studio ready, managing the equipment needed, paperwork, their actual clients, and casual rehearsals.

Which meant less sex for me.

Not *zero*.

It had been raining all week, so when we were home, we were inside and not going anywhere else.

Ben and Rylan pulled me down to the pool and took turns teasing me with the underwater jets and their tongues before they took me together. A game of pool turned into all five of them fucking me on the table, and probably ruining the surface of it forever.

But it was less with the distraction of what was coming. And I understood it. This was an incredible opportunity, and I wanted it for them just as much as they wanted it. But I also wanted it to be over.

"Well," he said with a grin. "I have you now."

I looked up from under my lashes at him. "What are you going to do with me?"

Luke rubbed his thumb over my lower lip. "That's a dangerous question, little Omega."

"Is it?"

"You remember what I told you would happen?"

A shiver of anticipation ran down my spine. "Seeing how far down the rabbit hole I wanted to go."

"That's right. And it's up to you how intense this is."

After days of them being distracted and long nights at the studio, only having all of them home one night, I wanted fucking everything. "Show me all of it, and we can pull back if we need to."

Luke's scent deepened from a salty ocean breeze to the darker scent of water and night air. "I see."

We were in his bedroom, and he stood from the couch and closed the door before pulling his shirt over his head. The rest of his clothes came off with smooth efficiency, and I watched him from where I sat, drinking in the sleek beauty of his body and the length of him—already hard.

He sat on the end of his bed and looked at me. There was a different air around him. The quiet air of power that crackled when he stepped into this role. I fucking loved it.

"Stand up."

My body obeyed without me fully processing the thought.

"Take your clothes off. All of them."

I did, stripping out of my t-shirt and the shorts I was wearing, and leaving them on the couch along with my underwear.

Luke nodded in front of him. "Come here."

When I was standing in front of him, he smiled, but it was still full of that silent power. "What was the word you used with Kade? To stop?"

"Camera."

He nodded. "We'll use that then. If you need me to stop or check in, just say it, okay?"

"I will."

"Good." Reaching out, he brushed my arm. "I'm hopeful what we explore doesn't have to make you use it, but don't be afraid to."

Staring at him, I raised an eyebrow. "Are you stalling?"

His stare went from warm to steely.

Alpha.

The hair on the back of my neck rose under his stare, and everything tightened.

"Kneel."

My knees dropped out from under me, and I landed on the soft carpet. He dragged fingers through my hair and ran them down my cheek, lifting my face to his. "It's been too long since I felt your mouth, sweetheart."

His cock was level with my gaze, and I looked at it now, vividly remembering the way he knotted himself in my throat. Warmth and arousal swirled under my skin at the memory.

Luke's hand squeezed once, getting my attention. "Suck my cock, Omega. Don't make me tell you again."

Leaning forward, I took the tip of him between my lips and swirled my tongue around his head. No point in taking it slow—I dove down the length of him, taking most of him in my mouth.

"Fuck," he muttered. "I love Omega biology."

A laugh choked out of me in spite of my full mouth. There was very little we couldn't take, and we knew it. I loved it too, knowing I was prepared to accept whatever they had to give me.

The first time he fucked my throat it was with the others, and there'd been so much sensation I hadn't really been able to focus on just him. Rylan took my throat with casual arrogance I loved, and Kade was something different all together.

But Luke? With his quiet power and complete control? I wanted to feel what it was like with him. Pulling back, I looked up at him. "Am I allowed to ask a question?"

"Of course, sweetheart."

"I know you're in charge, and we're exploring it. But will you fuck my throat? Please? The way *you* want to?"

Luke's cock jerked in response, and his eyes widened. It wasn't what he'd expected, and I loved shocking him.

One corner of his mouth tipped up into a smirk. "Since you asked so sweetly."

He fit the head of his cock against my lips, and the

world changed. Both of his hands gripped my hair, guiding me down his shaft, all the way to his balls in one go.

Oh, fuck.

He was on his feet, keeping me pressed against his stomach. "Is this what you wanted, sweetheart? For me to take this throat and make it mine?"

Pulling back, he slammed in again, all the way to the hilt. And again. He cursed under his breath and unleashed himself on me, fucking my mouth just as hard as if he were in between my legs.

There was no air to be had, and just like with Kade, I accepted his choice, and everything felt hotter. More awake and alive. There was sharp pleasure under my skin and a *desperate* need for more of this. Of the taste of him and the brush of his cock across my tongue.

He yanked me off his cock and allowed me breath. I coughed, dragging in air and trying to steady myself.

"Do you need to stop?"

I shook my head.

"Good."

Luke made my throat his. I spiraled down into that gorgeous space of only reaction. Floating and light, blissful and content to give my Alpha pleasure. When he was so deep his balls pressed against my chin, it felt like he was meant to be there. When he held my head still and fucked, I tried to take him even deeper.

My thighs were wet with need, whole body spun tight waiting for the moment his pleasure would spill over into mine.

He pulled me back, fisted hand making me look up at him. "Whose throat is this?"

"Yours," I gasped. "It's yours."

"Good girl."

The thrill of his words sank through me just in time for him to pull me back onto his cock, all the way down. My lips sealed around the base of his shaft, and he held me still, fucking deeper. "That's it, sweetheart."

We stayed like that, frozen, as my supply of air diminished. I swallowed out of reflex, and Luke moaned. "God damn, Omega. Your throat is a fucking miracle."

He didn't move, holding me down. It was hard to describe the peace and joy zipping through my veins. It felt so strange to be drenched in euphoria with a cock down my throat.

There were no decisions to be made. Only an Alpha to be savored. He was giving me exactly what I asked for. Taking control and allowing me the freedom to do nothing but feel.

He pulled me off, and the world slammed back into full color with air in my lungs. It didn't change the feral, deep joy I was feeling. Lack of oxygen wasn't tainting my thoughts.

"I could fuck your throat all night, sweetheart. Maybe someday I'll watch a movie and you'll spend it on your knees for me. Would you like that?"

"Yes."

"Get on the bed."

He helped me, spinning me so my head hung into

open space. "Open. I'm going to use your throat to come before all my other plans for you."

I closed my eyes and opened my mouth. It was even easier to take him like this. Luke's hands landed on mine, pinning them to bed as his hips worked my throat in long, rolling strokes.

"Yes." He ground out. "Yes. Yes. *Fuck*, Esme."

The delicious heat of him filled my mouth along with and the delicate taste of the ocean. There was too much—leaking from between my lips and over my face. I didn't care. I was wanton and desperate. They could all come in and coat me with cum and I would welcome it.

They made me drunk on their very essence, and the lack of sex this week only made it more acute.

Luke stepped back, helping me slide onto the bed so my head was supported. His breath came in heaving lungfuls, and he stared at me in awe.

"You're fucking incredible, you know that?"

"I know." I licked his salt from my lips. "And I hope that wasn't all you had planned."

He laughed. "Not even close, sweetheart. You seemed interested, so I thought we'd try this." Luke disappeared briefly, and when he came back, two neat bundles of rope landed on the bed.

"To be clear, I don't need rope to restrain you. My hands work just fine. But this will feel different."

Being held down was incredible, and I intentionally didn't question my instincts when it came to sex like this. Being chased and held down, having my throat fucked into oblivion while I couldn't breathe... I liked it, and wondering if it was okay for me to do so was only going to twist me up inside.

I had enough of that in my life already.

And being tied up so he didn't *have* to hold me down? Yes fucking please. "What do I do?"

"Nothing." He circled his hand around my ankle, carefully spinning me around so my feet were at the end of the bed again. "I've got you. All the decisions are mine, all the work is mine." Rope circled my ankle, and he wrapped it carefully before slipping two fingers underneath the strands to make sure it wasn't too tight.

Suddenly, he leaned down, covering my clit with his mouth and sucking deeply. "More importantly, all your orgasms are mine."

"Fucking hell, Luke."

He laughed, muffled by the way his mouth was sealed to my skin, tongue working me in quick, fluttering strokes.

It wasn't nearly enough when he abandoned my pussy and went back to the rope. He pressed my knee upward to my chest, and I didn't realize what was happening until the rope twisted around my wrist, attaching it to my ankle. This was only one side, but when he did the other...

Arousal whipped through me, making me writhe. When he finished I would be completely open for him, and there was nothing more Alpha and Omega than that.

Luke was quick, repeating the process and checking to make sure things weren't too tight, but I was floating on a cloud like the pinned butterfly I was. I pulled on the rope to see if I could move at all, and nothing. My hands and ankles were going to be best friends for a while.

Pulling me to the edge of the bed, he knelt where I'd been before. "Where was I?" He murmured before licking me like an ice cream cone.

I couldn't reach for him and pull that amazing tongue and mouth closer. The way I was bound made it hard for me to even lift my hips and beg for it. I was simply here, bound for him to do whatever he wanted.

He spread me open with his hands, licking and sucking every part of me. Torturing my clit with his tongue before fucking me with it.

My arousal rose so much faster now because I couldn't move. There was nowhere to go to mitigate the need building in my core—I was simply going to tip over the edge and go screaming down the best roller coaster ever.

As I was cresting that peak, Luke pulled away, the orgasm fizzling into mist. "Wait, no—"

"Remember when I said all your orgasms belong to me?"

"I didn't know that's what you meant."

Luke's face appeared over mine, all Alpha. "It means you come when I say you can, and not before. It means, little Omega," he lowered his mouth to mine and kissed me with my own flavor on his tongue, "I can choose to take you all the way to the edge as many times as I want, and there's nothing you can do about it. You know what you can do to make me stop."

I nodded. "Yes."

"Do you want me to?"

Fuck me. The smirk on his face told me he already knew I didn't want to stop. I didn't want to be tormented with pleasure just out of reach, and yet I *did*. God, there was something wrong with me. "No. Don't stop."

His purr rumbled between us. "Good girl. Don't worry, Esme. I'm not *only* going to deny you."

"Just a lot?"

"I guess you'll have to find out."

He fit himself against me, pushing in, and the way I was spread made him feel bigger than he was, stretching me and making me moan. The bulge of his knot pressed against me from his first orgasm, but he didn't lock us yet.

"How do you feel?"

"I feel good," I told him. "Really really good."

The pleasure was right there, waiting for me to come to it again, pulling me up into pre-orgasmic bliss like a slingshot.

"Esme, you don't have permission to come," Luke said. "If you have to, you will ask, and asking doesn't mean I'll say yes."

It was right there, barely out of reach. "Please?"

"Please what?"

"Please may I come?"

Luke's lips grazed over my neck. "Not yet."

He slowed down his pace, my climax fucking evaporating, and I moaned, the loss nearly painful. "Cruel Alpha."

I felt him smile. "Absolutely."

Pushing my bound legs wider, he fucked me again, a ruthless driving pace carrying me toward ecstasy. Again, I could see the blinding fireworks from a distance, and again, Luke told me no, letting everything wink out into darkness.

"You're going to kill me," I breathed. "Please, Luke."

He stared down at me, stormy blue eyes cold with power. "Please what, Omega?"

"Please fuck me, Alpha, and make me come." The last word was shaky and breathless. He didn't have to say yes. He could keep me here all night and say no. Why did that thought bring me so much closer to going over?

Luke thrust deep and hard, bringing back the fireworks in full force. No matter if he said no this time, I wasn't sure I could hold myself back. The orgasm train was already on the tracks at full speed, and the brakes were out. "You can come, sweetheart."

"Thank fuck," I moaned, and I barely heard his low laughter through the rushing in my ears. Rapture rolled into me, an ocean tide as strong as his scent, carrying me away with the force of all the pleasure he'd denied me.

His knot thrusting into me and locking us together started the wave all over again. My head was floaty and fuzzy, all of this fizzing through me and hovering, waiting for me to come back to myself.

"Why do you like it?" My words were slurred slightly. "I mean, I know why *I* like it, but I want to hear it from you."

"Well," Luke said softly, "for one, seeing you orgasm

like that is better than any movie in the world. Second, it feels good here." His hand slipped between our bodies and pressed to the center of his chest. "That my command is more important than your desire for pleasure." A kiss on one cheek. "Or your need for air. Holding that power is like holding a live wire."

He moved slowly, releasing the ropes from my limbs and rubbing them, easing the stiffness and working blood back in. "And I hope I don't have to tell you that sex with you is incredible."

"Back at you." The awake part of my mind—the piece which wasn't currently in control—rolled her eyes.

Luke lifted us together, moving us to the head of the bed where the pillows were. "But it's more than being tied up, or even me saying you can't come. It's an exchange. You coming to me and knowing for a little while you don't have to make any decisions. You can just rest, and let me do it."

"It doesn't really seem fair to you."

"We choose what's fair, sweetheart. If you were *forcing* me to do it, then no, it wouldn't be fair. But you're not. I'm offering. Holding power and those decisions for you makes me feel the same way letting go does for you. It feels like I can finally breathe."

He kissed my forehead, and together we did breathe, slowly easing back from that exchange to just the two of us. Words were in my chest, but the fear was still there, even if I hated it. Still, I couldn't let this moment pass without saying something.

"Luke?"

His eyes flicked to mine.

"You know I have a hard time saying things sometimes, right? It doesn't mean I don't feel them or want to say them. Everything gets stuck in my throat and it feels like I can't breathe, but it's still there."

For a second, he froze. Then he pulled me close, wrapping his arms fully around me so we were tangled together.

His purr nearly overwhelmed the whispered words in my ear.

"I love you, too."

CHAPTER THIRTY-NINE

ESME

"Sure you're going to be okay?" Eva's voice came over the phone. She was back in town, but we hadn't had a chance to see each other yet.

"I'm sure I'll be fine. It was going to happen sometime or another. Might as well get it over with."

Mom called me and asked me to come over for lunch. Specifically not go out, but come to the house. We hadn't spoken since dinner, so hopefully her inviting me over for lunch meant she actually wanted to talk about what happened and not have to have our public faces on the way she'd insist on at a restaurant.

Eva sighed. "I wish I could be there to run interference."

"You can't be a shield between me and Mom every time we have a disagreement, Va-va. I need to do it myself."

"Yeah." Her voice was quiet. "I just wish you didn't have to."

I was staring into the long mirror on my bedroom wall. On the floor in front of it actually, doing my makeup. My phone was propped against the wall, and I could see her on video. There was a silence, and I took the risk. "I went to see dad."

"You did?"

"Yeah."

"Are you... are you okay?"

"No, not really."

She blew out a breath. "Yeah, I was going to say. That's probably been a long time coming."

"Maybe."

"No maybe, Esme. I know dad's death hit me hard, and I'm not going to apologize for it. But it hit you harder, and you wouldn't admit it. Dad was your person, and Mom has always been mine. We both know it."

I laughed. "I thought something similar while I was there. But it seems disrespectful to say they have favorites."

"Parents always have favorites." Eva rolled her eyes. "Unless there's only one kid. Fair? No. Real? Yeah."

"Don't wear my pack out too much today, okay? I need them. This screen test has been distracting and I haven't been getting nearly enough attention."

She could hear both the truth and the exaggeration in the statement. "I won't wear them out. It's only a screen test, there's nothing strenuous about it. And they're *your* pack now?"

I couldn't keep the smile off my face. "Yeah, they are."

Luke and I hadn't talked about it this morning, but I was planning on telling them all together tonight. I was one-hundred percent in love with them, and had been for a while. I didn't ever want to leave, and now that I knew, I wished I'd told them sooner.

Eva shrieked and did a little dance. "I'm so happy for you!"

"Don't say anything. I'm telling them later."

"My lips are completely sealed."

A text popped up on the screen—Wes telling me he was outside whenever I was ready.

I sighed. "I should probably go. Mom's going to be annoyed if I'm late."

"Tell me how it goes?"

"I will. What's your schedule like?"

She grinned. "Now that I'm home I'm free as a bird. I would promise to steal you away for some twin time, but if tonight goes well I don't think you'll be leaving the house for a while."

"Here's hoping."

"It's going to be great. Now send those boys over. The faster everything gets going, the faster they can come home to you."

I stuck out my tongue. "Talk to you later."

"Bye."

Quickly putting away my make-up, I checked myself. I looked nice. A cross between what my mother expected of me and what I was now wearing to please myself. The asymmetrical skirt was long, a blue green ombre, and the gray top I had on matched the tones but was a little more severe.

The guys were all in the kitchen when I came down, and they stopped talking when I walked in. "Am I interrupting something?"

"No," Kade said quickly. "Just last minute talking points before we get in the car."

"You know you're supposed to be *natural* on camera, right?"

Avery stood and hugged me. "We know, baby girl. We're just nervous."

"You're going to be great. And Eva says get over there so you can start."

He chuckled. "Yes, ma'am. Say hello to your mom for us?"

"I'm not sure if that would help or hurt."

They all touched me as they left, brushes on my shoulders or across my back. They *were* nervous if that was all they did. It made me smile.

One good thing about living your life in the public eye was you forgot about stage fright. I couldn't remember the last time I'd been nervous and not annoyed to have a camera pointed at me.

Luke kissed me on the cheek as he passed. "See you later."

"Bye."

The house was still with them gone, and I was tempted to bask in it instead of going into the lion's den. That would only delay the inevitable. Plus, Wes was waiting for me.

He smiled when I came outside. "How are you?"

"I'd be better if we weren't going to see Mom."

Opening the door, he let me slide inside. "Your mom loves you, you know."

"I do know that. Doesn't mean it's easy."

"Very true."

He sat up front with Henry, and I realized he'd been doing that for a while. As soon as it looked like I might stay, he didn't feel like it was appropriate. It was sweet.

The sky was overcast with dark, brewing storm clouds, just like it had been for the last few days. It was going to rain later, no question.

A couple of cars I didn't recognize were in Mom's driveway, but that wasn't entirely unusual. One of the meetings for her foundation could be running late. They were held here since she couldn't bear to go to the head-quarters downtown. It reminded her too much of dad.

I let myself in without ringing the bell. "Mom?"

She appeared a second later from the sitting room, completely polished. Clothes, hair, and make-up. Definitely having meetings today then. "You're here. Good. I'm glad."

She hugged me quickly. "How have you been?"

"Good. Really good, actually." While I spoke, she led the way to the living room. "I was actually hoping we could talk about some things since we're home and not out at—"

I walked into the living room and it was full of people.

Katarina stood near the far wall, looking every bit a bitch as the last time I'd seen her. And on the couches, there was a cluster of men. One of whom I hoped I would never see again.

"Mom, what is going on?"

"Come, sit down."

I held my voice steady. "I will not sit down until you tell me what the *fuck* is going on."

Mom glared at me. "Language, Esme. This is the Solery pack. They've come to interview with you. They were gracious enough to come on short notice, and of course, you already know Aaron."

For the first time in my life, I understood what people meant when they said they saw red. My voice was deadly calm, and every head in the room turned to look at me when I spoke. "How dare you."

"Excuse me?"

"Not even a week ago I was here with the pack I am courting. It's unclear to me why you would set this up, knowing I'm in the middle of that process. Wait, scratch that, I'm at the end of the process."

"What?" My mother gasped. "What do you mean?"

"I mean tonight I'm telling them I've chosen."

My mother's voice turned to fury. "You can't do that, Esme. I will not allow it."

"Good thing it's not your fucking decision, is it?"

"You can't bond to a pack of *tattoo artists* for god's sake. Do you know where some of them are from? Places I wouldn't let you go in my wildest dreams. Covered in ink like it means something. 'World-renowned' art that will never be in a museum. Tattoos are bad decisions that get blurry with time. They won't be able to give you the life you want and deserve. The Solery pack will, and you already know one of them."

I scoffed and looked at the Alpha now smirking at me.

"Ah, yes. Aaron Gardelli, the Alpha who took me on a date and told me I was nothing in comparison to Eva and I should own being the slutty, knock-off twin before trying to feel me up under the table." My gaze snapped back to my mother's. "Is that what you mean by knowing one of them?"

To her credit, shock and horror showed on her face. Of course I hadn't told her. What difference would it have made?

Then her face changed, and my stomach dropped. The woman looking at me wasn't my mother. It was someone filled with rage and pain, and she was no longer interested in what I had to say.

"The pack courting you is the same, Esme. They're artists trying to get to the top. You don't think they're courting you because they want the connection to Eva? You told me yourself she's helping them get on television."

"That's not true." I glanced at the others in the room. Everyone except Aaron looked embarrassed. Even Katarina, though it wasn't nearly enough to make me like her.

"Isn't it?" She asked. "Go ahead. Tell them you want to spend your life with them and see what they say. They won't bond you. They'll make excuses and string you along until all the contracts are signed and then leave you."

Panic built up under my skin. She knew it was the thing I feared most, and I never thought she would use it against me, but she was, and it was working.

The room blurred, and I blinked quickly to push the tears away. "What happened to you?" I asked her.

"Nothing happened," she said. "This is who I've always been, and whether or not you believe it, I want what's best for you."

I nodded slowly. "Then, despite being my mother for twenty-eight years, you haven't known or understood me for a single day. It doesn't take much to look and see that what I want and what you want are different, mom. And I do love you. But I'm done."

She took a step toward me and I took one back. "Esme, be reasonable."

"You know what's fucking *reasonable*? Talking to people. Not ambushing them with Alphas who tried to assault them." My heart cracked into pieces, but I had to do this. Otherwise it wouldn't stop. "Don't text me. Don't call me. Until you realize what it is you've done and are ready to apologize, I'm not speaking to you."

Her whole body went slack with shock, and I turned to the pack and Katarina. "I assume you already signed the NDAs?"

"They did," Katarina answered for them.

"Good. If I hear a single breath of this outside this room, I have all of my inheritance and access to very good lawyers, do you understand?" Despite everything, I wasn't going to embarrass Mom in the media. *That* was her worst nightmare, and I wasn't that cruel.

I turned to leave the room and stopped, looking back at my mother one last time. Eva's sentiment echoed in my head, and I couldn't stop myself from saying it. "I'm so disappointed in you."

Before I completely lost it, I left the house. My breath was coming in short gasps, and I was barely keeping myself from crying. This morning they'd stopped talking when I entered the room, and then barely touched me when they left. On the way to the screen test.

My mind swirled, finding every moment of the past week when they'd been distracted or busy, focusing on this instead of me. Which wasn't fair. This was an amazing opportunity and I *wanted* them to have it.

But Mom had hit the target she aimed at. Every other pack—every other Alpha—was more interested in Eva than me. Why would this be any different?

Luke told me he loved me last night. Was it something I could trust? Did he love me? Or the paths I opened for him?

Stop it.

I needed to see them. Now.

The screen test wouldn't last long. I could just wait in their office in the back until they were done. Lifting my bracelet to my nose, I inhaled their scents in order to calm down.

They were mine. I knew they were mine, and I'd known it far longer than I'd been willing to admit it. If something went wrong now, I wasn't sure I would survive it. Just the thought—

I choked back the sob and wiped away the tears.

Wes did a double take at my appearance. "Miss Williams?"

"Take me to the Nautilus studio, Wes. Right now, please."

"Of course."

I didn't even wait for him to open the door for me, and I slammed it behind me.

Fuck. I used my phone to check my make-up. I'd been blissfully free from the press, but Eva was there. Where she went, cameras followed. Wouldn't they love that, me showing up in streaked make-up?

I fixed the streaks and tried to control my thoughts. It wasn't working well. I *knew* they loved me. I knew it. And I suspected the only reason they hadn't said it yet was because they were waiting for me to choose. As if I could choose anyone but them. As if I wasn't hurting them now by not telling them I wanted all of their marks on me.

Sure enough, paps were outside the studio. Inside there were *bright* lights, and that was about all I could see. Again, I didn't wait for Wes. I didn't want him to ask me if I was okay.

The first few drops of rain hit me on the way inside.

Esme, what are you doing here at the studio? Can't trust your pack with your sister? Enjoying finding a pack willing to go all the way in public? Will we finally see the ice queen on fire? We want more sexy shots.

The questions burrowed under my skin.

Can't trust your pack with your sister?

Can't trust your pack?

Can't trust?

I pushed past them and through the door, heaving in

a breath. The atmosphere was hushed but lively. The lights were facing away from the windows, and things were illuminated, but none of the pack were in sight. They were in one of the private tattooing rooms. I saw them on a small monitor where they were talking and laughing.

Jasmine stood there. I hadn't seen Eva's manager since the night of the party, but she grinned when she saw me. "Hey, Esme. We weren't expecting you."

"Is it a problem? I wasn't expecting to come, but my plans changed."

"Not a problem at all."

The small image showed the five guys standing and leaning casually in the room, but Eva wasn't there. "Where's Eva?"

"In the office," Jasmine said. "She got a call from Brian."

Eva's agent. When he called, it was important, even more than a screen test like this one. Hell, it was probably *about* this.

Jasmine looked at me. "Do you want to listen in? They were just asked about you."

"Really?"

"Yeah, here." She took the earpiece out of her ear and held it out to me. I put it in. It took a second for me to focus on what they were saying. Ben was the one talking right now.

"Oh, that was totally by chance. We keep her around cause she gets the job done, but..." He shrugged and the rest of them laughed.

The interviewer cleared his throat. "So there was never any chance of making that situation permanent?"

Kade snorted with laughter. "No. Absolutely not."

The earth fell ten feet beneath me, and there was nothing I could do to stop the rest of it from crumbling.

"No," Avery smiled with a shrug. "She's a friend, nothing more than that. We're definitely going to reward her though. She did a lot to make all of this happen." He gestured at the lights and the cameras. "We at least owe her one for that."

"Too bad," the interviewer said. "Audiences go nuts over a love story."

"The audience will have to go without," Luke said. "This has been, and always will be, only about the tattoos."

I ripped the piece out of my ear and handed it back to Jasmine, hands shaking. "I'm sorry, I just realized I have to be somewhere."

"Oh. Everything okay?"

"Yeah." My voice squeaked, high-pitched and scrambled. "Sure. I'll see you later."

Bile was rising in my throat. I was going to throw up, and I had to be away from everyone when it happened. The rest of me was numb. Like I'd been struck so hard I couldn't feel anything.

Mom was right. All they wanted was her. Eva and her connections so they could make it bigger.

I ignored the paparazzi as I moved away from the studio. One of them went to follow me, and someone else pulled them back. The warning had stuck, and they weren't going to follow. Thank god.

Speeding up, I power-walked around the corner and bent over, vomiting onto the sidewalk. There wasn't much for me to lose, but it was all gone.

I needed to get the hell out of here. And somewhere they weren't going to come find me. There was nowhere. They were in *everything* in my life and I let it happen. I let them in and believed them.

Fuck. Fuck. *Fuck.*

A cab was coming down the street, and I hailed it. It stopped, and I hoped it wasn't someone who recognized me. I realized my face was wet. I was crying and couldn't even feel it because I was trying to hold my soul together with both hands.

"Townsend park," I told the driver.

I hadn't been to the place where I ran since I met the pack. First because of the press attention and then because... I didn't know. I'd been busy. Where Kade took me hadn't been the park. But it was the one place in my life they hadn't touched. They'd even found me at my father's grave, and I'd believed everything they told me.

Stupid, naïve, hopeful Omega.

Turning my face away from the driver, I tried to keep myself calm. It wasn't working. This was everything, *everything*, I'd been afraid of. The fact that Mom and the press were both right on top of it only made the knife twist deeper.

Can't trust your pack?

They'll make excuses and string you along until all the

contracts are signed and then leave you.

Maybe Aaron was right. Maybe I was only as good as being Eva's knock-off, but he would still never have me. I would simply be alone. For one brief, shining moment I thought I had a future, and everything I'd ever wanted.

But like everything, it was too good to be true.

It felt like forever to get out of the city. The sprawling park which went for miles was the one place I had left. On the whole it wasn't that far, and when I was ready I could walk home. Right now I needed to be as far from everyone as humanly possible so I could shatter.

I already knew I wouldn't be able to pick up the pieces.

"Here you go," the driver pulled up to the entrance of the park.

"Thanks." I quickly paid the fare, and opened the car door, grabbing my phone.

Wes could track my phone—he had permission as my security. It would lead them right to me, and I knew what I wanted. I would buy another one later. It's not like my disappearance would make a difference.

They got what they wanted.

I slipped the phone onto the floor of the cab and got out, shutting the door behind me.

Thunder clapped overhead, and the rain was starting to get harder. There were shelters throughout the park. I would be fine.

So I waited until the cab was out of sight, and I did the only thing which had never failed me.

I ran.

CHAPTER FORTY

RYLAN

*T*he producer Eva had brought with her smiled at us. "I think that's a wrap. Thanks, guys. This is going to be really good."

"Thank you." Luke extended a hand, and the guy shook it. "What's next in the process?"

"We cut it together and make something like a mini-episode. We don't have the tattooing parts of it, obviously, but the banter will be enough. We'll write a pitch too, and Eva's helping with the placement."

"You bet I am." The woman of the hour breezed in and kissed the man on both cheeks. "Thank you, Lamar. Brian's going to call you."

"Sounds good."

The small crew started to break down the equipment, and Eva turned to us. "Sorry I was MIA for most of it. Brian, my agent, called to talk about this. I hadn't told him and he was a bit blindsided by the idea that I want to get tattooed on television."

"So how'd it go?" Kade asked.

"Not great at first. But the amazing thing about Brian is he's always willing to listen. Trust me, not all agents are like that. So I explained my reasoning to him, and he agreed it makes sense. He's not *totally* sold on the idea of the tattoo yet, but he's willing to hear it out, and regardless of what's on my skin, he's going to see what he can do for you guys."

Ben shook his head. "That's incredible, Eva. Thank you."

She grinned. "I might have told him you're my sister's pack. It helped."

"I hope we're her pack." I said it automatically. The rest of the guys looked at me like they wanted me to shut the hell up, but it was the thing in the back of my mind every second of every day.

"I wouldn't worry about that too much," Eva said.

"Really?"

She put a finger to her lips and shook her head. "Anything else, take up with May-may."

The crew was fast, and since there wasn't much equipment, everything was nearly back to normal in twenty minutes, and Eva's manager left with them. We'd canceled all our appointments and gave Daisy the day off. Probably for the best, given the way we'd razzed her in the interview.

Daisy kept the place running, and none of us harbored any illusion she wouldn't grab us by the balls and set us straight if we crossed her. We kept her around for way more than keeping the place running. An honorary member of pack Nautilus even if she already had her own.

"Do you guys need anything else from me?" Eva asked.

"I don't think so," Avery smiled. "You've done more than enough. We'll walk you out back. We're ready to go too."

"Perfect." Her smile was just like Esme's, and yet it was entirely different. Esme's smile made my heart flip in my chest and gave me the desire to drop to my knees. Eva's was pretty, and I appreciated it. But nothing more.

Luke was the first one out the back door, and he froze. "Wes, what are you doing here?"

The bodyguard looked up from his phone where he was relaxing under an umbrella in the sputtering rain. He was next to Eva's car, where her security was waiting. "I'm waiting for Esme." Then he scanned our group. "She's not with you?"

"No," I said. "We never saw her. She was here?"

"I dropped her off more than an hour ago. Things didn't seem to go well at her mom's, and she said to come straight here."

Eva was already retreating into the studio, and we followed. Wes, too.

"Jasmine, was Esme at the studio?" She looked up at us, relief clear in her eyes. "She was?" Pulling the phone from her ear, she flipped it to speaker. "Sorry, Jasmine, say that again. You're on speaker."

"Esme came in, and she was with me for a few minutes. I let her listen through the monitor, and then she suddenly said she had to be somewhere and left."

"Did she seem okay?"

Jasmine made a non-committal sound. "It happened

451

so quickly I didn't get a good read on her, but no, I wouldn't say she was happy when she left."

"Thanks. If you think of anything else, call me." She ended the call and looked at Wes. "What happened at Mom's?"

He shook his head. "I don't know. I wasn't inside. Esme was barely inside ten minutes, and when she came out, she was crying."

I noticed he'd switched to calling her by her first name. He never had before, but the switch told me everything I needed to know. Wes cared about Esme as more than a bodyguard. Their whole team did. They were long-standing employees, and they were treated well. It was more than just security.

Panic clawed at my throat, and I tried to push it down. "Maybe she went home," I said. "If something upset her, and she didn't wait, maybe she went back to the house. Or her studio." The words came out of my mouth, but they rang false. Something was wrong, and I didn't know what.

Ben had his phone out. "She hasn't unlocked the door at home," he said quietly. "I obviously don't know about her house."

"No," Eva said. "If she wants to avoid people, she wouldn't go to the first two places people would look. But Wes, call Neil and send someone to Esme's studio to check. Now."

"On it." He stepped away with his phone to his ear.

I wanted to sprint out the door and start looking.

Calling her name to make sure she was okay, and I couldn't do that. She wasn't anywhere close by now, and all it would do was alert the fucking photographers something was wrong.

Anger sizzled through my veins until I was rigid with it. I wanted to hurl something across the room or punch the wall. Everything about those people outside made me seethe. Hadn't they done enough? Now they were keeping me from—

"*What happened?*" Eva snapped. She was on the phone again, and this time I had a feeling I knew who it was.

"No, you don't get to do that. You're going to be quiet and answer my questions one at a time and then maybe I'll let you talk, Mom. Now what happened?"

She listened for a second and her eyes went wide. "Are you out of your *fucking mind?* Why on earth would you do that?" I wasn't the only one shaking with rage now. "Yeah, spare me the excuses. Esme is missing, and it's at least partially your fault. Is it so hard to accept we're not like you? And yes, I said *we*."

Another impossibly long silence as she listened.

"Well, Mom, I guess you're going to have to live with your actions just like the rest of us. Now I'm going to try to find my sister and undo the damage you did. I'll call you when I know something."

She closed her eyes when she ended the call, taking a slow, even breath. "My mother set up a pack interview today. Esme had no idea and walked straight into it."

All of us stared at her before it clicked. "No wonder she was upset," I said.

"Yes," Luke said. "But that doesn't explain why she's not here."

"Esme isn't at her house," Wes said. "But I tracked her phone. It's moving. Not far from here."

"Let's go," Kade said.

Ben held out a hand. "Hold on. You said it's moving?"

"Yeah."

"Okay, let's give it a second and see if it stops because I want to think about this. Wes, Eva, excuse us for a second." Ben led the way into the main studio, and I was right on his heels. "Sorry," he said. "I know Eva is her sister, but I didn't feel like talking about Esme's emotions so casually in front of both of them."

"No, it's a good call," I said. It was the same reason we'd passed over the question about Esme when we were asked by the producer.

"Esme already knew her mom wasn't a fan of ours. Walking in on that would have been shocking, but I don't think it would make her run," Luke pointed out. "And she came *here*. Whatever made her leave happened here."

"Maybe she just needed air," Kade said. "We know where she is now. We can ask."

"Yeah." Avery nodded. "That's for the best. Let's not try to guess."

I led the way back into the office. "We're going to

find where she is using the phone. Eva, thank you for your help."

"Oh, I'm coming with you."

Wincing, I held out a hand. "I don't think that's a great idea. Esme loves you, but if this is about her history with packs..."

Eva cursed under her breath. "You're right. Okay, I'll go home. Please call me as soon as you find her. I need to know she's okay."

"We will," Avery promised.

She went out to her waiting car, and I watched the car pull out through the alley.

"The car is getting closer," Wes said. "It's just around the corner."

Kade was already moving. "Let's go. Which corner?"

"North."

There were still photographers outside, but fuck them. I didn't care anymore. It was raining harder now, the drops cold in spite of the warm weather.

"It stopped," Wes called. "Right there on the corner."

Looking ahead, there was a cab. Parked on the corner. A man was getting out, umbrella and briefcase in hand. No sign of Esme. "It's the cab?"

"It should be."

Shit. Shit, she wasn't in it. Which meant her phone could be. But there was no way we were going to make it down the entire city block before it pulled away, and with the increasing rain, I couldn't see the cab's number.

"Did she ditch the phone?" Ben asked. "Do we think she'd do that?"

Kade growled. "Why would she?"

"I don't *know*," Ben exploded. "All I know is something is wrong and I'm panicking. Nothing about this feels right. You don't sense it?"

"You're fucking *right* it doesn't." Kade's voice was just as angry, and he stepped into Ben's space. "You want to tell me how to feel right now?"

"Stop it, both of you," Luke said. "Yes, something is wrong. Last night I told Esme I loved her. She told me she had a hard time saying things, but it didn't mean she didn't feel them. So yes, something is fucking wrong."

"Hello?" Wes answered his phone. I was the closest, and he handed it straight to me.

"Esme?"

"No, it's Eva. Jasmine remembered something else."

My heart stuttered in my chest. "Tell me."

"When she came in, and Jasmine let her listen, it was right after you guys were asked about her. Jasmine said she told Esme you'd just been asked about her, and that's when she gave her the earpiece."

"But we didn't—oh my god."

"What?" Eva asked, voice desperate. "What did you say?"

"I'll call you back." I hung up and handed Wes his phone. Right after we'd declined to answer the question about Esme, the producer asked us about Daisy. The whole discussion of Esme took maybe ten seconds. And she would have heard us... *fuck*.

"Wes, where would she go?" I begged. "If she needed to not be with anyone at all, where would she hide?"

"Let me think about it for a second."

The guys were staring at me, and I was glad it was pouring now so they couldn't see the frustrated tears I couldn't hold back.

"That was Eva," I told them. "I know why she ran."

CHAPTER FORTY-ONE

ESME

The cold water felt good on my skin. My muscles and lungs burned with the effort of running on soft earth and keeping myself upright.

My bag was slung across my chest and the sandals I'd worn were long behind me. I would rather run barefoot than slip around on those. This park was well maintained —I would be fine.

The only thing keeping me going was the burn. The pain I loathed was the only feeling which made sense. It was the only thing I would allow myself to feel. The physical pain was replacing the shredding happening in my chest. It was ripping me open, slowly.

My truth was burning me alive. Tied to the stake of my own naïve dreams.

I stumbled, slipping on the wet grass, and caught myself. "*Fuck.*"

It was truly pouring now, and I needed to turn around at some point and go home. I couldn't stay out here forever, even if that seemed like the more appealing option at the moment.

The river was getting close. The Slate River divided the city in half and curved out of it, turning back south a few miles later. This park was nestled in the bend of it. I would turn around when I got there. It was at least a couple miles back to the entrance and then my run home. By the time I got there, I wouldn't have enough energy to keep my eyes open, which was the entire idea.

We'd had so much rain in the last week, the water was building up on the ground because the dirt was already saturated. I was splashing behind me nearly as much as a car, but I kept going. The soreness I would have tomorrow would keep me occupied.

This was foolish, one piece of me acknowledged, but I couldn't stop. If I stopped now, I would break. Movement was keeping me together just a while longer.

The sound of the river reached me long before I saw it. It was overflowing, rushing with brown, dirty water and debris because of all the things it was collecting on its way. It smashed around the curve of the park, almost looking like an amusement park ride on the other side the way it splashed up and slammed back down.

It looked exactly the way I felt. Spinning, dizzy, angry, overwhelmed, and full of things I didn't want to be there.

Slowly, I moved over to one of the trees dotting the upper bank for a bit of shelter. I could stay here for a minute and listen to the crashing noise. It was a nice replacement for the roaring in my head.

The banks were high here, carved away from erosion and intentionally trying to keep park visitors away from the river. It was fast on calm days, now it would be a nightmare.

Water gathered around my ankles, puddles at least an

inch deep. I laughed once as my foot sank into the mud. If I was going to be out here, at least I could get a mud pedicure out of it. Had to make the best out of things, right? That was going to be my life now.

I shoved my other foot down into the mud, and felt the squish between my toes. It grounded me. Let me breathe. My chest still ached like there was a knife in it, lungs trying and failing to take a true even breath after all the running.

The water around my feet was running down, sinking past them and draining the puddles. I pulled my feet out and lost my balance, the mud thicker than I realized.

Vertigo hit me again, and I tottered to the side, realizing too late it was the ground moving, and not me. I lunged for the tree and missed, the bank crumbling beneath my feet, disintegrating and tumbling away, dissolved by the water I'd let into it with my feet.

There was nothing to hold on to. Grass and dirt caked under my fingernails, and I couldn't even scream. I fell with the avalanche of dirt, rocks battering me and chunks of earth catching on my skin.

Pain seared through me like fire, my ankle suddenly in so much pain I *had* to scream. It was lost in the sound of the rain and the river.

Oh, fuck. I wasn't moving, but I was hanging. Partially suspended under the precarious overhang of the bank by my ankle. It was caught on a root of the tree, bent at an angle it shouldn't go.

My head was in the dirt, and every movement sent a

new wave of pain through me. Blood was rushing to my head. I was going to pass out if I stayed like this, and I needed to be free. I needed to get away from the water and away from the overhang.

Think, Esme.

At least I wasn't hanging. When I got myself free, I would only fall on dirt. Small blessings.

But the way I was hanging, I couldn't reach my foot. It was too far and too awkward, and it was wedged between the crossing of two roots that didn't want to move. The only way it was going to move... was if I moved it.

Even preparing to move it was agony.

It's that or pass out, May-may. You can do this.

It was Eva's voice in my head. I could do this. I had to do this. I was broken and devastated, and I wasn't sure my soul would ever recover, but I wasn't going to give up and die here.

Passing out and dying hanging from a tree root was unacceptable.

I took three big breaths, counting myself down, and I shoved upward, screaming as I did. My ankle might as well have been made of glass for all it felt shattered.

The dirt was slick, and I kept falling, rolling down the bank too fast to control.

Please stop, I begged. I couldn't go in the water. I wouldn't be able to get myself back out. I didn't even think I could walk.

I hit the bottom of the curve, slamming into the

rocks on the shore too hard. But I was no longer moving. The water was close, but I wasn't going to slip into it.

Everything hurt, and I couldn't keep my eyes open. My body gave in to the pain, and I faded into black.

CHAPTER FORTY-TWO

LUKE

The rain splattered against the windshield as we drove too fast.

Omega. Omega. My Omega.

My heart pounded with the word. I couldn't breathe, because I didn't know where she was, and in this weather...

Something felt wrong. On the same base, primal level where I knew Esme was mine, I knew something was very very wrong.

We'd already looked everywhere we could think of. She wasn't home, and she wasn't at her father's grave. We'd checked her favorite restaurants while Wes worked on tracking the cab with her phone. When he finally caught up to the driver and found her phone, he'd said where he'd taken her: Townsend park.

The place where she used to go running, and a place we'd never been with her. It fit the bill.

Last night she'd been so peaceful and content in my arms. The thought that she was hurting tore me open inside. If what we thought happened was true, my little Omega felt like the world was crashing down on her.

I couldn't say I wouldn't have run too.

We nearly spun out turning into the park entrance. There was so much fucking water we could barely see.

"This place is huge." Ben's voice was desolate. "How are we going to find her?"

"Comb every inch," Kade said. "We don't have too much time before it gets dark."

It was still the afternoon, but with this kind of weather it was already dark, and even dying daylight would make it impossible to see.

"Follow her scent as best you can," I said. "Do we split up?"

Rylan nodded. "I think we should. We'll cover more ground, and we have our phones. Just be careful."

"Her scent?" Avery asked. "In this rain?"

"*I know*," I snapped. "Just try. It's all we have."

The car went silent.

"Sorry."

Avery put his hand on my shoulder. "I know. Let's just find her."

We got out of the car and headed into the park. Immediately, I saw a smudged footprint filling with water. "Look."

"Okay," Rylan said. "Start in this general direction and fan out?"

"Sounds good." Kade was already walking, and his roar penetrated the pouring rain. "*ESME!*"

I chose a path a few degrees away from his, and started walking, looking for any other signs of her foot- steps or traces of her scent.

Come on, sweetheart.

True terror rested in my chest. We needed to find her. We *had* to. She was ours, and I loved her more than I loved my own breath. When we found her, I prayed to the universe she would let us explain. Tell her it wasn't what she heard, and there was nothing we wanted more than to be hers. We would give everything up for it.

Everything.

In the distance, I heard Kade's voice, and I found my own, calling for my Omega.

"ESME!"

Please, let us find you.

CHAPTER FORTY-THREE

ESME

*A*gony.

Blazing, piercing agony was the thing to wake me. My ankle felt hot and swollen, and one move to look at it confirmed it. It looked like someone had shoved an orange under my skin, red and angry though the rest of my skin was turning blue.

I wasn't moving anymore, and the pain was too much. Everything was too much.

A sob worked its way out of me, and I couldn't hold it back. Deep, ragged sobs that *hurt*.

I felt so stupid and so broken and so alone. There was no one to come help me, and there wouldn't be. Not after today. I would go back to my house and my half-hearted heats. Trying to get through life on the small joys of my art, and it would have to be enough.

It would have to be alone.

Moving felt like jagged glass beneath my skin, but I couldn't stay here. Somehow I needed to get to the road. Somewhere someone would see me.

My whole body was shivering, and it felt like I'd never get warm again. It was my own fault for doing this. I left my phone on purpose. I hadn't made the bank fall on purpose, but it was still my fault.

I dragged myself away from the river, allowing myself

to make as much sound as I needed to. It was pure torture. As long as I lived, I would never call anything sexual torture again.

The thought crashed down on me. No matter what, I wouldn't be able to. Because they'd never been mine.

I whined, my Omega finally understanding it was real. This was real.

"Please wake up," I whispered to myself. "It's a bad dream. Please wake up."

But no pain like this—physical or emotional—could be a dream.

One tiny movement at a time, I forced myself toward the bank and the impossibly steep incline. If my ankle were fine it would be easy. As it was?

A sound made my head snap toward the park. Was that someone's voice? I couldn't hear anything with the river and the rain.

I was probably imagining things, desperation and fear creating what I wanted most.

But it was there again. It was a voice, even though I didn't know what it was saying. Maybe they would help me. Take me home.

"*ESME!*" The call was faint, but it was my name.

I sagged on the ground, hoping with everything in me someone had figured out where I'd run and at the same time unwilling to accept it was real.

"*ESME!*" The voice was closer now.

"I'm here," I said. "I'm here!"

I couldn't force my voice any louder. There was too

much sound and there wasn't enough air in my lungs with all the pain.

"I'm here," I said, only loud enough to the answer the voice in my head. "I'm here."

"Esme?" The panicked voice called down from above. Clattering rocks followed. "Fuck. Fuck fuck fuck. Baby, talk to me, baby."

It was Kade. He was here, turning me over and looking at me.

Sobs burst out of me. The damp version of his scent was so beautiful, and my body and brain didn't understand we were broken. He was here and it wasn't fair for him to be here when it wasn't fucking real. "No," I managed through the tears. "No, no, no."

"I'm here, baby, and I am so sorry. It's not what you think. We'll explain, but I need to get you out of here. Shit, you're burning up."

"I'm freezing."

He swore again, pulling his phone out of his pocket. "I found her. By the river. Her ankle is fucked up and she's got a fever that would burn down the world. I'm getting her up the bank."

Beyond my sobs, I cried out at the pain when he lifted me. "You can leave me at home," I told him. "Then you're free. It's okay."

He grunted, pushing us both up the steep embankment before setting me on the ground again to get himself over the edge. I was in his arms again in seconds, and I hated myself for how safe I felt, and the comfort in his arms.

Then I closed my eyes and savored it, knowing it would be the last time. They felt guilty, so they found me. It would be enough.

"We're not leaving you at home, Esme. We're not leaving you at all."

"You already did."

Kade lifted me higher, and his voice cracked. "Baby, I am so sorry. None of what we said was about you. I promise. It wasn't you."

I curled into his chest, trying to lessen the pain in mine. Maybe he was right and I did have a fever. I felt like I was floating now. Everything still hurt, but it was easier to ignore now. I was too cold.

Kade kept talking, his voice painting a different background to the pounding rain. "I've got you, baby. We're going to take care of you, I promise. You're going to be okay."

"*Esme.*"

I knew that voice, and I somehow couldn't place it.

"She's out of it," Kade said. "We need the hospital."

No, we didn't. That was silly. "No hospital," I murmured.

"Let's go. Be careful of her ankle."

The slamming of car doors and warm air had me drifting again. I didn't want to fall asleep. It smelled safe, but I knew I wasn't. I wasn't safe.

I wasn't safe.

Fluorescent lights were bullshit.

That was my first thought as I opened my eyes. An off-white drop ceiling and fluorescent lights were above me, and there was a beeping somewhere to my left.

"Where am I?"

A startled sound, and I looked to my left and saw Eva curled in a chair. She stood, looked at me, and burst into tears. "Oh my god, I am going to *kill you* now that you're awake."

"I'm sorry."

"Please just tell me one thing, May-may. Please tell me you weren't trying to kill yourself."

I shook my head and stopped because it ached. "No. I just wanted to run. It was an accident."

"Good." She shuddered and sat, pulling her chair closer to the bed. "Good. That's good."

Moving, my body screamed at me. It wasn't as bad as it had felt before, mostly soreness, not unlike what I'd woken with after Kade's chase. My ankle though...

It was elevated and wrapped, and at the moment I barely felt it. But if I moved my leg at all it was a shock of pain. "Is it broken?"

"No, thank god. Severe sprain. Won't be able to walk on it for a couple of weeks, but the doctor said you'd make a full recovery."

"Okay." I sighed. "I guess I'll have to stay with you if I'm not allowed to walk on it."

She touched my hand. "Don't be silly, you're going to go home with your pack."

"I don't have a pack." My voice broke.

"Yes you do. *Yes*, you do," she insisted when I tried to interrupt her. "You've got so much up in your head, sis, and I understand it. What Mom did was shitty, and what you heard at the screen test was the worst case of wrong place wrong time I've ever heard, but you need to listen to them. For me, if not for yourself."

I let my head fall all the way back onto my pillow, staring at the ceiling. "It broke me, Eva. I don't know how to come back."

"You're not broken. When you hear what they have to say, you'll see why."

Closing my eyes, I filled my lungs with air and breathed it all back out. It would be better to do it now. Faster was better. Rip the bandaid off now. "Okay."

"Just listen," she said softly. "I promise it will be okay."

Her footsteps retreated, and five sets entered the room. I kept looking at the ceiling, not looking at them. Their scents were now filling the room, and it was making my eyes fill with tears.

"Hey, sweetheart."

I swallowed. "Eva asked me to listen, so I will."

Avery cleared his throat. "There's only one thing that will make it clear, so here it is."

Suddenly, I heard them laughing. It was a recording, and my entire body went rigid. The producer's voice.

"Okay, so now I have to ask the question. You've been publicly connected to Eva's sister, Esme Williams. It's said you're courting her. How's that going? Will we get a peek inside the relationship for the show?"

"No." Luke's voice. "We prefer to keep our private life private. Too much of it is already out there, and for everyone involved it's better if it's not talked about."

"Fair enough." The producer laughed. "What about your receptionist, Daisy? Seems like she was made to be a part of the studio."

Ben's voice. "Oh, that was totally by chance. We keep her around cause she gets the job done, but..." Laughter.

Shock rolled through me.

The interviewer cleared his throat. "So there was never any chance of making that situation permanent?"

Kade snorted with laughter. "No. Absolutely not."

"No," Avery said. "She's a friend, nothing more. We're definitely going to reward her though, she did a lot to make all of this happen. We at least owe her one for that."

"Too bad," the interviewer said. "Audiences go nuts over a love story."

"The audience will have to go without," Luke said. "This has been, and always will be, only about the tattoos."

"Not to mention she has her own pack," Rylan said.

The recording ended, and I couldn't breathe. I hadn't heard that last bit.

Shock and shame crashed down on me in a wave, and I was crying. They'd been talking about Daisy. Sweet Beta Daisy with her wild blue hair. She'd helped them set up the studio, and that was what they meant by making it all happen.

"Oh, baby girl." Avery was by my side, pulling me

475

into his arms as best he could without moving my injured leg.

"I'm sorry." My voice was barely recognizable. "I'm so sorry."

"Esme, you were blindsided by your mom and then heard your worst fear come to life. The universe has a bitchy sense of humor for that kind of timing, but the last thing you need to do is apologize." That was Rylan.

I let Avery try to wipe my tears. "I feel so stupid. If I'd waited, or trusted you—"

"Stop, sweetheart." Luke's words were ragged. "It's not your fault. I swear it's not. It's just..." He turned away for a second, shoulders heaving. "If something had happened to you and you thought that we didn't love you, I would never have been able to live with myself. Because we do. I do. I meant it when I said it."

I closed my eyes, unable to look at them and speak. "I love you," I said, my entire chest releasing. "I was going to tell you I chose you when you came home. Eva knew about it, but no one else, and I'm sorry."

Kade came up on the other side of the bed and wrapped one of my hands in both of his. He lifted it to his lips and kissed my skin. "You've apologized enough, baby. We're just happy you're safe."

"You found me."

"We did. Scared the hell out of us."

Pressing my lips together, I blew out a shaky breath. "I'm going to feel embarrassed for a while. Figure it's best to warn you."

Ben stepped forward, and Avery laid me gently back,

letting Ben close. "You're not the only one." He pressed his forehead against mine, and I breathed in the sweet scent of vanilla. "I was the one who answered first, and that's what you heard, right?"

"Yeah."

"I'm the one who's sorry," he whispered. "I can't even think about it, knowing it was my voice that broke your heart."

Reaching up, I got my arms around his neck, though the angle was awkward. "I should have known," I breathed. "None of you gave me a reason not to trust you. It was my own fucked up brain, and it felt like everything was falling apart."

They were all touching me now, somewhere on my body. I was still weepy because it was like whiplash. Shame was and would cling to me while it was raw, but they were here, and I knew they weren't going anywhere.

"So you're coming home with us, baby girl?" Avery finally asked.

"Yes, please. And—" I stopped myself from blurting out the thought.

"Oh no," Luke said. "What was that thought?"

I looked at all of them one by one. "I don't really want to wait for a bonding ceremony. I just want all of you."

Kade grinned. "The press will be so disappointed."

"Yeah, well, they can go fuck themselves," I said.

"That's my girl," Ben said.

Eva poked her head in the doorway. "Everything going okay in here?"

I laughed at the suspicion on her face. "Yes, it is."

"Thank all the fucking cupcakes in the land. I was going to have to smack all of you down if you said differently."

Raising an eyebrow, I stared at her. "Oh really?"

"Don't give me that look. I can take you down."

"Only because I have a sprained ankle," I muttered, and Ben coughed to cover his laughter.

Eva stepped inside. "But I came to tell you there's someone here to see you."

Just beyond the door, I saw my mother. She was looking at me, and I barely recognized her. There wasn't any polish. She was soaked with rain, clothes messy, and it looked like she'd been crying.

I looked back at my sister. "You talked to her?"

"Yeah, I did."

"And?"

She swallowed and nodded. "I think you should talk to her."

My heart stuttered. "Okay."

Ben leaned down and kissed my hair. "We'll be right outside if you need us."

"Hopefully making it so I can go home?" I asked.

Luke nodded. "On it."

They filed out past my mother, and she smiled hesitantly at them. But that's what it was. Hesitance and not something fake.

She hovered in the door until Eva left too, shooting me an encouraging smile.

Mom shut the door and looked like she was steadying

herself. Finally, she turned to me, eyes watery. "I owe you an apology, Esme."

"Yes, you do." I wasn't going to sugarcoat it.

She took a step closer. "I'm sorry. Especially for this morning. I... I honestly don't even know what I was thinking. It was so clear, and now I can't find a single reason that makes sense."

"I just don't understand why, Mom."

She smiled briefly. "I won't make excuses for it, but I was trying to protect you in my own way. Your dad and I —" She broke off and cleared her throat. "We had a plan for how we were going to help you guys find packs. It still involved a matchmaker, but the way we'd talked, it was going to be led by the two of you."

Slowly, she walked around the bed and sat in the chair Eva had been in. "When he passed, I still wanted to do everything we planned. And then Eva met her pack, and I was running out of time. I thought—I had myself convinced the best way for you to find someone was the way we'd designed. And when you brought them over, it was like..." She shook her head. "It was like I was being replaced? Like everything I'd tried to do wasn't good enough. Like your father's spirit was right there telling me I'd failed you by not finding you a pack."

"Mom, Dad would *never* say that."

"I know." Her eyes were glassy with tears. "I know that."

We sat in silence for a moment, and she found her voice. "When you left earlier, it was like someone had finally turned a light on in my head. How did I get to a place where both my daughters were disappointed in me? How did I manage to lose the only two people I have left? And I looked at myself. *Really* looked at myself. I haven't been a very good mother to you, Esme."

I blinked back my own tears. "I miss him too, you know. It hasn't been easy doing it without him. The stuff about people wanting Eva had started before he died, and the stuff with Aaron, but it got so much worse. And it was like I was disappearing."

"I don't hate you, Mom. I just want you to see me."

She stood, dragging me into a hug. "I see you, Esme. I promise I see you. And this pack you've chosen, they're a good one. I looked at the files. They came in handy even though my intentions weren't good. It was hard to watch you and them because I recognize what it's like. Both you and Eva, you have what I had, and I *miss it*."

"Yeah."

She held me for a long time, and I couldn't actually remember the last time we'd done this—been this close for this long. My mom's scent was delicate. Like lilies. It was where the floral elements of my and Eva's scents came from.

"I hope you can forgive me," Mom said. "I want to know your pack, and I want you to be so much happier than you've been."

"I am happy," I whispered. "Today notwithstanding. And yes, I forgive you. It doesn't mean it won't hurt for a while."

"I know."

When she pulled away, I looked at her, wrinkled and

mussed. It was the first time I saw my real mother in a long time.

"When Eva told me you were gone, I didn't know what to do with myself."

"I lost my mind a little. But that wasn't all on you. I've got it back now."

She laughed softly. "Good."

"Also, don't kill me, please."

"Why?"

"I don't want a bonding ceremony."

Mom waved a hand. "That, at the very least, I knew. Getting you to do a big event would have been like pulling teeth. I'll only ask one thing."

I waited.

"After it's done, have some pictures done with all of you. You'll want them later. I promise."

Nodding, I held out a hand, and she took it. "We can do that."

She looked at the door. "I don't want to take you from your pack for too long. Eva told me what happened. I'm sorry you've had to go through all of this. And I'm sorry for all of it, but even in my desperation, if I'd known what happened with Aaron, I never would have brought his pack in."

"Thanks, Mom."

Patting my hand, she started for the door. "Lunch once you can walk again?"

"Yes. But please, for the love of *god* can we go somewhere other than Aurelia's?"

She made a face. "I'll think about it."

Outside I heard soft words, my mother's voice and others. They were too quiet to be heard, but I hoped she was apologizing to them, too. She would love them once she got to know them.

Rylan poked his head inside. "You okay?"

"That depends on how long I have to stay in the hospital." I wasn't a fan of hospitals, and I wasn't dying, apparently. So I wanted to go home.

Avery came in. "They want to keep you overnight."

"Why?"

"Because you were delirious and had a fever when we brought you in. They want to make sure you're not developing an infection even though the fever broke."

I sighed deeply. "Fine."

"Don't worry, baby girl." Avery leaned down and kissed me lightly. "We'll all be here with you."

"You don't have to be," I said. "Hospitals aren't comfortable, and all five of you don't need to have sore backs because I'm an idiot."

Avery's eyes hardened as much as they could for a teddy bear Alpha. "If you keep calling yourself that, I'm going to spank you when we get home, and it will be one to remember."

"Promise?"

He laughed. "Don't say I didn't warn you."

"How did you end up down there?" Kade asked. "It didn't seem voluntary."

"No. I was just standing watching the river. I was about to turn around and head back. There was too much water built up. I sank into the mud and the hole I made must have allowed all of it to dissolve the dirt. The bank crumbled underneath me. My ankle got caught on the roots of the tree on the way down."

"You're lucky it wasn't worse."

"I know. What did my mom say?"

They all sat, some of them bringing in chairs from the hallway in order to do it. "She apologized, and said she wants to redo dinner without her being an asshole," Luke said with a grin. "Her words, not mine."

"It'll be a little while," I said. "I forgave her, but I'm not ready for that."

Avery had my hand, thumb drawing circles on the back of it. "If you're still tired you can sleep. We're not going anywhere."

I was tired, but I didn't want to close my eyes in case I lost them again. Still, like his words lifted the exhaustion to the surface, it fell over me like a heavy blanket. "Don't let me go?"

He squeezed my hand. "Never, Esme."

CHAPTER FORTY-FOUR

ESME

*L*uke carried me up the steps and into the house, the mixture of all of our scents meeting me like an old friend. This *was* home now, not just me wondering if it was.

I was home.

Tucking my face into Luke's neck, I held him tighter. He seemed to know, squeezing me right back.

"Hungry?" Avery asked.

"Not for food."

Ben laughed. "I feel like we should make this more romantic. There's nothing saying we all have to bond at one time, or right away."

Looking over Luke's shoulder at him, I pinned him with a stare. "We're going to have all the time in the world for romance. I want to *feel* all of you. Please?"

I'd informed them before we left the hospital we were bonding when we got home, and I still wanted it. They were mine and I was theirs, and I didn't want to wait anymore. They even agreed to a photoshoot like my mom wanted. That was, if I agreed to the sexy photoshoot *they* wanted to match the pictures I had with Ben. Or rather, to go further than the one I had with him.

Whoever ended up taking those photos would sign a

hell of an NDA if we didn't end up taking them ourselves.

Ben kissed me over Luke's shoulder. "If you're sure."

"I'm really fucking sure."

Luke laughed. "Nest?"

"Yes, please." I couldn't imagine anywhere else for it.

My nest. It was a relief to say it now. Everything was mine. I almost couldn't breathe with all the joy packed into my chest right now.

"I've been thinking about where I want to bite you," Luke whispered.

Arousal dropped through me like a stone in a clear pond, creating ripples through everything. "Did you decide?"

"Not yet. I've got a few places in mind."

"And they are?"

He smirked. "Secret. For now." I made a face, and he laughed. "I'm sure everyone else has been thinking about theirs."

We entered the nest and he lowered the lights before gently setting me on the cushions. The hospital gave me crutches, but I was pretty sure if they were around I wasn't going to be allowed to use them. Maybe if I went to my studio, but that was it. They hadn't even let me sit in the wheelchair, passing me from one set of arms to another.

I put up a fuss, but I loved it. Being held by them was another reminder this was real and I was theirs. Soon, there wouldn't be any doubt for any of us.

"Does my bite on Rylan act the same?" I asked as they filed into the room. "Is it touch sensitive?"

Rylan nodded. "From what I know, yes."

Rubbing my hands together, I grinned. "Interesting. Any requests?"

"Nope." He tugged my shirt up over my head. "Bite me wherever you want."

Thankfully, I'd showered at the hospital. It hadn't been easy, and I'd had to do it mostly sitting down, but I was glad to have all the mud off me, and it made this faster.

I still felt a bit awkward after everything. But they wouldn't hear of it. They were too understanding, and too good.

And they were *mine*.

"You know," Ben said. "Some packs exchange rings and some don't. We had another idea. A gift for the bonding."

I leaned back, allowing Rylan to pull my skirt off my hips. "You don't have to give me gifts for every occasion, you know."

"That's debatable," Avery said. "But for this one? Yes. Yes, we do."

Ben knelt in front of me as I sat back up next to Rylan. "We'd love to give you a sleeve. Made up of all of our styles. It's not something that can be lost or taken off, and it's even more visible than a claiming mark."

My mouth popped open. "Really?"

"Really." He grinned. "And we'd each get something

as well. Not all of us have room for sleeves, but something."

"*Yes.*" There wasn't any hesitation. I didn't care about the pain. I wanted them on me. "Yes, absolutely. And I want it before Eva gets her tattoo because like hell is my pack going to tattoo *her* before me."

Ben climbed over me, pushing me back onto the cushions. "You know mine's going to be a cupcake, right?" He traced a hand down my arm. "And it's going to be so realistic people will want to take a bite out of your arm."

I burst out laughing. "That's going to be so weird, but I can't imagine anything else."

My Alpha kissed along my jaw, working his hands beneath me to take my bra off. "We're *all* getting tattoos with you. Matching ones. Your choice."

I couldn't even fathom all the options there. "Maybe I could design something."

"Hell yes," Ben said, tossing my bra aside. "And None of us are going to knot you now. Because after we're finished bonding with you, that's only the beginning."

"What do you mean?"

I was breathless, already overwhelmed by the feeling of him and the scent of all of them and the realization this was about to become permanent.

"It means we have to be careful of your ankle, but other than food, we're not planning on leaving the nest tonight."

The frenzy Eva mentioned. Like a heat, but not quite. "Yes."

Ben's hand skimmed down my stomach and beneath my underwear, finding my clit and teasing me. "It doesn't matter what order we do this in," he whispered. "Choose who feels right. We're all going to bond with you, and I can't *fucking wait* to make you mine."

A moan slipped out of me at the same time he slipped a finger inside me. "Do it," I breathed. "Make me yours."

Thumb circling my clit, he kept teasing me, drawing me into pleasure and arousal, enough to overcome the soreness in my body and the occasional pulse of pain from my ankle.

I shuddered and arched, impatient for all of him. "Ben, I'm going to need you to fuck me."

"Bossy little Omega." He removed his fingers and stripped my underwear off to toss them aside. Kade caught them and inhaled right where my pussy had been. A combination of embarrassment, shock, and lust ignited in me.

Ben bent his head, licking up the center of me and sucking my clit between his lips briefly. "Just needed a taste."

"I—"

His stare held me still, and it felt like he grew taller as he stripped. "You told me you'd suck a dick all day if it tasted like a cupcake. Well, turns out since meeting you I *love* tea." Bracing himself over me, he brushed my lips with his. "And I will suck a clit all day if it tastes like tea."

"Fuck," I moaned.

"Yes, ma'am." And he slammed into me.

Oh. My. God.

There wasn't a warm-up, and I didn't want one. Ben unlocked all of his Alpha, fucking me with every ounce of his strength. Raw, wild, and deep, my Omega woke up and took over.

This was different, and we both knew it. Claiming in every sense of the word. Marking himself inside just as he was about to with his teeth.

"Bite me," I gasped. "Bite me, Alpha."

Ben growled, moving faster. Harder. Untamed pleasure was a storm inside me, breaking open for him. I didn't need to climb the peak, I was already there soaring through the clouds.

I bared my neck for him, turning my head to the right, and arching. He hadn't told me where he wanted to bite me, and I didn't care. I just needed him, and I needed it *now*.

His mouth moved over my skin, drawing a whine from me. "I love you, Esme Williams," Ben said.

And then he bit me.

I came, the pleasure a fucking fiery tornado ripping me apart and putting me back together the same and differently. Suddenly I didn't just feel myself, I felt *him*. In the center of my chest, there was a joy and a sweetness that *felt* like Ben.

He was drowning in just as much pleasure and awe as I was. And Love. There was so much love it stole my breath. It went down to the core of his being, rooted there so deeply it couldn't be shaken.

Me.

He loved me.

"Yes," he whispered in my ear, both of us trembling with the newness of this. "I love you. I love *you*."

"I love you, too." It wasn't hard to say it now. The words were the most natural thing in the world. How could I have held them back?

Ben licked over his claiming mark, sending another blizzard of pleasure swirling through me, strong and sharp. "I'm going to like doing that," he murmured. "Every day."

"Every day?"

"Every fucking day." He kissed me and finally pulled back far enough for me to breathe. I could still feel him in my chest like a miracle. Nothing I'd ever heard about mating bonds made them sound like this. Like souls being twisted together so tightly they could never separate.

It was incredible Eva and her Alphas made it all the way through the ceremony.

My other men were already naked, and I was feral. Rylan was the closest, and I didn't wait for him to come to me. I was barely conscious of the movement but for the brief pain in my ankle.

Shoving him back onto the cushions, he laughed, catching me before I collapsed and helping me ease down onto his cock. "God, yes."

"You gonna ride me, Esme?"

I couldn't answer him—I could only move. Rolling my hips, I took him all the way down to the place where his length could reach, making stars shine behind my eyes.

My first orgasm still lingered under my skin, new pleasure catching it and spinning up into everything new. I was an addict needing a fix of each of them. It wouldn't be enough. Not nearly enough until I carried all of them with me.

"Ry," the word barely made it past my lips.

He was looking up at me never away. In his eyes I saw everything we didn't need to say—everything he'd already told me. That I was pack and belonged with him, and he belonged with me.

Pleasure stole my strength, and I collapsed against his chest, following the instincts driving me. He was my Beta. *My* Beta. The place where his neck met his shoulder smelled the sweetest, and I bit before I could hesitate.

Rylan groaned, climax taking him a second after it took me. He was there in my chest alongside Ben now, and it was no less a miracle to feel him there. The way he looked at the world and saw me, so different, and yet the thread of love was the same.

"I choose you," I told him, gasping for the air in my lungs. It was what he'd told me that night, that he felt like I'd already chosen them, and I had. "I choose you, Rylan."

The emotion on his face was clear, echoed in our new bond. I turned, looking at Ben. "Can you feel him?"

He nodded. "An echo."

My smile was so wide it hurt. Not only would they be able to feel me, but each other. And that was incredible.

I kissed Rylan until neither of us could breathe and both of us were laughing before I slid to the side and off him.

An arm snaked around my middle and pulled me backward. "Come here, sweetheart." Luke was underneath me, my back to his chest, and Avery was there in front. They were entering me together, and I could no longer see a single thing.

"Oh *fuck,* I'm never going to get used to this."

"Better not, baby girl. Cause I like the sight of you squirming on two cocks."

Luke growled, and it was the hottest thing I'd ever heard. "Get her up."

They moved together, both standing while deep inside me, and gravity made them slide deeper. It was like I weighed nothing, trapped between them, both of them driving in. One and then the other, then together, and back again.

My head fell back onto Luke's shoulder. It was too much pleasure too fast. So, so good. "I can't breathe," I told them. "Too much."

"I decided," Luke said, grabbing my left hand and rubbing his thumb over the underside of my wrist. "Right here. So when I tie you to my bed, every time you struggle, you'll remember who you belong to."

He pulled my wrist to his mouth and bit, and I was

weightless in a crystal blue sea. Nothing but light and water and the scent of the ocean. Every particle and drop was filled with him and his scent and the pleasure ringing between the two of us.

Our bond settled in my chest—the calm steadiness of who he was. All that power and dominance, and love so strong it felt like steel.

Pain spiked through my other hand followed by another wave of orgasm. Avery's teeth bit into my palm below my thumb, filling me with warmth as our bond locked into place as surely as his knot. The four of them echoing inside me—it felt like chaos, and yet it wasn't.

It was right.

"You're mine now, baby girl," Avery whispered. "Can't get rid of me."

Luke kissed me under the ear before he stepped away, and Avery pushed me against the cushioned wall of the nest, thrusting deep once more. I was dripping, a mess with all of them, and I wanted more.

Avery held me long enough for Kade to take his place, still pinning me to the wall, my knees at my shoulders, all of me open for the taking.

And take me he did.

Every ridge of his piercings made me moan, and they were lost in his kisses. The ring in his lip was another reminder of who he was, anchoring me as I slowly lost myself to the frenzy of the moment and the newness of bonding with the men I loved.

"The next time I chase you—"

"Next time?"

494

He growled, thrusting harder. "I hope you didn't think it was the only time."

"I'm glad it's not. *Oh!*"

Kade's hands gripped under my knees, pressing me more into the wall so I was held there more by his cock than anything else.

"The next time I chase you, it will be far harder for you to hide."

The image painted itself in my mind, feeling him hunting me and the sharp, primal nature of his need. And he was going to feel *everything*. Every shattered breath and burst of fear. It would make him hard, and every step he took toward me, stalking me like prey would make me wet.

I came, spasming around his cock and throwing my head back against the cushions and baring the other side of my neck. "Yes. Please, please, *please*."

"Always, baby." Kade's teeth sank into my neck, the twin bite to Ben's, and I exploded.

My vision went dark, and I heard my ragged cries echoing through the nest as I took what I needed, thrusting against Kade just as hard as he was fucking me. All of them were there with me, bonded, permanently a part of me, and the orgasm wasn't done with me. I was merely a vessel for all the sensations, going on forever and rippling through the entirety of our pack.

Our pack.

I had a pack.

Tears were on my cheeks when I came back to myself, curled on my side on the cushions with Kade behind me.

"Happy tears," I said. "Happy fucking tears."

Their happiness echoed in my chest, and it made mine brighter. "Wow, that's going to take some time to get used to," I said, sitting up.

"No kidding," Ben laughed. "We've been a pack for years, and I feel like we're brand new."

"You're the strongest," Luke said to me. "But the others are there too. Dimmer, but I can still feel them."

"I love that." My whole body flushed pink with pleasure. "I love you."

Kade reached out and ran a finger over his bite. Instantly, I was a puddle between my thighs and desperate for a knot. "How long will it be like that?" I asked. "Not that I'm complaining, but if I collapse into an orgasm whenever you touch my bites, none of us will *ever* leave the nest."

Rylan snorted. "And that's a bad thing?"

"I almost bit you here," Avery reached over and slapped the back of my thigh, just below my ass. "So I could use it when I spank you. But it was too tempting. I'd have you over my lap every day."

"You're all going to kill me," I moaned. "Death by orgasm."

Ben laughed, the sound filling the room. "But what a way to go."

Bringing my knees up to my chest, I looked at all of them. "I know you don't want me to say it anymore, so it's just this once. I'm sorry. I know there are reasons I reacted the way I did, but I still shouldn't have run. I promise from now on the only time I'll run from you is when Kade is chasing me."

He purred in response. "Name the day, baby. I'm ready to hold you down and fuck you till you scream."

Now that we were bonded, he felt every detail of how much I liked his idea.

"I love you," I said, addressing all of them. "And it didn't just happen. It's been happening for a while, and I'm so—"

A sob choked off my words.

I'd cried more than enough, but I was so relieved and so happy to be here with them. To have a pack and have a family. Now I didn't have to say the words for all of them to feel it.

"We love you too, baby girl," Avery's voice held wavering emotion too. "You're *our* Omega now."

All of us moved at once, suddenly a tangle of limbs and mouths. Rylan was kissing me and then Luke's mouth was there. So many hands on my skin it felt like heaven.

All of their marks were touched, and I was simply an inferno. "We're not leaving the nest, right?"

"We are not," Ben confirmed.

"Thank fuck," I said. "Because I need a knot wherever I can take one. And Rylan—"

"Oh, I forgot." Rylan sprinted out of the nest like his ass was on fire, and we all laughed. But he was back in less than a minute, holding something I'd only seen in ads. "I can knot you too."

He slid the toy onto his cock, where it rested,

forming a knot at the base, and my eyes went wide. Rylan smirked. "Surprise."

I swallowed. "Then what I said stands. I need knots wherever I can take one. Until I can't anymore."

Luke took my hand and kissed his claiming bite, making me dissolve into nothing but need. "As you wish, sweetheart."

The frenzy took us, and Ben was right.

We didn't leave the nest.

EPILOGUE

ESME

SIX MONTHS LATER

"Fuck you," I snapped. "Fuck every single one of you."

Ben pulled the tattoo machine away from my arm and leaned in for a kiss. "I'm almost done. I promise. And you know this is the last one. You don't have any more."

I grit my teeth. "It doesn't make it any less painful, Ben."

He looked down at Luke. "She needs more."

"What if someone finds out about this?" The words were more a moan than anything else as Luke went back to consuming my pussy like it was his favorite meal. Which it was, according to him and the rest of my pack.

Kade chuckled from across the room. "Find out we fucked our Omega in our studio? What are they going to do about it?"

The sleeve on my arm was almost complete. We started right away, with them designing it. It began with tentacles like Kade's octopus flowing over my shoulder, and one of Rylan's calligraphy lines coming out of them and spinning around my arm down to my wrist. That one had hurt like a bitch, with the concentrated black.

But they'd come up with what they thought was an excellent plan—fuck me through the sessions, giving me pleasure to combat the pain. And it was as delicious as it was hot, but it didn't make the agony of tiny needles being jabbed into my skin any better.

Avery's watercolors covered the rest of my skin, with geographic shapes, leaves, and the traces of animals peeking out in his trademark style. Luke's swallow flew away from Rylan's line, chasing it across my wrist—right over his claiming bite.

He'd had a good time with that one.

Now Ben was finishing his cupcake on the side of my forearm. The piece was stunning, and I *loved* having their ink on my skin just as much as I loved their bites. But fuck, I was ready for it to be over.

Luke sealed his mouth over my clit, drawing deep and reaching out to stroke over his bite at the same time. I jerked in the chair, the combination of stroke and tongue setting me on fire. "What are you doing to me?"

Sitting back, Luke licked his lips. "I thought it was obvious, sweetheart. But If I'm not distracting you enough, clearly I need to try harder."

He slid two fingers inside me and continued with his tongue, still stroking my wrist with one hand, forcing me up and over the edge far, far too easily.

The little private room echoed with my orgasm.

"Good girl." He licked my clit slowly and lazily, like it was a lollipop. "Now stay still for Ben."

Buzzing sounded next to me, and I closed my eyes. It was almost over. They were right. I could make it. And the orgasms did help, even if it felt weird to be entirely naked in their studio.

Being wholly naked wasn't necessary, but they insisted.

But after tonight, we would have to be careful. The show started filming next week, starting with Eva's first tattoo appointment. She'd wanted a full back piece, but her agent said no, so she talked him into a half-sleeve.

There wouldn't be cameras in the studio all the time, but like hell was I getting naked in here, just in case.

Regardless, people were excited about the show, and it was going to be amazing both for Eva and my guys. A win for everyone. Eva got her edgier image, the studio got exposure, and I got to watch everyone I loved shine.

Eva and I had quietly swapped images, slowly switching, so by the time the show aired, she'd be in full bad bitch mode, and I got to wear the soft pretty things I'd always wanted. And no one was calling me a copycat now.

Biting my lip against the pain, I looked over at the wall at the pictures. I used them as a distraction every time I was in here, sinking into memories and trying to relive those instead.

There were pictures from our bonding session, which we ended up doing in Thompson Park, ironically. And they were stunning. The other photos were darker and hotter, cropped so you couldn't totally see they were us, but we'd done the shoot they wanted with a photographer Eva knew who did sexy photos for the stars and had a reputation for zero press leaks.

So far, her reputation was intact.

The full photos were in the house in various places. I couldn't convince them to take them down, but whenever my mother came over, I managed to hide them.

In one photo you could see a tattoo peaking out on Rylan's shoulder. It was the matching bonding tattoo I'd designed for them—a nautilus shell, but in my classic, chunky style of painting. The shape and colors were a little different for each of them, but they had my art on their bodies just like I had theirs.

I hissed, and Ben held my arm still. "Almost there. It looks great."

"Okay. I'm talking to distract myself. Avery, do we have what we need to cook for Mom?"

"Yes, we do," he said, coming to stand beside me. "Is there something you're worried about?"

"No, just... trying to make conversation."

Mom had been trying, and it was getting better. We had dinner once a week at either our house or hers. And predictably, every one of my pack had won her over. I was pretty sure she liked them more than she liked me now.

Avery leaned down and kissed my forehead. "You've got this, baby girl."

I did have it. A few minutes later, Ben shut off the machine. "Done."

"Really?"

"Really." He grabbed a mirror and held it up so I could see the final product, and a laugh burst out.

It was a cupcake. So real it looked like he'd stuck it

beneath my skin. Yellow cake, vanilla frosting, just like I'd wanted the first time I met him. "It's amazing."

"I know."

I rolled my eyes and grabbed my pants, putting them on. "Aww, why?" Rylan asked. "I was enjoying the view."

"You can have more of the view at home," I laughed. "I have a question, and I need to be dressed for it."

All of them looked at me, and I felt the sudden anxiety. Not about the question, but about whether I was okay. "I'm fine," I answered, still not fully used to living with other people's emotions in my chest.

It was strange, but it made everything better. There were fewer fights because we already understood where everyone was coming from, and it made sex absolutely unbelievable. And it had been amazing before.

"I found this at the house." When I said that I meant my house. As well as working on paintings, I'd slowly been going through my house and moving everything over to ours. I was getting rid of a lot of old stuff, but there was plenty I wanted. Like the little note I found. "It's a note from my dad."

Through our bond, their emotions turned sad and careful. "It doesn't even matter what it said. It was a reminder not to be home too late because of some kind of dinner we were having. But he signed it 'love you, dad.'"

Ben was the first one to understand. I felt it. "Esme."

"I'm not sure which of you would be the best one."

"The best what?" Rylan asked.

Kade scrubbed a hand over his face. "To tattoo it. Right, baby?"

I nodded. "Here." The inside of my other wrist, where I could always see it. "It's his handwriting. I just thought…"

Pushing off the wall, Kade came over. "I'll do it. I'm probably the best at mimicking like this. Me or Ben."

Ben put up his hands. "I'm better at the photographs. Handwriting is all you."

"It won't take long," Kade said. "Promise."

I took a breath. "For this, I can take the pain. And now you know why I couldn't be naked," I laughed to lighten the mood.

"Yeah," Rylan chuckled. "Definitely."

Kade took the note and scanned it and made a transfer before fitting it to my wrist. "Does that look good?"

"It's perfect."

"Good." He turned my face toward him and kissed me briefly. "Thank you for letting me do it."

I couldn't speak now. It was already too much seeing his handwriting on my wrist. He positioned my arm, and the buzzing started, and the pain. But this was bearable.

He hadn't lied, it only took a few minutes with the simple lines, and when I opened my eyes, it was there.

Love you, Dad

. . .

I blinked away the tears as Kade took me in his arms. "Thank you."

"You're welcome."

All of them came to me, embracing me and burying me in comfort. "I love you."

The responding purrs broke the somber mood and made us all laugh. The tattoo was perfect, and it felt like finally, I was dealing with it. He was always with me, even though he was gone, and I knew—I *knew*—he'd be proud of where I was.

"Okay." I hopped off the table. "Home? I'm starving."

"Same," Avery called. "And I don't want to cook. I'll order ahead."

"Chinese, please. And add some cupcakes?"

He nodded, pulling out his phone, and I stumbled on the way out of the private room, catching myself on the door frame. Luke was by my side instantly. "You okay?"

Pain pulsed low in my stomach. Sharp, accompanied with a burst of warmth.

Shit.

"Yeah," I sighed. "I'm fine. But my heat is coming."

Luke's concerned face turned into a smile. He was beaming. They were all fucking beaming.

"Why are you all so happy about this?" I asked.

"Because." Rylan hugged me from behind. "It's your first bonded heat. Just *imagine* how it's going to feel."

God, I wasn't going to survive it.

Another pulse of pain had me bending over, which

conveniently shoved my ass right into Rylan. "I mean, we can start early if you like."

"Smart-ass," I said through my teeth. "At least we won't have to rush to get the nest ready this time."

"Nope. Whenever you're ready, we're ready. Now let's get you home and some pain meds." Avery guided me out the door with a hand on my lower back. "I've got a whole heat stash of gifts waiting."

I laughed. "You did that?"

"It was going to happen sooner or later. Best to be prepared."

The burst of love from all of them through our bonds nearly put me on the ground. "Thank you."

Ben picked me up and carried me to the car as another stab hit me. "You don't ever have to thank us, Esme. You're ours, and we've got you."

I curled into his chest, letting his purrs soothe the rising pain, and hid my smile.

I was theirs, and they would always have me.

The End

ello beautiful readers!

Thank you so much for reading my very first Omegaverse! I had an amazing time with Esme and her pack, and I'm so happy to share her story with you. I have more Omegaverse books planned, and I hope you'll love them!

In the meantime, I'd love to meet you! Sign up for my newsletter for updates and sneak peeks, and the occasional dessert recipe!

I also have a Facebook group where we share memes, I share snippets of works in progress, and everything in between. Come join the Court of Fantasy! I hope to see you there, and there will be more books very soon!

Devyn Sinclair

PLAYLIST

This is a playlist of some of the songs I listened to while writing *Knot Your Damn Omega*.

The playlist is available on Spotify.

- **Bad Love** — Tropic Gold
- **Black and Blue** — Hurtwave
- **Bleach** — Hurtwave
- **Blue** — Versus
- **Breathe** — Tropic Gold
- **Candle** — SayWeCanFly
- **Caviar** — Two Feet
- **DARK** — A Foreign Affair
- **Eclipse** — Last Heroes
- **Feel Alive** — Linko
- **Fever Dream** — Hurtwave
- **For Granted** — Lauren Spencer Smith
- **Frost** — SayWeCanFly

- **Glass Heart** — Caskets
- **Godless** — BANKS
- **Go Low** — Taylor Watkins
- **Grey** — PALESKIN
- **Heavier** — Rain City Drive
- **Here's My Heart** — SayWeCanFly
- **Hollywood's Bleeding** — Post Malone
- **If I Had an Airplane** — SayWeCanFly
- **IN TWO** — PALESKIN
- **Lonely** — Justin Bieber
- **Love/Hate Letter to Alcohol** — Post Malone
- **Lovely** — Time, The Valuator
- **Lovely** — Billie Eilish
- **Mascaron** — Lissom
- **Mesmer** — Valiant Hearts
- **My Father Said** — Hurtwave
- **The Night We Met** — Lord Huron
- **Out Loud** — Fairlane
- **Outta My Head** — Tropic Gold
- **Pavement** — SayWeCanFly
- **Phases** — Dan Lancaster
- **Reputation** — Post Malone
- **Roses** — Awaken I Am
- **Runaway (U & I)** — Galantis
- **Savagery** — Lissom
- **Savagery - Hahlweg** — Lissom
- **Sever** — Hurtwave
- **Signs** — Caskets
- **Signs - Dreamchaser Remix** — Caskets

- **Silent Prey** — Glasslands
- **Someone Else** — Loveless
- **Starseeker** — Time, The Valuator
- **Sweat** — Myles Erlick
- **Telescope** — STARSET
- **Walking Disaster** — SayWeCanFly
- **Where the Light Fades** — PALESKIN
- **Where You Are** — Portico

ABOUT THE AUTHOR

Devyn Sinclair writes steamy Reverse Harem romances for your wildest fantasies. Every sexy story is packed with the right amount of steam, hot men, and delicious happy endings.

She lives in the wilds of Montana in a small red house with a crazy orange cat. When Devyn's not writing, she spends time outside in big sky country, continues her quest to find the best lemon pastry there is, and buys too many books. (Of course!)

To connect with Devyn:

ALSO BY DEVYN SINCLAIR

For a complete list of Devyn's books, content warnings, bonuses and extras, please visit her website.

https://www.devynsinclair.com/